Love's Sure Dawn

Eagle Harbor Book 3

Naomi Rawlings

Love's Sure Dawn: © Naomi Mason 2015

Cover Design: © Clarissa Yeo 2014
Cover Photographs: Shutterstock.com
Editors: Melissa Jagears; Andrea Strong
Formatting: Polgarus Studio

To my daughter, Eliana Rose. I'm so glad to have you safe and whole after the many months of tears, prayers, sickness, and worry it took to bring you into the world. May you grow in grace and knowledge of our Savior, Christ Jesus. And may your future be as bright and sure as the dawn.

Chapter One

Eagle Harbor, Michigan; June, 1883

How much was a year of someone's life worth?

Very little when it resided at the bottom of Lake Superior.

But Gilbert Sinclair hadn't just lost one year, he'd lost four.

He sighed as he stared out his office's open window at the calm waters of the harbor, where one of his steamships had just arrived from Chicago. The afternoon sun painted the water a turquoise blue, though the shade could change from turquoise to dark blue to gray in a matter of hours. The waves, lapping gently at the sand for the moment, could change even quicker, unfortunately—just as they had on the day the *Beaumont* sank two months ago.

His gaze drifted to the west side of the harbor entrance where the bow of his once-prized steamer stuck up from the water like a beacon while placid waves washed it against the rocks. If only it hadn't been carrying four years' worth of his work when it went down.

Salvors would be here any day to dredge what was left of the *Beaumont* out of the rocky shallows of Lake Superior, and the insurance company would soon write him a check for a new ship.

Or rather, seventy-five percent of a new ship and lost cargo, as that was all his maritime insurance would cover.

Which left him in need of precisely $11,341.

If he intended to get that money, then there was only one way to do so.

Unfortunately it meant leaving Eagle Harbor. In the summer. With its glistening bay and leafy trees and wildflowers aplenty.

From his open window, Gilbert drew in a breath, long and deep. It smelled of lake and sun and foliage, all so very different from the packed streets and thick, smoggy air of Chicago.

But Chicago was where the money was.

The door to his office burst open, and he turned to scowl at his assistant, Stanley Harris, for bothering him when he'd asked not to be disturbed.

Except it wasn't Stanley.

"I'd heard the *Beaumont* had wrecked." His older brother's smooth voice filled the office. "Looks worse than I'd imagined."

"Why are you here?" Though really, he shouldn't be surprised. The only surprising part was it had taken two months for Father to send someone to fetch him home to Chicago.

Gilbert straightened and adjusted his waistcoat, even though doing so was futile. He never looked quite as impeccable as Warren, who stood just a few inches taller, had hair just a touch blonder, and eyes just a hint bluer than his own.

And considering how Warren was just a little better at landing business deals…

He let his shoulders fall back into their relaxed position. Why did he try keeping up with his brother? He would only fail in the end.

He looked out the window at the *Lassiter*, which was certainly preferable to watching Warren. His workers were unloading the supplies that would be sent via rail to the copper mines farther inland. He would have rather filled the space Warren occupied aboard the ship with cargo. Then he'd be making a profit.

"So you lost one of our most valuable ships?" Warren's voice mocked as he approached the window.

Gilbert sighed. His brother was nothing if not predictable. "The *Beaumont* wasn't ours, it was mine." Father had signed it over to him last year along with the *Lassiter* and two other ships, just as he had signed over four similar ships to Warren. "Why aren't you in Chicago?"

Warren leaned against the side of the window and smirked. "I see you've got a pretty view of the *Beaumont* from your office—or rather, what's left of her since your inept crew decided to smash a forty thousand dollar vessel."

"*I* was piloting when we hit those rocks." Piloting in a blizzard. Without the aid of the Eagle Harbor Lighthouse to guide him to harbor. The truth sounded inane even to him. The ship never should have been on the water during such a storm.

"So it's all your fault, is it? Either way, Father's livid. He wants you back home."

"Yes, well…" Gilbert fiddled with a small scratch in the smooth molding along the window. "Perhaps I don't want to see him."

Warren smirked again, that taunting grin which compelled women all over the Great Lakes to fall into his arms the moment he arrived in port. The one that made Mother beam and Father sign over the better ships to Warren.

Gilbert held back his sigh. Was he the only one who saw the mocking curl at the edge of Warren's lips? The cold glint in his eyes?

"Good luck avoiding Father." Warren surveyed the street below as though he were some medieval lord and the land below his fiefdom. "So has anything interesting happened around here?

Besides you sinking the *Beaumont*, that is." He muffled a yawn. "It looks the same as always."

If Warren only knew. Gilbert turned away from the window and strode to his desk. "Boring as ever."

"For someone who finds it boring, you sure spend a lot of time here."

Gilbert plopped down and took up his pencil without glancing at his brother. "Why do you care?"

"I have to run my part of the business from here for a bit."

How was it that he was leaving Eagle Harbor when he'd rather stay, and Warren was staying when he'd rather leave?

"Your office is next door." Gilbert jutted his chin toward the far wall where a sofa piled with paperwork and reports sat. "Your business would be better handled over there."

Warren straightened and looked around the office. "Tsk. Tsk. You're awful quick to get rid of the brother you haven't seen in three months."

"I've work to do." He moved the ledger he'd been studying closer, the one that proved he needed to come up with over eleven thousand dollars to replace the *Beaumont* and its cargo. And that wouldn't cover the extra five thousand dollars insurance wasn't going to pay him for the prototype of a shipping crane he'd had aboard, the crane he'd spent the past four years of his life inventing, perfecting, and—finally—building.

Talking to Warren or facing sixteen thousand dollars in debt. Choices, choices.

"I see your old friend is still fishing." Warren leaned back against the window molding as though he hadn't been asked to leave. "I'm surprised one of you hasn't killed the other by now."

Gilbert's hand stiffened on his ledger. His brother could only be talking about one man. "Cummings and I have made amends."

4

"Amends? That sounds interesting." Warren drew out his words, his head cocked to the side.

"It's not." And he was a liar, because amends didn't begin to describe what had transpired between him and Elijah Cummings, and his brother would find the story very interesting.

Though he'd probably hear the tale the second he headed to the brothel tonight.

"How long did you say you were staying again?" *Please let him leave tomorrow. I'll even endure a trip to Chicago with him on the* Lassiter *if it means I can get him away from here before he hears the scuttlebutt.*

Warren shrugged, but the movement was stiff and jerky. "A month. Maybe two."

Two months in Eagle Harbor? His brother? "Maybe I should be asking you if anything new has happened. You must have really erred if you have to stay so long."

The little muscle on the side of Warren's jaw clenched. "What about Cummings's sister? Always was a looker. She married yet, or is she still tromping around in trousers like a man?"

Had Warren seen Rebekah? Gilbert shot out of his chair, knocking his neatly stacked pile of steam engine diagrams to the floor. Even if Warren was looking at Elijah's fishing boat, he shouldn't be able to recognize Rebekah from this distance given the way she dressed as a man and wore that overlarge hat low on her face.

Not that Gilbert ever had trouble picking her out from afar. "Leave Rebekah alone."

"Rebekah, is it? Not Miss Cummings?" Warren chuckled, low and deep. "Don't tell me you've finally taken a mistress, Gil, and one who wears trousers to boot."

"She's not my mistress." Gilbert peered out the window,

though doing so positioned him entirely too close to his brother, and looked toward the stretch of beach to the left of the dock. There she was, all right, her movements swift and efficient as she took the trays of fish from the boat and dumped them into crates.

"Then why is the back of your neck red?"

Brothers. Had a worthwhile one ever walked the earth? "It's not like that. We're just…"

What? A vision of her came to him. Her face smooth and creamy, her auburn hair thick, and her grass-green eyes shooting little sparks at him over some imagined affront. What did one call the woman he'd nearly kissed a month and a half ago? The woman he thought of far too often?

The woman who hadn't so much as looked at him in three weeks. Gilbert fought back a cringe at the memory of their last conversation, the one that had ended with her storming away from a rainy beach, her jaw set and shoulders stiff.

"You're just what?" Warren taunted. "Lovers?"

"Friends." And that's all they'd ever be.

"Friends." Warren tipped back his head and laughed, his eyes gleaming the way they did whenever he walked into a saloon and spotted a pleasing woman. "I'm rather interested in finding out just how friendly she can be."

"You're the last person Rebekah Cummings would waste her attentions on." And he was. But Gilbert suddenly wanted to wrap her up and take her to Chicago with him if only to keep her away from Warren. In all his years, he'd never once seen his brother treat a woman as anything other than an object to lust over and then discard. Or worse.

But Rebekah wouldn't have to fend him off by herself. She had two brothers that looked out for her, and she was smart enough to see past Warren's charm—even if most of the other women who lived in port towns couldn't decipher Warren's compliments from his taunts.

"Feeling protective?" Warren flashed another mocking smile.

"No," he gritted, because there was nothing to be protective of. Sure, he might think of Rebekah from time to time—if lying awake every night counted as time to time—but he meant every word when he told Warren they'd only ever be friends. Their worlds were too different to meet.

"Well, I must admit that I rather enjoy seeing a woman's legs— though not encased in trousers. Put Rebekah Cummings in silk dresses during the day, and she'd be a sight to behold." Warren shoved himself off the wall and moved to study the bookshelf in the corner, the one filled with drawings, equations, and prototypes for cranes and derricks and the steam powered engines that ran them. "We'll see how committed she is to you once you've gone to Chicago to beg Father for money to replace the *Beaumont*."

"I keep telling you, she's not—" Gilbert clamped his mouth closed. He was better off not uttering another word. His brother was likely toying with him, and he'd fallen into Warren's traps one too many times over the years. "I'm not going to Chicago to beg Father for anything."

Warren turned away from the bookcase and raised an eyebrow. "No? It might be the last chance you have to get any money for your silly ventures, seeing how Great Northern Shipping will be mine in another year or two. I won't be so generous with business associates who run ships aground during a snowstorm, relatives or not."

The business will be Warren's. The business will be Warren's. He'd been hearing that his entire life, and he didn't doubt for an instant it would happen. But neither did he intend to acknowledge it, at least not today. "You sound rather sure of yourself considering

Father sent you away."

It was just a guess that Father had sent Warren here, but Warren's eyes suddenly turned hard. What had his brother done?

"Watch yourself, Gilbert." Warren leaned his elbow casually on the top of the bookshelf, except there was nothing casual about the movement. It sent an entire pile of papers scattering across the floor, a one hundred-and-twenty-some page study on friction drums and the benefits of using two drums or three in a hoist.

Who needed to read it in order anyway?

"My being in Eagle Harbor is a misunderstanding, that's all." But the tightness in Warren's jaw said there was no misunderstanding. "My mistake will blow over a lot sooner than yours, and when all is said and done, I'll be the one controlling Great Northern Shipping, not you."

Warren stalked across the floor toward the door, not bothering to avoid the papers he'd spilled as they crinkled beneath his polished shoes. The office door swung shut with a thud that could likely be heard across the street on the *Lassiter*.

Gilbert bent to pick up the mess off the floor. Maybe Warren would end up with Great Northern Shipping, but there was one thing neither his brother nor his father knew.

He wasn't going to Chicago to ask his father for money—he was going to find himself an heiress.

One with a dowry of at least sixteen thousand dollars.

⌐.⌐.⌐.⌐.⌐

Rebekah Cummings woke as she did every morning, in the dark of predawn, curled on her bed with her beaver pelt quilt. She rubbed at her bleary eyes and slipped quietly from under the covers, pulling on an open-collared shirt and a pair of trousers. Her hand stilled as she reached for the carpetbag she'd packed the night before.

No time to doubt herself now. She'd put things off long enough.

She clasped the handle and tiptoed to the edge of the loft where she slept above the kitchen. Careful to hold her carpetbag so it didn't bump the ladder, she climbed soundlessly down into the sitting room and then padded to the kitchen on her stockinged feet. A quick glance at the first door down the hall told her the lamp was still out in Elijah's room. He was usually up by now to launch the *North Star* while dawn broke over the water.

Except today was Sunday. He and Victoria were likely still abed together, and Ma wouldn't be up for another hour yet.

She cast a wishful glance at the kettle sitting atop the stove, her mouth watering at the thought of a cup of strong coffee. But she needed to leave before anyone else awoke, so she set the brief note she'd written last night on the table. Hopefully God would forgive her for the lie it told, the one that would buy her enough time to leave Eagle Harbor.

She silently opened the door that led from the kitchen to the entryway and slipped on her boots before tiptoeing down the rough plank floorboards and letting herself outside. The sounds of waves rolling into rocks and the first birdsongs of the morning greeted her as she rushed across the yard. She didn't pause to look back at the rambling log cabin her pa had built on the shore of Lake Superior or the vast lake beyond. Instead, she tightened her hold on the carpetbag until her nails dug into her palm and hastened down her family's long, winding drive until she reached North Street.

The Pretty Penny brothel sitting just outside the town limit was all shut up for the morning, as was the bar, mercantile, barber shop, haberdashery, and telegraph office. She kept her gaze on the ground as she rushed past them.

She wouldn't miss any of this—she absolutely refused. Elijah had left the family for two years while he'd sailed the world. Now he was settled with a wife to care for. But someone needed to leave, and it was her turn, like it or not.

She was determined to like it.

Because she couldn't stay any longer in a town where everyone saw her as the half-crazed woman who ran around in trousers, nor could she stay with two brothers who thought she had nothing of value to offer the family.

She had something to offer, and she wasn't going to sit around while Elijah and Isaac relegated her to mundane tasks like cooking, sewing, and icing fish. She'd let people keep her from doing what she knew had to be done once before, and her pa had ended up dead. She wasn't about to make the same mistake again.

She'd seen the bills lying on the kitchen table and knew Elijah had emptied the family's savings to rebuild his ruined surfboat this spring. She'd even wiped a tear or two from her eyes after he'd put in a full day of work on the lake and then turned around to help unload cargo ships for two straight weeks so he could purchase the small gold wedding band Victoria now wore on her finger.

But yesterday the representative who sold their catch inland said he could only give them seventy dollars for four months' worth of fish. How could she not fear for her family when they were getting less than a third of what they'd brought in last year with the same haul?

There was no help for it. Her family needed money, and she was done—

"Oof!" She stopped short as she slammed into tall, lanky male body.

"Easy there." A soft southern voice wrapped around her, and gentle hands gripped her shoulders as she attempted to straighten herself. "You should look where you're going."

In the growing light of dawn, she stared up into a narrow face that always seemed to be wreathed with compassion. "Sorry, Dr. Harrington. I wasn't expecting anyone out this early."

"It's Seth. How many times must I tell you?"

"Seth, right." Why didn't she ever remember to call him by his Christian name? Her gaze fell to the black medical bag at his feet, which he'd probably dropped to keep them both from falling. "I trust everything is well this morning?"

"I'm afraid Tressa Oakton is still having trouble with her pregnancy." He nodded toward the lighthouse to her left, then moved his somber green gaze back to her.

Rebekah shifted, not quite sure what to do with the odd way her belly curled whenever he looked at her like that. Maybe that look had something to do with him being raised in the South. They certainly did things differently down there.

She swallowed and turned to survey the red brick structure that jutted out from the rocks lining the outside of the harbor. Though Tressa's husband Mac might not carry the last name of Cummings, he was something of an adopted brother, having moved in with them when he was ten years old and staying until he took the assistant lightkeeper position. She'd miss him and Tressa and their children while she was gone.

And now she'd have to wait until November before she met her newest niece or nephew. "Will Tressa be all right?"

"I pray so, but I'm afraid I don't know what's wrong with her, not really. Lots of fainting, lots of lightheadedness, and low blood pressure, but as for what's causing it?" His brow furrowed and his lips twisted together. "Sometimes I wish this town had a midwife. I'd gladly defer to her in such situations."

Since she wasn't likely to have children anytime soon, Eagle

Harbor's lack of midwives wasn't on her list of worries. Getting to the *Lassiter*, on the other hand, was. "You're a good doctor. I'm sure you'll see that she has a healthy baby in a few more months. Now I best be on my way."

She moved to step around Dr. Har—Seth, but stilled when his hand clasped onto her arm.

"And where are you heading so early on a Sunday morning?" He ran his eyes down her in that assessing way again, but this time his gaze lingered on her carpetbag rather than her face. "Not fishing, I assume."

No, she hadn't been fishing in the three weeks since Elijah had told her he didn't want her anywhere near his rescue boat during a recent storm, though she'd helped ice his catch every day after he returned from fishing. "I've taken a post."

"One that requires a traveling bag and a trip at dawn?"

She drew in a deep breath. Speaking the words shouldn't be this hard. After all, she had little trouble expressing herself when she'd been hired yesterday. But she'd been discussing leaving town with a stranger, not a family friend. "On the *Lassiter*, as the cook."

"I'm surprised your brothers would let you do such a thing." The furrow on his brow deepened, and his southern accent grew thicker.

She tore her gaze away from him and looked past his shoulder toward the ship with its lanterns burning. "Yes, well, I best be going."

She attempted to move around him again, but his hand stopped her once more.

"Your family doesn't know, do they?"

"Really, Seth. I gave word I'd be there at dawn. I don't have time to talk." She pulled her arm from his hold and rushed across Front Street and onto the pier where the *Lassiter* was docked.

"Wait. Rebekah, come back!" Footsteps thudded on the wooden planks behind her. "At least let me write to you while you're gone."

She paused at the top of the gangplank leading from the dock to the steamship and turned. "Whatever for?"

Even in the gray light, she could have sworn his cheeks turned red as he stood on the pier below her. "It's what ladies and gentlemen do sometimes when they're apart, hardly an odd notion."

Yes, but why her? The odd fluttering in her belly started again, and she nearly pressed her hand to it. With his sandy blond hair, clear green eyes, and gentle southern manners, Dr. Seth Harrington had probably caught the attention of every marriageable woman in town—who could all be counted on one hand.

She liked him well enough, but to let him write her? That was as good as letting him court her. And if they wrote, when she returned to Eagle Harbor at the end of shipping season in November, he'd certainly have expectations concerning her.

They'd be wasted. She was too rough. She'd trample his kindness and compassion in a matter of days.

Certainly some other woman in town would be better suited for him. Like Ellie Spritzer. Dr. Harrington would make her a good husband, and Ellie surely needed one. "Seth, I think—"

"There you are."

She glanced over her shoulder to find the shipmaster who'd hired her yesterday approaching.

"I was starting to worry I'd need to assign kitchen duties to one of the sailors." Captain Steverman's droopy blond mustache covered the corners of his mouth when he spoke and nearly hung down to his chin.

"I'm sorry, Seth. I have to go. And I think it's probably best if we don't write." She stared at his chin rather than his eyes so that she couldn't glimpse whatever emotion flashed across them.

"I assumed you'd say as much, but I wanted to ask nonetheless. Don't feel bad for your answer."

She pressed her lips together. Here she'd just refused him, and he was the one comforting her. If that didn't prove he'd make a good husband, she didn't know what would. If only she could be as good to him in return. "Have you thought of calling on Ellie Spritzer?"

"Ellie? She's rather young yet, and I'm afraid since there're so few women..." He blew out a breath and met her eyes. "How about we try this? Should you change your mind, you're welcome to write me any time. If you happen to write, and I'm courting someone else, I'll let you know straightway."

"I can agree to that." She glanced over her shoulder at the shipmaster, who'd taken a couple steps toward the hatch that led below deck. "Now I have to go. Goodbye, Seth."

"Goodbye." He held up his hand in a somber sort of farewell before turning and heading down the dock.

"You coming, lass?" Captain Steverman asked.

"Yes, I just needed a moment to say goodbye."

"Got a sweetheart, I see." He settled his hands on top of the belly that protruded over the waistband of his trousers as he watched Seth step off the pier.

"Not a sweetheart." At least she didn't think he was a sweetheart. "Just a good friend."

She picked up her carpetbag, pausing to look back over the town she'd known her entire life. The town she'd never left once.

The lighthouse stood proudly on the rocks at the edge of the harbor, the beam powerful as it cast its rays over the water despite the brightening dawn. Behind the lighthouse, the town of Eagle Harbor sat, the buildings an odd collection of clapboard and whitewash intermixed with log structures.

"I'll show you the galley whenever you're ready."

And look at her being maudlin. What a fool. Leaving town was best for her family, and she wasn't going to stand around and regret it.

Even if she might miss the place where she'd grown up a tad more than she'd expected.

Chapter Two

"Welcome aboard, Mr. Sinclair. I know the accommodations aren't quite what you're used to on the *Beaumont*, but I hope the *Lassiter* suits you well enough for your journey."

The shipmaster stood in his quarters—quarters which Gilbert had taken over this morning—his shoulders uncomfortably stiff and his gaze straight ahead, pinned to some point on the wall above where Gilbert sat at the desk.

Did the man think every ship he'd ever traveled on had been as lushly appointed as the *Beaumont*?

Gilbert glanced around the small but adequate captain's quarters. He didn't know Captain Steverman personally, though his business assistant had hired the man last year on excellent recommendations. "The accommodations are fine. I appreciate you giving up your room for me, though I am a bit concerned about yesterday's drama. I assume you've split kitchen duties among the crew until we reach Chicago."

"No, sir." The man kept his shoulders straight and his hands clasped tightly behind his back, as though he were a private in the army rather than the master of a steamship—except Gilbert had never before seen a soldier with such a protruding stomach. "I found us another cook, and I think she'll work out right good.

Sure was a shame about Fred heading inland and trying his hand at mining though."

She? He'd hired a woman? And one from Eagle Harbor? Gilbert could perhaps see one of the vagabond men who came through town having the ability to cook for a crew of mariners, but Eagle Harbor wasn't exactly teeming with women. Did the new cook know what she was getting into?

Even if she was a decent cook, a woman on a ship full of men didn't always make for the best situation. "I'd have rather you hired a man for obvious reasons."

The side of Captain Steverman's mustache twitched, causing a good portion of his lips to disappear beneath the thick blond curtain. "Couldn't find any man willing to do the job."

"Tell the crew I expect gentlemanly conduct toward the new cook."

The captain cleared his throat. "I believe they know, sir, but I'll send 'round a reminder anyway."

Good. If there was a woman aboard, then as far as he was concerned, the sailors he employed couldn't be reminded of his policies enough. His strictness had cost him a skilled sailor or two over the past year, but the rules were well worth keeping. He'd little interest in employing men who would take advantage of women, even if his father and brother didn't share his concerns.

Or rather, maybe men like his father and brother were the reason he had the policies in the first place.

"I best get back to the deck, Mr. Sinclair, but I assume you want your breakfast served here rather than in the galley?"

Gilbert looked back at his desk where drawings of the crane now resting at the bottom of Lake Superior lay neatly stacked. "Please."

"Very well." Captain Steverman spun on his heel with the

precision of an army private performing a drill and headed for the door. He turned back and paused just inside the doorframe. "Mr. Sinclair, sir, for what it's worth, I was sorry to hear about the *Beaumont*. I'd never been on her myself, but I'd seen her. She was a beaut."

"Thank you." Now if only he could erase Warren's words from his mind.

Tell me, brother, how does it feel to sit at your desk and view the forty thousand dollar ship that your crew smashed?

The door clicked shut, and Gilbert turned back to the diagrams spread over the desk. How much was a prototype of a crane worth? Should he count the four years he'd spent developing and building it? The cost of the materials and the labor he'd needed to assemble it? And what about the previous prototype that helped him make this one a success?

It was all worth nothing, at least according to the insurance company. They'd only pay him for the iron in the crane, which their divers would soon salvage.

At least he had a set of extra diagrams so everything wasn't lost when the *Beaumont* went down. He searched through his papers until he found the section with the friction drums. Should he use three drums instead of two when rebuilding? The hoist would certainly be more powerful if he did, but it meant longer pistons and bigger wheels to turn the drums. Maybe he was better off going with a more compact engine.

A knock sounded at the door.

"Come in," he called without looking up. His crane would already be overly large on a normal pier, but if it was put on a smaller dock like the one in Eagle Harbor, the dockworkers would—

Crash!

He jolted, his pencil dragging across the paper as his breakfast spread across the cabin floor.

"What are you doing here?" An irritated female voice demanded—a voice he recognized far too well.

He dropped his pencil and pressed his eyes shut. Rebekah Cummings was not standing in his quarters. She couldn't be. He'd only imagined her. First she'd started by haunting his dreams at night, and now her voice had decided to haunt him during the day. In another moment, he'd open his eyes and find a fat, old cook with wrinkles, graying hair, and a stomach protruding almost as far as Captain Steverman's.

Instead he opened his eyes to find a porcelain face with thick auburn hair and shrewd green eyes surveying him. "This is my ship. I'm the one who gets to ask what you're doing here, not the other way around."

"I'm the new pilot." She gestured to the food at her feet. "Why does it look like I'm here? You, however, are supposed to be in Eagle Harbor."

He stood and stalked to the door, stepping over the mess of flapjacks, syrup, and coffee covering the floor before he made it into the hall.

"Wait." Rebekah reached out and grabbed his arm. "Where are you going?"

"To get Captain Steverman. I'm turning the *Lassiter* around."

"Because of me?" Her eyes grew round, and he tried not to look into their familiar green depths, into the slight panic that lurked there.

"Yes, because of you. Your brother will throttle me if I don't return you to Eagle Harbor, and this time I'd deserve it."

"But—"

He held up his hand. "Don't bother explaining further."

"I need this job."

Of course she didn't listen. She never did.

"And you need me as your cook. It's not like you'll find anybody else in Eagle Harbor for this job, and the crew liked breakfast."

He raised an eyebrow and glanced pointedly down at the mess at his feet. "I wouldn't know, considering I didn't get any."

"Oh, don't be so insufferable. I've extra in the kitchen."

He knew how sailors ate. The only food likely to be in the kitchen would be the plate set aside for Rebekah herself. "Don't bother. I'll eat when we get back to Eagle Harbor."

"No!" She fairly screeched the word, her fingers digging into his arm through the fabric of his suit coat. "I can't go back."

He sighed and rubbed a hand over his face. He hadn't been serious yesterday when he'd thought of trundling Rebekah off to Chicago, but somehow she'd ended up on his ship anyway. "Does Elijah know you're here?"

She took her hand from his arm as though he'd burned her. "I don't see how that's any of your concern."

"Oh, I assure you it's my concern." The man had saved his life. Delivering Elijah's sister back home was the least he could do in return. "And your family's as well."

She crossed her arms over her chest and raised her chin in a stance that had become far too familiar over the years. "Elijah left to sail for two years and no one balked. Now it's my turn."

"No, it's not." And he wasn't going to let her tell him any different. Rebekah needed to be safe at home with her mother and two brothers. Or better yet, married to a man who could keep a handle on her and give her a whole passel of little ones to keep her busy. "You should be home finding yourself a man to marry."

"For as much as you and Elijah fight, you sure are annoyingly similar. 'It's time you get married, Rebekah. Settle down. Stop wearing britches and start behaving like a lady.'" She mimicked, her voice a gross approximation of Elijah's.

"He's right. You should have been married five years ago." Would likely have saved herself and her family a heap of trouble had she settled down as soon as she'd finished school.

She made a rather unfeminine snarling sound. "If marriage is so important, why aren't you married yet?"

He clamped his jaw together. "That was cruel, even for you."

"I'm sorry. I… I wasn't thinking." Her face grew white and she reached for the sleeve of his coat again, but he pulled it away.

She probably hadn't meant to rub his face in the fact that her brother had stolen his fiancée from him, yet her jab had still smarted.

"Go pack your belongings." He pointed down the hallway.

"Gilbert, please. I only meant—"

"I said go."

Her eyes turned large and sad, so similar to the way she had looked at him a decade earlier, when he'd brought friends to the fishing spot she'd shown him and then told her that girls weren't allowed to fish with them. He'd expected her to rage or fight or scream. Instead she had looked at him with the largest, most sorrowful eyes, and left without a word.

Which was precisely what she did now. Turned and headed toward the galley without another word, her chin down, and her usually determined shoulders slumped.

Confounded woman. It wasn't his fault she didn't make any sense. At least she wouldn't be his problem for much longer.

~.~.~.~.~

Rebekah tromped down the corridor toward the galley. Of all the idiotic, imbecilic, ridiculous notions. Why did men have to be so stubborn? So controlling? Did Gilbert really think taking her back to Eagle Harbor meant she'd suddenly become the kind of woman Victoria and Tressa were? There would surely be another ship needing a cook. Or she could take the train to Chicago and find work. Of course, that would require saving enough for a passage first.

Her eyes filled with unexpected moisture, and she blinked it away. Cooking until the end of the shipping season would've earned her a hundred dollars. Surely once her family saw how much help she could be by working until November, they'd happily send her off again next spring. Goodness, the first twenty-five dollars she sent home to Elijah after a month's work would likely convince him this was a good thing.

Gilbert had been the boy who'd come to school every fall with a fancy new suit and shiny shoes. The boy who'd have roast beef and pudding in his lunch while she, Isaac, Elijah, and Mac only ever had fish, fish, and more fish. He wouldn't understand how desperately their family needed money now.

He'd also been the boy who'd steal Billy Tubbin's lunch pail and the ribbon out of Nancy Rinker's hair just because he knew he'd not get in trouble.

And that's why he'd never had any friends.

Though Gilbert seemed different now. Older, more mature, owner of ships and cranes and probably a slew of other things she didn't have a clue about. If he didn't have friends today, it was because he didn't want them.

He'd certainly turned down her friendship when she'd offered it ten years ago.

Leaving her plate of food on the table untouched, Rebekah glanced around the galley for a bucket. But was she truly about to return to Gilbert's quarters to clean up his mess while he turned around the ship for the sole purpose of booting her off? Instead of grabbing a bucket, she pumped water into the basin and tossed in the dirty dishes from the crew. Though really, why bother with that either? She should leave both messes for the next cook.

But Gilbert wasn't going to find another cook in Eagle Harbor on such short notice, even she knew that. So the kitchen duties would be split among the crew until a new cook could be hired. At least the crew would thank her for cleaning up, even if Gilbert didn't.

The man was so rich, he probably thought dishes washed themselves.

Maybe he didn't realize some people truly needed money and had to work hard to get it. Maybe if she explained everything to Gilbert, he'd let her stay on as cook.

She had nothing to lose by asking.

She set the plate she'd been scrubbing on the table and headed down the corridor that led to the deck. The *Lassiter* hadn't turned yet. Could she catch Gilbert before he found the shipmaster?

Her feet barely touched the stairs as she flew up them. A brisk summer breeze greeted her, tugging at the knot in her hair. She squinted against the morning sunshine. She might not be aboard her family's little mackinaw sailboat, flying across the waves with the wind, but she'd never tire of being at sea, of the reflection of sunlight on water and the endless expanse of blue before her, the rugged shoreline of pine trees and rocks to the south, and in the distance, the shadows of what must be the Huron Mountains. She'd never seen the rolling hills before. While she'd sailed west hundreds of times to fish, she'd never before sailed this far east of the Keweenaw Peninsula.

"Did you need something, Rebekah?" A youth who looked like he still belonged in short pants rushed up to her, a thatch of brown hair flopping over his eye. "I can haul water somewhere if you need it. Or maybe help—"

"Where's Gilbert?"

The boy blinked at her. "Don't have no one by that name on the crew."

She surveyed the deck to find several other sailors standing still, their attention locked on her for some reason.

"Gilbert's not on the crew. He's the owner."

"Oh, you mean Mr. Sinclair."

She caught sight of him standing in the pilothouse with three other men, one of which was probably the captain. "I found him."

She headed toward the group without another glance at the boy.

"I can't turn this ship around." The captain's voice floated from the open door to the pilothouse. "We're already running a day behind, and I've every intention of making that time up before we reach Chicago."

"When you told me you'd hired a woman cook, I didn't realize it was Rebekah Cummings."

"Which shouldn't make a difference one way or the other." Rebekah stepped into the pilothouse. "I'm as fine of a cook as anyone else you could get, probably better."

The bearded mariner at the helm glanced at her. "Her flapjacks were right good this morning."

She smiled. "Thank you, Enfield."

"I agree." Stanley Harris, Gilbert's business assistant, stood in the corner, his red hair bright even in the shadows.

"You are not staying." Gilbert glared at her, his words clipped and terse.

Well, so much for calmly explaining herself to him. "I'm not a child to be sent home at your whim. You've got a boy of no more than ten and five working for you, but you won't let a woman of two and twenty aboard your ship?"

"I don't care how old anybody is." Gilbert jabbed a finger in her direction. "You're not working on this ship."

Had a more exasperating man ever walked the earth? "You heard the captain. You're running behind schedule, and you need a cook, at least until you get to Chicago. Whether you care for it or not—"

"Enough!"

~.~.~.~.~

Gilbert clenched his jaw and rubbed his hand through his hair despite the stiff feel of the pomade he'd used on it that morning.

His shout caused the pilot to take a step back from the wheel and the captain to edge nearer the glass. Rebekah, on the other hand, had crossed her arms over her chest, her chin tilted in a defiant angle, and her eyes sparking green fire.

Why did his anger only seem to make her more stubborn? If she had any sense, she'd be cowering in the corner right now, or better yet, pleading with him to turn the ship around and drop her off at the nearest port.

"It's not fair, Gilbert, and you know it. You're singling me out because you know my family, not because of my abilities. I'm a fine cook and an even better sailor, and you—"

"Just stop talking," he gritted. "Please."

Her jaw moved back and forth for a fraction of a second, then she opened her mouth, and he braced himself for another diatribe. But rather than talk, her lips snapped back together, her jaw as tight as the cable on a loaded crane.

"Have you cleaned up the mess in my quarters yet?"

She cringed. "Not yet."

"Go." He pointed toward the door. "Now."

She pressed her lips together and stalked out, walking so briskly the rest of her hair slipped from its updo to trail behind her in the morning breeze.

Every sailor on deck watched her go, her stride confident and her gait tense enough to shatter the blocks of ice stored in the cargo hold.

And she wondered why he didn't want her aboard? Even if he ignored the debt he owed her brother, a steamship with a twelve man crew was no place for a woman with expressive green eyes and long auburn hair, especially not one who wandered about in trousers.

He had no doubt Rebekah Cummings was an excellent sailor, and she appeared to be a decent cook, but a cargo ship wasn't any place for a woman as innocent to the ways of the world as she. He couldn't watch her every moment, couldn't promise a sailor wouldn't approach her in one of the narrow corridors and attempt to take liberties despite the rules.

"I-I think she should stay," the pilot stammered.

Gilbert cut him a sharp glance, and the man's gaze moved back to the sea.

"Not that my opinion matters, sir."

"She's a good cook. And it seems like she'd do a rather good job of keeping you company." The captain winked at him.

And that was exactly why he couldn't have her aboard. "If she stays, she won't be keeping me company—or anyone else company. I thought I made myself clear in my cabin earlier."

The captain cleared his throat and gave a curt nod. "Very clear, Mr. Sinclair, sir. And I've already told the boys how she's to be treated. But her cooking is still to be commended."

He rubbed the side of his forehead where a soft throbbing had started. Why did she have to be so oblivious about the ways of men and women?

Perhaps you should try kissing your fiancée instead of me. Her words from two months ago came back to him, quick and sharp as they'd stood on North Street together one night, where music from the distant brothel, his anger at Victoria, and Rebekah's pointed tongue had haunted him until his lips had gotten within an inch of hers.

Then that shrewd tongue of hers had turned him away.

Perhaps she wasn't completely naive. Yet she certainly seemed to think every man she met on the *Lassiter* would treat her with respect, and he could guarantee no such thing.

"So am I turning the ship around?" the pilot asked. Enfield winced when the captain gave him an evil glare.

Was taking Rebekah home worth getting to port late? His crew just might mutiny if he attempted it. Furthermore, she did have a point about her age making her old enough to form her own choices.

He rubbed at the throbbing in his head again and looked at the captain. "You'll need to find a new cook once we reach Chicago, a man this time." The last thing he needed was another pretty, naïve woman traipsing aboard the *Lassiter*. "Rebekah will disembark with me, and I'll send her home via rail." He'd see that she was headed back to Eagle Harbor within an hour of arrival. "And call a meeting of the crew. I personally want a word with them regarding their conduct toward Miss Cummings."

The only question was, would he be able to keep his conduct toward her gentlemanly for the next five days? He'd already nearly kissed her once this spring, and that didn't take into consideration all the other times he'd imagined kissing her.

Gilbert blew out a breath. Gentlemanly conduct. Five days. He could manage it. He'd better manage it. He was, after all, headed to Chicago to find himself a wife.

Chapter Three

Elijah Cummings let himself inside his family's cabin, stomping the dirt from his boots as he walked through the entryway and into the kitchen. He wiped the moisture beading at the back of his neck and left the door open to let in the air. After a cool spring, it looked like they might be in for a hot summer.

"Victoria?" With Ma still in town working on some beautification society project or another, maybe he should have come home right after church to help Victoria get lunch ready. He glanced at the biscuits, cheese, and jam set out on the table for lunch and cringed. Something told him Sunday lunch in the Donnelly household was more along the lines of roast beef, gravy, fresh rolls, dessert, and probably a few dishes with fancy names he didn't know how to pronounce.

Not to mention servants to wait on Victoria and her family.

Now she didn't even get meat with her Sunday dinner.

"Victoria?" The Cummings family home might be big for what had once started as a one-room cabin, but it wasn't so large his wife couldn't hear him. He moved into the hall that led to their bedroom. "There was a letter for you at the general store."

"From m-mother?"

Was that a sniffle he heard in her voice? She kept her back to him as she worked to strip the bedding off the mattress. Yet another thing that had changed since she'd married him. She hadn't complained any about the housework she'd taken on, but he'd bet his fishing boat she'd never changed sheets before in her life.

"No, from your sister."

"Oh." That word was definitely accompanied by a sniffle.

"I'm sorry checking on Mac and Tressa took so long. You should have seen him trying to manage the young'uns while Tressa was resting. Jane and Grace were running circles around him." He stepped over the pile of soiled bedding on the floor and wrapped his arms around Victoria's middle, pulling her back into his chest.

"D-don't touch me like that, not right now." Her voice was quiet, nearly strangled.

Don't touch her? During the three weeks they'd been married, he'd discovered many things about his wife, seen and heard several things he hadn't expected. But she'd never once told him not to touch her.

She slid her hand below his arms and pressed it to her belly.

Rather than let go, he held her tighter. "Are you really so upset with me for being home late?"

She shook her head. "I d-don't care about that. There's no b-baby." Her voice broke on the words.

"No baby?" As in, she wasn't pregnant? He turned her to face him, but she kept her eyes down and her hand pressed to her flat stomach. "Victoria, sweetling, we've not even been married a month."

"We st-still had enough time together for me to…" She sniffled and moved her other hand over her first on her belly. "But I didn't."

That was what had her so upset? Not his being late or the paltry offering of food spread on the table? If every woman fell into the family way after only a month, Eagle Harbor would be overrun with young'uns.

All the world would, for that matter.

He sat on the bed and drew her into his arms though she was still standing, then he looked up into the soft hazel eyes she was so determined to hide from him. "I didn't realize you were in such a hurry to start a family."

"Beatrice got pregnant with little Timothy right away. And now she and Timothy Sr. are trying for another."

Beatrice. He should have guessed. The month Victoria had spent with her sister before she'd married him had only increased her determination to have a family. To be more genteel. To overcome her stutter. And to change a slew of other things that he loved about her. Why, if there were some highfalutin' way for her to make her stature shorter or change her hair from its rich brown to Beatrice's blond tresses, she'd try it just to be more like her sister. "Maybe I like spending time with my new wife just how we are. Maybe I want a year or two with you before we have a passel of little ones."

"You w-want to wait an entire year?" she squeaked.

He tugged her down onto his lap and placed a kiss against her strong, square jaw that he loved so much. "I'm enjoying having you all to myself."

Or rather, he did when he was actually home to enjoy her and not working twice as hard as usual to provide for her, build a boathouse for his volunteer life-saving crew, and make up the money he'd lost on his spring catch.

And considering they lived with his ma and sister, he really didn't have Victoria all to himself. Maybe next year they could build a little cabin on the far side of the property. Still in view of the lake, but with quite a few trees between where his family lived and where he and Victoria could start a family themselves. If he didn't have a boathouse to build. If his fish had brought a better price. If he hadn't needed to build a new surfboat or pay for damages to the mercantile from a brawl that had erupted at the store last month. If he didn't need a couple new fishing nets, and the roof over the bedrooms didn't need to be repaired…

And the list went on.

He might finally be married to the woman he'd loved for fifteen years, but the next few months weren't going to be easy on either his pocketbook or his time. And since it didn't look like the price of fish was going up anytime soon, he just might have to look for extra work around town.

"I'm enjoying our time together too." Victoria rested her head on his shoulder. "And you're likely right, and I'm worrying about a baby for nothing."

He breathed in the scent of her, rich and sweet and warm like the summer breeze, then nuzzled his nose against her hair. She was definitely worrying over nothing, but he wasn't fool enough to tell her so when she was on the verge of tears.

"But Tressa also got pregnant right after she was married, and she's about to have her third with Mac. Is it so t-terrible of me to want the same th-th-thing?"

"Tressa and that third child of hers need a lot of prayer at the moment. Mac said Tressa fainted again last night, and they had to call Doc Harrington."

"Is that why they weren't at church?" She lifted her head from his shoulder and bit the side of her lip in that charming little way she had. "Oh dear. Maybe I should m-make up some soup and an extra batch of biscuits for them."

Now that was the wife he knew, always thinking about how she could help others.

"Ah, I'm sure they'd appreciate the soup." The biscuits, however, were another matter. Though he had to give Victoria credit for trying. It couldn't be easy to spend twenty-two years of her life living with a cook on staff and then having to learn to cook herself. But at least cooking would give her something to do this afternoon. Maybe if she paid Tressa a visit, she'd forget about her own troubles.

Or maybe the visit would only make things worse, seeing how it seemed his wife would gladly trade places with Tressa and be confined to bed for a week if it meant a babe was growing in her belly.

Victoria stood. "I'll go gather Rebekah's bedding to wash, then start the biscuits and put on the soup. I can do the laundry while the food cooks."

He should tell her no, that it was too much. That she didn't need to work so hard. But the trouble was Mac and Tressa did need food, and the bedding needed to be washed and changed. Since Ma was gone for the afternoon and Rebekah had evidently decided to stay at Isaac's for a while, that left only his wife to do the work. "Some of the bedding could probably wait until whenever Rebekah gets home, or maybe even until tomorrow. And I think Rebekah made up a batch of biscuits last night. You might take those over to the lighthouse and concentrate on just the soup."

"Oh, I hadn't thought of taking Rebekah's biscuits."

Yes, well, Mac had better thank him later seeing how he was saving his best friend from eating biscuits that could break teeth. He stood and dug into his pocket for the letter from Beatrice. "Why don't you leave the sheets and sit on the sofa for a bit and read your letter?"

Victoria pressed her lips together and stared at the clean white envelope. "It probably has n-news of her being in the family way."

He smoothed a strand of hair away from her cheek and tucked it behind her ear. "Don't worry, love. God will give us a babe in time. Now speaking of sisters, have you seen Rebekah? She left that note on the table about going to Isaac's this morning, but I'd expected to see her at church."

Victoria shook her head. "Perhaps she and Isaac went into the woods, fishing or trapping or something. I've heard twins spend a lot of time together."

"Wrong time of year for trapping." Plus Isaac hadn't been on friendly terms with too much of anyone since Pa died three years ago—Rebekah included. And the note she'd left resting on the table before he'd gotten up that morn had been just plain strange. *Gone to Isaac's.*

For what?

"Maybe I should go check on them." Not that his younger brother was ever happy to see him, but it was time for a visit. And one that didn't include his wife since their brotherly chat was just as likely to end with a donnybrook as it was with a handshake. "Do you mind staying here and making that soup while I go?"

"Not at all. Maybe you c-can meet me at the lighthouse after you finish with Isaac, and I'll cook dinner at Mac and Tressa's."

He scratched behind his ear. "That's a fine idea."

If things went well, he and Mac might even be able to go work on the boathouse after dinner. He'd wanted to have the thing built by now, but he just plain hadn't had time to work on it.

"All right." Victoria stooped to collect the dirty bedding on the floor.

He clenched his jaw at the sight of his wife, all porcelain skin and smooth hands and perfect posture, gathering the soiled linens. He reached for the sheets. "I thought you were leaving those for someone else."

"Don't be ridiculous." She tucked them into a tight bundle against her dress—a fancy yellow one that he wouldn't be able to replace once it wore out. "I've already got these off. I may as well collect the others even if I'm not going to wash them."

"At least let me carry them."

She scowled up at him. "Do you have a problem with me doing housework?"

"Now you're the one being ridiculous."

She bit the side of her lip in that unsure way she had, and her eyes grew soft. "Am I? I don't mind helping. In fact, I'll feel bad if I don't. I want to do this."

"I'm sure everyone will appreciate the help." But he still hated to see her in this position when she'd been born into a finer world. Hadn't Gilbert Sinclair warned him about this before he and Victoria married? Except in Gilbert's version, Victoria was supposed to despise the hardships her new life brought.

Instead, she didn't seem to mind them overmuch, but he hadn't reckoned on feeling so guilty each time she tried to help with something.

Her arms full, Victoria headed out of the room, and his eyes strayed to the sway of her backside as she left. Maybe he was a fool for feeling guilty about marrying the most wonderful woman on the Keweenaw Peninsula—even if she did have to get used to a harder life and wanted babes right quick.

He shucked off his church-going shirt and hung the clothing on its peg before reaching for one of his plain, everyday shirts, then did the same with his trousers and headed out of the room. As he'd reminded Victoria earlier, they'd not yet been married a month. Maybe they were going through a bit of a rough patch, but things would work themselves out with time.

If only he could be so confident about things working themselves out with Isaac. Good thing Rebekah was going to be at his place. She seemed to have a calming influence on the two of them, which was strange considering his sister didn't rightly have a calming effect on anything else under the sun.

Father, please help our conversation to go well.

"Elijah!" Victoria called.

He paused, leaving him only a few steps away from the door. "What's wrong?"

Victoria's footsteps pounded on the loft floor above the kitchen, and he moved to meet her as she rushed down the ladder.

"It's R-R-R-R-R-Rebekah." She shoved a letter at his chest. "I d-d-d-don't think she's at Isaac's."

"Then where is she?"

Victoria's worried eyes met his, a sheen of tears already forming over them. "She d-d-d-doesn't say."

⌐.⌐.⌐.⌐.⌐

"Everyone aboard ship has taken to calling me Miss Cummings." Rebekah plopped Gilbert's dinner tray down on the desk, resisting the urge to bash it over his head—barely. "Care to tell me what that's about?"

Gilbert moved the tray to the side and fiddled with his pencil, his eyes never leaving the drawing at the center of his desk. "Since you're still aboard ship, Miss Cummings, and not back in Eagle Harbor facing Elijah, I wouldn't complain about the crew treating you like a lady."

"You expect me to thank you for meddling in my life?" Oh, Gilbert and Elijah were cut from the same cloth all right. Why had she never noticed it before? Sure, she'd been happy when Gilbert decided not to turn the ship around, but the fact that he'd considered doing such a thing in the first place still rankled.

"Seeing as I own this ship, I think your employment status is my concern." He sounded bored as he wrote a series of numbers on his paper.

"No one would speak to me at dinner beyond, 'Yes please, Miss Cummings.' 'No thank you, Miss Cummings.' 'The meal was excellent, Miss Cummings.' And they wouldn't even look at me when they spoke. What did you say to them?"

"I might have had a word or two with the crew about appropriate conduct."

She really should have bashed him on the head with his dinner tray. His breakfast had already ended up on the floor. Why not another meal? First she had to beg him for a job in front of the captain and pilot, and now she apparently had to beg him to let her talk to someone besides herself for the next four days.

Or rather, besides herself and Gilbert. But she'd hardly call her conversations with Gilbert pleasurable.

"While we're on the topic of proper forms of address, I'd like you to call me by my surname."

Sure he would. She narrowed her eyes at the dinner tray he was ignoring. Maybe it wasn't too late for smacking him in the head with it. "Am I not good enough to use your given name anymore?"

He rubbed at his temples and looked up at her. Finally. "Do you really understand so little of the world beyond the rustic little town where you live? Most women such as yourself would only call a man like me by his first name for one reason."

"They knew each other growing up?"

"They're paramours."

"Oh." And what was she supposed to say to that? "Well, we're childhood fr—" No. She wouldn't call them friends, not after what he'd done to her a decade ago. "Acquaintances. Being paramours is

36

the most ridiculous notion I've ever heard."

And it was. She might not know much of how things worked beyond Eagle Harbor, as Gilbert put it, but she remembered the sting of his rejection well enough. She'd been little more than twelve and he only fifteen, but time didn't take away the feelings of inadequacy and humiliation he'd caused.

Now if only she could forget the year they'd spent as secret friends before that.

"Yes. Utterly ridiculous." But his voice didn't sound as if he believed it to be ridiculous, and his clear blue eyes locked onto her lips until her cheeks began to warm. "I've no idea why people would think such a thing, but neither will I allow you to return to home with your reputation in ruin. I'm afraid you'll have to make do with calling me Mr. Sinclair."

"This is cockeyed. A month ago you would have been delighted to have me aboard ship and sully my reputation if for no other reason than to anger Elijah. Did what happened between you and my brother really change you so much?"

He glanced down at his paper, and she planted her palm smack in the middle of his desk. "Can you at least be polite enough to look at me while we talk, *Mr. Sinclair?*"

His shoulders slumped, the action causing his neck and back to lose their rigidness. "We're not talking about months ago, we're talking about right now, June 26, 1883. Two months ago, perhaps…" He shook his head before wincing and pressing a hand to his temple again. "It doesn't matter. You didn't come to cook on my ship then, you came now. And seeing that you're treated well and returned to Eagle Harbor as soon as we dock in Chicago is the least I can do."

"Returned to Eagle Harbor? But I thought—"

"That once you were in Chicago, I would let you find work on another ship? One that I have no control over? Where any drunken sailor might force his way into your cabin in the dead of night? Where the captain might take a fancy to you and demand you do more than cook for wages?"

This was laughable. Not every man on the Great Lakes was going to treat her so poorly, and if some scallywag tried, she could defend herself with the fishing knife tucked into the waistband of her trousers.

"So you plan to ship me back to Eagle Harbor." She shouldn't be surprised. He obviously viewed her no differently than Elijah or Isaac or anyone else.

"You'll take the train, most likely. It can take you to Houghton, and I'll see that you have transportation via water to Eagle Harbor."

"So Elijah saved your life, and you've suddenly decided to protect me, even if it means you're thwarting my plans to help the very brother who saved you?"

"Elijah and I should never have been enemies, but we were too stubborn to see it." He cocked his head to the side and ran his gaze down her in an arrogant, casual survey. "Probably much the same as you, too stubborn to see all the good you have in Eagle Harbor."

She crossed her arms over her chest. "I'm not stubborn."

He merely cocked an eyebrow.

"Fine. Maybe I can be a bit stubborn, but I'm trying to help my family." And if he thought she'd actually stay on whatever train he placed her, well, it was his own fault for being obtuse. She'd simply get off the train a hundred or so miles north in the port town of Milwaukee and look for work.

"By leaving town before daybreak without telling those you love where you're going?"

"You wouldn't understand."

"No, I'm sure I wouldn't." His voice was chillingly soft despite the constant thrum of the steam engines and the lapping of the water against the ship.

"I don't know why I even bother talking to you. I'll have Petie deliver your food tomorrow." The less she saw of him on this trip, the better.

She turned and stalked from the room, but that didn't prevent him from calling after her. "Miss Cummings, please remember to call Petie by his surname, Mr. Rumford."

~.~.~.~.~

Gilbert winced again as the door slammed behind Rebek—Miss Cummings. Was it so much to ask that she not go stomping around the ship and making a bunch of racket when he had a headache?

Probably. Something told him if she knew about the incessant throbbing in his head, she only would have slammed the door harder. He couldn't help the smile that curled the corners of his mouth at the thought of riling her.

What was wrong with him, mooning over a working class woman who did nothing but agitate him? But since things had been that way between them for a decade, they likely wouldn't change now.

No. No. No. His fascination with Rebekah had to change, starting tonight. He could hardly go to Chicago and pursue an heiress when he had the desire to kiss Rebekah every time she pressed her lips together in that stubborn manner of hers.

Which was why he needed to keep his distance. Out of sight, out of mind and all that. Once she was back in Eagle Harbor and he was busy finding a wife and rebuilding his crane, he'd barely think of her. And in the meantime, it was best to avoid her aboard ship. Having Petie deliver his meals tomorrow was an excellent idea, and she couldn't get mad at him since she'd suggested it.

He sighed and rubbed at his temples again. So why did he have the sinking feeling that Rebekah wasn't going to make keeping his distance very easy? Or that they'd both be better off if he'd have turned the *Lassiter* around and taken her back to Eagle Harbor?

Chapter Four

Gilbert yawned, the drawing before him growing blurry. In the two days he'd been aboard ship, he'd spent every spare minute studying his crane. How long had he been here tonight, sitting at his desk trying to make sure every last measurement was correct before he had another crane built?

Not that anything would get done quickly with the way he needed eleven thousand dollars simply to replace the *Beaumont*. He sighed. The harder he toiled over his papers and studies, the more elusive his dream became.

All the more reason he needed to get to Chicago and find a wife.

Confound it. His first crane was already supposed to be operational by now. How many dockworkers would end up with broken feet or hurt backs or even lost lives because of his delay? Heavy objects such as copper and gold needed a safer way to be loaded onto ships—something far more personal to him than most people realized—and yet no shipping companies and port authorities seemed interested in using machinery to load ships. Or rather, none of them wanted to pay the initial expense.

Why bother purchasing a piece of machinery when laborers are so cheap and plentiful?

His father had said those words to him dozens of times over the past four years after he'd switched his education at the University of Michigan from business to engineering and began studying cranes and derricks. He only needed one working crane to prove all the naysayers wrong—only one working crane to help people like the Marsdens—and it should have already been operational in Eagle Harbor by now.

Carl Mellar of Mellar Shipping in Chicago had been interested in his crane provided Gilbert could have the machine working and prove it would be a wise investment. Unfortunately, the possibility of making his first sale had sunk to the bottom of Lake Superior with his crane at the beginning of May. Mellar was likely still interested in purchasing a crane for his dock in Chicago, which was a meeting he'd have as soon as he reached the city, but Mellar's interest did him little good considering he didn't have a crane to sell and Mellar had never seen it active.

If his father had been using a crane like that in Eagle Harbor when Harold Marsden…

No. He wasn't going there. He'd taken that mental trip too many times to count by now, and revisiting it wasn't going to bring Mr. Marsden back from the grave.

Gilbert slumped to the desk.

God, why? Why allow my crane to end up at the bottom of Lake Superior? What did I do to deserve such a thing?

His cabin remained quiet, not that he expected an answer, but he wouldn't have complained about receiving some sort of indication from the heavens that everything would work itself out.

Then again, the fact that he drew breath might be all the indication he needed considering he was still alive when he should be dead.

He stood and pushed to his feet. He didn't need to think about that either, because reliving how Elijah Cummings had saved his life three weeks ago wasn't going to bring back his crane, nor would it help any of the dockworkers likely to be injured by loading overly heavy cargo.

He was the only one that could help them. He was the only one that could bring back his crane. And at the moment he needed to get out of this cloying little cabin.

He strode toward the door and down the corridor until he reached the stairs to the deck. He should see whether the *Lassiter* was making up time. If they didn't get to Chicago by Thursday afternoon, the load of pork and beef scheduled to arrive from several different slaughterhouses would likely be given to another ship, and the *Lassiter* would be stuck waiting at the docks until he or Stanley could find different cargo.

Gilbert reached the top of the stairs, the cool evening breeze ruffling his hair, and started toward the pilothouse. One of the lanterns at the ship's rail glinted off something dark and red. He paused, turning with a sinking feeling in his gut.

She couldn't be that dumb.

But she was Rebekah Cummings, and so she truly was that dumb.

He strode toward the edge of the deck where she leaned over the railing, the breeze that had ruffled his own hair tangling her long auburn tresses. Tresses she hadn't bothered to pin up before coming on deck. How long had her hair been like that? Didn't she know it was improper to let it down? How was he supposed to keep his crew away from her when she waltzed about the ship like this?

"What are you doing?" He nearly barked the words as he came up beside her.

She kept her head tilted up toward the night sky, her face half illuminated by a distant lantern and the other half cast in shadows.

"Looking at the stars."

"Your hair's down."

"I've never seen the stars from the lake before." She shrugged as though being out here in the dark meant nothing. As though the wind wasn't currently twirling the strands of hair nearest her face.

As though he didn't have his fists clenched in his pockets to keep himself from running his fingers through it.

"They're endless. You can't see this many in Eagle Harbor, too many trees." She craned her neck farther back, exposing the creamy white column of her throat. "But they're everywhere out here."

He opened his mouth to send her back to her quarters. Yet her face was so innocent, so sincere, so similar to the expression she'd worn a decade or so ago when she'd found him alone on the beach and offered to show him a fishing hole.

And just like that day ten years ago, he couldn't quite find it in himself to tell her no.

He tilted his head back, his eyes tracking immediately to the Little Dipper and the North Star, and from there to the Big Dipper and the Great Bear that completed Ursa Major before he shifted his gaze back to her. "You can't see them in Chicago."

"That's impossible. These constellations can be seen from anywhere in the Northern Hemisphere."

"In theory, yes, but the lights in Chicago are so bright they drown out the starlight."

"I don't think I'll like Chicago then." Her forehead drew together in a series of wrinkles.

His thumb ached to sooth the lines away. "I daresay you won't. There're people everywhere, and it's always busy, dusty, noisy."

"There has to be something good about the city, otherwise no one would want to live there."

"There's work. Factories upon factories making anything and

everything you can imagine. The smoke from them fills the air and makes it hard to take a deep breath at times."

She turned to him, the light from the nearest lantern casting shadows over her face. "I've never been somewhere with that many people."

No, and he didn't plan for her to be there long. "It's a lot more crowded than living in Eagle Harbor. You should see the tenements. Apartments after apartments stacked one on top of the other, filled with floors and floors of people who work in factories and have little besides the clothes they wear."

"And to think, sometimes I find Eagle Harbor rather crowded."

Eagle Harbor? Crowded? "Ah, would that be on Sunday morning when a whopping forty-five people attend church together?"

She chuckled and shoved at his elbow, causing it to lose its place on the railing and his balance to falter for an instant. "More like when a ship docks and all the mariners rush to The Pretty Penny."

He offered her a half smile and looked over at her. "Point taken."

Her face appeared nearly angelic in the mixture of star and lantern light, her usually tense body at ease. No sharp words flew from her mouth or stubborn tilt angled her jaw. For once in her life, she seemed completely content and at peace.

Was she like this often at home? With family and close friends? If only all his interactions with her were this way…

˰.˰.˰.˰.˰

Why couldn't Gilbert always be like this? Relaxed, well-mannered, a hint of teasing in his voice? This was the boy she remembered from their school days.

It was also the boy who'd always pretended not to know her

45

whenever more interesting friends were around.

She stared back over the lake. The absence of moon tonight made the lanterns from the steamer the brightest lights on the water. A perfect night for stargazing indeed.

"It seems like our house isn't big enough anymore, and we certainly don't live in one of those cramped apartments you mentioned." She didn't know where that confession came from. Perhaps the quiet of the night, or the way they stood separate and isolated from the handful of crew on deck.

"Your family home?" Gilbert edged closer, the scent of his expensive cologne mixing with the breeze off the water. "I thought it was rather large for a cabin."

"It would be if Elijah and Victoria stayed in their room. But they're always kissing and giggling and flirting. Last time I came home, Elijah's hands…" She clamped her mouth shut, but that didn't stop the heat from burning her face. One of these days, she'd learn to stop her tongue from rambling, and if she had any sense, it would be sooner rather than later.

The relaxed look drained from Gilbert's features.

Better yet, maybe she should just take the fishing knife from her waistband and cut her tongue out here and now. "I'm sorry, Gilbert. I wasn't thinking when I mentioned Victoria. I didn't mean to—"

"It's no bother." He moved away from her.

She hadn't realized he'd been standing so close, but her right side turned suddenly cold from his withdrawal.

"I'm sure she's happier with Elijah than she would have been with me. At least for the time being."

"For the time being?" What was that supposed to mean?

His hand clamped onto the rail and he looked over the water. "And now I'm free to find a wife in Chicago, one whose family I can forge an even more advantageous business arrangement with."

The coldness she'd felt when he'd left her side doubled, starting somewhere in the vicinity of her heart and swirling outward until her skin felt coated in ice. "Is that why you're going to Chicago? To find some rich heiress to marry?"

Gilbert met her gaze evenly, no hint of apology in his eyes. "It's one of several reasons, yes."

"Didn't you learn your lesson after what happened with Victoria?"

His jaw tightened. "Yes. Next time I'll have a lawyer thoroughly examine the finances of my fiancée's father so I know I'm not being lied to."

"That's not what I meant. Do you truly want to spend the rest of your life married to someone who came as part of a business deal?" She shouldn't care. She *didn't* care. They might have been secret friends a decade ago, but that was before he'd decided he was too good for her.

"Don't look so appalled, Miss Cummings. It happens all the time."

But the idea was appalling. Utterly and horrifyingly so. Did he think he could control his emotions so easily? Or those of his wife? That a marriage was only a cold, logical arrangement? "What if you fall in love with someone else? Someone who's poor or doesn't have the connections you want?"

"You women and your ridiculous romantic notions." Gilbert rubbed the back of his neck with quick, agitated jerks. "Love isn't something you helplessly fall into. It's something that grows out of mutual respect, often aided by shared living arrangements, and it's hardly necessary for a marriage."

Where was the boy she remembered? The one who'd gone fishing with her every day after school? The one who'd nervously given her that first kiss? The one with the tender heart who'd just needed a friend?

Or maybe not a friend, but someone willing to love him a little?

Even in the darkness, she could feel his icy blue eyes on hers. Maybe Elijah had been right to feud with Gilbert this spring. Maybe Gilbert had turned as hard as his father. "'Many waters cannot quench love, neither can the floods drown it: if a man would give all the substance of his house for love, it would utterly be contemned.'"

"Quoting one of your favorite poets now, are you?" Gilbert turned back toward the water.

"Not a poet. The Bible. So you might want to give the verse a moment's thought or two." She'd long thought that verse to be one of the more frivolous verses her father had them memorize at the dinner table, but it certainly served its purpose now.

"And you know so very much about love, seeing how you've never once had a suitor, and at the moment, you're running away from a family that loves you very much." Gilbert kept his back to her as he spoke, but that did little to soften the sting in his words.

The man was impossible. Was this how he'd be with his wife? Cold and icy? Making cruel remarks if he didn't like what she said? Ignoring her if he deemed himself too busy for an interruption?

And why did she care?

"There was a time when I would have been jealous of your wife—whoever she ends up being. With your grand house and fancy clothes and big inheritance, you're considered quite a catch, aren't you? But I can't bring myself to be jealous anymore. I pity the woman who ends up with you for a husband."

His shoulders straightened, and he turned at her words, but she was finished trying to talk sense into him. She stomped across the deck and down the stairs to her room.

Chapter Five

The wind whipped off the lake, nearly taking the hat from Elijah's head as he stood on the porch of the general store. A flash of lightning lit the sky over the water, and thunder rumbled in the distance. A quarter hour and the storm would be upon them.

If his sister wasn't missing, he would be fishing right now. But one glance at the horizon this morning told him he wouldn't have been headed onto the lake anyway.

The clouds had looked angry for the past two hours, the white-crested waves battering the rocks on the beach by their house. Aye, if he went out onto the lake today, it would be on his surfboat with his life-saving crew, not on his mackinaw fishing boat by himself.

More thunder rumbled, closer this time. He could almost sense the cold spray of water in his face as he rowed through the storm, the dip and swell of the waves, and the terrified people clinging to a sinking ship.

Elijah hardened his jaw as he surveyed the storm. A wave crashed over the pier that sat on the other side of the beach. Then another swallowed the end of the dock.

Was he crazy for almost wishing his sister was floundering aboard a ship amidst the waves? Then he could rescue her, bring her back to safety, and wrap his arms around her, holding her tight until he knew she was safe. But how could he rescue her when he didn't know where she was?

Or if she needed rescuing.

But of course she needed rescuing. Rebekah wouldn't just up and leave of her own choice.

Except she'd been angry with him since he told her she couldn't go out with his volunteer life-saving team on rescues.

But she wasn't angry enough to leave, was she?

Another gust of wind blew off the lake, and he smashed his hat onto his head lest he lose it. Where could she be? A day and a half of searching had yielded nothing, not even the slightest hint to her whereabouts. And he'd checked everywhere, from her favorite childhood fishing hole, to the upstairs apartment in Mac and Tressa's bakery, to the woods surrounding Eagle Harbor.

If he didn't find some clue soon, he just might have to knock on every door in the town in search of an answer.

Which would keep him from work for nearly a week.

And if he still found nothing? He shifted his gaze back to the water-slickened dock, and his stomach hardened into a tight little ball. Rebekah had been gone Sunday morning when he awoke, and the *Lassiter* had departed for Chicago that very day at dawn.

She wouldn't have left town completely, would she?

But it made too much sense. He'd told her she couldn't go out with his life-saving crew, and she'd refused to sail their little mackinaw fishing boat with him ever since. But Rebekah couldn't stay away from sailing forever. It was in her blood just as it was in his and Isaac's. Just as it had been in Pa's. And not only did Rebekah know the ins and outs of sailing, but she was a hard worker and a good cook. She'd be an asset to any ship's crew.

"Elijah, I thought you were coming inside with me. What are you doing out here?" Victoria appeared at his side, her basket laden with everything from flour and sugar, to marmalade and penny candy, to pink ribbons and lace—likely for Mac's girls.

Except they didn't have enough money for all that. He'd given her three dollars to get a few groceries for Mac, expecting change in return. By the look of things, she'd spent every penny—quite literally, since there was enough penny candy in there to last six months. And was that a dime novel in the bottom of the basket?

"Never mind. I found things to take to the Oaktons without you. But do you have two more dollars? The loveliest fabric just came in from Chicago over the weekend. I was thinking we could buy some and pay Jessalyn Dowrick to make Tressa a new dress. You should come inside and feel it. It's the softest cotton with little white daisies against a light blue background." Her eyes danced with excitement. "It'll look perfect on Tressa, and I'm sure she needs new clothes. The dress she wore yesterday was rather tight around her middle."

"I… ah…" He scratched behind his ear. How did he tell his wife she couldn't buy something for people who likely needed it? "We need to get to the lighthouse before the rain comes. Maybe we can come back later."

And hopefully she'd forget about the fabric by then.

"Oh, certainly." She looked around as though just noticing how strong the wind had gotten and how close the storm clouds were. "We should—"

"Elijah Cummings, just the person I wanted to see." Mrs. Kainner tromped up the steps to the mercantile, her small stature doing nothing to deter the authority in her voice and step.

"Yes, I'm glad we found you." Mrs. Ranulfson, twice Mrs. Kainner's size in both height and girth, moved slower as she approached. Normally Elijah assumed she walked slowly so as not to upset the precarious balance of ostrich feathers sticking out from her hat, but the wind had already bent the feathers down.

He looked between the two of them. The way they were looking at him with gleaming eyes didn't bode well.

"Good morning, ladies." He swooped his hat off his head, just like Ma and Pa had taught him, even though he'd rather pretend he was deaf and blind and didn't know they stood in front of him. "I was just on my way to deliver Victoria to the Oaktons before the storm blows in. Maybe we can talk later?"

Or maybe he'd be so busy searching for Rebekah that they'd find someone else to talk to entirely. And he wasn't about to ask these two gossips if they'd seen Rebekah, for then the news of her disappearance would reach legendary proportions before lunchtime.

"Y-yes. We don't want to get w-wet." Victoria smiled apologetically at the two women.

"Wet indeed. We were planning on shopping until the storm blew over. We might even venture upstairs and share some cookies with Mrs. Foley." Mrs. Ranulfson held up the brown paper sack that everyone in town recognized as coming from the Oakton's bakery.

"We best be going then." Elijah placed a hand at Victoria's back.

Mrs. Kainner huffed and bustled her way next to him. "You can wait a minute or two before dashing off. The storm's not upon us quite yet, and we need someone to head up the benevolence project for the Thimbleberry Festival in August."

Elijah dropped his hand from Victoria and took a step back, placing him right at the edge of the porch. For some reason he'd never been able to tell the little spitfire of a widow no, even though he probably should have a dozen times or so over the past few years. "Ah, I hope you find someone?"

"Don't be ridiculous." She waved her hand absently in the air. "We've already found someone. You."

Him. Sure. Why not head up the yearly benevolence project? It wasn't as though he was busy enough with a new wife, a search for his sister, a need to earn more money, sinking ships to rescue, a boathouse to build, the cabin roof to repair. "I don't think—"

"That sounds wonderful." Victoria's hazel eyes brightened, and his heart lurched. "I've always l-loved the Thimbleberry Festival. The festivals in Milwaukee were always so b-big and formal. But Eagle Harbor's is just p-p-perfect. What are you raising money for?"

Mrs. Ranulfson's glower softened into something of a smile— or rather, as close to a smile as the thickly built woman ever mustered. "Have you visited the school lately, Victoria? If so, you'll see it needs a new coat of paint, both inside and out, and the mathematics textbooks need to be replaced. The one Erik had last year was losing half its pages."

"Oh, it would b-be so hard to study from a t-textbook that didn't have all its pages, and especially for m-mathematics."

"Exactly." Mrs. Ranulfson seemed as excited as a raccoon that had stumbled upon picnic scraps.

Elijah drew Victoria to his side. If she didn't keep her mouth closed, she was going to commit him to heading up the benevolence project every year from now until he died. "Didn't you raise money for the school last year?"

The banker's wife huffed. "For the desks. This is different."

"Any extra funds we earn will go to the Spritzer family," Mrs. Kainner said softly. "They need whatever help they can get these days."

The Spritzers. Elijah swallowed and pushed away memories of the dark night that the oldest Spritzer boy had died—the night Lake Superior had claimed a life he hadn't been able to rescue.

Even with Ellie, the oldest daughter, now working at the bakery, the Spritzers had to be hurting for money something fierce. Mac and Tressa were probably paying Ellie half what Clifford had earned as a mariner.

But did he have the time to raise money for something else when he was in such desperate straits himself?

"L-let's do it, Elijah. I'm m-more than happy to help."

Victoria looked up at him with her bright, concerned eyes, and his heart gave another little twist. How could he say no to something that Victoria so clearly wanted to be a part of?

How could he say no to helping the Spritzers?

"I can go around to some of the t-townsfolk and ask for donations while you're on the lake each day."

Of course she'd volunteer such a thing, never mind how nervous she'd get making those calls by herself or how badly she might stutter as a result. When his wife saw a need, she was determined to put others first, just like she was putting Tressa and Mac first with the pile of things she'd bought them. It was one of the reasons he'd loved her for a decade and a half.

But none of that made his other problems go away. He still wasn't in a position to spend extra time between now and the Thimbleberry Festival in August raising donations.

"Have you talked to Gilbert Sinclair about heading this up?" Sinclair could probably get half the businesses in town to donate money by snapping his fingers.

Mrs. Kainner rolled her eyes. "Well, of course. He was our first choice."

"Didn't you hear?" Mrs. Ranulfson spoke over another boom of thunder. "Gilbert Sinclair left on the *Lassiter* last Sunday. I heard he expects to be in Chicago for the rest of the summer, maybe longer."

Gilbert Sinclair had left? On the *Lassiter*? The little ball Elijah's stomach had tightened into earlier was nothing compared to the cold, hard pile of copper ingots that lodged itself in his gut right now. He moved his gaze to the town dock being battered by white-crested waves. He'd been too busy quietly searching for Rebekah to pay attention to the scuttlebutt around town.

Had Rebekah left on the *Lassiter*—with Gilbert?

Please, God, let her be anywhere besides on that ship.

The fog bell clanged, not the constant ringing that warned ships of fog, but three quick chimes, a break, and then another chime: the signal for the life-savers to assemble.

Elijah smashed his hat on the top of his head. "I've got to go, ladies. Victoria, can you make it to the lighthouse on your own? If not, just stay here until the storm blows over."

If he had hustled Victoria to the lighthouse straight away rather than staying to talk to these two women, then she'd have been safely at the lighthouse by now. But he didn't have time to play gentleman and escort his wife about town when people needed to be rescued.

He stepped between Mrs. Kainner and Mrs. Ranulfson, but something tugged at his sleeve. He turned back to find Victoria grasping his shirt, her eyes large with worry.

"Be careful out there."

He pressed his lips to her forehead, and cupped the side of her neck with his palm. "As careful as I can be, sweetling."

Then he dashed down the steps of the mercantile without a backward glance. He'd learned never to look back when he first started going on rescues, because the last thing he needed was the worried faces of loved ones haunting him while he battled the waves.

⌐.⌐.⌐.⌐.⌐

Fruitless. Gilbert stared at the diagrams spread across his desk. The entire notion of accomplishing anything while Rebekah Cummings was somewhere aboard ship, smiling and teasing and laughing with the crew, was utterly fruitless. He hadn't even been able to correctly add the columns in his ledger this morning and had come up with a different sum each time he made an attempt.

He ran a hand through his hair and pushed himself away from his desk. Maybe he needed fresh air, a change in scenery. They should be approaching the Sault Ste. Marie locks shortly.

But if he left his cabin, he was bound to run into Rebekah. He had enough memories of her from last night, her hair a mixture of auburn tresses and starlit highlights. Her face calm and content, her laughter soft and relaxed.

But none of that compared to her parting words.

There was a time when she'd have been jealous of his wife?

Why?

Or maybe more importantly, when?

Was she talking about some school girl crush from years ago, or had she been jealous when he'd been engaged to Victoria this spring?

Or did she mean she'd only be jealous of having his money?

And why did it matter? He couldn't marry a woman who barely had twenty dollars to her name. And even if she had the money he needed, he still couldn't envision her by his side at a dinner party while he courted investors and manufacturers for his business. The woman had no self-control. Rather than smile and be polite, she'd haul off and slap the first man who said something slightly offensive. She'd probably slap the first woman who was mean to her as well, and it wouldn't be long before one of the snide women who filled the upper echelons of Chicago society said something insulting.

Then, even if by some miracle he and Rebekah could overcome her lack of money and manners, marriage to her would still mean fights.

Lots of fights.

Infuriating fights. Amusing fights. Entertaining fights.

Strangely, that idea bothered him much less than the notion of her slapping a woman at a party. At least she stood up to him rather than bent to his every whim. And did she have any idea how breathtaking she was when mad? The corner of his mouth inched up into a half smile.

A smile he let die. What did it matter if she stood up to him or made him smile? He needed to approach marriage like he did everything else in life—with precision and logic. Emotions and dreams and wishes would get him nowhere.

Rebekah might stick her nose up at him and spout Bible verses about love, but she'd never before been in a position where she needed thousands of dollars. If he wanted to build cranes, if he wanted to keep dockworkers from getting injured when they loaded heavy cargo, if he wanted to prevent unneeded deaths, then he needed to get his crane into production. There were only two ways to do that: beg his father for funds, or marry someone who already had them.

He didn't need ten seconds to decide which was the better option.

A knock sounded, and his door cracked open.

"Gilbert?"

Of course Rebekah would be the one to peek her head into the room. It couldn't be Stanley or Petie or Captain Steverman.

"What?" he growled.

She rolled her eyes at him and opened the door the rest of the way, leaning her shoulder against the frame.

Good. He hardly needed her any closer, even if her hair was tucked up under her hat rather than hanging freely down around her shoulders.

"The captain wants you to know we'll be approaching the locks in another hour."

"Thank you." He stood from his chair and made his way around the desk.

"Do you want me to take your breakfast tray?"

"No. You can…" But it was too late. She was nearly to the desk before she'd finished asking, her gait light and quick, and her trousers doing little to hide the gentle sway of her hips.

He scowled. "I want you wearing a skirt for the rest of your time on the *Lassiter*."

She plopped the tray back down on his desk. "Do you now? And why, precisely, do you think you have control over what I wear?"

Was it too much to hope that one day he'd tell her something without her turning it into a battle? "Would you stop arguing?"

"I don't have a skirt."

"You what?" He'd known she liked to wear trousers, and as odd as her attire usually was, he couldn't exactly fault her for donning them on her brother's fishing boat. But for walking around town or even around a steamship as large as the *Lassiter*?

Rebekah shrugged. "I have one or two at home but didn't think to pack them."

He'd have to buy her one before sending her back to Eagle Harbor, though that wouldn't exactly help either of them at the moment.

"They get in my way when I'm trying to work."

He ran his eyes slowly down her. Dressed in trousers, boots, and a loose shirt, she looked much the same in his quarters as she had last night on the deck.

But her lips... he could see them better now, in the clear daylight that streamed through the porthole, soft and pink and full. He'd tasted them once before when they were little more than children, so long ago that he couldn't remember much other than the fact of their kissing.

Perhaps you should try kissing your fiancée instead of me.

She'd been right to set him in his place two months ago, the last time he'd almost kissed her. But now that he didn't have a fiancée—or more particularly, now that her brother had married his former fiancée...

What would kissing her be like now that she was a grown woman? He'd already forgotten the taste of Victoria's kisses. If he kissed Rebekah, how long would the flavor of her lips linger in his mind?

"Why are you looking at me like that?"

He pulled his gaze away from her mouth. "Last night on the deck you said there was a time when you would have been jealous of whomever I married. Why?"

She turned away, picking up a fork that had landed on his desk when she'd set the tray back down. "I let my mouth get the better of me, that's all."

He put his hand on her arm to stop her from lifting the tray again. "Your blush is giving you away."

She twisted her arm out of his grip. "Well, that's all I'm going to tell you."

"Is it my money?"

Her face turned redder yet. "I should slap you for saying such a thing."

Yes, she probably should. It would hardly be the first time she'd done so over the years, but if he was going to endure the sting of her palm against his cheek, then it should be for a much better reason than asking her questions. Besides, he had questions of his own that needed to be answered.

Except his questions couldn't be asked with words.

He moved a step nearer—close enough to trap her between the edge of the desk and the wall—then brushed his lips against hers, and braced himself for the slap.

A slap that didn't come.

He brushed across her lips again, slower this time, longer.

A shaky breath shuddered out from between her lips and fanned against his mouth, warm and honest, like the woman before him.

He raised his hands up to clasp her arms, holding her in place as he settled his mouth over hers yet again, and for more than a simple brush of lips upon lips.

She tasted sweet, but not sickeningly so. Strong, yet somehow vulnerable.

This was nothing like kissing Victoria. No awkwardness and stilted efforts. Rebekah was all gentle, soothing movements with energy burning just beneath.

Her hands reached up to wrap around his neck, and he drew her closer. How many times had he dreamt of this? How many times had he wondered how it would feel to hold her in his arms? To rain kisses on her forehead and cheek and neck, to bury his face in the soft, thick waves of her hair?

He tore his lips away from her mouth to do just that, starting with a whispered kiss at the back of her jaw.

Whack!

The sharp sting of flesh on flesh stung his cheek. He pulled away only to find the tip of a fishing knife poking him in the stomach.

"How dare you?" Fury coated her voice, and her eyes flashed a heat intense enough to smelt a ton of copper into ingots. "Really, Gilbert? You spend all this time telling the crew how to treat me, and you're the one who acts as if I'm one of the girls at the Pretty Penny? I've half a mind to shove this into your stomach."

The tip of the blade tore a bit of his shirt.

He took a step back, out of the range of her knife. "I'm sorry. I wasn't thinking. I just…" He rubbed a hand back and forth over his hair, searching for the right words. "You… you tasted so good, and—"

"I tasted good? Do you think I'm some type of confection? I don't taste like anything, thank you very much. And neither am I a toy. Are you bored and in need of some entertainment on the way to Chicago, and I just happened to be the only available woman?"

"Rebekah, no, it's not that way. I promise."

"You promise? Why should I believe your promises? You, who threaten every man aboard with losing their job if they treat me wrong, yet has no trouble breaking all those rules yourself."

He gritted his teeth. "Don't act so innocent. You're the one prancing around the ship at all hours of the night, with your hair down and wearing clothes that show off your legs. I'm not a saint. And you didn't say no when I kissed you. I seem to remember you wrapping your arms about my neck and kissing me back."

Her face turned whiter than the gulls that circled the docks over Chicago's harbor. "Don't blame this on me. I never asked you to kiss me, and I'll thank you to keep your grubby mitts off me for the rest of the trip." She turned and fled toward the door.

"And I certainly hope you treat your future wife better than you treat me." The door slammed closed so hard the crew on deck surely heard it.

He stared at the door for a moment, then buried his head in his hands. *God, what have I done?*

He hadn't meant to frighten her, to take liberties he ought not. But she'd been right there in front of him, with that odd combination of strength and naivety, and all those questions about her being jealous had tumbled through his mind. How could he help but hold her?

Kiss her?

Even though I intend to marry another.

She was right. He was a scoundrel, and he still had nearly three days left with her aboard ship.

How was he supposed to control himself now that he knew how perfectly she fit in his arms? How sweet her lips tasted?

And how, oh how, was he supposed to go to Chicago and find himself a wife with memories of Rebekah Cummings spinning through his mind?

Chapter Six

From her hunched position on her tiny bed in the cook's quarters, Rebekah pulled the last of the pins from her hair. Since Gilbert had tugged half of her tresses down during their kiss, simply pushing the pins back in wouldn't work. Had she really let his hands tangle in her hair before she had sense enough to pull away? She must have, because the simple twist she'd thrown her hair into this morning was now a mess.

She let the thick tresses fall in a curtain about her face, then wrapped her arms around her knees.

What had Gilbert been thinking to kiss her like that?

What had she been thinking to let him?

He wasn't even her friend, let alone her beau. Yet as soon as his lips had touched hers, she'd forgotten everything, from the arrogant, commanding way he treated her to his intention to marry another.

She'd befriended him once before and that had turned out disastrous. Why did she think befriending him, kissing him, even thinking about him would turn out any different now? Elijah was right about him. He was a rich, snooty scoundrel who cared for nothing and no one, save himself and his business pursuits. Perhaps he'd once had a soft heart, but it had turned to ice during the time he'd been gone from Eagle Harbor.

She sniffled and raised her head to look around the cramped cook's quarters. The room that sat off the galley was no bigger than a closet, but it allowed the cook to be near the kitchen and made it easier for the *Lassiter* to employ a woman cook. She still had three days and two nights left aboard ship. How was she ever going to survive being around Gilbert?

She reached down to finger the hilt of her small fishing knife. She could always use that again. If only next time she remembered to unsheathe it when he started the kiss rather than when he was nearly finished.

No. There wouldn't be a next time. No matter how pleasant it felt to have his arms around her or how much her lips tingled afterwards.

A knock sounded on her door.

"Leave me alone." Was it time for lunch already? She'd barely finished breakfast before she'd gone to tell Gilbert they were nearing the Soo Locks.

Even if it was lunchtime, the sailors could feed themselves for one meal. Mariners weren't helpless. And what could Gilbert do? Throw her overboard for not cooking?

He couldn't threaten to fire her when he'd already promised to do just that the second they docked in Chicago.

The knock sounded again.

"I said, 'Leave me alone.'" She wasn't about to get up and unlock that door for anybody, even if the steamer was sinking.

The lock clicked anyway, then the door opened.

"Get out." She scrambled to her feet, shoving her hair back from her face and wiping furiously at the tears on her cheeks.

"Not before we talk." Gilbert stood in the doorway, his shoulders relaxed and his eyes soft and concerned.

She should hate him. Wanted to hate him, wanted to find the fact that he'd invaded her room as unforgivable as Elijah would have.

But as tears burned her eyes and a lump stuck in the back of her throat, her stomach did a little flip. Then her heart stopped for the briefest instant before it started beating again.

He'd come for her. Her slap a few minutes ago hadn't scared him away, nor had her threat to use her fishing knife. Who else would come after her when she threw such a fit?

Oh, but they were a bad pair. Like the drunk who stumbles into a bar every night and keeps asking for one more pint though he's dead broke. The two of them were going to break each other if they couldn't find some way to pretend the other didn't exist for the rest of the trip.

"I'm sorry, Rebekah. I didn't mean to frighten you." He ran a hand through his hair—his perfectly combed hair.

A sure sign he was upset if he dared mess up his pristine appearance.

She swallowed the knot lodged in her throat. "You need to leave. Now. I'm not some strumpet whose room you can barge into at any time."

"Blast it." He stalked farther into the tiny room. "I never said you were."

She shifted so she had a clear path toward the door, which he'd at least left open—though that wouldn't necessarily stop the sailors from talking. "Then why'd you treat me like one?"

"I didn't…" His hand found his hair again, rubbing vigorously back and forth this time. "It wasn't my intention to treat you in an unbecoming manner."

As though that explained anything. She wrapped her arms around her middle and wiped a stray tear from her cheek. "Then what was your intention?"

He slid his gaze away, and she stomped her foot on the floor. "Don't stand there like some mute schoolboy. Look at me, Gilbert, and explain yourself."

~.~.~.~.~

Gilbert pressed his lips together and tipped his head back to stare at the ceiling. He couldn't start explaining himself to her. Doing so would reveal entirely too much.

He drew in a breath and glanced into her green eyes, still moist with tears. He owed her some type of explanation, if nothing else. "I kissed you because I wanted to."

"But you hate me."

He hated her? Did she truly think that? He reached out a hand toward her shoulder. But touching her would only make matters worse, so he dropped it. "I've never hated you."

She sniffled again and wiped at her eyes. "Sure. That's why you threatened to kick me off your ship two days ago."

"You shouldn't be here. First because your family doesn't know, second because the shipping industry is no place for an innocent like yourself, and third because the two of us are… are…"

"Going to kill each other."

"I was thinking rather the opposite."

Her head shot up, her eyes round and questioning.

He reached for her again, better not to touch her, yes, yet he'd always been a trifle helpless to control himself around her. He laid his palm on her cheek. "I mean it, Rebekah. Every time I'm near you, I want to…" *Kiss you. Hold you.* "Take liberties I ought not."

She heaved in a large, shaky breath, a breath that reminded him of the one that had fanned his cheek when he first attempted to kiss her…

And someone knocked on the door.

Rebekah jerked away from him, her face white.

He whirled to see Stanley standing in the doorway, his eyes moving back and forth between him and Rebekah, a question etched onto his brow.

Gilbert rubbed his hand through his hair again and let out a sigh. At least his assistant knew how to keep his mouth shut. Had one of the other sailors interrupted them, rumors would be flying about the ship before he climbed the stairs to the deck.

"What do you need?" His voice came out rougher than intended, but wouldn't anyone's after being interrupted in such a fashion?

"Uh, we're slowing down to approach the locks. Miss Cummings was supposed to let you know a half hour or so ago."

The locks. Of course. That was what originally brought Rebekah to his quarters. "Tell Captain Steverman I'll be right there."

Stanley's gaze flickered past him to Rebekah. "Of course." Then he headed out of the kitchen.

Gilbert turned to find Rebekah standing against the far wall of her tiny room, her rich auburn hair cascading down her shoulders and her arms still wrapped about herself in a forlorn sort of embrace. "Rebekah, I need…"

She shook her head at him. "Just go. I don't want to talk about it anymore. I'll try my best to stay out of your way until we get to Chicago."

Earlier that morning, he'd intended to call her up to the deck when they reached the locks, even if it was time for her to be making lunch. Living in Eagle Harbor all her life, she'd surely be fascinated by how the water levels in the locks raised and lowered so ships could traverse the once-dangerous rapids that led from

Lake Superior down the St. Mary's River to Lake Huron. But he could hardly call her up to the pilothouse now.

He pressed his eyes shut and rubbed at his forehead. And she was probably right about ending this conversation. Talking wasn't likely to accomplish anything, and he'd decided on the first day of their journey that avoiding her was the best course of action.

So why did he leave the room feeling more guilty than when he'd come?

～.～.～.～.～

"Don't blame yourself. You're not that dense."

Elijah looked at his best friend and adopted brother, Mac Oakton, as they trudged up Front Street together, mud from the storm that had just blown over sucking at their boots. "How can you say that when our sister is missing?"

Mac stepped into a puddle, sloshing water on the hem of his trousers. "Because she's old enough to make her own choices."

"And you expect me to stand around and wait for her to return?" Frustration tinged his voice. Mac might be able to wait patiently for Rebekah since he wasn't the one who'd told her she deserved a switchin' for wanting to help with his last rescue, and that was right before he chased her off the beach.

"No, don't stand around. You're supposed to lay down and wait. Doctor's orders."

Elijah looked over his shoulder at the log house Dr. Harrington had converted into his office. Inside, the doctor was treating a family that had come down from the Central Mine to spend the day boating and got stuck on the rocks.

It was Merrick's day off. He could still hear the mother protesting when he'd asked what had possessed them to take their three young'uns out in a canoe on a day like this.

We couldn't have gone tomorrow.

The storm clouds looked far away.

A thick, Cornish accent had coated their words. One would think they'd come from a country surrounded by land and not a rocky peninsula that jutted into the Atlantic Ocean. What was it with the Cornish? Give them a pickaxe, and they could burrow down any hole and come up again with copper, iron, silver, gold, or anything else a person could mine. But give them a canoe, and it was splintered on the rocks before rain even started. A handful of Cornish were good sailors, his pa being one of them, but the majority of them were better off underground than on the waves.

"Elijah?" Concern laced Mac's voice. "Are you sure you're all right? Do you need to go back to the doc's?"

"I don't need to go to the doc's, and I don't need to lay down either. I'm fine." Though he stretched his shoulder a bit, aching from where a wave had washed him into a rock as he'd reached for one of the crying children.

"The only thing I need to do is find Rebekah." He refused to believe she was gone—never mind the note she'd left. Would his sister really up and leave because they'd had an argument? He and Rebekah had been arguing all their lives, and she'd never gotten the notion to run off before.

"Why don't you start asking people if they've seen her then? There's Mr. Ranulfson." Mac pointed to the owner of the bank.

"Confound it, Mac." Elijah scowled and left Front Street, starting up the path to the lighthouse and not quite caring that he took such quick steps he splattered mud onto his and Mac's trousers. "If I start asking everyone whether they've see her or not, the whole town is going to know she's gone within the hour."

"And what's wrong with that? Rebekah did leave, after all."

Did Mac hear himself? How could his friend talk about

Rebekah being gone with the same casualness that he discussed what direction the wind was blowing. "Isaac hasn't returned from checking Pa's old trapping cabins yet, and he was supposed to stop by Central to see if she'd gone there."

Please, God, let her be holed up in one of the trapping cabins.

Mac opened the door to the lighthouse and climbed the few steps into the kitchen. "Central's crowded enough that she could hide there half a year before Isaac found her."

"Thank you for that reminder." Elijah climbed the steps behind Mac and rubbed at his temple. Maybe Mac was right and he was crazy for holding out hope that this was all a misunderstanding and Rebekah would be at the cabin when he returned home.

"You're back!" Victoria rushed across the kitchen to him and threw her arms around his neck.

Elijah wrapped his arms around her and burrowed his face into the place where her shoulders and neck met. He'd taken to keeping a dry change of clothes at Doc Harrington's—half because Lake Superior was so cold the doc insisted hypothermia would set in if he didn't get his wet clothes off right away, and half because his wife ended up soaked when she hugged him after one of his rescues—though she'd never once complained. "I'm safe and sound, even standing on my own two feet."

"I love you." She spoke the words on a sigh.

"I love you too." He gave Victoria one last squeeze before releasing her.

"How did the rescue go?" Tressa, Mac's pregnant wife, lifted a plate of cookies off the hutch and headed for the table with them, but she only made it a step before she swayed.

Mac dashed across the kitchen in two strides. "Do you need to lay down? Elijah and Victoria can go if you're not up for visiting."

Tressa reached out and braced herself on the hutch, then

shrugged Mac's hand off her shoulder. "I'm fine. I just lost my balance for a minute."

But she didn't look fine. With her pale face and thin cheeks, she looked ready to fall over.

"Dolly want to swing! Dolly want to swing!" Jane rushed into the kitchen and pulled on her mother's skirts, a ragdoll clutched in her arms. "Go outside. Go outside."

"Not now, Jane. Your mother isn't feeling well." Mac looked around the kitchen. "Where's your sister? And is Colin still at the Spritzers?"

"Gracie's sleeping," Jane answered solemnly, her hands clutching her little rag doll. "Colin's at his friends."

"Why don't you men take her outside? Then Tressa and I can sit on the sofa and visit some more?" Victoria squeezed his arm and gave him one of those pleading looks he hadn't figured out how to say no to.

"Go outside, Uncle 'Lijah. Go outside!" Jane bounded toward him.

He swooped the little girl off her feet and over his shoulder. She let out a fit of giggles that echoed overly loud in the somber kitchen.

"Go on, Mac." Victoria moved between the quarreling couple and laid a hand on Mac's bulky forearm. "It will be a nice break for her."

Mac looked from Victoria's relaxed form to Tressa's stiff shoulders and back again. "All right, but don't let her—"

"I said I was fine," Tressa snapped.

Mac heaved out a breath and took a step back from his wife, then turned and headed for the door that led outside. "Come on, Jane. Your ma needs some quiet."

With Jane still slung over his shoulder, Elijah snagged a couple cookies from the platter Tressa had set back on the hutch and popped one in his mouth before heading outside.

The rocky hill on which the lighthouse sat gave a clear view of the wide, narrow harbor below and the open lake beyond. Summer, winter, autumn, and spring, a constant breeze blew over the water to the north, sometimes causing white froth to cap the waves even on the sunniest of days.

Right then, the lake was still rough from the storm, even though the sun had peeked out from behind the clouds. The air hung thick and muggy, and the humidity that had plagued them for the past few days had only grown worse with the storm.

Across from them, on the opposite point of the harbor, the boathouse sat, its frame nearly up. Once it was functional, it would make launching the surfboat into rough waters quicker and easier. No more heaving the boat into the water from the beach.

If only he had time to work on it.

"I'd thought things were getting better with Tressa—until her recent fainting spell." Mac kicked at a stray stone. "She likes to pretend nothing's wrong, but something is. There has to be. I can see it in the puzzled look on Doc Harrington's face when he looks in on her, in the constant paleness of her skin. She's always short of breath these days and sways half the time she walks from one room to another, but if I tell her to lay down, she just glares at me and goes about her business."

"Let me down, Uncle 'Lijah. Let me down." Jane squiggled in his grip. "Dolly want to swing."

He slid the child to the ground and gave her a pat on the head. "Be careful now. Don't go near the rocks."

She nodded, her brown eyes wide and serious. "I won't, Uncle 'Lijah." Then she squealed and darted off toward the wooden swing set that Mac had set as far back from the rocks as possible, her golden brown hair flying behind her and her pinafore so long it nearly dragged on the ground.

Mac kicked at another stone. "Yesterday when I told Tressa to rest, she tromped into the kitchen and baked up three batches of cookies."

Elijah popped his second cookie in his mouth. Probably wouldn't do to tell Mac the cookies were right fine.

If only there was something he and Victoria could do. Something Mac could do. But none of them had the ability to make Tressa and the child inside her well. "The baby's due in September, right? That's just two more months."

"October. And it feels like we'll never get there."

Well, yeah. When he put it like that...

"Elijah, there you are."

Elijah turned to see Isaac striding up the hill.

"I've searched half the town for you, and that's after searching for Rebekah." Isaac's hair stuck out at odd angles from beneath the brim of his hat, the same reddish-brown shade as Rebekah's, though since he appeared dry, he must have escaped the storm.

"Did you find her?" Worry swirled in his gut as he headed to meet his brother.

Isaac held his hands open. "Does it look like she's with me?"

"You didn't find any sign of her? Not even in one of Pa's trapping cabins?"

Isaac slung a hand low on his hip. "She certainly hasn't been to any within the past couple days, and the handful of people I talked to at Central hadn't seen anyone resembling her."

"Huh." Mac scanned the beach and road as though suddenly expecting to catch sight of Rebekah. "I figured she'd be holed up in one of them for some reason or another."

Jane's laughter echoed from the swing, where she was setting her doll on the seat only to have it fall off as soon as she gave it a push.

"She's probably in Chicago," Isaac muttered. "It's the only other choice."

No. Chicago was too far away, and if she'd left on the *Lassiter*, then she'd be on the ship with Gilbert even now. He might not be fighting with the rich scoundrel anymore, but he didn't cotton to the idea of his sister being with him for an entire trip to Chicago either. "What if she's somewhere else? Somewhere we haven't checked yet?"

"Like where?" Isaac raised his hands in question. "It would take months to scour the Central and Delaware mines well enough to be sure she wasn't at either of those. And what would she be doing there anyway? You're sure no one around town saw her headed to the dock Sunday morning?"

Elijah knocked the brim of his hat askew as he scratched behind his ear. "I don't know."

"What do you mean, 'you don't know.' Haven't you been asking people while you searched the town?"

He shrugged. "I didn't want everyone knowing she was gone."

"So you didn't ask anyone?" Isaac thundered loudly enough that Tressa's restful afternoon had probably just been disturbed. "It's not like you can keep her leaving a secret in a town the size of Eagle Harbor."

"Doesn't mean you have to ring the church bell and announce it from the top of the steeple either."

"You should be lying down, Elijah," a fancy-sounding voice with a southern accent interrupted.

Elijah looked over Isaac's shoulder to see Dr. Harrington approaching, his black medical bag in hand.

Isaac turned to the doctor. "Lying down? Why would he be

lying down in the middle of the…"

Isaac's voice trailed off as he turned to survey the rough, gray water. "You went on a rescue, didn't you?"

Confound it. Why did Harrington have to come tromping up and announce the rescue to Isaac? Ever since their father had died, his brother was miffed each time he set foot upon a boat. "Had I not gone out, a whole family would have died."

"And what happens when you die trying to rescue complete strangers?" Isaac's green eyes shot accusations.

He told himself not to clench his jaw or grind his teeth. Told himself to take a deep, long breath rather than yell at his brother.

"When the Good Lord calls me home, then I don't reckon there's much I'll be able to do about it." The words tumbled out anyway, not quite a shout, but they were still a far piece from being kind and brotherly. It was an argument they'd had hundreds of times since he'd started his volunteer life-saving team. One of these days, Isaac might find some sense and realize he wasn't about to give up his missions, nor should he. If he'd been home when Pa's boat capsized and had tried to rescue him, then their father might well be alive today.

How could he sentence another person's family to the same grief his own had gone through when he had the ability to prevent people from dying? Isaac might be fine with sitting around safe and dry while others perished, but Elijah wasn't about to carry that guilt on his shoulders.

Jaw hard and shoulders rigid, Isaac turned to face Dr. Harrington. "I don't suppose you have the afternoon free to go knock on doors with me?"

Elijah forced his jaw to relax and hands to unclench. There was no point arguing over his rescues with a more pressing matter to worry about. And since they'd done all they could to search the town on their own, he couldn't prevent his sister's disappearance from being the most popular topic of conversation around dinner tables much longer. "Rebekah's run off, and we have no idea where to find her."

"You're looking for Rebekah?" A faint flush of pink stole across the doctor's cheeks. "She left on the *Lassiter* Sunday morning. Got a job as a cook."

Elijah's jaw fell open while Isaac's snapped shut.

"Huh, didn't think she'd actually do it." Mac readjusted his hat on his head and glanced at the swing, where Jane had stopped pushing her doll and was now twirling her way toward them, arms spread wide and dress flaring.

Elijah crossed his arms and took a step closer to Dr. Harrington. "Care to tell me how you know that, and why you didn't tell us sooner?"

The doctor's cheeks were definitely pink now. "I ran into her on my way back from checking on Tressa Sunday morning."

Elijah's stomach plunged. He couldn't deny it anymore. Rebekah was on the *Lassiter* with his enemy—or rather, his former enemy. But at the moment, the truce he and Gilbert had made didn't seem near as important as the fact that the snake was sailing with his sister.

"Why'd she leave?" Isaac snapped. "Did it have something to do with Elijah?"

Elijah took a step back. He might not have been all that kind to Rebekah about not going out on his rescues, but he certainly hadn't prodded her into running off with Sinclair.

Deep breath, Elijah. Deep breath. Hadn't Doc Harrington said she was working as the cook? So she didn't run off with Sinclair, but why'd she take that job?

Was she concerned about the family's bills?

76

That didn't settle much better than her running off because she was mad.

"I don't know why she left." Dr. Harrington shifted his medical bag from one hand to the other and glanced toward the lighthouse, where he'd probably been headed to check on Tressa. "She didn't tell me."

"Maybe the way her brothers go at each other, like two wolf pack leaders warring over turf, has something to do with it." Mac gave Elijah's shoulder a little shove, then bent to heft Jane up on his shoulders. She'd twirled herself smack into the back of her pa's legs.

"I suppose it doesn't really matter why she left." Isaac heaved out a breath and squinted at the open water to their north. "Either way, you've got to go get her, Elijah."

"Go get her?" Elijah looked at his brother. Isaac expected him to drop everything he was doing and head down to Chicago? "I can't. I've got a boathouse to build, a benevolence project to head up, fish to catch…"

The list was endless, and he surely didn't have money to buy passage to Chicago either.

But this was his sister they were talking about. He'd sell the *North Star* if it meant keeping her safe.

"Rebekah's two and twenty." Mac settled one of his big, bear-like hands on Isaac's shoulder, the other hand firmly gripping Jane's skinny leg. "That means she's old enough to make her own choices, same as you. She wanted to leave, so she left. Doesn't mean anyone should chase after her."

"Chasing after her wouldn't work anyway," Elijah muttered. "If she's working as a cook, then she won't be in Chicago for more than a day. She'd be gone long before I arrived."

"Great. Just great." Isaac's eyes met Elijah's. "Why did you have to run her off? Can't you get along with anybody?"

"What makes you think she left because of me?" But what if he had been the reason? What if snapping at her for her nonsensical desire to be involved in his life-saving rescues made her run? Or what if she'd seen some of the bills and taken it upon herself to earn extra money?

"A hunch I have." Isaac studied him for a moment, his green eyes entirely too similar to those of his missing twin sister. "If something happens to her, I'm holding you responsible." With that, Isaac whirled and stalked down the hill, leaving a slight ripple in the thick air that clung to the town.

Elijah sighed. If something happened to Rebekah, he'd hold himself responsible too.

Chapter Seven

Rain slanted sideways through the dark afternoon, hammering the deck of the *Lassiter* while lightning slashed the sky above. Gilbert hunkered beneath his wide-brimmed hat and braced himself for the loud boom of thunder as he made his way across the rocking ship to the pilothouse.

"How far are we from a harbor?"

Captain Steverman shook his head and pointed to the nautical chart pinned to the wall. "We're better off riding her out than trying to change course in this wind. She should blow over in an hour or two."

Gilbert glanced at the chart, indicating the deep waters of Lake Michigan all around them. The captain was right, not only would they need to go out of their way to seek shelter, but with this kind of wind, they also risked wrecking on any number of sandbars and rock reefs as they approached shore. Summer storms that lasted a matter of hours didn't pose near the risk of day-long blizzards with snow so thick a person couldn't see the bow of the vessel they stood on. Riding the storm out was the best option by far.

Still, the last time he'd been on a steamer during a storm, he'd lost his most prized ship, not to mention his crane. If that didn't give him reason to be anxious, he didn't know what did.

Another slash of lightning streaked the sky, followed by a crack of thunder. Gilbert paced behind where the captain and pilot stood, four steps in one direction, a whirl, and four steps in the other.

The captain shook his head but clamped his mouth shut beneath his droopy mustache. Gilbert turned and paced again. Perhaps he was being a bit ridiculous. After all, even in the driving rain, he could see the bow and stern of the ship, the wild waves that rocked her to and fro, the crew hunkered down on the deck making sure the sails they'd taken down stayed secured in the gusting wind. The ship and crew didn't need him hovering. He should go back to his quarters and—

"Mr. Sinclair." Young Petie stepped into the pilothouse and pointed to the starboard railing. "It's Miss Cummings. I've asked her twice now, and she won't go below deck. Insists on standing right there."

Gilbert followed the direction of Petie's finger, and sure enough, a lone figure in a wide-brimmed hat and slicker stood at the rail.

"Thank you," he growled at the youth before leaving the shelter of the pilothouse and stalking off across the deck.

He hadn't seen her since their kiss yesterday morning—a good thing that, since the last words he remembered speaking were something along the lines of wanting to kiss her every time he was near her.

At the moment, however, she deserved to be throttled.

The wind caught a few strands of her hair, dragging them into the rain as she stood at the rail looking out over the waves. The rain itself didn't seem to bother her though, nor did the rough swaying of the ship. The waves weren't large enough to reach the deck, let alone wash her over. A fact she likely knew before she'd decided to stand there, but that didn't take away the overall stupidity of standing at a ship's rail during a storm. What if she slipped? What if the rocking caused her to lose her balance?

"Miss Cummings," he barked, coming to a stop beside her. "I want you below deck, immediately."

She turned and drew her gaze up. Red, swollen eyes rimmed with tears met his.

Perfect. Not only did he have a crazy woman on his ship trying to get herself washed overboard, he had an emotional one to boot.

"Come." He gripped her upper arm and tried tugging her toward safety, but she refused to let go of the rail.

"Do you think this is what it was like for Pa when he... when he..." She sniffled, her eyes still filled with moisture that couldn't be mistaken for raindrops. "I should have gone to help him. The Foley's dingy was sitting right on the beach, and he was so close to the harbor. I wanted to take it and go get him, but Isaac and Mac wouldn't let me."

Her father. Gilbert swallowed. He hadn't been in Eagle Harbor when her father, Hiram Cummings, had drowned three years ago, but he'd heard the story. A quick and violent storm. An experienced fisherman who almost reached harbor. And three siblings standing in the lighthouse tower, watching as the little fishing boat capsized just shy of calm waters.

He cleared his throat. "Isaac and Mac were right to keep you safe."

She couldn't possibly think it wise to go out in a little dinghy by herself in a storm such as this.

"Not you too." She jerked away from him. "Just because I'm a woman doesn't mean I should stand by and watch people die, stand by while my own father dies."

The tears flooded her eyes again, and this time there was no stopping the deluge.

He shouldn't be out here arguing with her, had already made up his mind not to be near her again. But what was he to do? Leave her alone in the storm while she sobbed for her father?

She put on a strong, determined front for the world, but vulnerability lurked just under the surface—it always had. Maybe that's why she always presented herself so fiercely. She didn't want anyone discovering the softness underneath.

They weren't so different, him and her.

"Let's get you away from the railing." The wind and waves muffled the sound of her sobs as he led her toward one of the smokestacks in the center of the ship. He reached inside his oil slicker and found the handkerchief buried in the pocket of his suitcoat. "You did nothing wrong that day."

"How can you say that when Pa's dead and I didn't try to save him?"

"There's no need to blame yourself." He took a step nearer, close enough that to most of the crew they probably looked like one form hunched along the side of the smokestack. The thunder boomed above, and the rain showed little sign of lessening.

He took his handkerchief and trailed it down her tear-stained cheeks. It was soaked by the rain before it could do much for her tears. He held it against her cheek a moment longer than necessary, not quite ready to take it away.

He may have grown up in a fancy house with expensive servants, but his family had never been like the Cummingses. Hiram had always been on the beach building sand castles or mediating a snowball fight between half the children in town. His own father locked himself in his office, too busy with papers and figures and numbers to even look up when Gilbert had a question for him.

"Is this the first time you've sailed in a storm since your father's accident?"

She nodded and returned her gaze to the sea. "It's harder than I thought, being out here, imagining what must have gone through his mind. Elijah goes out on rescues all the time. I don't know how he manages."

"As I said before, your father's death isn't your fault."

Her chin trembled. "But it is. Don't you see? I should have gone out. I should have helped. Instead I listened and did what I was told. And look where that got me." She swiped a fresh bout of tears from her cheek. "I'm done asking permission and doing what I'm told. Elijah needs money something fierce after buying Victoria a ring, paying for a new surfboat, paying the bill for damages at the general store, and everything else that happened this spring."

Gilbert held back a groan. How much of that money trouble was his fault? He had never offered to help replace Elijah's surfboat, though he'd certainly been tied to its destruction. Never offered to pay the full extent of damages after the fight between his crew and Elijah's life-saving team broke out at the mercantile.

Not that he had a surplus of money lying around. But if he could get sixteen thousand dollars for the *Beaumont* and his crane, couldn't he spare an extra hundred dollars or so to help smooth over some of the trouble he'd caused? Elijah had saved his life, after all.

"If I asked Elijah's permission before I left to find work, do you think he'd say yes?" Rebekah's voice turned fierce.

Gilbert stroked a strand of tangled, wet hair away from her cheek. "If I had a sister, I'd not let her go." Especially to work in the shipping industry.

"That's the problem. What am I supposed to do? Stand around

and watch my family struggle because they don't want me to work? Because they've got too much pride to let me help? For as long as I live, I'll always regret not trying to help Pa. If my family complains when I return at the end of the shipping season with a hundred dollars in my pocket, maybe I'll leave for good and move somewhere people will appreciate me."

His heartbeat stilled. She couldn't leave her family. Didn't she see how much they loved her?

But as she'd just reminded him, she was a grown woman and able to make her own choices.

So why did the notion of Rebekah leaving her family bother him?

He should have asked her reason for leaving home sooner. He could have found a hundred dollars to give her that first day aboard ship—on the condition that she go straight back to Eagle Harbor after he turned the *Lassiter* around. Then he'd have gone to the mercantile and paid Elijah's portion of the bill for damages. He wouldn't have even needed to argue with Elijah about taking the money that way.

"Let's go." He took her by the shoulder and wrapped his arm around her back. "You need to get below deck where it's warm and dry."

She looked out over the lake one more time, bracing her legs with the adeptness of a mariner who'd spent the past thirty years at sea. "I still wish I wouldn't have listened to Isaac and Mac when they told me not to go out."

"They love you, Rebekah, and they were just trying to protect you." Though he couldn't argue with some of her reasoning. He'd probably have killed himself trying to rescue his own father in that situation, and Byron Sinclair wasn't half the man Hiram Cummings had been.

But if Rebekah would have gone out that day, she likely wouldn't be standing in front of him now, and the thought of the world without Rebekah Cummings seemed sad indeed.

He tugged on her shoulders. "Let's go. Standing here and staring at the sea will do you no good."

⁓.⁓.⁓.⁓.⁓

Despite the dry clothes she now wore, a chill raced up Rebekah's spine as she slipped into a new pair of stockings and set to braiding her hair. She sniffled and swiped at her eyes, which still insisted on tearing up.

Stupid eyes.

Stupid tears.

Stupid her.

What had she been thinking standing at the side of the deck and crying like a baby? And in front of Gilbert, no less. Hadn't she told him just yesterday that she didn't want to see him for the rest of the trip?

She also seemed to recall saying something about using her fishing knife to gut him if he touched her again.

But there he'd been, his eyes gentle and concerned, his face etched with soft lines rather than its usual hard planes. He'd even wiped away her tears—or tried.

She put on her boots, pulled open the door to her cabin, and stepped inside the galley. She couldn't start dinner given how the ship rocked violently back and forth with the tumultuous waves, but perhaps she could scrounge up a leftover biscuit and some coffee while she waited out the storm.

"Ouch!" A clatter sounded to her left.

She looked over to find Gilbert, mug in hand, fighting his way through the swaying cast iron pans that hung from the galley ceiling.

"What are you doing?"

He stepped to the long trestle table bolted to the floor so it didn't slide across the galley in rough seas. "Trying to make you tea."

A small smile tilted the corners of her mouth. Did he even know how to make tea in a normal kitchen? "Figured you went back up to the deck."

He shrugged, and if she wasn't mistaken, the back of his neck turned slightly pink. "Seemed like you needed some tea. Mother always says it calms the nerves. And up on deck, you were…" He blew out a breath and looked around the galley. "But it's impossible to make any with how the ship's rocking."

Actually, it was possible. The kettle fit securely into its notch on top of the cook stove so that it wouldn't fly about the ship, and like the table, the stove was bolted to the floor. But starting a fire and heating water just for her was hardly worth the effort.

Would he go through the trouble if he knew how?

And why was she asking herself such ridiculous questions? Sure, they'd kissed yesterday, but then she'd threatened to use her knife on him. End of story. It changed nothing.

Besides, they'd kissed once before and nothing had come of it. She'd been twelve—not that she was particularly keeping track of how old she'd been when various men had kissed her.

Except various men hadn't kissed her. Just Gilbert. And just that once.

Until yesterday.

Her cheeks suddenly felt as though a cook stove fire had ignited beneath her skin. "There's a little coffee left from this morning in the kettle." She nodded to the stove.

Gilbert strode to the kettle, his gait sturdy and determined despite the swaying ship.

Had she expected anything else? He'd been sailing on vessels like the *Lassiter* for as long as he'd been walking.

Gilbert filled the mug and then returned to the table, a scowl on his face as he handed it to her. "It's cold."

She plopped down onto the bench, bolted to the floor like everything else on the steamer. "That's what happens when the fire goes out. Coffee gets cold."

He stood at the edge of the table, his gaze moving from her to the stove and back as she took a sip.

"Would you like to get yourself a cup and join me?"

"Coffee. Right." He pivoted with the precision of someone in the military and marched back over to the kettle, where he poured himself a cup before returning to the table. He didn't even attempt to take a sip. "Are you feeling better?"

"Yes, thank you. I'm sorry about earlier though." She took a long gulp of coffee, and glanced out the small porthole at the gray water. "Do you think Elijah's on a rescue?"

"The storm's not that big."

She knew it, but one day there would be a storm big enough to cause trouble, and she wouldn't be around to help if Elijah needed it.

But Elijah didn't let her help, not even though she could sail better than most of the life-savers on his crew. That was part of the reason she was on the *Lassiter* in the first place.

"Don't."

She looked up at Gilbert.

"You're worrying about things you have no control over." He reached out his hand and covered hers on the table. "Don't."

Her gaze dropped to his hand, large and strong and warm, calloused from spending too many hours holding a pencil, but not from hard labor like her brothers' hands were. "Why can't you always be like this?"

His brow drew down into a frown. "Like what?"

"Like how you are now." She tilted her mug slightly. "You got me coffee."

"It should have been tea," he muttered. "Coffee will only make you more nervous, not calm you down."

"But you got it for me. And up on deck, you didn't shout at me for being a dunderhead and then lock me in my quarters until the storm passed. You… you… just, well, thanks."

"I'm sorry about your father. I don't think I've ever told you that before, or anyone from your family, for that matter." He sighed and tilted his head up to the ceiling as though fighting his own memories—which didn't make sense. He'd always seem to resent her father. "Hiram was a good man. I'll never understand why God took him early."

She took a long sip of coffee to moisten her suddenly dry throat. "I'm not sure any of us will."

"Well." Gilbert removed his hand from hers and stood. "It seems like the storm's abating."

He gestured toward the porthole, and she turned to see the sky lightening with orange rays of sunlight breaking through the clouds in the distance. And now that she thought of it, the ship had stopped its harsh rocking and was moving with the waves in a gentle, lulling motion.

"I need to go check that the wind hasn't blown us off course and we're still able to make port by tomorrow evening. Do you need anything more before I leave?" He headed to the sink to dump out the coffee he hadn't touched.

Only for you to stay a little longer. "Are you offering to cook dinner for the crew?"

He looked back over his shoulder and grinned. Not smirked or half-smiled, but an honest, full-out grin. "The crew will throw me overboard if I attempt it."

She smiled back at him. "I suppose I'll do the cooking then."

"That's probably best." He returned to the table, and the pleasant smile left his face, replaced once again by that serious, somewhat baffled look he got when he watched her. He studied her for one moment, then two and three, but as always, his eyes gave no indication what he was thinking.

"Have a good evening, Rebekah," he rumbled in a deep, barely recognizable voice. Then he walked past her and headed into the corridor, his brisk stride causing him to disappear far too quickly.

Why, oh why did he have to be so nice? It was almost easier to have him mean. Almost easier to look at him and see only hard determination, hear him spout off about how he would marry the first heiress that could help him reclaim all he'd lost when the *Beaumont* sank.

But the compassion in his eyes when he'd looked at her on deck, the way he'd gotten her coffee and then complained that it wasn't warm and he couldn't make tea, the way he'd said her father was a good man…

What if he wasn't as hard as she'd thought? What if all the sweetness and softness that he'd had when he was younger was still there, lurking somewhere beneath the cold, hard exterior he now showed the world?

She tilted her head toward the ceiling and drew in a deep breath. It didn't matter. She couldn't let it matter. By this time tomorrow, he'd be dragging her to the train station and sending her back to Eagle Harbor. It hardly made a difference if he wasn't as cruel as he'd led her to believe. He still wanted to be rid of her.

So why did her stomach churn at the notion of him sending her away and marrying for money rather than love?

Chapter Eight

"What do you mean no train can take her farther than Milwaukee tonight?"

Rebekah turned away from where Stanley Harris and Gilbert stood arguing with the ticket clerk and looked around the massive Union Station in Chicago. Echoes filled the air while lines of passengers stood waiting to purchase tickets. Each railroad company had its own special area. Some signs and arrows pointed to the Pennsylvania Company terminal while others pointed to the Chicago, Burlington and Quincy Railroad. Gilbert stood discussing matters with a clerk for the Chicago, Milwaukee and St. Paul Railway. And there were signs for the Chicago and Alton Railroad on the other side of the giant corridor-like room.

How did a person keep from getting lost in here? Never mind how confusing it was to find the station in the first place with all the dusty roads and similar looking buildings that made up Chicago.

And it was hot. The breeze off Lake Michigan wasn't nearly as cool as the one off Lake Superior. It also appeared Gilbert had been right about the air itself. Dust and smoke hung thick, and not even the series of doors leading into the station seemed to keep the filthy air out.

The chugging of trains outside mixed with the shouts of children and lectures from mothers and fathers, all of which echoed tenfold through the cavernous room. Some commuters had purchased their tickets and headed straight out of the numerous back and side doors to the platforms—platforms with so many trains she was more likely to get on the wrong one than the right. And Gilbert said some of the trains even entered the buildings behind the station's main terminal so passengers didn't have to wait outside.

Stanley approached her. "It should just be a few more minutes." Why had he accompanied them to the train station? Surely he had plenty of things to do back on the steamer. The *Lassiter* was set to leave tonight for a series of smaller ports along the northern portion of Lake Michigan—Traverse City, Petoskey, Charlevoix—all places she'd never heard of.

And would never get to see if Gilbert had his way.

"I don't understand why Gilbert wouldn't let me stay on as cook."

Stanley scrubbed a hand over his mouth and looked around the station. "He didn't explain?"

He had, but the reason hardly seemed good enough when Gilbert well knew her family needed money.

"Come." Gilbert appeared beside them, his jaw hard. "I can only get you as far as Milwaukee with the trains left tonight."

That was fine with her, considering that's where she meant to stay.

He took her hand and planted it firmly on his arm before striding through the crowd.

She struggled to keep up. "Not everyone has legs as long as you. And you left Stanley behind."

Indeed, Gilbert's business manager was nearly swallowed by the crowd behind them as he walked along with her bags.

"Sorry." Gilbert slowed as he held open the door to the station and guided her through.

She took a breath of hot, choking air. Maybe she'd been wrong about how much of the dust and smoky haze these doors kept out.

Somehow, despite the throng of people headed every which way, Gilbert's fancy carriage sat on the street only a few steps away. He barged straight toward it, tugging her along like an anchor that was too small to hold its ship in place.

"Where are you taking me?"

Ignoring the driver scrambling down from his seat, Gilbert opened the carriage door and waited for her to climb inside before he settled on the seat across from her. "To my parents."

She nearly choked, and not on the air this time. "Y-your parents?"

"Unless you have a better idea of what I'm supposed to do with you."

Do with her? Did he view her as nothing more than unwanted cargo? Who said she wanted to go to his parents anyway?

"If I put you on a train tonight, you'd have to stay over in Milwaukee before departing for Green Bay in the morning. If we wait until tomorrow, I can purchase connecting tickets all the way to Houghton without any overnight stays."

Stanley climbed inside the carriage, and the door swung shut behind him.

She slumped back against the seat. It looked like Gilbert was giving her little choice about where she went for the night, and she wasn't foolish enough to fight him on it. Best to save her energy for when she ran away tomorrow. Besides, if she insisted on finding a place of her own for the night, she'd have to pay for it, and that meant less money to give Elijah.

But it was all a bit much, really. The Chicago docks had been so busy they'd nearly given her apoplexy, then the noise of Union Station had nearly turned her deaf, and now she was headed to the Sinclairs' Mansion?

She'd been anxious to see the city, yes, but absorbing everything in an hour or two wasn't what she'd had in mind. Would the Sinclair house in Chicago be bigger and grander than their Eagle Harbor mansion? It had to be. Everything seemed bigger and grander in Chicago. But what kind of house would the Sinclairs own? Was it possible to have a better house than the one she'd already seen?

And look at her letting her imagination run away with her. It hardly mattered what their house would be like. She wasn't staying any length of time. Knowing Gilbert, he'd take her around back to the servants' entrance, drop her off with the cook, and give her a little closet of a room to sleep in until it was time to stick her on a train tomorrow.

Except he hadn't exactly treated her like that during the storm yesterday, had he?

She blew out a breath and slanted him a glance. It was almost easier to deal with him before, when he'd been all authoritative and arrogant. What was she supposed to think about him now that he was halfway nice?

Hopefully he would take her to the servants' entrance. Then she'd have reason to be miffed with him again.

Silence settled over the carriage—if you could call it silence given the way the noise of other carriages, horses, and passersby filtered inside. She looked out the window at the dizzying array of streets and people and vehicles.

"I wonder if Lindy Marsden is still living here." She hadn't thought of it before, but one of her friends from Eagle Harbor had moved to the city after her father died five years ago. She and Lindy had traded letters for a while, but she'd never been very good at making herself sit still long enough to write a letter.

"She lives in Bridgeport," Stanley answered.

She turned to Stanley. How would he know? Had he kept track of Lindy? That didn't make sense, since he wasn't from Eagle Harbor. Gilbert, on the other hand, had known her before she moved. "Do you ever see Lindy?"

"We visit on occasion."

Well, wasn't that lovely? She didn't remember Gilbert and Lindy ever talking when she'd been in Eagle Harbor, but now they visited? She crossed her arms and stared at Gilbert. "Too bad I'm not staying long enough to visit her."

"Yes, too bad." Gilbert moved his gaze back out the window, which was fine with her. She wasn't in the mood to talk to him anyway.

She shifted in the seat so she could better see Stanley, and if that meant she didn't have a clear view of Gilbert anymore, she wasn't going to complain. "Are you staying at the Sinclairs' too, Stanley?"

"No," Gilbert answered—as though his business manager didn't have a tongue of his own. "We'll drop him off at his apartment on the way."

She frowned and kept her gaze pinned to Stanley. "Then why did you come to the train station in the first place?"

Stanley shifted and looked between her and Gilbert. "I'm escorting you back to Eagle Harbor."

"You are?" She couldn't help the panicked edge to her voice.

Gilbert turned from the window and raised an eyebrow. "You thought I'd leave you to go back to Eagle Harbor by yourself?"

She snapped her jaw shut and glared, which was just as well, since Gilbert glared straight back at her.

"If I was concerned about your safety aboard ship, you can't possibly expect I'd send you five hundred miles north by yourself."

"I'm not some helpless ninny who needs to be followed around. Or did you forget about my fishing knife?"

His haughty gaze dipped to her waist. "I don't think I'll ever quite forget your knife—or anything else about that incident."

A sudden burst of heat flamed in her cheeks. What a scoundrel to bring up their kiss. And he didn't seem the least bit repentant. Ugh!

"However," Gilbert continued. "Were I to send you on a train to Houghton by yourself, you'd disembark at the first stop north of here."

"I would not." She crossed her arms and slumped back against the seat—the rather comfortable cushioned leather seat—but she wasn't about to compliment Gilbert on his carriage.

He tilted his head to the side and surveyed her. "You're many things, Rebekah Cummings, but a liar isn't one of them."

The comment brought a new type of heat to her cheeks, one of shame rather than embarrassment. "I wasn't lying." Milwaukee would have been the third or fourth stop.

"Looks like we're here!" Stanley's overly bright voice filled the small space inside the carriage.

Rebekah looked out the window to discover they had stopped at a massive stone building that towered... six stories high? Everything in this city was bigger and grander than Eagle Harbor by tenfold.

"We'll pick you up at a quarter after six tomorrow," Gilbert said as Stanley jumped down from the carriage. "The train leaves at seven."

"Sounds good." Stanley gave a little wave before the carriage door slammed shut. He exchanged a few words with the driver, and a moment later the vehicle lurched back into traffic.

"So you weren't lying to me about disembarking on the first stop north of here?" Gilbert tapped her foot with the toe of his shoe.

Why couldn't Gilbert let Stanley's departure be the end to their conversation? Especially now that she needed quiet to devise a plan to sneak away from her escort at some point tomorrow. "No."

"No?"

"At least not completely."

He waited, and the silence that filled the carriage hung thick and awkward. She squirmed in her seat and stared out the window at the endless buildings and streets and people, and still, Gilbert didn't utter so much as a word.

The lout.

"I was going to get off in Milwaukee," she muttered. "Not the first stop north of here."

And she still probably would, though doing so would be more difficult now.

Gilbert was quiet for a moment, his head tilted to the side in that peculiar way of his. "Will going back home truly be so terrible?"

"Going home?" An image of the calm harbor waters flashed through her mind, followed by another of her family's cabin on the rocky southern shore of Lake Superior. "There's nothing terrible about home."

"So why leave it?"

"Did you listen to nothing I said yesterday? I don't have a choice."

"But you do."

"Not if I want to earn money." She should have never told him her reason for leaving. It hadn't swayed his opinion in the least.

"What can I do for work in Eagle Harbor?"

"What you've been doing all along. Fish with your brother."

He made it sound so simple. So easy. The man who'd never wanted for a dollar in his life, much less a penny.

She gripped her hands together on her lap. "For a third of the price our fish brought in last year? How will that help anything? Besides, Elijah doesn't want me on the lake. None of you do."

"Because your family loves you." Gilbert surveyed her up and down, his jaw no longer tight and his shoulders forgetting to be rigid. "Because they care. If they didn't, they'd let you on the lake rain or shine, storm or calm. I'd hardly complain that God gave you a family who loves you enough to protect you."

Wasn't it kind of him to make her family sound so perfect? But he didn't have to live with them. "Protect me is all they want to do. They don't want to let me help. I'm twenty-two and just as capable as you, Elijah, Ma, or anyone else. And no, I'm not going to go back to Eagle Harbor like you want. You can stick me on a train and send Stanley to watch me, but he can't be with me every second, and I didn't come all this way only to be sent home." She slumped back against the seat again and crossed her arms.

"What if I gave you a hundred dollars?"

"What?" She nearly screeched the word, then cringed as it reverberated through the carriage.

"Yesterday you said you planned to work through the shipping season and then bring home a hundred dollars. What if I gave you the money now on the condition you return home with Stanley tomorrow?"

"I... I..." What to say to such an offer? A yes meant she'd be home tomorrow. Perhaps she missed the forgotten little northwoods town more than she expected. And she didn't like wondering about whether Elijah was out on a rescue. "But I wouldn't have earned it."

"You would, by going home like I asked."

"It's not the same thing. You're paying me to cooperate, not to work. And that's the point of my leaving, to prove that I can care for myself, that I can be a help."

"Rebekah…" The way he said her name, all warm and familiar and gentle, sucked any further protests from her mind. Then he looked at her with eyes that had changed from intense to soft without warning, just like how he'd looked at her before he'd kissed her in his quarters. "No one who knows you would ever say you're not helpful."

"Then why does no one want my help?" She looked down at her shoes. "Why is everything I do wrong?"

"Hey." He nudged her toe with the tip of his shiny leather shoes again. "Just because you go about things differently than others doesn't make it wrong."

It sure felt that way.

The carriage rolled to a stop, and a glance out the window told her she'd been mistaken about the Sinclairs' Eagle Harbor mansion being as grand as their Chicago one. Fancy wood siding covered the largest house she'd ever seen—or what would have been the largest house, except mansions just as large and grand lined the entire street. Perfect flowers had been planted beneath the windows and around the trees in the yard, and the front door—

"So will you take that hundred dollars and return home?"

She tore her gaze away from the sprawling house complete with a stone base, turrets, and more windows facing the street than were used in all of Eagle Harbor's houses combined. "You're serious about giving me a hundred dollars?"

"Of course."

"That doesn't make sense. If you can give me that much money just so I'll go home, then why do you need to marry an heiress?"

The driver opened the door to the carriage and stood ramrod straight as he waited for them to alight.

Gilbert didn't get up but tilted his head back against the top of the seat and stared at the roof. "Because what's a hundred dollars more when you already need sixteen thousand?"

The air rushed from her lungs. Sixteen thousand dollars? Who'd ever heard of that much money?

And could he really find someone to marry who would bring him such a large sum?

Chapter Nine

"Mother, you remember Rebekah Cummings, don't you? Hiram and Mabel Cummingses's daughter from Eagle Harbor?" Gilbert gestured toward Rebekah, who stood beside him in the foyer of his parents' South Prairie Street mansion.

His mother should have remembered Rebekah, but the thin set to her lips gave little indication one way or the other. Even with Eagle Harbor being as small as it was, she hadn't paid attention to the townsfolk when they'd lived there, and she hadn't been there in nearly a decade.

"I thought you'd brought me a serving boy with pretty hair." Mother arched her eyebrow and perused Rebekah the way a captain might inspect his ship's log before turning it over to a clerk.

Feminine voices and the clink of teacups on saucers floated from the open door to the salon, where mother must be hosting some kind of tea.

"So she's here to work?" Mother waved her hand toward Rebekah, causing the fabric of her elegant rose gown to rustle— likely a new gown purchased solely to impress the ladies she was hosting. "I'm surprised your father listened when I sent him word that I needed a new serving girl."

To work? The last thing he needed was Rebekah working under his parents' roof. She should've been on a train to the Upper Peninsula at that very moment, not standing in the foyer with him.

But Rebekah staying a night in Chicago was only one of many things that hadn't gone his way today. The *Lassiter* had barely made it to port in time and had lost one of its shipments of beef as a result. And as soon as he'd disembarked, one of his clerks from Great Northern Shipping's Chicago office had been waiting to tell him that his insurance check covering seventy-five percent of the *Beaumont's* losses hadn't arrived yet.

Now Mother wanted Rebekah to work for her? No.

No. No. No. No. No.

There simply weren't enough no's in the world to express his thoughts. Rebekah needed to go home to her family. He at least owed that much to Elijah for saving his life.

"I am here to find work, though I'd intended to be working as a cook on one of Great Northern's ships." Rebekah refused to look at him as she spoke. "But if I—"

"That's not accurate." Gilbert stepped between his mother and Rebekah, forcing Mother's gaze on him. "She sneaked onto the *Lassiter* as the cook without my knowledge, but I can't keep her on. I'm sending her back to Eagle Harbor in the morning, so she needs a place to stay for the night."

"I'm not going back to Eagle Harbor." Heat from Rebekah's glare bored into his back. "My family needs money, and one way or another, I intend to find work and—"

He reached behind him and squeezed Rebekah's arm. Hard.

"Why are you dressed as a man?" Mother's features appeared sharp in the lighting from the gas chandelier above. With her thin figure and prominent cheekbones, she could almost be a worker in the tenements who ate porridge for three meals a day rather than a member of the upper crust who could order up a feast with an hour's notice.

Rebekah jerked out of his hold and stepped beside him. "Because I—"

"Rebekah found it easier to cook and move about the ship in trousers." Gilbert gripped her arm again.

Wait.

Had he just defended Rebekah's choice of clothing? And to his mother, no less?

"Would you consider a serving job, Miss Cummings?" Mother's shoulders lost their rigidity, though she still managed to maintain proper posture, as always.

"Shouldn't you be attending your guests?" Gilbert nodded toward the salon, where Aileen, one of the servants on staff, had just entered with a tray of snacks.

"What would working here entail?" Rebekah cocked her head to the side.

"No."

Mother didn't even glance his direction as she rattled off a list that included everything from serving meals to cleaning the dining room.

Gilbert blew out a breath. Calm. He needed to stay calm. Maybe having Mother list Rebekah's duties was good. A woman in trousers wouldn't want to polish the family silver. Being a maid was probably the least enticing job in America to a woman like Rebekah Cummings.

"How much does it pay?" Rebekah asked.

He tightened his hold on Rebekah's arm until he had to be cutting off the blood to her hand. Had the rough seas yesterday tossed Rebekah's brain about until she'd gone daft? Hadn't she heard Mother's list? "She wouldn't be right for this job, Mother."

"Fifteen dollars a month."

Rebekah twisted her arm away from him. "I can earn twenty-five a month working aboard ship."

"No, you can't." At least not if he had anything to say about it. "I'll pay you twenty dollars." Eyes narrowed, Mother tilted her head to the side much like Rebekah had earlier. "But only if you earn it. I won't pay you to stand around and flirt with the footmen."

Rebekah coughed, or maybe it was more like a choke. "I wouldn't flirt, Ma'am."

"Would you two listen to me?" The back of his teeth ground together as he spoke. "Rebekah can't work here."

"The lady is of an age to choose for herself." Mother crossed her arms, looking like a queen with her silver-streaked blond hair and her deep rose gown that shimmered wherever a beam of the chandelier's light touched it "Have you worked in service before?"

"Does feeding mariners count?"

Mother let out a small huff. "I suppose. Miss Niebert, the head housekeeper, will teach you etiquette. She usually does the hiring and will see to whatever training you need."

"Or you could teach her nothing at all and send her back to her family, who are likely sick with worry." Gilbert glanced back and forth between his mother and Rebekah, two mirror images of stubborn females.

In truth, he couldn't force Rebekah to listen to him any more than he could force his mother, though he'd certainly tried over the years. Both were too stubborn to listen to good sense.

Didn't Rebekah know what she was likely doing to her family? How blessed she was to have one that cared about her?

But as much as he might want to see her safely back in Eagle Harbor, his mother was right. Rebekah was old enough to make her own decisions. Wasn't that one of the reasons she'd said she'd left Eagle Harbor in the first place?

I'm done asking permission and doing what I'm told. He remembered far too well her words during the storm as they'd huddled together on the deck of the *Lassiter*.

What am I supposed to do? Stand around and watch my family struggle because they don't want me to work? Because they've got too much pride to let me help? For as long as I live, I'll always regret not trying to help Pa.

He'd explained that they were just trying to protect her. But for some reason, she didn't see it, and he couldn't make her.

"Come, I'll introduce you to Miss Niebert, and she can show you the servants' quarters." Mother gestured for Rebekah to follow.

"I haven't agreed to take the job." Rebekah's lips flattened. "It's still five dollars a month less than I'd earn aboard ship."

Mother's arms went back across her chest. "I'm not in the habit of giving money away. I don't pay any of the regular servants that."

"How about this, we'll say twenty dollars a month, but I want a list of extra things I can do each week to earn a dollar. If I finish the list, I get the dollar."

Gilbert pressed his eyes shut and sighed. "No."

It was more a prayer than anything, but he opened his eyes to find both women looking at him.

"You're refusing to let me hire a servant?"

But both he and his mother knew she wasn't going to listen if he refused, though she didn't have to look at him as though he'd lost his brain somewhere between Eagle Harbor and Chicago.

"Yes, you can have a list."

"I'll take the job then." Rebekah gave a firm nod.

Gilbert sunk his head into his hands. "It'd be better to go home, Rebekah." He inwardly cringed at the pleading sound in his voice, but it was his last chance she'd listen. "Please."

"No." She planted her feet into the Turkish carpet beneath her faded shoes. "I want to work. And you've no reason to worry about my being unsafe and alone if I'm working for your parents."

Alone? No. Unsafe? He blew out a breath. At least Warren was in Eagle Harbor. But having her under his parents' roof did mean he could watch her—at least until he got married and bought a house of his own. Plus now he wouldn't need to worry about her sneaking away from Stanley on the way back to Eagle Harbor.

"Enough nattering. I don't pay my servants to stand around and argue with my children. Come, Rebekah, I'll introduce you to Miss Niebert, and she can find you a uniform." If the way Mother was glaring at Rebekah's trousers were any indication, Eagle Harbor's most determined tomboy was soon to don a dress.

But as much as he'd like to see Rebekah in a skirt, even a serviceable, black one, he'd rather have her wear trousers if it meant she'd return to Eagle Harbor and her family.

~.~.~.~.~

"You lost the *Beaumont*."

Gilbert barely managed to resist gritting his teeth as he plopped into the seat across from his father's ornate desk. "It's nice to see you again as well, Father. What's it been? Three months?"

Byron Sinclair didn't bother to look up from the stack of papers he riffled through. "When I signed the *Beaumont* over to you, I expected you would see that she was properly staffed, especially considering she's one of our newer ships—or was."

"She was properly staffed. I was piloting her when we hit that rock reef."

That got his father's attention, at least for a moment. He set down his sheaf of papers and steepled his hands in front of him.

"*You* were piloting."

"Yes."

The smack of his father's palm against his desk reverberated through the room. "Then how did the ship wreck?"

Gilbert thought back to the dark night that had drastically altered the next few months—if not years—of his life. "There was a blizzard. I probably should have sheltered up in Copper Harbor, but we were almost to port." He'd been a fool that day. But his father had figured that out years ago, hadn't he? "I didn't know the lighthouse was out, or that—"

"The lighthouse was out?" Father's voice cracked through the room like a whip.

"Yes."

"You made certain the lightkeeper got fired then?"

He shifted in his chair, never mind how comfortable the plush cushions and velvet upholstery were supposed to be. "The issue was addressed."

Father's thin lips firmed into a straight, pale line. With his balding head, graying hair, and pointed nose, he almost looked like one of the eagles that swooped fish from Eagle Harbor. "That's your way of telling me the Oakton fellow who runs the light still has his job. You've always been too soft."

Only compared to the rest of his family.

"Was that all you wanted me for?" Gilbert pushed himself up from the chair and turned for the door.

"You're not going to ask for money?" Surprise flickered through Father's voice—probably the most emotion he'd shown all night.

Or rather, the most emotion he'd shown his family. He would have displayed plenty of emotion when he'd gone to visit his mistress after leaving the Great Northern Shipping office earlier, which explained why they were having this conversation at ten-thirty at night.

Not that Gilbert was complaining about putting it off.

The door to Father's study opened, and in walked Rebekah, balancing a tray of refreshments with the same brisk efficiency she used in everything from gutting fish to fixing a meal for his crew. Dare he tell her the china tea service on the tray was worth more than the fish she and her brother caught in an entire year?

"Tea?" Her eyes flickered up to meet his.

As much as he might want to exit, he wasn't about to leave Rebekah alone with his father at such a late hour. He sighed and nodded. "Please."

She swept past him, her black service dress swishing about her ankles. His tongue turned suddenly thick, and though he should return to his chair and let her serve him, his feet seemed glued in place. How long since he'd seen her in a dress? Not since her father died, and that had been three years ago. Before that, he'd been in college and rarely had time to travel to Eagle Harbor. She'd worn trousers on her family's fishing boat for as long as he could remember, but when had she started wearing them all the time?

And look at him. Gaping after a woman in a serving dress, of all things. He'd been surrounded by plain black serving dresses and white aprons since the day he was born.

"You have to need money." Father tapped his fingers on the desk, seemingly oblivious to Rebekah—for the moment. "I know you aren't carrying I&P insurance on your vessels."

"Actually, I am." Now. It was the first thing he'd seen to after the *Beaumont* sank. Beforehand, he'd simply carried maritime insurance, which only covered seventy-five percent of his losses. Most ship owners then banded together to form protection and indemnity clubs that would cover the extra twenty-five percent of the losses, should a need ever arise. If only he'd bought into one of the clubs sooner. "But I didn't have it on the *Beaumont*, no."

Teacup in hand, Rebekah slanted him a glance and then looked at the chair he'd vacated.

He might as well get the conversation over with tonight. Father would hound him for information later if he didn't. Plus he could get a sense of how Rebekah was managing after being in his mother's employ for a few hours.

But if the efficient way she'd poured tea without spilling a drop and handed him the cup was any indication, she was getting along just fine.

Was that good? Was it possible she'd spend the next four months working for his parents? What if she liked working here and wanted to stay longer?

He sat back down.

"You weren't carrying proper insurance on the *Beaumont* because you wasted all your extra money on that wretched machine of yours." His father surveyed him, his eyes the same cold, fierce blue as Warren's. "I hear it's lost now, which is for the best. I can write you a check to cover your losses, of course, but I'm not sure I will. Maybe this ordeal will teach you to focus on shipping rather than cranes and foolhardy business endeavors."

The tea sloshed in his cup. A stupid reaction on his part. Of course Father watched for any reaction he might have, and he should have expected such cruel words. "A crane for loading heavy cargo onto ships is hardly a foolhardy notion. They're already used for trains."

"We've dockworkers aplenty for such tasks. And they're cheap. No need to start tampering with a system that works."

Gilbert plunked his teacup down in its saucer without taking a sip. "There is when some of those workers end up dead or maimed."

Rebekah slid a teacup and saucer onto his Father's desk. "Did you want a sandwich or cookie? Perhaps a piece of cake?"

"No tea." Father slapped his hand on the desk again, spilling a trace amount of the liquid onto the polished mahogany surface. "Port."

Rebekah opened her mouth, her green eyes sparking fire, then clamped it shut and glared. His father was thankfully too preoccupied with his bank book to notice.

Gilbert bit back a smile. She hadn't spilled tea or broken his mother's china, but watching her attempt to play the docile servant might well prove amusing.

She pulled a rag from the folds of her dress and wiped up the spill. Something about her quick, efficient movements must have caught his father's eye, because he drew his gaze away from his precious banking information. When Rebekah turned and headed toward the liquor cabinet, Father's gaze trailed down her back.

Gilbert nearly growled. Hadn't Father just been to visit his mistress? He hardly had need to ogle the help.

Rebekah surveyed the liquor in the glass-fronted cabinet then turned back to them. "Which is the—"

"The narrow bottle on the right. It's a red wine," Gilbert answered. "Bring the whole thing. My father will pour it."

Father glanced back and forth between the two of them before turning to Rebekah again. "You look familiar. Have you worked here before?"

"I'm from Eagle Harbor." She set the wine and two goblets on the desk.

"Ah, yes. That's where I've seen you. The Cummings girl, correct?"

The slightest bit of pink tinged her cheeks. "Yes, sir."

"You've come to Chicago with Gilbert?"

"Just looking for work, sir. This happened to be the first position I found, other than working as cook on the *Lassiter*, that is." She sent Gilbert a glare.

Father leaned back in his chair and ran his gaze down her once more. "You worked as a ship's cook?"

"It was a one-time arrangement." Gilbert shoved his now-cold tea onto the tray, causing the china to clatter.

"If you'd rather work as a ship cook, I can make arrangements on one of my vessels. It pays better than house service."

No! But Gilbert gripped the arms of his chair. If Father knew he had the slightest interest in protecting Rebekah, she'd become a pawn in one of his father's endless games—games he always lost.

"I…" Rebekah bit the side of her lip and slanted him a glance. "I'm planning to see how things go here first, but thank you for the offer."

Gilbert drew in a breath of air. His father didn't have nearly the same standards of morality on his ships that Gilbert maintained, nor had he ever seen a lock on the door to the cook's quarters.

Which brought up another matter, did Rebekah have a lock on her room here? And not merely a lock, but a bolt on the inside that couldn't be opened with a key?

"Let me show you how to pour the port so you can serve us next time." Gentleness and understanding dripped from Father's voice, and Gilbert tried not to squirm. "Then perhaps you can return here and dust. I noticed the maid missed some spots this morning."

Dust? At eleven o'clock at night?

"Yes, sir."

Father's eyes tracked Rebekah's departure from the room with a satisfied gleam.

He needed to distract Father before Rebekah returned. "You

were saying you see no need for a crane to help load ships?"

"Not in the least." Father rubbed the bridge of his nose. "Honestly, Gilbert, why can't you be more like Warren? At least he recognizes tomfoolery like this crane obsession of yours when it's placed under his nose."

"Does he? Then why did you send him to Eagle Harbor?"

Rebekah opened the door again and came silently into the study, but father was too busy fiddling with the newspaper on the corner of his desk to notice.

"A misunderstanding, that's all. It'll blow over soon enough." Father tossed him the paper.

Gilbert unfolded it to find his brother's name printed boldly across the top of the society page. "Warren got the mayor's daughter pregnant?"

Father pressed his eyes shut, continuing to rub at his nose. "Her father wasn't the mayor at the time. And she has nothing but sensational stories. She doesn't remember doing anything that would lead to a child with Warren, just drinking a little wine with him and then having no memory of the rest of the night. Now she's pregnant and claiming Warren is the reason."

"Is he?" His mouth was suddenly dry.

"No!"

If only he could be so sure of Warren's innocence. "The mayor's daughter would certainly be the most high profile woman he's dithered with. So he's in Eagle Harbor until this settles?"

"Keep in mind none of us were expecting her father to win the special election three weeks ago. He's from a working class family, son to a meat plant worker who got started in politics and so on." Father waived his hand distractedly.

"So Warren impregnating this woman would have been fine if her father wasn't the new mayor?"

"You know what I mean."

Yes, unfortunately he did.

"And this new mayor is already causing problems. Says he's going to clean up Chicago. Claims factory workers and dockworkers and other common laborers should be treated fairly." His father gave another absent wave of his hand. "Safe working conditions and unions and so forth. What a bunch of rubbish."

Rubbish indeed. How dare the owner of Great Northern Shipping be required to treat his dockworkers well.

"It'll be a disaster if the dockworkers unionize." His father's eyes narrowed, and he leaned back in his chair, tapping his fingertips together. "Actually, this new mayor sounds rather like you. Maybe you should meet with him, talk about how you're both so concerned about the laborers and whatnot. You might end up with a shipping contract from the city. They must need lumber or coal or something imported."

"You want me to meet with the mayor and procure a shipping contract after Warren impregnated his daughter?"

Father slammed his hand on the desk. "Allegedly, Gilbert. Allegedly."

⌐.⌐.⌐.⌐.⌐

Rebekah slid into the corner and concentrated on dusting the bookshelf. Why had Mr. Sinclair requested she come back? Did he really think a servant needed to be present for such a conversation? Then again, Mrs. Sinclair had been rather clear that the household staff were not to speak of the family's affairs—especially if Rebekah was going to earn that extra dollar.

Gilbert and his father were back to discussing the *Beaumont* now, Mr. Sinclair stringing one berating sentence together after another as he talked about how Warren would have never lost a ship, how Warren had made a forty-two percent profit during the year he'd had control of his four Great Northern vessels while Gilbert had only turned a seventeen percent profit. And Mr. Sinclair certainly didn't think much of Gilbert's crane.

And Gilbert was so cold, so distant. No emotion crossed his face or heightened his voice. If anything, he couldn't act more bored.

She poked her tongue into the side of her cheek and stood on tiptoe to reach the top of the bookshelf with the duster. What would it be like to have Byron Sinclair as a father? Nearly everyone in Eagle Harbor despised him, though he was far too powerful a man for anyone to tell him so. But to grow up with him? He wasn't the type of man who'd smile if Gilbert had brought back a perfect score on his cyphering or a large whitefish he'd caught on his own.

He wasn't even the type of man who'd look at his son unless he wanted something.

Rebekah swallowed. And that's what she'd seen in Gilbert all those years ago. A need for a friend. A need for a family. A need to be loved.

Her duster clattered to the floor, and she pressed a hand to her hot cheek. What was she doing thinking of such things? That had been years ago, and in the end, Gilbert had wanted nothing to do with her.

He still might have some softness buried inside him though. After all, he'd offered to give her a hundred dollars so she'd return home. And he seemed more interested in building that crane to help dockworkers than to make himself wealthy.

She glanced at the liquor cabinet, the only thing left to dust besides the desk where Mr. Sinclair sat. Surely she could come back and finish up those two things in the morning. Mr. Sinclair had a rather disturbing manner of watching her. She wasn't prepared to say Gilbert was right and every man living along the Great Lakes wanted to take advantage of her, but something about his father's look made her stomach clench. She wasn't about to parade up to the front of the office and start working if she could avoid it.

If Isaac were here, he'd needle her about this being the first time she was content to stand in a room's corner rather than in its center.

But she was here alone, and the one person she knew was rather distracted at the moment, though it did appear he and Mr. Sinclair were back to talking about money again, and Gilbert was about to get a heap of it from his father. Was that a good thing? She couldn't imagine a man like Byron Sinclair giving anyone sixteen thousand dollars without making demands.

Tucking her duster into her apron, she crept over to gather the snacks both men had left untouched. She lifted the tray, eliciting no more than a swift glance from Mr. Sinclair before he launched into another rant, and fled the room.

Now if only she could remember how to get back to the kitchen. All the halls looked the same—dark, gleaming wood walls and floors with fancy rugs and tapestries. Who knew wood could be so shiny? Never mind that the Sinclairs must have had shanty boys cut down half a forest just to build this house.

She turned left down a hallway. Was this the way she'd come? A house shouldn't be so confusing. If she could just find her way back to the servants' staircase, she could make it to the kitchen.

She ended up at a window overlooking the street. Stately lamps cast their light over the shadows so that it seemed dawn was approaching rather than the blackest part of night. This must have been what Gilbert meant when he'd said a person couldn't see the stars because of lights from the city.

Unfortunately none of this did her any good in getting back to the kitchen. She huffed and turned, heading back the direction she'd come.

She found the servants' staircase at the end of another hall and trudged down the steps, her pace slower than normal. Evidently the Sinclairs weren't the type to care if their staff had been up at dawn to cook breakfast for a crew of sailors. They expected to be served whenever they wanted, even if it was nearly midnight.

She stepped off the last stair, rounded another corner, and headed toward the swinging double doors to the kitchen. Finally. If she found herself with a spare quarter hour tomorrow, she was drawing herself a map of this mammoth house.

With only a step to go before she reached the kitchen, the door flew open into the tray she carried.

"Ouch!" The tray flipped up and into her stomach just before it…

Crash!

"Ach, ye shoulda' been watching where ye were going." The lilting Irish voice of Aileen, one of the servants she'd met earlier, floated through the plain white hallway.

Rebekah looked down at the tray, the fancy teapot with the little purple flowers now shattered at her feet along with one of the teacups.

"Mrs. Sinclair isna going to like this."

A sick lump formed in Rebekah's stomach. Would Mrs. Sinclair deduct money from her pay to make up for the tea service?

She knelt down and tossed the broken shards of china onto the tray. Why had she chosen such a fancy looking teapot in the first place? She doubted Gilbert cared whether he drank out of a cup with dainty, perfect flowers or one that was plain white.

"Though the mistress has so many tea sets, she might not

notice. Probably best not to tell her anything so she doesna' see what ye've done." Aileen stood over her, her robe cinched tight around her nightdress and the gas lighting reflecting on the long red hair that cascaded about her shoulders.

"Are you telling me to lie to Mrs. Sinclair?"

Aileen offered a dainty shrug. "I'm only trying to help."

Helping would involve getting down on her knees and picking up the mess she'd helped cause, not watching while someone else did all the work.

"Thank you for your advice, but I'll be going to Mrs. Sinclair first thing in the morning and telling her what happened."

Aileen's lips pressed into a firm white line. "Suit yourself, but don't come complaining to me when she makes ye pay for the teapot and then fires ye."

Fire her? She wasn't the only one to blame, and surely Mrs. Sinclair wouldn't fire them for such a simple mistake. Was Aileen purposely trying to frighten her? "Well, when I speak with Mrs. Sinclair, I'll be sure to explain that you bumped into me while rushing out of the kitchen, not the other way around."

"Me?" Aileen took a step back. "I do na' see what I've to do with any of this. Ye're the one who dropped the tray."

"You ran into me." Rebekah finished picking up the last of the china but left the tray on the ground while she stood. No sense dropping it a second time in front of Aileen. Though now that she thought of it, it was rather odd for Aileen to be in the kitchen at this time of night. It's not like she'd been up working late, seeing how she was dressed in her nightclothes. "Or did you expect me to lie about why I dropped the tray too?"

"I never told ye to lie," the other woman snapped. "As someone who's worked here for several months, I was just trying to help because ye're new. But I can see how much ye want me advice."

"I've no interest in 'advice' that tells me to be dishonest."

"So now I'm dishonest, am I?"

"What were you doing in the kitchen? And in your nightclothes to boot?"

"Our conversation is done." Aileen raised her chin and whirled, her robe swirling about her legs.

Rebekah reached out and grabbed her arm, halting the other woman's steps. Aileen jerked backwards, and two lumpy napkins fell to the ground.

Rebekah bent and swooped them up. "Ham and biscuits?" Miss Niebert had been very clear about Mrs. Sinclair's rules for the kitchen. The staff got three full meals a day, and other than that, the kitchen food was to be left alone. "You're breaking the rules."

Aileen's freckles stood out against her pale face, and she held out a shaky hand. "Give it back. I need it."

Something about the sincere way Aileen spoke, about the extra hint of moisture shimmering in her brown eyes, made Rebekah pause, the biscuits and meat still in hand. But no. Rules were rules, and she truly would get herself fired if she was deceitful. "We both know I can't do that."

Aileen blinked, and the moisture left her eyes, making them dull and flat. "Then I hope the mistress fires ye first thing tomorrow."

Aileen stormed down the hall towards the servants' staircase, her steps so brisk that her white robe flowed behind her. Rebekah rubbed her bleary eyes and then bent to pick up the tray, tossing the ham and biscuits in with the rest of the ruined food and china.

Why did she have the feeling she'd just made an enemy—one who might bring her more trouble than the broken tea service?

Chapter Ten

"I'm interested in your crane, son, but I'm sure you understand my position." Mr. Mellar leaned back in his chair, his thin gray eyebrows drawn low over his eyes. "I can't purchase something of that magnitude without first seeing it operational. Your business plan looks sound, just as it did a few months ago, and I'm still willing to make an investment for a percentage of the profits, but you don't seem open to that possibility."

Gilbert tightened his grip on the fancy leather chair seated across from Mr. Mellar's desk. "Last time we talked, you were only interested in investing if I gave you controlling share of my crane."

Had he really expected a different offer this time?

Expected, no. But hoped?

Ah, hope was a dratted thing. Giving a person just enough promise to keep pressing on, even when the end goal was unattainable. Still, he'd had to try this one last route before he called on a certain young woman this afternoon.

"I see your point, Gilbert, but I hope you can see mine as well. A project of this scope would be quite an undertaking, and were I to go through the effort, it's not something I'm willing to lose money on."

Gilbert glanced out the window overlooking the myriad docks

and blue waters that made up Chicago Harbor before he drew his gaze back to one of the most powerful shipping company owners in the Midwest. "I do understand."

But he also wasn't about to hand control of the past four years of his life over to someone. Mellar was a businessman, yes, and he could probably describe in detail every function of a steamship from its boilers to its propellers to its pilothouse. But did he understand engineering? Did he understand the calculations needed when determining the length of a hoist or the difference between a friction drum and a clutch drum?

And even more, did Mellar understand the need for his crane? The why of it? The way getting this crane operational haunted him at night? Even when he'd agreed to marry Victoria and tried to take her father on as a business partner, the partnership had only involved his ships, not his crane.

Perhaps in the future, if he continued to invent other machinery rather than focus on the production of this crane, he could take on investors and hand over shares—though probably not ever controlling shares.

But this crane was too important, and no one could do this project as well as he. "I was hoping you'd purchase one of my cranes outright."

"I see." Mellar twirled the pointy edge of his mustache and surveyed him, but not with the cold gleam his father's eyes always seemed to hold. "You understand why I can't do that before you have an operational one to sell me."

Understand? He wasn't quite sure he understood, when having such a crane would mean safer working conditions for the tumult of men currently visible through Mellar's office window. However, from a business standpoint, Mellar's decision made perfect sense. "If I were in your situation, I'd likely make the same choice, yes."

"I heard you weren't carrying I&P insurance when you lost the *Beaumont*."

The back of Gilbert's neck heated. Why was Mellar asking about the *Beaumont*? Hadn't discussing it with his father last night been enough? "No, sir."

"I assume you needed extra capital until you sold your first crane, which you'd nearly accomplished given my interest in your endeavor."

The padded leather chair he sat on suddenly seemed as hard and cold as the ice-encrusted rocks that lined Eagle Harbor's shore every winter. "I'm aware it was a poor business decision."

Mellar leaned forward, placing his elbows on the diagram of the crane Gilbert had brought, and tipped his head to the side. "Lake Superior has hard storms, but even so, the chances of you losing both a steamship of that magnitude and your crane, well, they were slim. It happens sometimes. Every business has its own inherent risks, especially one like shipping. Furthermore, every businessman decides what risks to take, both with his business and personal finances. I don't think yours was a poor one just because you lost."

Gilbert's head shot up. Mellar wasn't going to sit there and berate him for—what had his father said at the end of their conversation last night?—ah, yes, *making foolhardy choices led by asinine dreams.*

"Every shipping company owner in the country has lost a ship at one point or another. Including me and your father. It happens." Mellar shifted, and Gilbert cringed as his diagram crinkled under Mellar's elbows. "You're smart, you're determined, and you've got a sound head for business. Everything will come together. And as before, my offer to invest is open at any time, should you choose to take it."

"Thank you." And he meant it. Not every businessman in the

world was like his father, nor was every businessman inherently evil—though he'd be hard pressed to ever convince the residents of Eagle Harbor of that. Still, coming to Chicago, sitting at a desk with a man like Mellar, well, something felt intrinsically right about it, even if he did have to put up with being under his father's roof.

He stood to go. "Might I collect my papers, please?"

"Of course, of course." Mellar stacked them into a neat pile, paying little attention to their order, and handed them across the desk.

"Thank you for your time." Gilbert picked up the suitcoat he'd draped over the back of the chair due to the stifling summer heat and then blew out a breath. Without taking his father's money and without opening up his crane to investors, he really had no other choice than to ask. "Before I go, I have a question of a more personal nature."

Mellar leaned back in his chair and crossed his arms over his chest, his expression not nearly as cordial as it had been a moment ago. "Go on."

"Might you be opposed to me calling on Marianne?"

The corner of Mellar's mustache twitched. "Marianne? I suppose that's one way to finance your crane."

This time the heat that stole up the back of Gilbert's neck burned so fiercely his skin might well break into one of those big beach fires Eagle Harbor's residents were always so fond of. "I've met her before, spoken and danced with her more than once."

"Yes, I suppose you have." Mellar pressed his two index fingers together and tapped them against his lips. "Most men in your situation wouldn't bother coming to me first but try stalking her at that fancy ball scheduled for this weekend."

There was a ball this weekend? He'd have to get the

information from Mother. "I'm five and twenty, Mr. Mellar. Crane or not, it's time I find a suitable wife. I've no way of knowing whether Marianne and I will be... ah... compatible unless I get to know her better."

Compatible. If Rebekah heard him describe his future wife in such a manner, she'd start spouting that Bible verse from Song of Solomon about a flood not being able to drown love. Well, she might be willing to save herself for a marriage that had love so strong it wouldn't sink amid a flood. But while she waited half her life for a love she might never find, he'd make himself content with "compatible."

"You can't pretend as though Marianne's marriage settlement has no impact on the situation, especially given what happened to the *Beaumont* and your crane." Mellar was nothing if not direct, which was likely one reason his business did so well.

"She's the daughter of one of the wealthiest shipping barons on the Great Lakes. Her marriage settlement will factor into any offers she gets. The only way to avoid that is to disinherit her." Gilbert cringed as the final words left his mouth. They might be true, but had he lost his mind speaking such things to Mellar?

But Mellar didn't stand up and cast him out of the office. Instead he leaned back, his hand doing a poor job of covering the grin that spread across his face. "Gilbert Sinclair, if I didn't already have six sons to help with my business, I'd hire you out from under your father this very day. The business world is sorely lacking in men who can speak plainly."

Speak plainly. That was one way to put it.

"Let me tell you a bit about Marianne. My wife waited years to have a daughter. Six boys and not a single girl. I think we'd both given up hope on ever having one." Mellar stared out the window, his gaze not on the busy docks and endless ships, but pinned to an unknown spot in the sky above. "Eleanor was thrilled when Marianne was born, but never regained her strength afterwards. She died before my daughter's first birthday. I suppose I spoiled Marianne when she was growing up, and now that it's time for her to find a husband... let's just say she hasn't taken well to the suitors who've approached her. If compatibility is what you seek, she might not be the right woman for you.

"But you can call on her, yes. And if she takes an interest in you..." Mellar nodded to the papers under Gilbert's arm. "I've a feeling that crane of yours is going to do well, very well, one day. I've no doubt you'll be able to provide for my daughter. Then you'll be something of a son to me, won't you? And I just might steal you away from your father after all."

That was as close to a blessing as he'd ever get from a man like Mellar. At least the shipping baron hadn't immediately shut him down.

"Thank you, sir. I'll call on her later today." Gilbert nodded his goodbye and turned for the office door only for it to burst open.

"Mellar. There you are. Your clerk claims you've been in a meeting for a deuced hour."

"Mr. Frobisher." Gilbert extend his hand to the rotund man with a tuft of fuzzy white hair sticking up from his ever-balding head.

"Well, well, if it isn't Gilbert Sinclair." Frobisher ignored his hand and scratched the top of his head instead—likely the reason for the wild tuft of hair in the first place—then he thumped Gilbert on the back. Hard. "You ready to come work for me yet, boy?"

"Ah, not precisely, no."

"What you got there?" He gestured to the papers under Gilbert's arm.

"The crane I spoke with you about several years ago."

Frobisher frowned, his hand heading back up to his scalp again. "That isn't built yet? Figured you'd be selling so many of those you'd make me look like a destitute farmer by now."

Last he knew, Frobisher wasn't that far off from being destitute, though that changed a couple times a year. He'd invent something, sell the rights to it and make a pile of money, then pour every last bit of that money into a new engineering feat of some sort. If only the man was as brilliant with business as he was with engineering.

"Are you having trouble with her? Let me have a look." Frobisher reached for his diagram.

"Allen." Mr. Mellar's voice cut through the room. "Leave Gilbert alone. He's not interested in selling a partnership in his crane, otherwise I'd have bought into it already. What did you come see me for?"

"See you for?" Frobisher squinted at Mellar and then wheezed out a breath. "Oh, yes, the docks. We need to build a new one."

Mellar looked pointedly out the window. "The last thing the harbor needs is another dock."

"Now listen here." Frobisher rapped his fist on Mellar's desk even though he already had the man's attention, then plopped himself in the chair Gilbert had just vacated. "I ran some calculations last night—I was a bit bored, you see—and if we increase the length of that south pier there by twenty-seven and a half percent, we could try…"

Gilbert let himself out of the office while Frobisher went on about how building a longer, wider dock would allow for ships to be unloaded quicker if they ran some kind of pulley system down the center.

Frobisher was likely right about the pulley, but that didn't mean the man was sane. Was this how he appeared to his father?

Always yammering about one invention or another? Always coming up with ideas to improve things, even if impractical?

Except there was nothing impractical about his crane. And he wasn't Frobisher. If not for losing the *Beaumont*, he'd be in a better financial situation than Frobisher at the moment.

But none of that helped him get his crane built. Calling on Marianne Mellar, on the other hand, would.

The question was, could he do so without the image of a stubborn, auburn-haired woman appearing in his mind?

⁓.⁓.⁓.⁓.⁓

"Care to tell me why my mother is asking whether you've been caught stealing before?"

Rebekah paused, the dust beater raised in her hand, and looked over her shoulder to find Gilbert standing in the yard behind her, a small paper sack in his hand. She turned back around and swung. Hard.

Thwack!

And again.

Thwack!

A third time.

Thwack!

"You do know mother expects that rug to be cleaned and back on the floor of her room tonight. Without holes beaten into it."

Rebekah gripped the beater doubly hard.

Thwack!

Thwack!

Thwack!

"I knew this wasn't going to work. Just take my money and go home, Rebekah. We can get you and Stanley on a train first thing tomorrow."

She turned at that, the dust beater raised once again to swing—at Gilbert this time rather than the rug. "Then maybe you could have warned me about Aileen and her habit of telling lies about other servants before I accepted the position."

A bird chirped nearby, and the noonday sunlight cascaded over Gilbert, highlighting his strong cheekbones and jaw while turning his honey-blond hair various shades of gold.

Not that she cared about how handsome he appeared or the color of his hair.

"So you didn't break Mother's tea service last night?"

She dropped the stick to her side. "It was more like Aileen broke it. I just happened to be holding the tray when she crashed into me."

Gilbert drew his forefinger and thumb together and rubbed between his eyebrows. Even as a boy, he'd done that whenever he had a headache. "Yes, and I'm sure you were walking docilely as you balanced a tray full of precious china."

She should raise the dust beater again and swing it at him. Maybe it would knock some sense into that arrogant head of his. "I was handling everything until Aileen ran out of the kitchen and straight into me. She was stealing food, by the way, and wasn't supposed to be in there at all. Though that's not the story she told your mother. In her version of events, I was the one to drop the tray and sneak food from the kitchen. Furthermore, I apparently told Aileen something about how I wasn't going to confess what had happened to the teapot to your mother or the head housekeeper and hoped neither of them noticed."

The vixen had gone straight to Mrs. Sinclair with her story first thing that morning. Rebekah had intended to wait until after she'd served breakfast to bring the topic up. That was going to be the last time she waited to tell Mrs. Sinclair anything. Aileen might be able to trick her once, but certainly not twice.

"I've no intention of getting into the middle of this, Rebekah. Now follow me. I've something you need."

"I'm not taking your money and going home just because someone lied about me," she snapped.

"Of course not." He rubbed his forehead. "That would make things too simple."

He started toward the kitchen entrance at such a brisk pace that she had to drop the beater and scramble to keep up with him.

"Aileen probably hates me because I'm not Irish like her. I bet that's what it is, though that doesn't explain why she'd let herself work for you, being English. Then again, she probably hates you too. Probably got fired from her last job because—"

"Enough." Gilbert held open the door to the servants' entrance for her. "And she doesn't hate me," he spoke beneath his breath, likely so the fancy French chef working in the kitchen couldn't hear.

"She's probably just good at hiding it," she whispered back.

Gilbert led her through the kitchen. "That's hardly the case, and if you expect me to defend you to my mother the next time there's an issue, then I suggest you stop making accusations about a woman you hardly know."

"Making accusations! Of course, I'm in trouble for 'making accusations' when she can go to your mother and tell blatant lies."

"You need to calm down."

"What do you think I was doing by beating the rug?" she nearly shouted at him.

He slanted her a sideways glance, his face impassive and unreadable. "I wouldn't call that calm, no."

She huffed. He was right. Aileen likely didn't hate him. How could anyone, with his golden hair and blue eyes and firm, determined jaw? Not to mention all the money his family had.

No. Aileen just hated her.

Rebekah ignored the hot prick of moisture at the back of her eyes. Unfortunately Gilbert picked that moment to look at her again. She blinked away the threatening tears and stared straight forward, practically marching like a soldier. What was wrong with her? This whole ordeal with Aileen was a stupid thing to get upset over, and she was even stupider for nearly crying in front of Gilbert.

A firm hand landed on her shoulder, pulling her to a stop. "Look at me."

She turned to face him.

He stroked a strand of hair behind her ear, his skin cool against her flushed face. "Breathe, Rebekah. Take a deep breath and breathe."

Breathe. Right. Except she really couldn't do that. Not with him standing so close she could smell that fancy cologne of his, not with his hands gripping her upper arms in a way that made her wish he'd wrap his arms around her and hold her. Kiss her.

That's what had happened the last time they stood this close.

Every time I'm near you, I want to take liberties I ought not.

Then she'd threatened to gut him with her fishing knife if he tried to kiss her again.

The trouble was, if he kissed her now, she wouldn't be the least bit tempted to reach for her knife. Should she tell him? Should she simply raise up on her tiptoes and kiss him? Would he want to kiss her back?

Oh, how did a regular woman know what to do at a time like this?

Or maybe a regular woman wouldn't be trying to kiss him at all—at least not if he was still planning to marry an heiress.

But hadn't his father given him the money he needed last night? So did he still need to marry an heiress?

Probably. She couldn't imagine him taking a normal person to wife like Ellie Spritzer or Aileen or... her.

Definitely not her.

"There now. See." Gilbert drew back from her. "You're calmer. That wasn't so hard, was it?"

It was hard, but in another kind of way. And she wouldn't say she was calmer, either. But her agitation had changed from a boiling rage at Aileen to...

Well, if nothing else, her blood was still rushing hot. "You believe me about Aileen, don't you?"

Gilbert rubbed the back of his neck and glanced away. "It's not like Aileen to lie."

"So you don't believe me then? Or you don't know which one of us to believe?" Moisture pricked behind her eyes again, but she tightened her jaw and held it back.

"I asked Mother to hire her this spring, and there's never been any trouble with her before now."

Gilbert had gotten Aileen the job? Why did that make her want to slap him? "Then tell me, have there been other girls who've come to work here for a day or two before Aileen had some story about them stealing or breaking something?"

He grew still. "I don't know, though Mother has certainly had trouble finding help of late."

"The next time either a servant quits or your mother finds reason to fire one, you might ask the poor girl being fired what part Aileen had in the situation. Your mother probably can't keep help because she's firing the wrong girl."

"I have enough to worry about without coming home to a war between you and one of the other servants. Just calm yourself and let whatever happened last night between you and Aileen rest." He rubbed a hand through his hair. "Now which room is yours?"

She paused and glanced at her surroundings. How had they ended up here? In the narrow, plain hall, lined with servants' rooms barely bigger than the size of her cook's cabin on the *Lassiter*. "What are we doing down here?"

And why hadn't she noticed their whereabouts sooner? She'd merely been following Gilbert, assuming he knew where they were going while she'd been stewing over Aileen. But Gilbert had no business being down here, and he certainly had no business being down here with her. She took a step away from him. If Aileen saw them together, she'd be fired. In fact, if any of the other servants spotted them alone, she'd be out of a job.

"I asked which room is yours."

She took another step away from Gilbert. "I'm not allowed to have men in my room, and Miss Niebert never said you were an exception."

Gilbert reached into a paper sack he'd been carrying and pulled out a deadbolt and a screwdriver. "There are bigger dangers in this house than a servant lying about you. You need a lock on your door. Now show me where to install it."

"Oh." Something inside her softened as she stared at the cast iron hardware. Surely she wouldn't get in trouble with Mrs. Niebert or Mrs. Sinclair for letting Gilbert install a lock, especially not if she stood in the hallway while he was doing it. She pointed toward the next door down on the left. "It's right there."

Gilbert stepped forward, opened the door, and pulled out the screwdriver. "How much did Mother end up docking your pay for the tea service?"

Rebekah leaned against the outside of the doorframe. "Ten dollars."

"Then you have much to be thankful for." Gilbert narrowed his eyes at her wall. "That tea set cost over a hundred dollars."

"A hundred dollars?" she squeaked. "Just for fancy cups to drink tea in?"

"It was Wedgewood. A set made in England that I gave her for Christmas several years ago."

"You gave it to her? I'm sorry Gilbert. Truly I am."

He looked up at her, his eyes twinkling. "And here I thought it wasn't your fault and you had nothing to apologize for."

"Oh, stop it already." She took a step into the room to see whether he was almost done, but his shoulders and back blocked her view. "I wish I'd picked another set. Your mother certainly has enough to choose from."

"As she should—she collects them."

"The lilacs painted on the set were just so pretty," she muttered.

"Rebekah Cummings, I'd never guess you to be enchanted with pretty flowers."

She scowled at his back, an effort that was lost on him since he didn't bother to turn around. "They reminded me of home, that's all."

"There aren't a terrible number of lilacs in Eagle Harbor." Frustration tinged his voice.

Because he grew upset with installing the deadbolt? Or because he was still frustrated with her? It probably had something to do with her again. That was the only thing they seemed good for—frustrating each other.

"You'll probably find more lilacs on this street than the entire Keweenaw Peninsula."

"The beautification society planted some at the edge of the cemetery. You can see them from Pa's grave."

"I see." He fell silent, still fiddling with the screwdriver.

She sank onto the edge of her bed and dropped her face in her hands. Teach her to be sentimental and pick something pretty. "How am I going to repay a hundred dollars?"

"You're not. Didn't you say Mother was only charging you ten dollars?"

"She must have meant ten dollars a month and I misunderstood." Would she have to work here for ten months just to pay everything back? How was she going to get a hundred dollars to her family now?

"My mother might not be the most compassionate of persons, but she's not a shrew. She knows you won't be able to pay the money yourself, and she's funds aplenty to purchase another one. I daresay the ten dollars is to teach you a lesson rather than help with the cost of replacing anything." He attacked the trim beside her door with the screwdriver once again.

"Do you know how to put in a lock?" She stood from her bed and approached him. "Because I don't think what you're doing is working."

"I can handle installing a deadbolt, thank you." Gilbert glared at the screw he was trying to twist into the wall, but the screw slipped from his fingers and dropped to the floor.

She snatched it up before Gilbert had the chance to bend over. "Let me try."

He held out his hand for the screw. "The store clerk said it was easy."

"It probably is—if you know what to do with a screwdriver."

"I've engineered and designed a crane. I'll thank you not to be so insulting."

"Yes, but how many screws did you put in that crane yourself?"

"Fine. Have at it, then." He stepped aside and waved his hand at the place in the trim where his efforts had scratched the paint and nothing more.

"Give it all here." She held out her hand, and he placed the sack in it. "And stop stomping around behind me and glaring over my shoulder. I've seen those drawings of your crane. Your mathematics equations have more letters and symbols than they do numbers. So you can't hold a screwdriver, but you can cypher with letters. Cyphering with letters is probably a better skill to have anyhow— at least for you."

Laughter sounded from behind her. "Are you trying to placate me? That's darling."

Darling? Her? Was he being sarcastic or honest? She shifted awkwardly and focused on the last of the screws, the warm blood that rushed through her earlier when Gilbert had stood too close suddenly returning. Somehow she didn't think darling was the first word most people thought of when describing her.

But Gilbert thought it. She swallowed as heat crept into her cheeks.

She finished with the final screws and slid the beam cleanly into place before trying to open the door. Everything held tight.

She handed the screwdriver back to him. "You didn't need to do this, but thank you."

He stepped closer and opened his mouth as though he were about to say something, maybe even reach out and push her hair behind her ear again. But then he backed away, undid the bolt, and walked into the hallway. "I hope you're right. I hope you never have need of the lock. But if something happens, anything at all, while you're here, come get me straightway. Do you understand?"

She opened her mouth to tell him she'd do fine with her fishing knife—and she would—but he'd just gone out of his way to not only buy her a lock but install it himself. Besides, with the way his father had looked at her last night, maybe the lock was needed. She nodded. "I'll let you know if anything happens. I promise."

He glanced down the hall to Aileen's door.

Had it been slightly ajar before? She hoped so, because she could only imagine the story Aileen would relay to Mrs. Sinclair if she'd seen the two of them together.

"And do try to get along with Aileen. You two could be fast friends."

"When she's stealing food and costing me ten dollars on my first night here? 'Friend' isn't the word that comes to mind."

"She hasn't been in America a year, and her brother died this spring, leaving her alone. She needs a friend regardless of whatever happened last night."

"But you don't understand. She went to your mother and—"

He clamped his hand over her mouth and moved close enough she could see the dark blue outline that rimmed the lighter blue of his eyes. "I seem to remember your brother quoting me a Bible verse about your enemies being at peace with you when your actions please the Lord. I seem to remember that happening right after he saved my life, even though I'd given him no reason whatsoever to save me."

She tried to speak, but he only pressed his hand tighter, his gaze holding hers. "Let's say, for the sake of argument, that everything you claim about Aileen is true. She broke the china, she went to Mother and lied, she tried to get you fired. Don't you still have an obligation to act peaceably towards her? Don't you still have an obligation to love her even if she's your enemy?"

She pressed her lips together behind his hand, and he finally released her.

"Fine. I'll try to be nice. But that doesn't mean—"

"'When a man's ways please the Lord, he maketh even his enemies to be at peace with him.' That's what it means, peace. Not anger or resentment or fighting. And trust me, Aileen needs peace right now. She's not just here for a few months like you, and she doesn't have a family she can return to whenever she wants."

Rebekah blew out a breath, her shoulders deflating with the action. Peace. Her father had made them memorize a good number of Bible verses about peace, and Gilbert was right to call her out on it. She needed to try harder with Aileen, even if it was the last thing she wanted to do. "I'll attempt to befriend her."

The corner of Gilbert's mouth tipped up into a soft smile, one so tender she suddenly needed to lean back against the wall lest she melt into a puddle on the floor.

"Thank you." Then he turned and was gone, all glimpses of tenderness vanishing with his brisk, determined stride.

She heaved in a breath and stared after him until he disappeared up the stairs. If only she could figure out how to make him smile at her like that more often.

Unfortunately, it seemed she was much better at pulling scowls from him.

Chapter Eleven

Gilbert glanced at his timepiece and shifted against the carriage seat. He'd spent too long with Rebekah just now, and if he wasn't quick at Lindy's, he might not make it to the Mellars' to call on Marianne today. He supposed he could put off visiting Lindy for another day, but he hadn't seen her in three months. Had the *Lassiter* gotten to port earlier yesterday, he'd have stopped on the way home, may have even brought Rebekah since Rebekah had asked about her. Something told him Lindy would enjoy a visit with an old friend from Eagle Harbor, and he could well imagine the way Rebekah's eyes would sparkle and how a smile would claim her face.

Did she realize how beautiful she was when she let herself be happy?

Then again, she was beautiful when mad, as this afternoon had reminded him. He leaned his head against the back of the seat and stared up at the carriage ceiling. What was he going to do with her? She'd never been a liar, nor was she the type to get caught up in some kind of spiteful battle with another woman.

"Mr. Sinclair? You did mean for me to drive you to Bridgeport, correct?"

Gilbert glanced at the carriage driver, who stood with the door ajar outside Lindy Marsden's home. "Yes, yes, of course."

Teach him to get distracted by thinking about Rebekah. Clearly he needed to go visit Marianne Mellar sooner rather than later. Once he had a suitable wife to focus on, his thoughts of Rebekah would surely fade. He only hoped she found a good man sometime soon. A man who deserved her. A man like—

"Mr. Sinclair?"

He disembarked from the carriage into the squalor and rank air that made up the Bridgeport tenements. A gang of boys rushed past, the youngest nearly plowing into him as they shouted to each other in a language he couldn't identify.

"Excuse you," he muttered under his breath before striding up to the tiny house made of flimsy wooden boards.

He knocked once, twice. No answer. Was that good? Perhaps she'd picked up extra hours down at the stockyard, or maybe her shift had changed and she now worked in the afternoon.

He knocked again only to be answered by a deep coughing. No good could come of that sound. Why hadn't he stopped here yesterday?

He opened the door and stepped into the house's single small, dark room. "Lindy?"

He moved across a floor so dusty it needed to be scrubbed thrice over and knelt beside the pallet on the floor. "Your cough's back."

Her body shook as her lungs tried to expel the wet phlegm trapped inside.

He bent his head until it nearly touched her shoulder. *God, why? Am I doing something wrong? She deserves better than this.*

She'd been healthy when he left Chicago. Was he hoping for too much by wanting her to stay well this time? "Does this mean you lost your job at the stockyard?"

She slumped back onto her pillows—something he'd made sure she had a lot of the last time she'd gotten sick. "What do you think? All anyone has to do is point at me and mention the word *tuberculosis,* and I've lost my job. And no, I'm not going to a sanitarium, so don't ask."

He should have known this would happen. It had happened too many times before for him to think otherwise. Each time her cough faded, each time she grew well and strong enough to work, it all came flooding back within a few months' time. "How long have you been sick?"

"I won't see another doctor, either. So don't try to sneak one in here like last time."

"You need help. Am I supposed to do nothing while you..." She wasn't dying. In the five years since her family had left Eagle Harbor, he'd seen her like this numerous times before. She'd get better from this cough, just like she had with all the others—for a few months at least.

And no, he wasn't going to think about the lung infection or pneumonia or whatever it was that had taken her mother's life. Lindy didn't have that.

Please, God, don't let her have that. "How long since you lost your job?"

She wheezed, her lungs struggling for air. "Six weeks, maybe more."

Another bout of coughing shook her body, and he helped her sit up, though he'd seen enough of her illness to know her position did little good. Lying, sitting, or standing, the murky sounding coughs were still vicious.

"And the money I left in case this happened?"

She rolled her eyes. "I told you hiding it under the floorboard wasn't going to keep the thieves from finding it."

He gritted his teeth. It was frustrating. Beyond frustrating, really. Every time she got well enough to work, she'd be sick again in a few months. Every time he brought a doctor, they claimed she had tuberculosis, never mind how her lung ailment seemed to go away and then return again in cycles. He didn't need to be a doctor to understand tuberculosis got progressively worse.

And most frustrating, every time he left food or money, someone stole it. How was he supposed to help her when he couldn't even give her food without someone taking it? His only other choice was to put her up in a house and pay for everything. Not only did he not have the funds given his current financial straits, but she would never agree to that. Furthermore, it would look an awful lot like she was his mistress, and neither of them needed to deal with those rumors.

"How's my sister?" She coughed again, though not as rough this time.

"She's well."

"As well as anyone can be for a prostitute, you mean." Even through her illness, her words shot sharply into the room.

He sighed. When Lindy's father had died, she and her sister had made very different choices, Lindy journeying with her mother to their aunt's house in Chicago, and Betsy choosing to remain in Copper Country, earning her keep in the same way many other women who'd fallen on hard times chose. "There's not much you can do when a person chooses that life."

"And my nephew? How's he?"

He should have never told her she had one. Knowing that the boy grew up in a brothel while both of them were helpless to stop it was perhaps more heartbreaking than Lindy's recurring illness. "He grows bigger, or so I'm told. It's not like I'm able to see the boy when I check on your sister."

Lindy pressed her eyes shut against the news, her face void of any emotion, which was probably best. This was the type of situation that emotions were best left out of, and while he might not be able to help Lindy's nephew, he could still help Lindy. "You should marry."

"What?" Her eyes fluttered open, and she pushed herself fully up from the bed before leaning against the wall.

"You need a husband, someone to work a job and support you when you get sick. Riffraff will be less likely to bother you if they know you have a husband to contend with."

She tipped her head back to stare at a ceiling so thin it couldn't possibly stop the rain from falling inside. "I'm too sick to marry."

"But you'll get better." He'd make sure of it, just like he'd start working on a way to get her out of this tenement.

"And just as assuredly as I'll get better, I'll get sick again. This might go on for days or decades, but eventually I'll stop getting well, and it will be just like Ma."

No. He wouldn't let her end up like her mother. "I'll find you a better doctor. One who can diagnose what's wrong. One who can help."

She stared at him with hazel eyes only a shade or two darker than Rebekah's, but they looked a decade older than Rebekah's vibrant irises. "Tuberculosis. It's what they all say. I have a cough that won't go away, so it has to be tuberculosis. And I refuse to go to a sanitarium. If you want to help, build more cranes so that this doesn't happen to anyone else."

Gilbert looked down at the rough planks he kneeled on and swallowed. "I lost the crane. The ship I was using to transport it sank during a storm, and the crane with it."

"You lost it? You said you had a buyer."

"I did, until that happened." He reached out and took her

hand, frail and bony. "I'm sorry."

She pressed her lips together, her eyelids closing, though whether due to tiredness or sadness, he couldn't tell. "How are the workers at the docks?"

"Much the same. Someone broke their foot last week loading one of my father's ships. The top crate fell while the stack was being tied down."

Her eyes filled with a familiar kind of sorrow. "Tell me you're helping him."

"I sent Stanley over this afternoon to see if his family has need of anything and to pay whatever doctor's bills he incurred."

"Will he be able to walk again?"

If ever he wished to lie, it was in moments like this, when the sick and injured looked at him and asked for an answer that would give them hope. But he'd seen Lindy go through too much over the past five years to start lying now. "I don't know."

"Does he have a wife, children?"

"A wife and two children, yes."

She closed her eyes again, but not before a single tear slipped down her cheek. "I hope he walks. And I hope you get that crane built soon, that it helps people, and that you sell a thousand of them so that dockworkers all over the country can be helped."

He reached for her hand again and squeezed it. "Have you heard about the new mayor?"

She gave an absent shrug, her eyes drifting shut once more. She was likely tired then, not just upset.

"He claims he wants to make the docks a safer place for workers. And the factories. Probably even the stockyard."

Her eyes sprang open at that. "Have you met him? Is he a man to be trusted, or will he forget about all the workers the moment a businessman walks into the room?"

"No, I haven't met him." And he doubted he ever would if there was even the slightest truth to the rumor about Warren and the mayor's daughter. "I don't know what kind of man he is, though my father has taken a disliking to him."

She smiled faintly. "That has to be a good omen."

He couldn't help but return the smile. "You're probably right."

Another coughing spell claimed her, and he sat by her side, her hand in his, until the coughs finally subsided. "Thank you for coming by, but I'm tired now."

"I see that." He pushed himself off the pallet and headed toward the small icebox and single cupboard that sat by her equally tiny cook stove. "Why don't you eat something before you sleep?"

"Not hungry," she muttered as she lay down, her long blond hair fanning out beneath her on the pillow.

The cupboard held a single bag of dried peas. What was he supposed to do with those? He lifted the lid to the icebox, but it didn't even have ice, let alone food. He'd have to bring some tomorrow, and he'd bring Rebekah to visit and clean the house as well. Maybe if he slept on it, he could figure out a place to leave money that the various ruffians who ran through Bridgeport couldn't find.

"Why don't you come home with me? We can put you in one of the servants' rooms and you can..." But she was already sleeping, and even if she wasn't sleeping, he couldn't envision her saying yes. He'd asked her this same question the last time she'd gotten sick and lost her job.

It was probably just as well. He could only imagine what Mother would say if he brought home a sick woman that appeared to have tuberculosis. Still, he had to find a way to get her out of this place. But what could he do when she didn't want help?

What could he do when his funds themselves were so limited?

Maybe he couldn't do anything more today or even tomorrow, but one day he'd do exactly what Lindy had said. He'd build his crane and sell it. Then he'd build another and another and another. With each crane he sold, he'd be keeping people safe. And he hoped she was right, hoped he ended up selling a thousand cranes or more to harbors all over the country. Then he'd take that money, and he'd make things better for people like Lindy.

But first he had to marry an heiress.

⁓.⁓.⁓.⁓.⁓

"Where have you been?"

Elijah blinked wearily at his wife as he plopped down onto the kitchen chair and peeled off his boots. Who knew that a person's feet could ache so much?

"Elijah." The tips of Victoria's pink shoes appeared in his line of vision—expensive shoes he wasn't going to be able to replace once they wore out.

Just as he wasn't going to be able to buy her another yellow dress like the one her shoes matched.

"Elijah." Victoria crouched down in front of him, her large brown eyes filled with concern. "Are you all right?"

"I'm fine." Or he would be, after he drank a gallon of water and had himself a long night's sleep. "Just tired. And thirsty."

"You look as though you haven't slept for a week." Victoria rested a hand on his leg for a moment, then jerked it away. "And you're drenched in sweat."

It wasn't all sweat. He'd doused himself in water before leaving the sawmill earlier. If only explaining wouldn't take so much effort.

Victoria moved away, and he closed his eyes as he listened to his wife's familiar gait while she padded around the kitchen.

"Here."

He opened his eyes to find a glass of water and a plate with a slice of ham and a heaping of potatoes on the table beside him.

"See if this helps."

He drained the water and set the empty glass on the table.

"Are you sure nothing's wrong?" Victoria sat in the chair beside him, a pretty vision of dark hair and pink ruffles despite the scarred wooden table she sat at and the rough log walls of the cabin. "You look as though something happened."

"I'm tired, like I said." He took one bite of ham, then another, energy slowly seeping back into him as he ate. "Since my fish are bringing such a low price, I went looking for work. Got hired in at the sawmill."

"You're this tired from working at the sawmill?" Her eyebrows drew together in a frown—one he'd normally kiss away, but doing so would require too much movement right then. "Maybe you need to find a different job."

"I start there at noon, so I can fish in the morning. They leave off work at six, but on the way home I saw a ship had docked." He rubbed at his droopy eyelids, then reached into his pocket and pulled out a dollar. "Earned a little extra money that way."

"And now you're ready to fall over." Ma stepped into the kitchen, her graying hair hanging over her thin shoulders in long, loose strands.

Was it really late enough Ma had taken her hair down for the night? How long had he spent unloading that ship? And he still didn't have enough money to pay the bill he owed Mr. Foley for damages done to the general store during his brawl with Gilbert.

"You missed the planning committee meeting." Ma moved to the stove and put on the kettle, likely for the cup of tea she had every night before bed.

How could she drink something so hot on a night as warm and

muggy as this? "What meeting?"

Ma turned to him. "For the Thimbleberry Festival. Mrs. Ranulfson said you were heading up the benevolence project this year."

"I forgot about the meeting." He slanted a glance at Victoria, who was looking down, the side of her lip tucked beneath her teeth. "I'm sorry."

She settled a hand over his.

"Your wife is quite good at making excuses for you." Ma sat at the table with a biscuit while the kettle warmed behind her. "I don't think Mrs. Ranulfson suspected you forgot."

Hopefully not, or the woman would be pounding down his door before he got out on the lake tomorrow.

"Trudy's not used to all those fancy words Victoria's set uses when they beg off."

A heavy silence fell around the table, and Victoria's cheeks grew red. He scowled at his ma, who looked a bit mortified herself. Usually they did so well pretending Victoria was one of them.

Not that he ever forgot the differences between their backgrounds for long.

Victoria cleared her throat and smiled a little too brightly. "D-do you have to work at the mill on Saturday, or can we still go on our picnic?"

Their picnic. Elijah dropped his fork to his plate. "I forgot." *Again.*

Her gaze fell once more. "That's all right. If the sawmill needs you, I understand."

"No, not the sawmill, the boathouse for the life-saving station. I'm having trouble getting it built myself, so I scheduled a work day." After he'd promised his wife a picnic. He rubbed his hand across his forehead. Of all the callous, ignorant things to do.

They'd only been married six weeks, but the longer he and Victoria were wed, the less time they spent together.

He glanced at Ma, quietly eating her biscuit. Pa had always had enough time for her. Even when things were lean, he never once remembered Pa refusing to go on a walk or picnic with Ma—or even with the whole family.

And now he had a wife of his own, sitting beside him in her pretty dress, a pair of combs tucked into the curls at the top of her head. He didn't need to ask whether they were real gold, and the little yellow and green stones embedded in them would be some kind of expensive gems, though he didn't have an inkling what their names were.

The door to the entryway opened and then thumped shut, followed by the familiar sound of boots on the entryway flooring.

"Looks like everyone's here." Isaac appeared in the doorway to the kitchen. "Good. You'll all want to see this telegram." He pulled a piece of paper from his pocket and set it on the table.

"Did Rebekah send a note?" His weariness fled as he snatched the paper and skimmed the telegram—from Gilbert, not Rebekah. His heart thudded harder with each word he read. "She's working in Chicago? For the Sinclairs?"

"She is?" Victoria reached for the paper.

"Appears so." Isaac stalked over to the stove, where he removed the kettle and set it down with a thunk. "I can't see Sinclair lying about something like this."

"No, he wouldn't lie." Victoria shook her head.

And his wife would know, seeing how she'd been engaged to the scoundrel this spring. Was this some kind of payback on Gilbert's part? Since Gilbert had lost his fiancée, he'd decided to go after their sister? Something hard tightened in Elijah's stomach.

"Well, at least now you can do what we talked about earlier and go get her." Isaac poured a cup of tea for Ma and nearly spilled the boiling water on his hand when he slammed it onto the table. "I just hope you get there before Sinclair compromises her."

Yes, now that they knew she was staying put, he was certainly capable of retrieving her. But should he? He'd just been hired at the sawmill, had only been married for a few weeks, and Mac had made a decent argument about her being old enough to do as she pleased. "I don't want Rebekah to be gone any more than you do, but charging off after her isn't going to solve anything."

"Who knows what trouble Rebekah will get herself into somewhere like Chicago." Isaac poured another cup of tea and snagged a biscuit from the platter on the table. "And do you trust Sinclair with her?"

He didn't. Not for an instant.

Gilbert was probably deriving some twisted pleasure from ordering her around whenever he wished.

But that wouldn't bother Rebekah. She was likely the hardest worker the Sinclair family had ever hired.

"Gil would never d-d-do anything to hurt Rebekah." Victoria stared at the table as though the old wooden boards held some sort of secret message.

Did she realize she'd just used a nickname for her former fiancé? One that no one else in the town used? Elijah turned toward his wife. "You don't know that."

"Seems that if Gilbert Sinclair had ill intentions, he wouldn't be sending us a telegram." Ma wiped up the droplets of spilled tea with a rag and took a sip. "My only question is, why did we hear from him and not Rebekah?"

Isaac dusted biscuit crumbs off his hand and leaned back against the sink. "Probably because Rebekah doesn't have money to send a wire."

Kindness and philanthropy didn't exactly drip from the Sinclair family. "If Gilbert's being nice to Rebekah, then he's getting something in return."

"All the more reason for you to get her from Chicago." Isaac downed half his cup of tea as though he were guzzling water.

"Quiet, the both of you." Ma's voice resonated through the room, soft yet firm. "Isaac, why are you insisting Elijah bring Rebekah home?"

Isaac's face turned pale, and he set his tea down. "Certainly you don't expect me to sail down there, though I suppose I could take a horse to Houghton and then go by train."

"Th-this is probably why she left without a w-w-word." Victoria used the tip of her finger to trace a scratch on the table, still not looking up when she spoke. "She knew both of you would stop her from g-going if she said anything."

"Of course I would have stopped her," Elijah growled. "I'm with Isaac in thinking she ought not be prancing about Chicago with Sinclair, but I'm sensible enough to know that if I drag her back here, she'll only leave again."

"Then we'll just have to keep her from leaving a second time." Isaac clenched the ledge of the sink, his knuckles turning as white as his face.

"How do you propose we do that?" Elijah ran a hand through his hair. "Chain her to the cabin wall?"

"She needs to be married. If she were settled, she wouldn't be off gallivanting around."

"And who's she supposed to marry?" Ma raised her eyebrows and looked at Isaac.

"Not Sinclair, that's for sure."

"I agree." Elijah thumped his fist on the table.

Victoria jumped when the table moved beneath her finger. "I d-doubt Gilbert's much of a threat. He's quite set on marrying to advance his business prospects."

Elijah ran a hand through his hair, damp from a mixture of water and sweat. If only he could be so sure about Sinclair. But there'd been something between him and Rebekah this spring, something about the way they refused to look at each other, but when their gazes happened to meet, they stayed locked for too long.

"She should marry Harrington." Isaac finished the rest of his tea in one long gulp. "Have you seen the way he watches her?"

"You've noticed that too?" Victoria smiled.

"Oh, and isn't it nice of you to decide who Rebekah should marry?" Ma chomped on her biscuit as though she were angry at the flour, water, and lard rather than her family. "You'll leave her love interests alone just like you'll leave her alone in Chicago. She's twenty-two. If she were married and had a babe or two, you wouldn't think twice about letting her act like a grown woman. Each of you have made your own choices. No one's forced you into a boat since your pa died, Isaac, even though I'm sure Elijah and Rebekah both want to. And Elijah, your pa let you sail the Atlantic on your own, even though it grieved him. The lot of you need to let your sister make her own choices."

Elijah sat back. Five years ago he'd left town because he hadn't been able to stand by and watch the Sinclairs use their money as an excuse to run roughshod over Eagle Harbor. But how would he have felt if Isaac or Pa had followed him to Boston and dragged him back home?

"I suppose we have to let go, even if we don't want to." But he'd still worry about her; any good brother would. And the next time he saw Sinclair...

His hand clenched into a fist.

"Thank you for understanding, Elijah." Ma took a sip of her tea.

Isaac looked between the two of them and scowled. "As far as I'm concerned, there's nothing to understand."

"You make choices we don't have a say in." Elijah jabbed a finger at his brother. "So why shouldn't she? Even if I don't like it any more than you do."

"You had a hard time allowing me to make my own choices, but you're glad you did, right?" Victoria smiled at him, then reached for his hand.

He gave her arm a yank, and she tumbled forward into his lap. "I sure am." He wrapped his arms around her waist. "I can't imagine you would have stood for me carting you back to Eagle Harbor against your will."

She shook her head and pursed her lips, but the edges tilted up into an ill-hidden smile.

"But now that you're mine, I don't ever have to let you go." He held on tighter and nuzzled his face in the crook of her neck.

"Elijah, stop," she gasped.

"Thank you, lovebirds." Isaac rolled his eyes. "Can we go back to talking about Rebekah now?"

"We are talking about Rebekah. She needs to come back because she wants to, not because we force her to." Though going down to Chicago, hogtying her, and putting her on the first ship back to Eagle Harbor did have a certain appeal. "Just like Victoria came back here on her own because she couldn't keep away from me."

"You sound awfully sure of yourself." Victoria squirmed in his lap.

"I am," he whispered against her ear. "Just wait until later, and I'll show you how sure."

Isaac set his cup down with a thump. "But—"

"Elijah's right. If you force her home, she'll only leave again." Ma narrowed her eyes at Isaac much like she used to when they'd been in short pants and had made a mess that she wanted cleaned up.

"Am I the only sane member left in this family?" Isaac slammed his fist on the edge of the sink.

"More like the only insane one," Elijah muttered.

"I heard that."

"Enough." Ma raised her chin, her voice firm despite its quietness. "Sane or not, Isaac, you won't go and get your sister. It's not your place."

"If she comes back battered or ruined or both, don't blame me." Isaac whirled and stalked out of the kitchen.

The sound of the door slamming reverberated through the house. Elijah pressed his eyes shut against it and buried his face in Victoria's hair.

He was doing the right thing by letting Rebekah go, wasn't he?

Chapter Twelve

"She says she'll see you in the front parlor."

"Thank you." Gilbert handed the footman his hat and followed him through the Mellar's foyer, comprised of dark, polished wood much like the one that graced the entrance to his parents' house.

Marianne sat on a settee wearing a dress that looked to be made of light blue silk, the sleeves near her shoulders puffed in the latest fashion. He'd forgotten how stunning she was. With hair that was nearly black, and a petite, delicate frame, she was almost more china doll than living, breathing person.

She set down the lady's periodical she'd been reading. "Father mentioned you last night at dinner. He expected you to stop by sometime yesterday."

"I'd intended to, but a… situation came up that needed to be addressed." Situation? He nearly cringed. Lindy was a person, not a situation. But it wasn't exactly good form to tell the lady he hoped to marry that he hadn't called on her because he'd been in the tenements with another woman.

"Business, business. It makes the world go round, does it not? Still, Father says you've an excellent head for business and that your ideas are pointed in a good direction." She gestured to the chair across from the settee. "Sit. Shall I call for refreshments?"

Though she phrased it as a question, there wasn't much question-like about her suggestion. Yet another thing he'd forgotten about her. She didn't ask questions so much as give commands. "I was thinking we could go for a walk in your family's gardens."

"The gardens." She surveyed him, her eyes giving away little of her thoughts. "That's a rather romantic suggestion for your first call, don't you think?"

The gardens were romantic? What would she think of standing aboard ship and looking at the stars together?

No. He wasn't thinking about that—most definitely wasn't thinking about that. He doubted Marianne would ever sail with him, let alone stand on the deck with her hair down and stare at the sky. With a father worth half the state of Illinois, nothing short of diamonds would excite her.

"If I'm the first of your callers to suggest a walk in the garden, then you've been receiving the wrong callers."

A flicker of amusement shone in her eyes, and her prim little lips lifted in a half smile. "Most of my callers are far more interested in a discussion about how much money my father plans to settle on me when I wed than the color of our roses."

He took a step closer. "Then I think those callers are overlooking the most valuable part of the marriage."

She reached a delicate hand up to touch her throat. "I see."

He extended his hand to her. "Shall we?"

She took his hand and stood, revealing the full splendor of the blue silk gown she wore, and placed her delicate hand on his arm. "Only if you promise not to start quoting Elizabeth Barrett Browning to me."

"Elizabeth Barrett Browning?" He led her out of the salon and toward the back of the Mellar family mansion. "I was going to wait until tomorrow to start counting all the ways I loved you."

A laugh, small and clear like the tinkling of a little silver bell, escaped her lips. "You might fall behind some of your competitors then."

"You've had a suitor quote 'How Do I Love Thee' the first time he called on you?" He couldn't help his chuckle. "Tell me I don't know him."

"I'm afraid you do. It was Andrew Anderson."

"Andrew Anderson." Ah yes, he could just see the reed-thin son of the insurance agency owner doing that the first time he called. The poor woman. Andrew Anderson suited Marianne about as well as a sixty-year-old spinster suited Warren. "Well now, I better come up with something to quote, lest I fall behind. How about Christopher Marlowe? 'You can come with me and be my love, and we'll live…' in the hills or fields or mountains or wherever it is we're supposed to live."

They stepped outside into the sunlight, and she slanted him a glance, her lips still tilted up in a smile. "I do think I'm going to enjoy these calls of yours, Gilbert Sinclair. But please be aware that I've no intention of living in a field. Ever."

He bit back a smile. He should have guessed she'd have something smart to say in response. "I'm looking forward to spending time with you as well."

And he was. Marianne Mellar had always been a smart, lovely woman. Indeed, she would make him the most suitable wife in all of Chicago.

The only question was, would he enjoy walking through the Mellar family gardens and bantering with her as much he enjoyed standing under the starlight with Rebekah?

⌐.⌐.⌐.⌐.⌐

Rebekah stared out the window of Gilbert's carriage at the

crowded, dusty street. The drive was taking forever, especially since she didn't know where they were going. All Gilbert said was that he had something she needed to clean, then he'd trundled her off into one of his family's carriages.

"How are things between you and Aileen?" he asked from where he sat opposite her.

Rebekah scowled at him, letting the sounds of streetcars, trains, and other carriages fill the space between them before she answered. "Let's just say she's not as interested in making amends as you think."

His shoulders rose and fell with a silent sigh. "What happened now?"

Besides Aileen realizing Gilbert had been in her room and informing Mrs. Sinclair? Gilbert's mother must not have asked him about that, just lectured her about the house rules. Though evidently the rules didn't apply to carriage rides since the mistress had no trouble letting her go with Gilbert this afternoon.

Maybe one day society's upper crust would make sense to her. "Are things smoother now that your father gave you the money you needed?"

"I do notice when you abruptly shift topics." Gilbert's eyes lightened with a touch of mirth, and the corner of his mouth tilted up. "But no, my father didn't give me any money."

"Oh." It had looked as though he would when she'd left the room the other night. She reached across the carriage for Gilbert's hand and gave it a little squeeze. "I'm sorry, truly."

He turned his palm over so that her hand was engulfed in his. "Why are you sorry? I turned him down."

"Turned him down? But why would you—"

"My father does nothing out of benevolence, not even for his sons."

"Then how are you going to come up with... Oh. The heiress."
So he was still planning to marry for money.

"Now you see my predicament." He watched her so closely her
palm turned damp in his hand.

She tugged it away and planted both hands firmly in the center
of her lap. "It's still a ridiculous reason to marry."

"Only to you. Many women would marry a man for sixteen
thousand dollars, including the women in Eagle Harbor. Why is it
so terrible I marry a woman for the same reason?"

What should she say to that? It was true, wasn't it? In fact, if
someone offered her sixteen thousand dollars to—

No! She wasn't thinking about such a thing. First, no one
would make her that type of offer. She might have that kind of
value before God and her family, but someone like Gilbert Sinclair
certainly wasn't going to see it. Second, if someone was willing to
pay that much money for a wife, he'd want a woman who
preferred sewing to gutting fish. And third, well, *Many waters*
cannot quench love, neither can the floods drown it: if a man would
give all the substance of his house for love, it would utterly be
contemned. Did she really want to spend the rest of her life married
to someone who didn't love her?

Someone who assumed she could be bought?

Though if she ever married for money, her husband wouldn't
simply assume she could be bought, she'd have proven the matter
the day they married. And that verse from Song of Solomon was
pretty clear about love itself never being bought.

"Did I silence you? For once in her life, the sharp-tongued
Rebekah Cummings doesn't know what to say?"

She settled back against the seat and crossed her arms over her
chest. "I was mulling things over, that's all. And I think any bride
who'd marry for sixteen thousand dollars would come to regret her

decision, as would the groom."

"We're here." Gilbert looked out at the street as the carriage rolled to a stop, then thrust open the door and climbed out without answering her.

Was he in a rush? Or was he irked because she didn't agree with him?

She could just imagine the flattery he heard from half the women in Chicago.

"*Yes, Gilbert.*"

"*I'm sure you're right, Gilbert.*"

"*My, my, aren't you brilliant inventing that crane, Gilbert.*"

His future wife would probably be no different. If anything, she'd be even better at smiling serenely and agreeing with his every little thought, no matter how ridiculous.

"Are you coming?" Gilbert stuck his head back through the door.

"Yes, yes." She took a breath of hot, stifling air and climbed out of the carriage—where the air was even hotter and more stifling. And that didn't account for the rank odor wafting up from the trash scattered along the narrow street. She glanced down the road, packed with houses and apartments so hastily built that a good wind could blow the buildings over. "Where have you brought me?"

"To the Bridgeport tenements. You're here to clean, remember?"

"Clean? Here?" She looked around the narrow street once more. "I doubt cleaning will do much good. It's filthy."

A woman bumped into her shoulder and glared. "*Zejdź z drogi.*" She gripped the hand of the dirty little boy beside her and dragged him away.

"Sorry," Rebekah muttered.

"Let's get you inside." Gilbert took her by the elbow and led her toward a gray shack. He knocked once before opening a door with such wide gaps in its planks that she could see through the slits. "Lindy, how are you today?"

Rebekah blinked, her eyes adjusting to the gloom. Coughing emanated from the pallet in the corner, and a woman propped herself up on her elbows, her long blond hair falling onto the bedding behind her.

"You're back." Another bout of coughing shook the woman's slender frame.

"I told you I would be." Gilbert moved to her side, leaving Rebekah to stand in the middle of the... the...

House seemed too fine a word for the flimsy walls and sagging ceiling. A hovel, maybe? Or a hut?

"And I brought a friend from Eagle Harbor."

Rebekah's gaze snapped back to the woman. Stanley had said that her old friend Lindy from Eagle Harbor lived in Bridgeport. She sucked in another breath of hot, reeking air and headed toward the pallet. "Lindy Marsden, how are you?

~.~.~.~.~

Rebekah wiped the sheen of perspiration from her forehead as she stepped outside. Unfortunately her fingers came away not only sweaty but also smudged with a dusty gray film. She glanced at Gilbert beside her and wiped more grime from her neck. After scrubbing Lindy's house from top to bottom, she must look a fright.

And smell like a trash heap.

"Are you getting in?" Gilbert held the carriage door open for her.

She sniffed and then wrinkled her nose once again. "Are you

sure you want me to?"

"You gave that house a thorough cleaning. I don't expect you to smell like soap, and I'm sure I don't smell much better."

But he wasn't as sweaty as her since he'd sat and talked to Lindy the entire time they were in that stifling little house. She climbed into the carriage and sat on the fancy velvet seat that the dust on her skirt would surely smudge. "I'm not sure whether that's a compliment or an insult."

He settled himself across from her. "It's a compliment, I think."

She looked out the window at the row of squalid buildings while the carriage began to move, snippets of overheard conversation from Lindy's house floating through her mind. "Why didn't you tell me?"

"Tell you what?"

"Why you're so determined to build that crane?"

The air between them grew still, the temperature even hotter. "Does that matter?"

Of course it mattered. He wasn't building the crane to make himself famous or gain wealth, but because of Lindy's father. Because he cared about the dockworkers.

She'd never considered the dockworkers' working conditions until she'd listened to the conversation between Gilbert and his father the other night. But even then she hadn't envisioned people dying, nor thought of how the workers might be at greater risk if they worked long shifts.

She was a dunce, and not once over, but twice or thrice. She brought her gaze up to meet Gilbert's. "Yes. Why you're building that crane matters."

He stretched his legs out across the carriage floor and crossed them at the ankles. "You're the first person I've met who cares."

"No, I'm not. It matters to Lindy, and it would matter to

Elijah. It might not matter to the business men you have meetings with, but it matters to any decent person."

"And do these decent people have money to invest in my crane? Rich daughters I can marry so that I can put it into production?"

He didn't need to mock her for caring about his project. About his motives. She blinked back a hot bit of moisture—because a speck of dust must have gotten into her eye while she'd been cleaning, not because Gilbert was going to make her cry. Again. The lout.

"Leave it rest, Rebekah. The why behind my crane doesn't matter nearly as much as the how."

"You've spent the past four years of your life designing a crane so that what happened to Lindy's pa doesn't happen again. That makes the why matter a lot. It also makes you a hero."

He looked away, his Adam's apple bobbing. "I don't know what you're talking about."

"Plus you're paying Lindy's rent. Giving her food and money."

"When she'll take it, yes."

Rebekah glanced down and fiddled with the opening of the pocket on her apron. "I was wrong about you. This whole time I've been wondering what happened to the sweet schoolboy I went fishing with. But he's still there. You're just a lot better at hiding him now than you were all those years ago."

.⸱.⸱.⸱.

Gilbert glared across the carriage at Rebekah. Unfortunately she was about the only woman he knew besides his mother that wasn't cowed by that look. "Don't make more out of this than what it is. I plan to make money off my crane, not hand out charity."

"Have you been helping Lindy since she left Eagle Harbor?" Rebekah tucked a strand of dangling hair behind her ear, her eyes riveted to him.

Why did she keep asking these questions? Was it so impossible to believe he'd help someone who had suffered at the hands of his father? She was making it sound like helping others gave him as much business sense as Frobisher, who went bankrupt twice a year.

The carriage remained silent as she waited for an answer, and she probably wouldn't allow him to change the subject. "Yes. I've been helping her all this time."

"I remember her father's death."

Who didn't? The story had flown around Eagle Harbor. Lindy's mother had been sick for as long as anyone could remember, and her father had worked long hours on the dock, always trying to earn money for the never-ending list of medicines that Dr. Greely thought might make Mrs. Marsden well again. Her father had been working nearly fourteen hours when a crate fell on top of him and broke his neck.

Gilbert squeezed his eyes shut, not wanting to remember his father's callous treatment of the Marsdens.

"Lindy's sister went to work at Reed Herod's brothel up in Central." Rebekah wiped at a smudge on her cheek, and succeeded in spreading the gray film across half her face.

"I'm aware."

She wiped at the smudge again, spreading the grime down to her jaw this time. "And you didn't try to stop it?"

"What was I to do?" He'd only been eighteen at the time, and he had enough trouble thwarting his father's heartless decisions now. He'd been helpless to stand against his father back then. "Offer to set her up as my mistress?"

Her face paled, and she turned straight ahead. "That wasn't what I was thinking. Did you know Elijah proposed to Lindy after that?"

He dropped his head and rubbed his brow. "No."

Though he recalled the bloody nose he'd gotten after Elijah had approached him and asked what his father planned to do to care for the Marsdens. Elijah had said nothing about proposing to Lindy, but somehow he could see it. Elijah was sacrificial enough to marry a woman he didn't love and then be faithful to her for fifty years simply because he saw a need.

Gilbert shifted uncomfortably. He, on the other hand, was about to marry a woman so he could get sixteen thousand dollars.

And he wondered why Rebekah objected to his reason for marriage.

But then, when had he ever been as noble as anyone in the Cummings family?

Gilbert glanced over at Rebekah, who was studying him, tenderness evident in her clear green eyes just like it used to be ten years ago when she'd befriended him, the boy who never had any friends. But he was a grown man now, and he didn't need friendship based on charity and pity.

"I'm afraid the house might be a bit hectic when you get back." His suddenly restless fingers fiddled with the top button on his waistcoat. "Sorry for that. The dinner was rather unplanned, and mother had a fit when she learned I was taking you away for the afternoon."

"Dinner?" Rebekah's brow wrinkled. "Do you have company coming? I didn't know of it."

"That's because it was arranged only a few minutes before I took you to see Lindy."

"It must be important company, from the sound of it."

"Seeing how it's the woman I hope to marry and her father, yes, I'd call them important."

Rebekah's head snapped up, the tenderness in her eyes from

moments before now replaced with accusations. "I see."

He sighed. Did she see? Truly? Because something told him every inch of her body was fighting off the urge to start quoting that verse about floodwaters not quenching love and going on again about how he shouldn't marry for money.

But Rebekah didn't have the burden of helping all the people her father had wronged. And he didn't have any illusions that marrying for love would turn out well a decade or two from now.

Chapter Thirteen

She was perfect.

Rebekah pasted on a polite smile—at least she hoped it was polite—as she set a dish of crème brûlée on the table in front of Mrs. Sinclair.

Small, dainty, perfect. This Marianne Mellar lady was probably everything Gilbert wanted in a wife.

Rebekah set another dish in front of Mr. Sinclair and turned back toward the sideboard where the dirty dishes from the main course waited to be cleared.

They were probably about the same height, she and Miss Mellar, but Miss Mellar was thinner. Not in the sickly thin and underfed manner of Lindy Marsden, but in the delicate, porcelain china kind of way. Like that perfect icicle that hung off the roof in the winter. Clear and beautiful and stronger than it looked.

She didn't have any idea whether Miss Mellar was strong, but the woman was certainly rich, and that's what Gilbert wanted.

No, it was what he needed. Because if he didn't marry someone rich like Miss Mellar, he could wave goodbye to his dream of a crane and helping people like Lindy's family.

But that didn't mean she could watch them smile at each other or lean close and whisper without a lump forming in her stomach.

She jerked a tray of leftover gravy off the sideboard, causing the liquid to slosh over the side of the engraved silver bowl and spill onto the platter beneath. The soft chatter from the table continued undeterred. Evidently no one had noticed her blunder save Vincent, the footman standing to the left of the sideboard.

"Here, take the roast beef too." He handed her another fancy silver platter, this one filled with leftover meat cut so finely it just might disintegrate on a person's fork before they got it to their mouth. "And you best find Aileen while you're in the kitchen. I don't know where she got off to, but she should have cleared half the sideboard by now, and she hasn't taken a thing."

Rebekah blew out a breath. Knowing Aileen, the woman would find some way to pin her disappearance on Rebekah.

She balanced the two trays in each hand as she headed out the door and down the hall toward the servants' stairs. At least she wasn't carrying the fancy china plates. She couldn't exactly break the silver if she dropped it, though she could certainly make a big mess of prime rib and gravy.

She slowly descended the steps and used her elbow to open the swinging doors that led to the kitchen.

"Ah, zere's ze prime rib and gravy. I was starting to wonder if it got lost on its way back to ze kitchen," Cook blundered in her thick French accent. She took the trays from Rebekah and glanced at the door that led to the yard and gardens. "Aileen should be ze one doing zis. Ze sideboard must be a mess up zere without her to clear away anything."

"Yes, where is she? Vincent wanted me to find her before I headed back above stairs." She looked around the steaming kitchen, but the redheaded Irish woman was nowhere to be found.

Cook nodded toward the back door. "She ran outside at ze start of the main course. I haven't seen her since. You best find her and be quick about it unless ze two of you want an earful from Madame Sinclair later."

The two of them? Her prediction about Aileen blaming her for the disappearance was already coming true. Lovely. Rebekah headed outside, her stride brisk as she surveyed the immediate yard and then narrowed her eyes at the path that led into the garden. "Aileen? Where are you? You're needed inside."

A carriage clattering on the street was the only sound that greeted her.

"Aileen?" She headed toward the garden, but she'd not been in it yet, and she'd heard it was vast. Was it something she could get lost in at night? She glanced back toward the house, the lights on the first floor blazing even though the Sinclairs only had two guests for dinner, Miss Mellar and her father. If she didn't hurry back to the house, Margaret was going to be the only serving girl left.

But returning without Aileen wasn't going to bode well either.

"Aileen?" she tried one more time from the entrance to the garden.

Silence.

She dashed back inside, tucking the strands of hair that had come loose back into her updo as she rushed up the stairs and into the elaborate dining room with dark paneled walls, floor-to-ceiling drapes, and a rug just as thick and fancy as the one in the foyer.

From his seat at the table beside Miss Mellar, Gilbert lowered his brow and sent her a puzzled look.

She clapped her hands to her cheeks. Were they red? Was her hair askew? What?

"You're breathing heavy," Vincent whispered as he handed her a bowl of glazed potatoes and an oval dish that had been filled with elegant-looking green beans.

"Sorry," she whispered a bit more loudly than she ought, given the way she was sucking in breaths of air. Though she doubted any of the other servants would be behaving differently if they'd just run from the garden to the dining room.

"Where's Aileen?" Margaret came up behind her.

Rebekah shrugged, then pressed her eyes closed for a brief instant. Mrs. Sinclair had warned her about shrugging. *Not proper,* she'd said. Rebekah wasn't about to glance behind her and see if the mistress had noticed. Drawing Gilbert's attention was bad enough. "Cook said she headed outside at the beginning of the main course. I went as far as the garden but couldn't find her."

An overloud clinking sounded from the table. She and Margaret turned to see Mrs. Sinclair staring pointedly at her water goblet. So much for not getting noticed. Vincent lifted the crystal pitcher from the sideboard and headed to the table.

"Check Aileen's room when you go down next. Maybe she took ill," Margaret whispered before shooing her out the door with the dishes.

After stopping by the kitchen, Rebekah checked Aileen's room and found it empty with the bed made up. Only after dessert was finished and the family retired to... well, wherever rich families retired to after dinner, did she go out to the garden again. This time she had explicit instructions from both Cook and Mrs. Niebert not to return until she'd found Aileen.

Scents of flower nectar and fresh blooms floated through the air to create an almost peaceful environment despite the dense air and constant noise of the city. Gas lamps lit some of the larger trails, casting an orange glow on the bushes and flowers. Who had ever heard of lighting a garden? Wealthy folk got the strangest notions sometimes.

"Aileen," she called.

Still no answer.

She veered off the main path into a darker, unlit section of the garden and paused. Rustling sounded from the bushes in front of her, then the unmistakable sound of retching floated through the night.

"Aileen?"

The retching gave way to soft sobbing. Rebekah started forward again until Aileen's shadowed form appeared near a hedge. She undid the apron from around her waist and handed it to the kneeling woman. "Here, you might want to wipe your mouth."

Aileen kept her head tilted down in the darkness. "Go away."

Rebekah crouched beside her, ignoring the scent of vomit wafting from the bushes. It wasn't much worse than smelling fish guts, really. "How long have you been sick? Is that why you ran out on dinner?"

"I said leave me alone." Aileen dabbed at her mouth with the apron.

"Do you need help getting back to the house? You should be in bed."

"I'm fine. Just go."

"You can't truly expect me to leave you here, not in this state."

Aileen sniffled and wiped her mouth again. "I suppose dinner's done then? The mistress and Miss Niebert will be upset that I missed it."

"Not if you were sick." Mrs. Sinclair might have high standards for her servants, but the woman wasn't unreasonable. She was only docking Rebekah's pay by ten dollars for that shattered teapot, and she hadn't fired her when Aileen had tattled about Gilbert being in her room. "Do you think you can stand?"

Aileen groaned. "It's worse when I move."

"Here, let me help you." Rebekah pushed to her feet and held out a hand.

Aileen put her own palm in Rebekah's and slowly stood, then drew in a shaky breath. "Let's see if I can make it to me bed."

They started back towards the main path. Oh, Gilbert would be happy if he saw her now, helping Aileen even though the woman hadn't been kind. But how could she stay mad at someone so miserable?

"I think I need to…" Aileen darted off to the bushes again, but no retching sound followed. When she returned to the path, she drew in long, slow breaths. "I'm sorry. This must be such a burden on ye."

That had to be one of the most ridiculous apologies she'd ever heard. A person could hardly help getting sick. "I hope it passes quickly."

Aileen merely groaned.

"Do you have plans for Independence Day?" Gilbert asked.

Rebekah turned at the sound of his voice. Had he come to the garden to fetch Aileen too? Then why was he asking about Independence—?

"Just the usual." Marianne Mellar appeared in the opening where the main, well-lit garden path intersected with the dark, curvy trail they stood on. "We'll attend the fireworks display on the water and then head to the Carry's ball afterwards."

"*We* meaning you and your father?" Gilbert didn't glance at the dark trail where they watched from. Oh no, he focused every last bit of his attention on the beautiful woman by his side.

Or was there a word that meant beyond beautiful? If so, that was how to describe the small woman in the shimmering, pale blue gown.

"No, *we* meaning the whole family, at least for the fireworks." Miss Mellar had a voice like a bell, and not the kind of bell that the cook at a lumber camp rang for dinner. "My nieces and nephews love the display. It'd be a lot more boring to attend without the children. They shriek and yell as loud as the boom from the explosion. It's probably one of the only times I don't mind such noise."

"Probably one of the only times I don't mind such noise," Rebekah mimicked under her breath.

Aileen looked at her, a question written across her face.

"Sorry," she whispered as she took Aileen's arm. "We need to get you inside."

"No. Let them pass. I think the illness is starting to fade, and I don't want to disturb them."

Well, she wanted to disturb them, so much so that Marianne would head home for the night. Why couldn't they have come across each other on the main path, right about the time Aileen felt the urge to retch? Not that she wished more sickness on Aileen, but the look on Miss Mellar's face just might be worth Rebekah getting sick herself.

Did people as rich and perfect as Miss Mellar even get sick? Or were they too highfalutin for such things?

Gilbert and Miss Mellar neared the hedge of bushes that would soon block them from view, still chatting about watching the fireworks from the Mellar family yacht. Evidently watching them from the park where the rest of Chicagoans gathered wasn't quite uppity enough for people like the Mellars and Sinclairs.

Gilbert patted Miss Mellar's hand, which rested comfortably on his arm. He took smaller steps than she'd ever seen him use in her life, and seemed quite content about it, as though he had nothing better to do than stroll leisurely through the garden.

No cranes to build.

No injured dockworkers and their families to help.

Except he was strolling leisurely through the garden for that very reason. Because he wanted to build cranes. Because he wanted to help the injured and their families.

Oh, why couldn't he have found an heiress with teeth too big for her mouth and a forehead as broad as her hips? Smelling like fish and having a wart or two on her nose wouldn't hurt either.

Gilbert bent closer and whispered something to Miss Mellar, then raised the woman's hand and gave it a kiss.

Rebekah's stomach twisted as though it had suddenly been attacked by the same illness troubling Aileen.

..*.*.*

Rebekah yawned and rapped lightly on Aileen's door. It opened to reveal a bright-eyed Aileen with her hair pulled flawlessly up and her maid's uniform starched and ironed.

"Oh, I expected you to still be in bed after last night."

"Last night?" Aileen blinked at her, a pleasing smile on her face.

Rebekah raised an eyebrow. "You were rather sick, if I recall."

"I'm feeling better, thank ye for asking." Aileen pulled the door to her room shut. "No need to mention it to anyone if ye please. But ye best hurry and finish dressing if ye don't want to be late to the kitchen."

"Let me stop by my room for a minute, and we can head up to breakfast together." Since she'd thought Aileen would still be in bed retching, she'd padded down the hall in her stocking feet as soon as she'd pulled on her dress, leaving her apron, shoes, and dust cap all in her room.

"I can't imagine the family will be up with how late the Mellars stayed last night." A fact she didn't want to think about. When she'd gone to bed, everyone was still in the drawing room, Gilbert and Marianne seated far too close together on the settee.

She opened the door to her room and tromped inside.

"Ye have a bolt?" From where she stood just inside the room, Aileen's eyes flashed to the door and then back to her. "On yer door?"

Rebekah shrugged and tied the apron behind her. "Gilbert installed it."

"Don't ye mean Mr. Sinclair?" Aileen snapped.

"Yes, Mr. Sinclair," she gritted, though calling him by his surname behind his back wasn't nearly as bad as saying it to his face.

"None of the other servants have bolts."

Rebekah pursed her lips together. "I didn't ask for one, if that's what you're thinking."

"But he gave ye one all the same. That tells me enough."

It didn't tell her anything, but Aileen flounced out the door before Rebekah could respond. Not that she would have come up with an explanation that put the other woman at ease. She huffed. After all she'd done for Aileen last night, Aileen was probably headed upstairs to tell the mistress more lies about her and Gilbert.

So much for Gilbert's notion about them becoming fast friends.

Except now Gilbert was probably too busy with Miss Mellar to notice whether they fought.

Chapter Fourteen

"Rebekah." Basket in hand, Gilbert headed out the servants' entrance and around the back of the house, where he'd spotted her washing the outside of the drawing room windows.

How many days since he'd seen her? Two? Three? Between spending his mornings and afternoons at the shipping office and his evenings calling on Marianne, he couldn't quite remember the last time he'd spoken with Rebekah. Although Mother had come to him the other day asking if he was dallying with Rebekah and why there was a rumor he'd installed a bolt on her bedroom door.

Why his mother should mind so much, he didn't know, especially given Father and Warren's wandering attentions.

"Rebekah," he called again.

She turned, cleaning rag in hand.

"Could you do me a favor?"

"You're asking me for a favor on Independence Day? You know I've got the afternoon off, right?"

He did, though she was the only servant who'd dare remind him of such a thing. But if she left now, she'd have time to get everything done before her time off started. "I would have asked yesterday, but I didn't see you. Nor did I see you the day before that. The last time I remember seeing you was during dinner with the Mellars." He narrowed his eyes. "You came into the dining room panting and flushed while we were finishing dessert."

He'd meant to question her about that, but his mind was so full of shipping ledgers and insurance statements that he'd forgotten. "Why, exactly, did you look as though you'd just outrun a pair of pickpockets when you were supposed to be serving?"

"And why, exactly, were you and Miss Mellar walking in the garden after dark?"

The basket in his hand suddenly felt twice as heavy. "You saw us in the garden?"

"No, I guessed," she muttered.

How long had she watched them? And why did the air feel hotter than it had a moment ago?

"What did you need?" She gestured toward his basket, washrag in hand. "I doubt you're traipsing through the yard carrying that and shouting my name because you missed me."

"I need you to take this to Lindy today." But maybe he had missed Rebekah, just a little. She was, after all, the only person who had backbone enough to tease him about missing her.

Would Marianne tease him about such things one day? Somehow it wouldn't be the same.

Because he'd known Rebekah most of her life. That was why. It had nothing to do with the way they'd watched the stars together or how thoroughly she'd cleaned the house of a woman in need.

Rebekah took the basket and looked down at the various foodstuffs he'd had Cook put together. He'd tucked a series of five dollar bills beneath the cookies, but hopefully Lindy wouldn't find those until after Rebekah had left.

"Do I need to leave now, or is there time to finish washing the windows?"

"Leave now. The streets will be clogged with people and traffic for the fireworks display in a few more hours. And I'm sure you don't want to be late for the fireworks either."

Her jaw hardened. "Yep, don't want to be late."

"You are planning on going, aren't you?"

"Sure. Right after I wash the windows, mop the dining room, polish the silver…" She dug around in the pocket of her apron, pulled out a folded piece of paper, and opened it.

He swiped it before she could read more and glanced down. Eight chores were written in his mother's elegant scrawl. "This is the list you asked for from Mother. Your way to earn an extra dollar each week."

"Can I have it back?"

"And you're doing it all on your day off." He glanced around the empty grounds. Now that he thought of it, the other servants had apparently finished working for the day. Had Mother given everyone time off starting at noon? The staff's half days off usually began later than that.

He handed the list back to her. "Don't worry about visiting Lindy. I'll find someone else to run the food over, or maybe it can wait until tomorrow. Nothing in the basket can spoil."

"No." She wrapped her hand around the handle of the basket. "I'll do it. I want to."

"You won't have time to take this to Lindy's and finish that list, let alone go to the fireworks." And she should go to the fireworks. Eagle Harbor didn't have them, and he could only imagine the look on her face the first time she saw a burst of color explode over the night sky.

Would it be more captivating than the expression she'd worn that night they looked at the stars?

And why was he thinking about looking at the stars with Rebekah? Or watching fireworks with her? He was watching them with Marianne on her family's yacht, and he was going to enjoy that much more than he would enjoy watching fireworks with Rebekah.

He'd make certain of it.

"I don't mind. Lindy and I will have time to visit this way." Rebekah dropped her rag into the pail of water at her feet, set the basket down, then hefted the bucket and headed toward the bushes. "I've got another day yet to finish that list," she called over her shoulder. "And if I don't get everything done, I reckon Ma and Elijah would both rather get a dollar less from me and know I helped Lindy."

Yes, the Cummings family had always been that way, giving of themselves and their resources when they had so little to give in the first place.

Didn't Rebekah realize how special her family was? That most people would never have a family half as supportive as hers?

Yet instead of staying with people who loved her, she'd run from them.

"I'll take the trolley to the train to get over to Lindy's." Rebekah returned for the basket, her pail empty. "That way one of your drivers won't need to work."

"I'm going away on business next week," he blurted. "To Duluth to check on a shipping contract. I'll probably stop by Eagle Harbor on the way to look at accounts there. I don't suppose you'd like to come with me—I mean, go home."

What was he doing phrasing things like that? Yes, he'd enjoy Rebekah's presence on the ship, but last time, he'd ended up kissing her. Something he shouldn't have done then, and certainly couldn't do now that he and Marianne were coming to an understanding.

"You're leaving?" Rebekah ran her gaze up and down him.

Was she going to agree to go home? Or would she just say something about missing him?

"Who's going to look in on Lindy while you're gone? Stanley?"

Lindy. Of course she'd think of Lindy. Why would she think about missing him when he was pursuing another woman?

But if he wasn't pursuing Marianne, would she miss him then? No. No. No. He had to stop letting his mind wander in this direction.

"Gilbert." Rebekah let out a little, attention-getting whistle. "Do I need to go for the smelling salts? I think I lost you, though you happen to still be standing."

"Sorry." He gave his head a small shake in a useless attempt to clear it. "Ah, as my business manager, Stanley will be traveling with me. When I go away, I usually leave Lindy with food and money, but no one visits."

"Can I look in on her while you're gone?"

"Certainly." Why hadn't he seen that coming either? He scratched the top of his head. Maybe once he had a ring on Marianne's finger, things would calm down a little bit and his brain would start functioning normally again—though his father's endless stream of mistresses might well prove things didn't always work out so conveniently. Still, at least he could tell himself things would get better once he was engaged. "I'll leave instructions with Mother and Cook that you're to take a basket to Lindy twice a week. But are you sure you don't want to go home? Don't you miss your family?"

She swallowed thickly, her gaze dropping to her feet. "Yes, I miss them, but this is for the best. Even if I took your money, I'd still be an extra mouth to feed back home. And besides, I probably haven't been gone long enough to prove anything to Elijah. He's a mite bit stubborn, if you haven't noticed."

He'd noticed, all right. But Elijah certainly wasn't the only Cummings with a stubborn streak.

⁓.⁓.⁓.⁓.⁓

Gilbert hadn't been lying about the crowds that would clog the trolleys, trains, and roads on her way to and from Lindy's. Rebekah used a handkerchief to wipe the sweat from the back of her neck as she tromped down the servants' stairs to her room. It was a near miracle that she'd been able to get to Bridgeport and back with all the people. But as she walked through the mansion, she hadn't passed a single person. Never before had she seen the house so empty. It seemed every person in the whole of Chicago had gone to see the fireworks.

And to think Gilbert had suggested she go.

Fireworks indeed.

How was she supposed to enjoy herself knowing Gilbert was watching them with Marianne? And from the water, no less. If that didn't rankle. Was it wrong to be jealous of Gilbert simply because he was sailing?

Miss Mellar probably didn't have the faintest notion how to sail a yacht, and she got to watch from the water too.

If only knowing how to sail was a quality Gilbert wanted in a wife.

A retching sound filled the hallway. Was someone still here? She passed her room and headed toward the noise.

A loud groan sounded, the kind that made her stomach clench with sympathy. She stopped before Aileen's door and sighed. The Irishwoman had probably been lying about feeling well two mornings ago.

But did she really want to go in? Aileen had come up with quite the story to tell Mrs. Sinclair about her and Gilbert and why there was a deadbolt on the back of her door. No matter how kind she was to Aileen, the woman seemed dead set on getting her fired.

Another groan emanated from the room, and Rebekah knocked quietly.

"Aileen, are you all right?" She opened the door a crack and nearly retched herself at the sight of the blood on the bed. "What's wrong?"

She rushed into the room and grabbed one of the towels stacked at the foot of the bed.

Aileen lay curled in a ball. "Go away. I dona'…"

More retching cut off her words, but she lifted her head enough to spew into a chamber pot rather than on her bed. Rebekah glanced down at the towel in her hand. Having one seemed like a good idea, but where was Aileen bleeding from? And what should she do with the towel?

"It hurts," Aileen rasped as she sank back onto her pillow. "They didna tell me it would hurt this much."

"What hurts?" She took a step nearer. "Where are you bleeding? We need to stop it."

"No." Aileen groaned again, her arms wrapped low around her stomach.

Rebekah surveyed the bloody bed and the Irishwoman's crumpled form, pale face, and hairline beaded with sweat. "I'm going for the doctor."

"No." Aileen forced herself into a half sitting position. "I'm fine." She fell back and groaned again.

"You're clearly not fine, and I've no idea how to help." She glanced at the bottom of the bed where the blood was. She'd never seen so much blood before in her life, at least not human blood, and she wasn't quite comfortable comparing a living person to a pile of fish guts.

"It's just…" Aileen stopped talking to pant. "…Female complaints."

The woman didn't have to lie to her. "Say what you will, Aileen, but this is not your monthly."

But what if it were something worse? The blood, the groaning, the vomiting and sneaking food from the kitchen her first day there. She'd never been in the family way before, but she'd seen Tressa go through the troubles of morning sickness three times. Plus she'd been six when her mother had lost a baby and had a vague enough memory of glancing into her parents' room, seeing the blood, hearing the groaning. "You're pregnant."

Aileen's face was already as white as fresh fallen snow, yet it seemed to grow whiter. "I'm not."

"That's why you were sneaking food."

"No." Aileen shook her head, but the word was weak.

"And why you were sick. You've probably been sick all along and hiding it."

"Just go like I asked, please, and forget ye saw any of this." Tears fell then, along with a gut-wrenching sob.

"You still need to see a doctor." Though Doc Greely certainly hadn't done anything to help her ma when she'd lost her babe. But Rebekah couldn't leave Aileen lying there, and she didn't have the first clue how to help the woman.

"I don't. I promise." Aileen gritted her teeth together and groaned as another pain came upon her. She panted through it and then fell back against the bed. "They said it would pass within a few hours."

"They said it would pass? Have you already seen a doctor?"

Aileen slanted her gaze away, but not before Rebekah caught the guilt in her eyes. "Aileen?"

"I've got the afternoon and evening off like ye, and I'll be back to work in the morning. No need to fetch the doctor. No need to tell anyone. It's all planned out."

Planned out. A sick sensation started in her stomach and roiled upward. "You planned this?"

She curled into a tighter position and lay back against her pillow. "I couldn't very well keep my job and be pregnant."

"Then maybe you shouldn't have been dallying around."

A tear slipped down Aileen's cheek, then another and another. "Ach, think what ye will." She wiped away the tears with her palm, only to have more streak her face. "That's why I had to get rid of me babe. Everyone will think I was dallying, and then I'll lose me job, and I've nowhere to go. Oh, why did I ever take this job in the first place? Gilbert made it seem like such a good plan, but he never warned me." She cast a spiteful look her direction. "And he certainly never put a deadbolt on me door."

"Aileen."

"No, ye listen to me. Go. Ye have to go. I don't know why the missus won't fire ye. She fired all the other girls, and goodness knows I've given her reason to fire ye time and again, yet she keeps ye on for some reason." Aileen was rambling now, the words falling faster and faster from her mouth while more tears coursed down her face. "But ye have to leave before he comes back. Ye're prettier than I am, and he doesna' listen when ye tell him no."

Rebekah moved to the head of the bed and wiped the sweaty hair back from Aileen's forehead. "What are you talking about?"

Her gaze dipped to the bed. "Warren. A deadbolt won't stop the likes of him."

Rebekah sucked in a breath as the pieces fell together. She'd never cared for Warren Sinclair, and it went deeper than their families not liking each other. There was something about the way he looked at her, as though he could see straight through her clothes to her body beneath. And he had that smirk like he knew something she didn't, the one that made her insides turn cold when he directed it her way. "Did you hear what the mayor's daughter is saying? That he got her pregnant and did something so that she doesn't remember what happened?"

"She's lucky then," Aileen whispered as another tear slipped down her cheek. "I wish I didn't remember."

Rebekah's heart stopped beating for so long she wasn't sure it would start back up again. When it did, a hollow ache filled her chest. "We've got to get you out of here before he comes back."

Aileen shook her head and groaned with another pain. "There's nowhere to go, or I'd have already left. Me brother died this spring, so I've got no family left in America. Passage back home costs too much, and even then, me mum is gone, so I've only aunts, uncles, and cousins, and none of them are better off than I am here."

Rebekah clenched her teeth together. "I hardly think they're being violated by their employer's son."

"There are other things that make life just as hard. They dona' own any land, just farm for the lord, and depending on the lord ye have…" Another groan cut off her words, and she wrapped her arms around her middle.

"Maybe we can find you a job in another house, one that doesn't have a son like Warren." Surely that thought had to have occurred to the other woman.

"What if they're all like Warren?" Aileen's eyes widened with fear.

They couldn't be. She refused to believe it. "Look at Gilbert. He's nothing like his brother."

"Aye, Gilbert was trying to do a good thing giving me work here after me brother died on the docks, but then he left town and Warren stayed. The more I'm around this rich society set, the more

I think most are like Warren and Gilbert is the exception. Even Mr. Sinclair gives me the chills sometimes, and he's got himself a mistress."

"You should go to the police. They can hold Warren accountable."

Aileen reached out and gripped her sleeve. "No. Ye can't tell anyone. I'll be fired, and there'll be no letter of recommendation, which means I'll not be able to find service work again in Chicago. I'd have to move to the tenements and look for work in a factory, and I'm not sure I'd fare any better there."

The image of Lindy, living in squalor as she lay on her bed coughing, rose in her mind. No, Aileen likely wouldn't fare any better in the factories, but there had to be some solution. "Why not look for service work now? There has to be an older couple with their children gone and married who need a maid. Will you at least try to leave? Because Warren will return eventually."

Aileen sniffled and wiped her damp cheek with her shoulder. "I suppose I can look through the classifieds in Mr. Sinclair's discarded papers."

Rebekah gave a curt nod. At least they had a plan, even if it wasn't the best one. "I'll think on it some more, see if we can come up with anything better."

"I'm sorry for treating ye so poorly, but I didn't want Warren to…" Aileen dropped her head back to the pillow.

Rebekah reached out for her hand and squeezed it tight. It was noble, really, the way Aileen had tried to protect her—and evidently a few other serving girls before her. "I probably would've done the same thing. Why don't I sit here until your pains pass, then we can clean up this room?"

Aileen drew in a deep breath, her eyelids fluttering shut. "I dona' deserve yer kindness."

She looked down at the pale Irishwoman, lonely and with nowhere to go. She was an arrogant fool for fighting Gilbert when he'd asked her to befriend Aileen. "I think you do, Aileen. I think you deserve a whole lot more kindness than you realize."

Chapter Fifteen

Rebekah blew out a breath and knocked on the ornate green door with dark, wide trim in front of her.

"Come in." Gilbert's voice resonated from inside.

She turned the knob to Gilbert's office at the Great Northern Shipping building in Chicago, walked through the door, and stared at Gilbert.

Just Gilbert.

She should probably look around, especially since it was the first time she'd been inside. But this was the first she'd seen him since he left for Duluth, and she couldn't pull her gaze away.

He sat behind a desk made of polished red wood that was very different from the plain one he used in Eagle Harbor. His gaze was focused on the papers spread before him, and the front of his hair stood up as though he'd ran his fingers through it one too many times. He absently fiddled with a pencil in his hand while his brow drew down in concentration.

She sucked in a breath, sharp and quick, and the already warm air in the office turned twice as hot. Two weeks. It had only been two weeks since he left on his business trip. And she hadn't missed him while he was gone—had barely even thought of him. So why was her heart thumping, and why couldn't she pull her gaze from him?

I haven't missed him?

Have barely thought of him?

She had to stop lying to herself. She'd thought of him every day, multiple times. Whenever she saw Aileen and wondered whether she should tell Gilbert what Warren had done. Whenever Cook handed her a basket to take to Lindy. Whenever she lay down at night and half-formed thoughts drifted through her mind as she fell asleep.

And she forced the thoughts away every single time. All she had to do was think of Marianne Mellar and her walk in the garden with Gilbert. Marianne Mellar and Gilbert staying out at some fancy ball until dawn the day following Independence Day.

Marianne Mellar and how she had sixteen thousand dollars.

"Did you find the files for the Umberg account?" Gilbert asked without looking up.

"Um, no."

His gaze shot up to her, and he bolted from his chair, causing it to screech as it slid across the shiny floor that the maid who cleaned his office probably spent hours polishing every night. "Rebekah, forgive me. I thought you were Stanley."

"You thought I was a man?" She tried to keep the squeak from her voice. Tried to sound calm and rational, as though her heart wasn't beating twice as fast as normal and the air whooshing in and out of her lungs wasn't scalding hot.

He scratched the back of his head, causing a tuft of hair to stick up. "That came out wrong. I was expecting Stanley, not you."

"Stanley with paperwork for the Umberg account."

"Yes." He glanced at the open ledger on his desk, then blinked at her. "But you're not Stanley."

Did he realize how adorable he looked with that baffled expression on his face?

"How have you been?" He came around the desk. "Well, I hope. Mother said you and Aileen were getting along."

That comment, at least, forced her gaze away from him. Why did he have to bring up Aileen?

Gilbert, did you know Warren raped Aileen? And not just once? He'd want to know, wouldn't he? He was the one who'd gotten Aileen a job working for his parents. And he'd never thought to put a deadbolt on Aileen's door—something that Rebekah had remedied the day after she'd learned what Warren had done.

But Aileen claimed nothing good would come of telling anyone, that she'd only be fired for dallying, and Warren was too rich to be punished. Hopefully there was no truth behind her fears. But what if the Irishwoman was right?

Aileen had a job interview tomorrow. The couple interviewing her weren't as well off as the Sinclairs, but it was still a job, and since they were older and childless, Aileen didn't have to worry about the likes of Warren. Aileen might move out of the Sinclair house as early as tomorrow evening, and then there'd be nothing to worry about.

Rebekah peeked up at Gilbert, who stared at her as though she'd gone daft. And maybe she had. After all, she was mooning over a man she couldn't have and keeping her mouth shut about a woman being forced. If Aileen didn't get that new position tomorrow, she'd tell Gilbert. Warren would be back at some point, and they couldn't risk Aileen still working for his parents when that happened.

"Rebekah?" Gilbert's voice resonated through the office, familiar and strong and deep. "I asked what brought you to the office."

The office. Right. Rebekah pulled a sheaf of papers from the satchel slung over her shoulder. "Your mother asked me to bring these by after I visited Lindy this morning."

"You've been to visit Lindy already today?"

She nodded. "I have a half day off every Sunday, and one of the churches near your house has a service that starts at seven o'clock. I go to that and then head over to see Lindy. She's doing better, by the way. Her cough is nearly gone now, and she's talking about finding work." That was one good thing that had come about while Gilbert had been gone. Now if she could just see Aileen settled elsewhere.

"I'll have to stop by and see Lindy myself this afternoon, but I'm glad to hear she's improving." He took the papers from her and glanced at them. "My shipping records from Duluth. Thank you. I hadn't realized I left them."

She shrugged. "Don't thank me. It was your mother's doing."

He opened his mouth, his gaze intent on her, but rather than speak, he pressed his lips together and set the records on his desk.

Was he waiting for her to say something? About Aileen and Warren? About her missing him? And now she was being ridiculous. He couldn't know either of those things—unless she slipped and told him.

She headed toward the window overlooking the harbor, half to get away from his gaze, and half because she never tired of looking at the water. The Great Northern Shipping building in Eagle Harbor was two stories like this one, but not near as grand. The polished wood floor beneath her shoes gleamed, the furniture was upholstered in a dark blue that suited Gilbert well, and the chairs were big enough that men like her brothers could sit in them without the legs snapping off. Fancy, but not too fancy.

She ran her fingers along the polished, dust-free window ledge and watched the people below rushing about the piers, a ceaseless commotion that never slowed as workers loaded and unloaded cargo. "You have a lovely view."

The docks spread out before her, an unending series of strips of wood that ran along the shoreline. Every pier had at least one ship docked, if not two or three. Steamers and schooners and vessels of all kinds filled the water, some old enough to be decommissioned and others sparkling as though they'd just arrived from the shipyard.

She'd never imagined so many ships together in one place. And why would she, when the town she'd grown up in could only dock one ship at a time?

"Do you miss the water?"

She looked up to find Gilbert standing beside her, watching her as though her answer were more important than the piles of papers and ledgers on his desk.

Which was a bit odd, since his question made little sense. "I'm still by the water, though I don't think I could ever move too far inland, if that's what you're asking."

"I meant being on it. Sailing."

She let her gaze drift back out the window, past the docks to Lake Michigan's expanse of rippling blue. "About as much as I miss the tall stand of pines east of our house, or the clean scent of the air. The sound of rain on our roof, or the sunset on the beach." She sighed. "I even miss that dratted lilac bush at the edge of the cemetery."

"I think you're lying." He leaned closer, nearly trapping her against the edge of the window and the wall. "I think you miss sailing more than all those things combined."

"All right, you win." The words came out as little more than a sigh as she stared up at him, his lips only a few inches from hers.

He stood still for a moment, so still that the faint puffs of his breath brushed her cheek. Then he shifted and glanced back out the window. "Father just purchased a new yacht. Would you care to go boating?"

"Truly?" Boating? And not just on a new yacht, but with Gilbert?

Except she shouldn't, not given the way she wanted Gilbert to step nearer again, not given the way he was determined to marry Miss Mellar.

She forced herself to shake her head. "I only have a half day off, and you've dinner guests tonight. I need to get back to the house."

His brow drew down. "Never thought I'd see the day you picked work over sailing."

Neither had she. But then, she'd never thought she'd see the day when her heart thumped erratically at the feel of Gilbert's breath on her face. Or the day that she was in Chicago working for his family while her own was home in Eagle Harbor.

"It'd be better if my work was sailing, of course, but…" Maybe next year the price of fish would be up, and with the family's bills paid, she could work for Elijah.

If he still wanted her to work with him after that spat they'd got into the last time she tried to go on a rescue.

"That settles it." Gilbert grabbed her by the wrist and tugged her toward the door.

"Wait. Where are we going?" She tried to pull away, but his grip remained firm.

"We'll be back from sailing before you're due home."

She huffed, but couldn't help the way her lips raised in a little smile. If he was going to insist… well, who was she to argue?

⌐.⌐.⌐.⌐.⌐

"It's so vast."

Gilbert watched as Rebekah's eyes scanned the lakeshore,

roving over miles and miles of city before trees reclaimed the land on the outskirts of Chicago.

She was beautiful, with the midmorning sun highlighting the golden tones in her hair and touching her skin.

But then, Rebekah Cummings hardly needed to be standing under the sun to be beautiful. Did the woman ever look in the mirror and notice how lovely she was?

Since she'd prided herself on wearing trousers for the past three years, something told him no.

"Do you miss the trees while you're in Chicago?" She tilted her head up to the sky, and more sunlight washed over her face while the wind toyed with tendrils of hair that kept slipping from their pins. "I hadn't realized how much I would miss home when I left."

And he hadn't realized how much he'd miss her while he was gone. Should he tell her that he'd thought about her often on his trip? That her cooking was better than that of the new cook Captain Steverman had hired for the *Lassiter*? That he'd stared up at the stars almost every night, wishing she was standing at the railing beside him?

That he'd avoided Eagle Harbor because he hadn't wanted to put up with Warren?

She'd care about that Warren bit, about how well he got along—or didn't get along—with his brother. Just like she cared about how well he got along with his father or how his crane was progressing. Just like she cared about a sick old friend living in a forgotten tenement.

Did Rebekah ever think of herself first? Did any of the Cummingses? Because nearly everything he believed of Rebekah could also be said of Elijah, and possibly even Isaac.

"So it looks like you were right." Rebekah leaned over the side of the rail, letting the tips of her fingers trail in the water. "As much as it pains me to say it."

He blinked. "I beg your pardon?"

He was right? About what? And even if he was right about something, why was Rebekah admitting it? That surely broke some kind of unspoken vow between them.

"I said you were right..." She looked at him as though he were simple minded—and maybe he was when around her. "...About me missing home."

Oh, that. He arched an eyebrow, and if his face appeared a little condescending, then so be it. "I'm sorry, but I'm afraid I didn't hear you correctly the first two times. Would you mind repeating that?"

She jabbed an elbow into his stomach so hard he stepped back and gasped a breath.

He'd grown too relaxed in his time away from her. Of course Rebekah wouldn't let a comment like that pass, and she didn't do anything half way. "I was about to say service work seems to suit you, but I don't know of any servant who goes around injuring her employer."

"You're not my employer."

Yet another thing he'd missed about her. She was the only woman who pushed back at his taunting.

"Besides, how would you know about service work agreeing with me?" She rolled her eyes at him. "You've been gone more than you've been here, and even when you're in the city, you're rarely home."

Yes, courting Marianne certainly took up most of his evenings and weekends, but the effort would soon pay off. He planned to visit the jewelers in search of a very specific ring come Saturday.

He cleared his throat and turned back to Rebekah. "I hear reports about your work from Mother and Mrs. Niebert."

She bit the side of her lip like she always did when uncertain. "Do they say good things?"

"They tell me you earned your full twenty-five dollars last month."

"And here you tried to talk me out of working for your parents when I first arrived."

"I still think you'd be better off at home. That hasn't changed."

She turned away from him and ran her hand over the sleek, polished rail of the yacht. "I've never seen such a lovely sailboat before, let alone been on one."

"Changing the subject again, are you?" He let his gaze roam over the new yacht nonetheless. Father had probably bought it in an effort to show up Carl Mellar or another of his business acquaintances. With its rich mahogany hull and deck, the two-masted ketch was a breathtaking display of opulence. And though a vessel of this size was only meant for day trips, it had a full cabin and galley below deck, all appointed in blindingly bright white and gold upholstery. Why anyone would want white upholstery on a boat was another question entirely. But knowing his parents, it was the latest style, and it did look rather grand against the ruddy wood.

Rebekah sauntered to the middle of the deck and abruptly flopped onto her back.

He narrowed his eyes at her. "Don't you think you ought to be manning the sails rather than taking a nap?"

"There's nothing around us to hit, but you can drop the anchor if you're worried."

"I'm more worried about your mental state. Most people don't suddenly decide to lie somewhere they can be walked on."

She let out a laugh, not the gentle restrained laugh that Marianne always used, but one deep and honest and full of life.

"Stop being so ridiculous and come lie down. Don't you ever stare at the clouds while you're out on the water? Nothing to block your view."

No. He hadn't stared at clouds since... well, he didn't think he'd ever done such a thing. He came toward her and sat on the bench closest to where she lay.

"It's not the same when you're sitting up." She stared at the sky as she spoke. "You need to be down here."

"I do not."

"Fine. Do it your way, but it won't be as good. That one looks like a duck." She pointed at a fluffy cloud.

It didn't resemble a duck in the least. "I rather think it looks like a cloud."

"A cloud in the shape of a duck."

He studied the cloud for another moment. "I was clearly right to question your mental state."

"It's because you're sitting up. You simply can't see it as well. There's the body." She pointed with her finger, but the fluffy cloud still looked nothing like the body of a duck. "There's the head, and there's the beak."

"I think you're telling me stories just to see whether I'm naïve enough to believe them."

She huffed. "Fine. If it doesn't look like a duck, then tell me what it looks like."

"I already told you. A cloud."

She rolled her eyes. "Are you trying to frustrate me? Or do you truly have such a limited imagination?"

"I don't think imagination has ever been my strong suit," he muttered.

"No, more like figures, diagrams, and math problems with more letters than numbers."

She didn't say it sarcastically, and he looked over at her, her auburn hair gleaming in the sunlight and growing messier with each moment she stayed aboard ship, her face shining with delight, and her mouth curved into a full smile.

He blew out a breath and stared back up at the sky, a much safer place to look. "Did your father ever make you memorize verses about the water or God's creation?"

"'The earth is the Lord's and the fullness thereof.'" She spouted the verse without a moment's pause. "Pa made us memorize Bible verses about everything and then some."

"So I've heard." The way Hiram had made his family recite Bible verses at the dinner table had taken on legendary proportions in Eagle Harbor.

"Elijah hated the one about 'When a man's ways please the Lord, he maketh even his enemies to be at peace with him.'"

Ah yes, he well remembered when Elijah had quoted that verse at him this spring. It had been only a couple hours after Elijah saved his life, and heaven knew he hadn't deserved to have Elijah, of all people, save it. "And which verse did you not care for?"

"I liked the one about 'By the grace of God I am what I am.' And proverbs..."

She quoted a list of verses as effortlessly as if she were breathing.

Was he half mad to be jealous of her?

Yes, he certainly was. Her family owned a cabin on the lake, and his owned a shipping empire. Yet he'd never been part of a family that memorized the Bible together.

And why, exactly, did that draw him? "You didn't answer my question. I asked which one you had the most trouble with while growing up, not which ones you liked best."

She smiled entirely too sweetly. "What makes you think I had trouble with any of them?"

He laughed. "It's God's Word, Rebekah. We all struggle with our Christianity at one point or another. Didn't the apostle Paul say as much?"

She pursed her lips together and mumbled a few words. Something about living peaceably with all men, perhaps? And something else about a sharp tongue.

He tamped down another urge to laugh.

She scowled at him anyway. "Pa said he was making us arrows, that's why we had to memorize so much Bible."

"Arrows?"

"'As arrows are in the hand of a mighty man; so are children of the youth. Happy is the man that hath his quiver full of them: they shall not be ashamed, but they shall speak with the enemies in the gate.'" Once again, the verses rolled off her lips. "We were Pa's arrows, and when we grew up and had children, we'd have the Scriptural knowledge to make our children into arrows too—or that's what Pa claimed. Memorizing verses went along with all the rest of it. Honoring your parents, loving your neighbors, and everything else."

"I think he taught you rather well."

She looked up at him, her gaze sharp, as if she'd thought he'd say something about how all her father's teachings had been lost on her. But they hadn't been lost, not on the woman who volunteered to go visit someone like Lindy Marsden.

What if he'd been born into a family that cared about helping others more than amassing their own wealth? What if his father had tried making him into an arrow rather than a cold, impersonal businessman? He swallowed thickly and stared back up at the sky, not to look at the clouds, but to clear his head. There was no point wondering such things. The die had been cast, the families he and Rebekah grew up in already determined.

And as for the families of their own that they'd each have one day?

Well, as enjoyable as a few hours on the water with Rebekah had been, he needed to get back to the office and keep working on his plans for his future. He stood. "We best head in. I'm supposed to stop by Marianne's this afternoon before her family comes to dinner."

Rebekah rolled to her side and stood before he could offer her a hand up. "You can't marry her, Gilbert. Don't you see how wrong that would be? You don't love her."

He pushed out a frustrated breath. She hadn't lectured him about Marianne since she'd learned the true reason he was building his crane. Was it too much to hope that she'd come to understand his side of things? "I fail to see how love factors into this."

"'Many waters cannot quench love, neither can the floods drown it: if a man would give all the substance of his house for love, it would utterly be contemned.'" She stepped nearer to him, close enough that the traces of her soap mingled with the breeze off the water. Close enough to hear each little intake of her breath. "God tells you love and marriage go together. How many times must I quote that verse to you? And still, you don't see it. Or maybe you do, but you choose to ignore it. You'll be as happy married to Marianne as your parents are with each other."

"I never asked you to care about my happiness." The words fell from his lips like sleet during a winter storm, a bit colder, perhaps, than intended.

"I'm your friend, and friends care about such things."

He clenched his jaw. "I don't understand you in the least. You spout verses about love and say that a relationship—a future family—should be built solely on that, and yet you ignore your own family. You want love? You have a family that already loves you, so much so that they want to protect you from harm, from having no choice about working like Aileen, or worse, being stuck in a hovel like Lindy. If you were sick like Lindy, what would your family do? How would they treat you? Would your aunt throw you out on the street? Would your sister turn to prostitution and ignore you?

"None of that would happen to you because your family loves you. They would sacrifice for you." He searched her face for any sign of understanding, but the content expression she'd worn a few minutes ago now seemed as distant as Eagle Harbor itself. "Your family is probably two steps away from coming down here and collecting you because they miss you and they worry about you. It doesn't matter that I'm watching out for you. It matters that you're here, away from a family who loves you.

"Not everyone has that, so be grateful and stop spouting off at me." He leaned his elbows on the boat's rail and stared out over the sun-drenched water. "Honestly, Rebekah, let me give you that hundred dollars, and you can board a train headed north tomorrow. It's where you should be. Leave the rest of us—the ones who don't have perfect families willing to cross the world for them—to ourselves."

She whirled on him, her eyes shooting those little green flames that he usually found so appealing.

Usually, but not today.

"How dare you talk like I'm so privileged, you who has china tea services, silver spoons—"

"Wealth isn't everything."

"Then why are you acting like it is?" Her voice likely carried over the water to the city with the way she was shouting. "Why are you willing to trade your future for money? Because let me tell you something, Gilbert, Marianne Mellar is not the right woman for you."

He clenched his hands into fists and shoved off the railing before stalking toward the boom. "You don't know that. Perhaps she's the exact person I should marry."

Rebekah followed him like a little yippy dog that chased after everyone's ankles. "Why? Because she has sixteen thousand dollars? You'll never have this loving family you speak of if you try building a marriage on money."

He rubbed his temples. "Maybe I'm not supposed to have a loving family. Maybe instead of having a wife who I talk to before bed every night and wake up next to every morning, who I write letters to and whisper sweet nothings in her ear—maybe instead of all that I'm supposed to build my crane. People are dying and families are being left destitute. How dare I chose a wife based on my own wishes and leave the workers to rot?"

She blinked and looked away, but surely that wasn't moisture welling in her eyes. "I never told you to leave anyone to rot."

"After seeing Aileen and Lindy and some of the others, I thought you'd understand. But you're too stubborn to take in the scope of everything. Too set in your own ways and too certain that you're right to see the needs of others around you. If I marry Marianne, maybe twenty years from now my family ends up looking more like the one I was raised in than the one you have. But right is still right. If God's given me the ability to help dockworkers, then I'm not going to run away because it requires a sacrifice on my behalf."

"I see." Rebekah said, but it didn't appear that she saw anything, not given the way her face had blanched and her jaw trembled. "Forgive me for interfering in your perfectly planned life."

She whirled and stalked to the mizzenmast at the aft of the

yacht, where she raised the sail with brisk, jerky movements.

Gilbert turned back to the mainmast and did the same. He was a fool for wasting precious hours of his day sailing with her. But he was an even bigger fool for thinking she'd understand his situation, that she would care enough about the dockworkers being injured to lay aside her own ideals and support him.

And that was definitely something he wanted in a wife—a woman who supported him.

Chapter Sixteen

Rebekah blinked away the tears that kept burning behind her eyes as she made her way from the street car stop toward the Sinclair mansion, but Gilbert's words rang through her mind as clearly as though they still stood on the deck of the yacht. *You spout verses about love and say that a relationship—a future family—should be built solely on that, and yet you ignore your own family. You want love? You have a family that already loves you, so much so that they want to protect you from harm, from having no choice about working like Aileen, or worse, being stuck in a hovel like Lindy.*

Compared to Aileen and Lindy—who truly did have no one—she had a wonderful family. Even Gilbert's family, with all their wealth, paled in comparison to hers.

She might not want Gilbert to be right, but he was. She preached to him about love and family, but she wasn't treating her family well. She thought she'd been doing right by leaving and helping to support them, but somehow she'd ended up running from the people she loved.

How had she made such a foolish mistake? But she didn't need to ask herself, not really. She'd made foolish mistakes all her life. If only she wasn't so headstrong, always rushing into things without thinking—or worse, without praying.

Always assuming her way was best.

Is that what she'd done when she'd left Eagle Harbor? She certainly hadn't prayed about leaving her family. She'd seen a need, grown frustrated with her inability to help meet it, and left to earn money.

So where did that leave her? Did she need to do as Gilbert said and return home? How could she earn her keep back in Eagle Harbor?

God, what do I do now? she prayed as she turned up the drive. Maybe she needed to send a letter. Gilbert had sent her family a telegram or two, but they'd be happy to hear from her personally, wouldn't they?

Unless they were too put out with her for leaving.

Oh, she was such a mess she could hardly think straight. Of course her family would want to hear from her. That had been part of Gilbert's point. Her family would love her through her mistakes, though that might not prevent one of her brothers from storming down here and dragging her back to Eagle Harbor when they got tired of waiting for her to return.

But would that be so bad? She did miss home, yet with her family needing money and her ability to earn it in Chicago, how could she leave?

Rebekah rounded the back of the house and headed across the well-worn path that led to the kitchen door. Maybe the best answer was to take Gilbert up on his offer of a hundred dollars. And if the thought made her heart ache? Made her feel as though she'd failed?

Her family was worth swallowing a bit of pride.

And here she was, making her own plans again without offering more than a quick prayer to God. Maybe she needed to make a new rule for herself: no more decisions without first praying for a week or longer.

"Well, well."

She paused at the smooth sounding voice and turned toward the hedge, dread settling in her stomach.

"If it isn't a little piece of Eagle Harbor come to visit me in Chicago." Warren stepped out from the bushes, his hair angelically blond in the afternoon sunlight, his gait both fluid and confident. "And such a pretty piece of Eagle Harbor at that."

"Mr. Sinclair," she snapped. "I see you've returned from your travels rather quickly."

Entirely too quickly. Why couldn't Warren have waited until Aileen had found another job to return?

A sick lump rose in her throat. Warren wouldn't try to prevent Aileen from leaving, would he?

"Come now." Warren stepped closer, causing every inch of her body to hum with the realization that he was standing far nearer than he should. "Aren't we a little too close to call each other by our surnames?"

There had never been anything close about them. "Not when you're my employer's son."

"That's right. I am your employer's son." His eyes traveled down her, lingering in places that made her cheeks burn. "A skirt becomes you, though I'd rather see you in a silk one. A moss green color, perhaps, to go with your eyes."

Her hand crept toward the fishing knife tucked into the waist of her skirt. "I haven't the slightest notion what good a silk skirt would do me, green or not. Now if you'll excuse me, your mother's expecting me back at the house."

"My mother isn't the only one with power around here." He grabbed her arm before she could turn and jerked her forward. His breath fanned hot against her cheek, and a chill skittered up her spine—so very different than the effect Gilbert's breath upon her cheek had on her body.

"I only answer to your mother."

"Rebekah, zere you are." The cook poked her head out the kitchen door. "We've been... Oh, Mr. Sinclair. I could only see Rebekah zough ze window with how ze shrubs are hiding you. So sorry to disturb you."

"It's all right." Rebekah met Warren's eyes, which were narrowed into cruel little slits, before jerking her arm away. "I was just coming in." She turned and walked steadily toward where Cook stood in the open door, her hand settling on the hilt of her fishing knife for good measure.

"Where's Aileen?" she blurted the second the door swung shut.

"I sent her to ze market when you didn't return. Now where have you been?"

Rebekah drew in a long, shaky breath. "How long ago did you send her? Does she know Warren's back?"

The cook eyed her, strands of stray hair hanging beside her ample, sweaty cheeks. "How should I know? But she better get back soon if she expects to keep her job. And you best find Mrs. Niebert if you expect to continue working here. Last I saw her, she was muttering something about ze dining room needing dusting."

"Yes ma'am." Rebekah scampered up the stairs to find the head housekeeper.

The next few hours flew by in a frenzy of dusting and mopping and laying out place settings. She only glimpsed Warren twice, and hopefully Aileen glimpsed him less than that. But avoiding Warren was only prolonging the inevitable, because they would both have to face him at dinner. And she had every intention of making sure Warren's attention stayed on her rather than Aileen. If she could keep Aileen safe until that interview tomorrow, maybe everything would work itself out.

~.~.~.~.~

"Yes, Mrs. Ranulfson." Elijah heaved in a breath, his arms bulging beneath the weight of the textile crate he carried. "I realize I only have six donations for the benevolence project, but—"

"But nothing. The festival is only three weeks away, and we've never before had so few contributions. How are we going to purchase new mathematics texts? The donations so far will barely buy four books."

"Move," someone grunted from behind him.

Elijah shifted his crate and turned to find Oliver Orrick behind him, the two crates in his arms piled so high he could hardly see over the top of them.

"Sorry," Elijah grunted, then he stepped off the pathway of packed sand that led from the dock to the warehouse.

Oliver merely glared as he moved past, and Elijah couldn't blame the man. After all, he'd stopped and parked himself right in the middle of all the dockworkers unloading the steamer that had just come in.

Or rather, Mrs. Ranulfson had stopped and parked him.

"Well? Don't you have anything to say for yourself?" The banker's wife moved her heavy girth to the side of the path, then planted a hand on each of her wide hips. "Why haven't you raised more funds?"

Elijah heaved in another breath and set the crate down before shaking out his burning arms. Never mind that there wouldn't be any strength left in them by the time he headed over to the boathouse after he finished unloading the steamer. "Reckon I've been busier than I expected."

"Too busy to take a few moments and serve the students of this town?" The ostrich feathers atop Mrs. Ranulfson's hat trembled with the indignation that seemed to sweep through her. "Really, Elijah. I expected better from someone who grew up here, from Hiram's son. The mathematics textbooks are in dire need of replacement."

Elijah wiped his moist face on the sleeve of his already damp shirt. What was he supposed to say? That he'd been too busy to put time into the project? That he had financial troubles of his own? That by the time he spent a few hours on the lake fishing and then put in six hours at the sawmill, he stank too much to talk to people about donations before he walked home? "I'll take tomorrow morning off from fishing and see if I can raise a bit more money."

"Warren Sinclair isn't even on here." Mrs. Ranulfson looked at the list of donations he'd given her that morning at church. "If anyone could have given money, it was Warren. Why didn't you ask him before he left town?"

Because he wasn't going to ask Warren Sinclair for anything. Ever. If Gilbert had been around, he'd have asked, and he'd have probably forced himself to ask Gilbert's father, Byron Sinclair. But Warren?

He'd rather drink dirty bath water.

"There's Mr. Foley. Why don't you ask him?" Mrs. Ranulfson pointed to where the mercantile owner walked down Front Street.

"I have a steamer to unload." And a boathouse to build. He looked over his shoulder and across the harbor to where his life-saving crew had already begun work. He was supposed to be there, but the steamer had docked just as church was letting out, and his crew had said they didn't mind if he helped unload the boat before joining them. He bent and hefted the crate, then started toward the warehouse. "Now if you'll excuse me, I need to get back to work."

"It will only take a moment to talk to Mr. Foley." Mrs. Ranulfson bustled along behind him. "Surely you can spare that."

"Actually, I can't." But only in part because he didn't have time. He still had half his bill for the damages to the general store to pay, and going to a man he was indebted to and asking for more money plain felt wrong.

"What about Mr. Fletcher? He's over there talking to Reed Herod. See him?"

He looked over the top of his crate at the corner of the warehouse, where Toby Fletcher indeed stood talking to Reed Herod.

"I'll talk to him when I'm finished hauling cargo." Hopefully the conversation wouldn't take more than five minutes, and he could skedaddle on over to the boathouse right afterward.

"You should talk to him now. Then you can ask Reed Herod for a donation too. That man's rolling in money."

Asking the brothel owner would be just as bad as asking Warren Sinclair. Did the woman not understand that?

"Maybe you should get someone else to head up this project," he grunted as he entered the warehouse, which was even hotter and stickier than the heavy air outside. "I'm not too keen on asking Herod or his ilk for handouts."

"But it's for a good cause. If Mr. Herod wants to make a fortune off sin and vice, then there's no harm in turning that money around for good."

Elijah plopped the crate down next to the others that held textiles and wiped the sweat off the back of his neck with his sleeve. "Then you ask him."

"Fine. I will." Mrs. Ranulfson whirled and stomped outside, the ostrich feathers in her hat quivering with each tense step she took.

Elijah sighed then hurried back outside, glancing at the

boathouse where two people had climbed atop the roof and started hammering. Maybe he should forget the money he'd earn unloading cargo and head over there now. His men might have said they could work on their own for a while, but he was their leader. How did it look to have him on one side of the harbor and his team on the other?

He was nearly to the dock when a familiar blue hat and dark hair caught his eye.

"Victoria?" What was she doing on Front Street? He'd thought she was going to the lighthouse for a visit with Tressa and then heading home.

"Victoria, sweetling." He headed toward her, but she kept her head down, her shoulders slumped as she carried one of the bakery's paper sacks in her hand. "What's wrong?"

He planted himself in her path, and she nearly ran into him before she stopped and looked up.

"E-E-Elijah?" Redness rimmed her eyes, and a handful of tears streaked her cheeks. She wiped some of the tears away and looked around, probably just now realizing that she was near the dock and warehouse. "I was g-getting some bread for Tressa." Victoria held up the sack. "She was too sick to make any this morning. But I d-d-didn't mean to b-bother you here. You can go b-back to work."

Not when she was crying. He might be a bit of an oaf sometimes, but he wasn't quite that big of an oaf—at least he didn't think he was. He laid a hand on her cheek and tilted her head up until her watery gaze fastened to his. "What is it?"

She wrapped her arms around herself and tried to pull her face away, but he kept his grip firm enough that she would have to take a step back in order to escape it.

"Tell me." He stroked a strand of hair back from her brow.

Her eyes watered anew. "Th-there's no b-b-b-baby."

No baby. He drew his wife into his arms, never mind that they were in the open where everyone could see.

She went willingly, without the slightest complaint about being held against his damp, sweaty shirt. "I j-j-j-just want a little one of our own."

"I know, love. I know."

Her bottom lip trembled. "Do you th-th-think there's something wrong with me? That I c-c-can't…"

"There's nothing wrong with you."

"That's n-not true. I already have my st-st-stutter. What if I c-c-c-can't have b-babies too?"

"Victoria…" He drew her name out, long and full. How many times did he have to tell her that he loved her how she was, stutter and all? "Come on. Let's go home. Do you need to lie down? Are you having pains?"

He glanced over his shoulder at the men working on the boathouse, then down at his wife. At this rate, he wasn't going to make it to the other side of the harbor to work at all.

"I d-don't care about the p-p-pains. I just w-w-want a b-baby."

"All right, then we'll go home." Never mind the extra dollar he'd almost earned for unloading cargo. His wife was more important.

It was time for dinner by the time he finally walked up the dusty path to the boathouse, but Elijah settled for eating a couple biscuits on the way—Ma's biscuits, not Victoria's.

"Anyone here?" he called.

"I thought you forgot about us." Mac came around the side of the boathouse, his shirt drenched with sweat and his broad body casting its shadow over the rock-strewn grass.

"I tried to be here earlier." He looked around the nearly completed building that would soon house their surfboat and life-saving equipment. "Are the others gone?"

"They took a dunk in the lake, then left about an hour ago. Not that I can blame them." Mac wiped his sweaty face with his hand. "It's deuced hot today."

"Were they upset I wasn't here?"

Mac slapped a hand on his back. "Naw, but they might needle you about it some."

Guilt lay heavy in his belly anyway. How could he take a group of men into a storm in a boat only slightly bigger than a dinghy when he wasn't responsible enough to show up and help them work?

"The boards need to be nailed up over on the west side." Mac tilted his chin toward the far wall of the boathouse "What do you say we work on that?"

Elijah shook his head. "Go on home to your wife. Tressa's got to be needing you after you've been gone all day. I know Victoria was supposed to keep her company, but something came up and she, er... had to go home."

"Is Victoria all right?" Concern lined Mac's sweat and dirt-streaked face.

"She'll be fine." At least her body would be. As for her heart...

Maybe he needed to start praying God gave them a babe, if for no other reason than to keep Victoria from getting so upset every month.

"Are you going to stay and work by yourself?" Mac looked around the building site littered with errant pieces of wood and a handful of stray nails. "I feel bad leaving you here alone."

"You've spent enough time here today." Elijah gave Mac's shoulder a little shove. "Though you might take a dunk in the lake before you go home if you want Tressa to let you inside. You smell worse than a she bear."

"After being stuck in the house all day with Jane and Gracie? She'll let me in." Mac wiped his face with the front of his shirt. "Phew. You weren't lying about how I smelled."

"Told you. Has Tressa been any better?" He'd meant to stop by the lighthouse sometime last week to see for himself, but since he'd picked up two other jobs on top of fishing, he didn't have time for coffee and one of Tressa's cookies.

Like he still hadn't found time to take Victoria on that picnic she'd been asking about.

It wouldn't be this way forever, would it? He just needed to get through this rough patch and things would start looking up.

"This babe can't come soon enough." Mac looked over the water to the lighthouse. "I'm praying both my wife and the child are all right in the end."

Elijah clamped a hand on his friend's shoulder. "I'm praying too, Mac."

Mac took his advice about a quick dip in the lake before he headed for town, leaving Elijah to nail boards onto the west side of the building by himself. He worked until his shoulders protested every movement and his neck ached from constantly looking up.

The sun slanted low in the sky, tracking a path of burning orange along the surface of Lake Superior. And the wind kicked up a bit, buffeting the shingles that had been nailed down earlier that day—or at least the shingles that were supposed to have been nailed down. It looked as though one or two had been missed. Elijah squinted up at the roof and then glanced over his shoulder at the lake. It didn't seem like rain was coming tonight or tomorrow, but the weather for the rest of the week was any man's guess.

His feet ached, and the muscles in his arms burned as though he'd rowed through ten-foot swells, but he wasn't about to leave the shingles loose so they could be blown off before someone came back to fix them.

With a groan, he hefted the ladder over his shoulder and carted it around the building before climbing to the roof. He bent to nail the first shingle, but the fog bell rang from across the opening of the harbor.

Fog bell? There was no fog. He turned to look and glimpsed the silhouette of a little girl running away from the big iron bell by the lighthouse at the same moment his foot caught on one of the loose shingles. He reached out to anchor himself to the roof, but he stumbled instead, his hand grasping only air as he careened off the edge…

And landed on the ground with a crack followed by a searing pain in his arm.

Chapter Seventeen

Gilbert scowled as Warren touched Rebekah on the arm, as brazen as could be, while she leaned in to serve his brother dessert. When she tried to move back, he held her there, using his knuckles to skim up her arm until they reached her sleeve.

Gilbert waited for the crystal dish filled with pear tart to clatter to the table and the sound of Rebekah's hand slapping Warren's cheek to resonate through the room.

But Rebekah did nothing. Nothing at all.

Or wait, had she just fluttered her eyelashes at Warren?

He would have said no, especially since Rebekah Cummings never fluttered her lashes at anyone. But seeing how he was sitting directly across from Warren, he couldn't deny what he'd just seen.

"Gilbert, darling, what has you so distracted this evening?" Marianne leaned closer to him and rested her hand on his forearm.

"Nothing. Nothing at all." He forced his gaze away from Rebekah and offered Marianne a small smile.

She looked resplendent in a blue gown, the same pale shade as her eyes. Her black hair was piled into a mass of fat curls on the top of her head, and gold combs embedded with sapphires and diamonds gleamed at him from the side of her updo.

"Tell me, how was Duluth?" She offered him a polite smile, her lips perfectly curved. "And while you were up north, did you stop in that little town where you grew up—what was the name of it again?"

"Eagle Harbor." He nearly glanced at Rebekah when he said the name, but forced his attention to stay on Marianne.

"Honestly, I don't know how you managed to live in a town such as that." Andrew Mellar, Marianne's brother who was attending dinner with his wife and their father, interrupted from where he sat on Gilbert's right. "I've been there once or twice to pick up a load of copper. There's nothing to that place."

"My sentiments exactly," Warren muttered.

"We're all happy to be away from there." Mother took a sip of her water.

"I've often thought we should sell the house we retain there."

Gilbert jerked his gaze to his father. Since when was Father thinking about selling the Eagle Harbor house?

Father dabbed his face with a napkin. "We hardly use it anymore, but the trouble is, who'd buy it?"

Warren smirked. "What, Father, you don't think a fisherman would give you a fair price?"

Everyone at the table erupted into laughter. Everyone, that was, except him. "The town might be tiny, but the port stays busier than most towns three times its size. Pulling out of Eagle Harbor would be a terrible business decision."

"I never said I'd pull out." Father set his napkin back on his lap and reached for his wine. "Just that there's no longer any advantage in retaining residence there."

"Did you like growing up in Eagle Harbor?" Marianne's voice floated over the table, as melodious as a flute.

Again, his eyes longed to seek out Rebekah. Again, he resisted. "Parts of it, yes."

What had Rebekah said in his office earlier that day? She missed sailing, of course, and the tall stand of pines to the east of her family's home. The clean scent of air, and the sunset on the beach. She'd even said something about the sound of rain on their roof, hadn't she?

"Are you going to tell us what parts you enjoyed?" Marianne's father asked him from across the table.

"Or did you disappear on us again?" Marianne offered him a teasing smile.

He dropped his gaze to the white tablecloth. Maybe if he stared at nothing, he'd stop getting distracted by thoughts of Rebekah. "I miss the trees and the air that doesn't smell like factory smoke or too many bodies. Sunset over the water is always stunning, and I enjoy being in a town where you see familiar faces rather than strangers everywhere."

Faces like Rebekah's.

So maybe staring at nothing wasn't going to keep his thoughts focused either.

"Doesn't a town that small lack plenty of conveniences?" Marianne's forehead furrowed in concentration. "Do they have a quality dressmaker?"

Would Marianne believe him if he answered that most women bought their dresses already made or sewed their own?

A commotion sounded at the buffet, and Gilbert raised his head to find Aileen racing out of the dining hall, her face as pale as snow. She nearly tripped in the doorway, which would have meant spilling the covered dish with the leftover sweet potatoes all over the floor.

What had happened? He swung his gaze to Warren, but Warren looked as bored and aloof as always.

Rebekah, on the other hand, was glaring at Warren from where she stood at the buffet. She then picked up the water pitcher and sashayed up to Warren, reaching across him to add two drops to his already full goblet.

"Gilbert?"

"No," he answered Marianne without looking at her. "I'm afraid you'd find the dressmaking options in Eagle Harbor lacking."

"Why don't we retire to the drawing room?" Father scooted his chair back from the table.

"Perhaps Marianne could entertain us with some piano music." Carl Mellar smiled at his daughter.

"That does sound delightful." Mother offered both Carl and Marianne one of her polite, society smiles. "I do wish I'd had a daughter and that she'd learned to play the piano."

Gilbert stood and extended his arm to Marianne as they filed out of the dining hall. He glanced at Rebekah, still standing by the sideboard, but this wasn't the time to ask why she'd been batting her lashes at Warren or what had happened with Aileen.

"You've been watching that servant all evening," Marianne whispered as he led her toward the drawing room.

Certainly not. He'd been watching Marianne—at least a little.

"Is something amiss?"

"Nothing spending more time with you won't cure." He patted her hand and directed her to the polished grand piano situated in the corner of the drawing room before settling himself in the closest chair.

Marianne played a classical composition of some sort. It was rather uncultured of him, but he'd never cared to learn much about the composers or the various types of music they'd written. Marianne, however, had a singularly elegant way of playing, one that pulled him in and made him forget the long hours he'd worked, the headache he'd gotten after sailing with Rebekah that afternoon, even the mess with the insurance company over compensation for the *Beaumont*.

"Would ye care for coffee, sir? Or maybe some port?"

Gilbert opened his eyes to find Aileen standing beside him and a silver tray with refreshments sitting on the side table. He swept his gaze quickly down her. "Is everything all right?"

Aileen glanced around the others seated near the piano. "I do believe so."

Apparently he'd been dozing for some time because everyone else had their refreshments—except for Warren, who was missing. "No, I wasn't inquiring about the refreshments, I was asking about earlier. You ran out of the dining room."

She stilled for a moment, her face growing pale once more. "I'm sorry if I caused a disturbance."

"I asked about *you*, Aileen. I'm not concerned about the disturbance, though I'm glad to see you're well enough to serve."

"Thank ye, sir. Now did ye care for some coffee?"

"No, thank you. Have you seen Warren?"

She swallowed, her jaw muscles growing tight and her eyes suddenly refusing to meet his. "No, sir."

He shouldn't be surprised since his brother's usual after dinner activities involved either women, gambling, or both. Had Warren left for one of his clubs, or was he still somewhere in the house?

And why did the notion of Warren prowling about give him a bad feeling? It wasn't as though he made it his habit to keep track of his brother's every movement.

But Rebekah was here, and not only had Warren shown far too much interest in her when they'd been in Eagle Harbor, but there'd been something odd going on at dinner.

Hopefully Warren had left altogether, but at least finding out whether Rebekah was safe could easily be resolved. He gestured for Aileen to step closer. "Is Rebekah in the kitchen?"

Aileen's brow furrowed, and she shook her head slowly. "No. I don't believe I saw her there."

"Then where is she?"

Again, Aileen shook her head.

The sense of foreboding clawed from his stomach into his chest. Mother was looking at him now, as was Carl Mellar. It was probably uncouth of him to leave the room while the woman he intended to marry demonstrated her talents on the piano—

No, it was extremely uncouth of him to leave.

But he stood nonetheless.

Marianne's playing continued behind him, the music sounding both elegant and effortless. He headed toward the door, muttering an "excuse me" that didn't satisfy either Mother or Carl Mellar, if the looks on their faces were any indication.

He was being paranoid. He likely couldn't stop thinking about Rebekah because of their argument earlier today and not due to any imminent danger from Warren. His brother had been living under this roof with various serving girls for years, and Warren had never caused trouble with them. Warren was the type to boast about it if he had, wasn't he?

Gilbert walked the path Rebekah would have taken through the house, using the servants' staircase and hallway as he headed to the kitchen. When he poked his head through the swinging doors, the cook straightened from her slumped position by the counter, and the scullery maid at the sink made a clattering sound with the dishes.

"Is Rebekah here?" A quick glance told him she wasn't.

"I haven't seen her." Mrs. Niebert's brow wrinkled as she looked around. "It's not like her to run off, though. What did you need her for? I'll send her up…"

The housekeeper's words trailed off as he headed toward the servant's stairway and the basement where their rooms were. At worst, Rebekah had taken ill and he'd find her in her bed. Or maybe she was too mad at him to tolerate being in his vicinity. After all, she had made her thoughts about him pursuing Marianne perfectly clear this afternoon. It probably irritated her to see him and Marianne together.

Though that wouldn't explain why she wasn't attending her duties in the kitchen.

He came to an abrupt halt the moment his feet hit the basement floor. "Rebekah?"

"Gilbert," she rasped without looking at him. She stared straight at Warren, who had cornered her against the wall near her room, his hand wrapped around her throat as he pressed his body against hers.

"Unhand her." Gilbert strode forward, fists at the ready.

Her hair had been pulled out of the bun Mother required of the help and fell about her shoulders in wild auburn waves. He half expected Warren to glance his way and smirk before forcing Rebekah into a kiss—or worse—but his brother stood still, his face white with strain, as though it took all his might to keep Rebekah in that position.

"I said, 'Unhand her.'" With one final step, he reached Warren and jerked him back by the collar. He didn't pause as he threw one punch, then another. Blood spattered his hand, and Warren yelped with pain, but he couldn't quite stop himself from throwing a third punch, and a fourth.

A hundred punches wouldn't be enough. His vision narrowed and a rushing sounded in his ears as he pummeled his brother. At some point, Warren slammed an upper cut into his jaw and landed a blow to his stomach. His brother might as well have hit him with a feather, he felt so little pain.

A hand yanked on his arm, pulling him back.

He fought against it.

"Gilbert, enough," Rebekah shouted, her voice breaking through the roaring in his head.

He paused for a moment, and another arm wrapped around him, its grip tight as someone pulled him farther back while barring him from throwing more punches.

"What are you thinking, son? Attacking your brother like that?" His father's voice boomed beside his ear.

"Yes, what is the meaning of this?" Carl Mellar demanded in his nasally tone.

Father was here? And Carl Mellar? Gilbert looked over his shoulder to find the shipping tycoon striding down the hall toward them with his son, Andrew.

Why had all the men from the drawing room traipsed down to the servants' quarters? Gilbert glanced at Warren, who was crumpled against the wall and holding his stomach, his face and shirt smeared with blood. Rebekah stood against the wall as well, but several feet away from Warren.

"Well, what was going on?" Carl went to Warren, though the small man wouldn't be able to hold off Warren if he lunged.

Not that Warren was in any condition for lunging. Gilbert glared at his brother. At least he'd bested him when it mattered.

"Yes." Father yanked back on his arms again. "Explain why Mrs. Niebert ran into the drawing room screaming that the two of you were down here killing each other."

"Tell them what happened, Gilbert," Warren sneered, then used the sleeve of his shirt to wipe blood from the side of his mouth.

Andrew Mellar stopped beside Rebekah and handed her a handkerchief. "Why were you down here in the first place, Gilbert?" Andrew's gaze shifted between him and Rebekah.

"I came to check on Rebekah after watching Warren ogle her at dinner. I found Warren strangling her." The urge to sink his fist into Warren's face rose up again, but Father kept his grip firm.

"Yes, Warren attacked me." Rebekah whispered, pressing Andrew's handkerchief against her throat.

Andrew's brow furrowed. "Are you all right?"

"Attacked?" Mr. Mellar ran his gaze swiftly down Rebekah and frowned. "Are you sure you didn't invite Warren down here?"

A cruel smile twisted Warren's blood-smeared lips. "She invited me."

"I did no such thing—!"

"She wouldn't dare." Gilbert shouted at the same time as Rebekah.

"Enough!" Father bellowed over their voices. "This is a family affair and doesn't concern the Mellars." He eyed Gilbert's bloody shirt. "Go clean yourself up and then get upstairs to Marianne, if she still wants to see you after you left in such a manner, that is. I'll have Rebekah brought to your mother's salon so we can get to the bottom of this."

"Fine." He jerked out of his father's hold but couldn't make himself move toward the stairs. Was Rebekah all right? What had happened between her and Warren before he'd found them?

Because if the haunted look in her eyes was any indication, he hadn't arrived soon enough.

⌐.⌐.⌐.⌐.⌐

"I'll explain everything." Rebekah shifted against the stiff, upholstered chair she'd been given in Mrs. Sinclair's private salon and tried to find a comfortable position despite the throbbing in her head, aching in her ribs, and soreness in her wrists. "He assaulted me."

She jabbed a finger at Warren, who was slouched on the settee across from her with a small glass of clear liquor.

"Don't tell lies." Though his lip was split and a bruise had formed along his jaw, Warren looked like a bored, arrogant prince presiding over his court. He glanced at her and yawned into his hand as though he deemed her no better than one of his serfs.

"I'm not." Rebekah turned to Mrs. Sinclair, who stood near the settee with Warren. Surely she would understand. Surely she wouldn't tolerate her son attacking one of her servants.

A rustling sounded from Mr. Sinclair where he leaned against the fireplace mantle and puffed on a cigar.

Did they realize they were lined up three against one? With the way the family all gathered in front of the fireplace while she sat alone in a chair?

If only Gilbert were here. He'd stand beside her the way Mrs. Sinclair did with Warren. He'd look at her with understanding in his eyes rather than accusations and hardness. Was he still bidding farewell to the Mellars? What was taking him so long?

"You invited me to your room. I merely took you up on the invitation." Warren took a sip of whatever spirits he was drinking, boredom still filling his face.

"He grabbed me outside the kitchen and dragged me down the stairs." She looked at Mrs. Sinclair again, not caring if her eyes gave too much away, if she looked a bit desperate. Didn't the other woman believe her?

The older lady's face revealed nothing, much like Gilbert's expressions.

Rebekah glanced at the door. *Gilbert, come quickly!* It seemed as though he'd been with the Mellars for an hour or better.

Though really, she had no idea how long it had been since Warren attacked her. She'd been whisked up here immediately after the attack only to wait for Warren to clean himself up and change clothes, and for Mr. and Mrs. Sinclair to make their appearance. She reached a hand up to rub the sore spot where Warren's hands had crushed her throat.

"Is that how you got from the kitchen to the basement?" The bejeweled combs in Mrs. Sinclair's silver-blond hair glistened in the gas lighting. "Warren forced you?"

"Yes." Plus he'd yanked on her hair, and not just once—which was likely what had given her the tiny army of miners currently chopping away at the inside of her head.

"It's not like she's innocent, Olympia." Mr. Sinclair puffed on his cigar. "She's been flirting with me ever since she arrived."

"I haven't." Hotness pricked behind her eyes, and she shook her head, though that only made it pound harder.

Would Mrs. Sinclair believe her husband and Warren simply because they were family? Even when Rebekah had bruises on her neck and wrist? And if the pain in her side was any indication, she'd develop a bruise there as well.

"I haven't flirted with anyone since I've come here." Not even Gilbert, though she may have wanted to, and not just once.

"Hmm." Mr. Sinclair took another long drag on his cigar. "That's not what I saw at dinner tonight. You and Warren looked rather friendly."

"That was different." She looked down at her hands, clasped tightly together in her lap. She should have figured others at the table would notice.

Had she been partly responsible for the attack? She'd been trying to keep attention off Aileen. Why hadn't she been prepared for Warren to take her up on her flirtations?

Because most other men stopped their advances when a woman denied them. But not Warren, which she'd already known. Gilbert was right. She was too naïve by half, and she'd been a dolt trying to take on a monster like Warren Sinclair.

But I wasn't trying to take him on, just distract him for a few hours.

Except Mr. Sinclair had seen her flirt with Warren, which meant the Sinclairs wouldn't believe her story unless she told everyone about Aileen and Warren.

No wonder Warren sat across from her with that cruel smirk on his face. She couldn't hurt him, and he knew it.

Gloated in it.

"Truly, Byron." Disgust rang through Mrs. Sinclair's voice as she turned to her husband. "Just because the help glances at you and Warren or asks how you want your coffee doesn't mean she's flirting."

"Perhaps, Mother. But in this case, Rebekah's invitation was rather clear. You can hardly blame me for taking her up on it." Warren ran his eyes down her, his gaze hot while he held his cruel smirk in place.

She shuddered and folded her arms over her chest. If only she could wrap herself in the robe hanging on the peg by her bed instead. She might be fully dressed in her servant's uniform, but Warren watched her as though he could see through her clothes and underthings to what lay beneath.

"Whether she's innocent or not, I can most certainly blame you." Mrs. Sinclair's gaze conveyed an entire lecture. "You well know I don't tolerate dallying under this roof."

Warren yawned again and rolled his eyes. "Yes, Mother, no dallying. We know."

Mrs. Sinclair crossed her arms and huffed. But what more could she do? Warren was a grown man. It wasn't as though she could take a switch to his backside no matter how badly he needed it.

"Maybe this is why you have such trouble keeping servants." Rebekah pressed her hands to the ache in her ribs and spoke through the pounding in her head. "Maybe I'm not the first person Warren's attacked."

The room fell suddenly silent, the ticking of the mantle clock above the fireplace the only sound.

Warren paused, his glass halfway to his lips.

Rebekah swallowed and shifted in her chair, but didn't look away from his furious gaze. Having her robe from downstairs would do little good now. The look Warren gave her would burn right through it.

She raised her hand to her throat once more and rubbed where the bruises from Warren's hands were sure to be forming. Was this how Aileen felt? Trapped in a house with a rapist and unable to fight back?

But she wasn't Aileen, and she wasn't going to sit here and do nothing.

"I'm going to the police." If she didn't report him, then there would be another woman. And another and another and another.

Warren leaned back against the settee and curled his lips into a vicious grin. "What do you expect that to accomplish? It's your word against mine, and I say you invited me to your room."

"If that's your story, then you should have been careful not to leave bruises." She shoved up the sleeve of her shirt and stretched out her arm, where the red mark around her wrist was already darkening to brown.

"If you go to the police, then you'll find yourself out of a job."

Mr. Sinclair straightened, the first time he'd bothered with proper posture since entering the room.

"Do you think I still want to work here? When your son could decide to attack me at any time?"

Mrs. Sinclair held up her hand and leveled her gaze at Warren. "I want to know if there's any truth to what Rebekah said. Are you the reason I have trouble keeping help? Has this happened before?"

"I'd like to know the same thing." Gilbert strode into the salon and straight for the chair where Rebekah sat.

"Don't be ridiculous." Warren took a sip of his spirits. "It's as I said, Rebekah invited me to her room. It's the first time I've dallied with anyone under this roof."

"You're lying again." Her eyes turned hot, smarting with tears not for her own sake, but for Aileen's.

"How would you know? You weren't even working here before I left."

She couldn't do this anymore, couldn't look into Warren's sneering face and pretend that everything was all right, pretend that he hadn't hurt anyone else.

"Because you've been raping Aileen for months." The words shot from her mouth like arrows from a taut bow.

Mr. Sinclair dropped his cigar to the ashtray with a hiss and turned to face his son fully, while Mrs. Sinclair stilled, her already perfect posture growing even straighter.

Oh, what had she done? Aileen would hate her now. But she couldn't be sorry for it, not truly. The family needed to know lest Warren attack someone else.

Gilbert reached out and settled a hand on her shoulder, his grip firm yet comforting.

"Warren?" Mrs. Sinclair's voice shook as she spoke her son's name.

"Falsehoods!" Warren jumped from his seat. "All of them. And I don't have to stay here and listen." He headed for the door, fury rolling off his body like waves during a storm.

Gilbert stepped in front of him. "Planning to run like a scared rabbit?" He shoved his brother in the shoulder. "Sit back down."

Mrs. Sinclair sank into Warren's vacant spot on the settee, her face pale save for two bright pink splotches along her cheekbones. "Someone send for Aileen. We need to know if this is true."

"You're going to take the word of servants over the word of your son?" Mr. Sinclair strode into the middle of the room. "Maybe that's where Gilbert gets his bleeding heart from, always wanting to help the underclass. Always taking their side."

"It's not a matter of taking sides, Father," Gilbert gritted. "Right is right."

"This whole thing is ridiculous." Warren turned for the door.

"I told you to sit!" Gilbert shouted so loudly the glass front on the china cabinet shook.

"You're not leaving before we hear from Aileen." Mrs. Sinclair pointed a finger at the other end of the settee.

It probably took minutes for Aileen to arrive, but it seemed like hours. Everyone stayed silent. Mrs. Sinclair sitting with her head slumped in her hands, Mr. Sinclair pacing, and Warren shifting uncomfortably on the settee.

Would Aileen even look at her when she came into the room? Probably not. She'd begged and pleaded for Rebekah to keep her secret, but crimes such as Warren's needed to be called out. Or at least, she thought they did. But she'd rushed ahead, blurting Aileen's business to everybody without even praying.

And this after promising herself that she wouldn't make any more decisions without praying for a week. Would she ever learn not to be so headstrong?

The entire household would know everything by morning, and Aileen would be humiliated. And though Rebekah had no desire to work here anymore, Aileen didn't have much choice.

Oh, why couldn't Warren have waited an extra day to return? If Aileen's interview tomorrow had gone well, this entire situation could have been avoided.

Until Warren forced himself on another servant.

A soft whispering sounded at the doorway, and Rebekah looked up to find Aileen looking nervously about the room before taking a step backward into the hall.

"Aileen," Gilbert held out his arm to her. "We need a few minutes of your time. Have a seat."

"I-I didn't do anything," she stuttered as Gilbert led her to the chair nearest Rebekah's.

Rebekah gripped her hands together. *Please, God, don't let her hate me. Help her to see the good in this. Give her the strength to speak of what Warren's done.*

"Aileen." Mr. Sinclair barked her name with a force that made Rebekah wince. "Has my son ever pressed unwanted advances on you?"

Aileen's sharp intake of breath could likely be heard in the hallway. She glanced up at Warren.

His gaze was riveted on Aileen, his jaw set in foreboding lines.

Aileen shook her head slowly. "I d-d-don't know what ye're t-talking about."

Rebekah stood, taking a moment to let her pounding head adjust to the movement before she walked to Aileen and knelt. "It's all right." She gripped Aileen's hand tightly in her own. "You can tell the truth. He's not going to hurt you anymore."

"Are you sure Warren's never forced you to do something against your will?" Mrs. Sinclair rose from the settee in a graceful sweep, her forehead lined with concern as she crossed the carpet to Aileen. "Nothing at all?"

Aileen looked up at Mrs. Sinclair.

"Go on, dear. It's all right." Compassion wreathed the regal woman's face.

"I… he…" Aileen licked her trembling lips.

The clock chose that moment to chime, ten endless dings that seemed to go on forever while Aileen moved her gaze nervously about the room and bit her bottom lip.

"Well?" Mr. Sinclair's voice rang out the moment the clock finished. "Did our son force you or not?"

Aileen glanced down at her lap, her eyes vacant, lifeless hollows, and she shook her head. "No. He d-didn't—"

"See." Warren stood and thrust his hand at her. "I told you Rebekah was lying. I want her gone first thing in the morning. Really, Mother, what manner of servants are you hiring these days?"

Warren strode toward the door, and this time Gilbert let him pass.

"I've heard enough as well, and I agree with Warren. I want her gone come morning." Mr. Sinclair followed in Warren's wake, slamming the door shut with such force that the walls trembled.

Rebekah looked up at Gilbert, who stared back at her with an unreadable gaze.

"I'm sorry. I…" But what was there to say? She'd told the truth, even if Aileen refused to verify it.

Rebekah squeezed Aileen's hand, which the other woman still rested in hers. "I'm going to the police and letting them know what Warren did to me tonight. Come with me, please. You can give a statement too."

Aileen didn't even attempt to speak, just shook her head for the third time since she'd entered the salon, tears blurring her bright green eyes.

Mrs. Sinclair turned to Gilbert. "How could I not have known?"

Gilbert shoved his hands into his pockets. "Because he's underhanded and without remorse."

"Come, dear, let's get you ready for bed." Mrs. Sinclair squeezed Aileen's shoulder. "Do you feel safe sleeping here tonight?"

Aileen wiped a tear from her cheek and nodded. "Th-there's a lock on my door. Rebekah put it there."

Gilbert crouched before Aileen and waited for her to look at him before speaking. "I'm sorry I didn't give you one sooner."

Aileen gave him a brief nod and then stared at the fireplace, empty and stark just like her gaze, until Mrs. Sinclair coaxed her to stand so they could go downstairs.

Chapter Eighteen

"I'm sorry." Gilbert repeated for the third or fourth time that evening as he held the door to the police precinct open. If only words were enough. If only he could go back five months' time and find a different job for Aileen. Go back to the minute he'd stopped fighting against Rebekah working as a maid and take a stronger stand.

"You didn't do anything." Rebekah preceded him out of the police station and into the damp night, her shoulders rising and falling on a shrug.

Most people would have assumed her unbothered. This was Rebekah Cummings, after all—the woman who didn't let anything defeat her.

Or rather, she didn't show anyone when she was defeated. But with her shoulders slightly slumped and her steps a touch slow and aimless, resignation laced the subtlety of her movements.

He reached out and gripped her shoulder, stopping her from heading toward the carriage despite the tiny water droplets misting her hair and shoulders. "The officers were terrible to you."

She shrugged again, the action far too flippant. "They were right. I didn't have proof."

His eyes met hers in the near darkness, and a lump stuck in his throat. *I don't know why they didn't believe you. I wish I could have forced them to.* But he settled for, "They still shouldn't have accused you of seducing my brother. I'm sorry."

If only saying the words a certain number of times would rid the guilt weighting his heart. Or better, reset his brother's actions so that he'd never harmed anyone.

Rebekah swallowed and looked down, her fingers fiddling with the band on her apron. "Aileen warned me it would happen. I should have listened."

How had it gotten to the point of his brother attacking Rebekah, of Warren repeatedly hurting Aileen? How had he not seen what was happening? Not stopped it? Gilbert slammed the palm of his hand into the precinct wall beside him.

"I wasn't lying about what happened, not to me, and not to Aileen." Muted gas lighting from the streetlamps drifted through the mist over Rebekah's pale features and thick auburn hair—hair she'd hastily pinned up before they'd left for the police station and that was now starting to fall. "You believe me, don't you?"

She'd relayed every last bit of her story to the police officers, including how she'd tried to reach for her fishing knife and Warren had noticed, which was when he'd thrown her against the wall and wrapped his hands around her throat. She'd also shown the police officer the bruises on her neck and on her wrists, and then told him there were rumors about Warren attacking other serving girls.

The eyes of the officer taking notes hadn't even flickered with compassion or interest, and Gilbert had barely resisted springing across the desk and wrapping his hands around the man's throat as Warren had done to Rebekah. Maybe if Officer Tabor felt his own lungs starve for air, he'd take more interest in Rebekah's claim.

"So you don't believe me." Rebekah took a step away from him.

"I believed your every word." He leaned an arm on the wall

beside her, bringing his head to within a foot of hers. "Did you think otherwise?"

She met his gaze. "Oh. I'd assumed... Well, you didn't say anything in your mother's salon, and you were quiet for so long just now. It's always hard to tell what you're thinking."

He was thinking that he hadn't gotten enough punches in when he fought Warren earlier. "I'm thinking my brother should be locked in a cell for a decade or better. I don't understand why the police refused to charge him."

He'd been frustratingly little help in the police station. Oh, he'd given his report of how he'd found Warren strangling Rebekah, but he hadn't seen what started the fight, and that was what the police were most concerned about. Was Warren acting in self-defense? Had Rebekah tried to provoke him, especially given that she'd been carrying a fishing knife on her person? Surely a servant such as Rebekah didn't mean to accuse Warren Sinclair of wrongdoing, did she?

His appearing at the precinct with Rebekah should have lent credibility to her claim. But it almost seemed as if Warren had already stopped by the police station and given his own version of the events—or bribed the policemen into not paying attention to Rebekah.

And perhaps he had. It was hard to say with his brother.

Or maybe it wasn't quite so hard. Warren wouldn't have the foresight to stop by the precinct and issue a statement first. But Father was trying to control the damage in the papers to the family name after Warren's stunt with the mayor's daughter.

He curled his hand into a fist against the wall of the police station. "I'm sorry it turned out this way."

Another futile apology. For all his attempts to help those wronged by his family, he was frustratingly inept at it, first with

Lindy and now with Aileen and Rebekah. No wonder Father thought his crane a farce.

"Stop apologizing. You rescued me, remember?"

"But not before Warren hurt you. And I didn't rescue Aileen at all." He pressed his eyes shut, letting his memories of Aileen working for his parents run through his mind. There had to be signs of what Warren was doing. How had he missed them?

"I'm worried about her."

He opened his eyes and peered down into Rebekah's face, now dusted with tiny droplets of water from the drizzle. She was worried about Aileen? Wasn't she the least bit concerned about herself? She'd been attacked so little time ago that her bruises were still darkening.

"I made things worse for her, and she has nowhere to go. I should have never brought her into this. Oh, Elijah's right. I have a wretched tongue—one that would be better off cut out of my mouth some days."

"No." He tapped a finger against Rebekah's lips, pushing aside thoughts of how soft they were. "If not for you speaking up, no one would know, and with Warren back home..." He couldn't bring himself to finish the sentence.

His brother had used women for one purpose only since the day he was old enough to walk into a saloon. But to force a woman? And someone like Aileen, who had no family to protect her, no relative to take her in?

Gilbert's stomach roiled with nausea. She never would have met his brother if not for him.

Rebekah's hand came up to rest on the side of his cheek, her fingers long and slim. "It's not your fault."

But it was. He pressed his hand over hers. "I thought you couldn't tell what I was thinking."

Her eyebrows furrowed together, and concern glinted in her eyes. "Every once in a while, it's obvious."

"She needs to go back to Eagle Harbor with you." He might not have stopped Warren from hurting Aileen these past months, but he could stop anything from happening in the future.

"With me?" Rebekah scanned his face. "What makes you think I—"

"You're going home. You have to. You said yourself you weren't going to keep working for my parents after what happened. Warren is furious with you, and I can't abide the thought of either of you staying in this city while he's here. He has unlimited resources at his disposal, and he's not the type to stop once he sets his mind to something. If he wants to find you, he will."

He waited for the sound of her foot stomping against the ground and the argument that was sure to follow. But she wasn't going to win, not this time. If she was too stubborn to see the truth, then he'd haul her over his shoulder to the nearest train depot and—

"You're right. It's time for me to go."

He blinked. "I am?"

She looked down at her feet. "I was thinking that even before I learned Warren was here. What you said earlier today—or I suppose it was yesterday now—it made sense. I didn't treat my family well. I was going to write them a letter and apologize, but with everything that's happened tonight, it's time for me to go." She peeked up at him, and the beads of water on her eyelashes glittered in the faint light. "Even if I didn't earn my hundred dollars."

"I'll give it to you."

She shook her head. "Keep it. Use it for your crane or to help another injured dockworker or something like that."

His eyes held hers for a moment, the green of her irises vibrant and intense despite the shadows and mist swirling about them. "You're the only person I've had to fight with about taking my money."

Her lips tipped up in a half smile. "That's because you've got better things to spend it on than me."

"I'm paying for both of your train tickets. And I won't accept a word of argument about it." He moved away from the building, clearing her path to the carriage. "Now let's get you out of this damp. It was ungentlemanly of me to keep you outside in this weather."

"Oh, yes, the horrors of a woman who grew up on a fishing boat getting her hair wet." She sent him that teasing grin that had become far too familiar over the past weeks. "However shall I manage?"

So tonight's ordeal hadn't stolen her spirit then, at least not all of it. He forced himself to smile back at her, though knowing Rebekah, she saw right through his faked amusement.

She strode ahead of him, and their driver hopped down from the carriage to open the door. But rather than climb inside, Rebekah stopped and turned back, her brow furrowed with wrinkles that his thumbs ached to smooth away. "Would you mind paying for one more ticket?"

"One more?"

"For Lindy. Only if she wants to, though. I haven't asked, but I hear the way she talks about Eagle Harbor. She misses her sister, even though Betsy's line of work is..."

"Disreputable." Yet another time where he'd failed to help a person in need. Much like Aileen's trouble at Warren's hands, Betsy's decision to prostitute herself after her father's death hung heavy in his mind. "I'll give you a key to my parents' house. Lindy and Aileen can stay there—at least until Warren and Father learn of it."

"No. They'll stay with us. We'll make room."

"Rebekah…"

"It'll be fine, and if it's not, I'll send you a telegram." She raised her chin in that stubborn manner of hers.

He blew out a breath. As long as they would all be safe, he wasn't going to argue about the specifics.

"Notify me if there's trouble." He gestured to the open carriage door. "Now climb inside. I want you ladies to leave quickly, and we've much to do before the first train of the morning departs."

~.~.~.~.~

She wasn't going to cry. She absolutely refused.

Rebekah blinked back a threatening tear and stared out the window at the fog that shrouded the city. She'd never seen Chicago's streets so empty, its sidewalks so devoid of passersby as this morn, while the carriage clattered over the road toward the train station.

"Are ye all right?" Aileen spoke quietly from where she sat beside Rebekah on the carriage seat.

Why did everyone keep asking her that? She kept her gaze out the window as she answered. "Fine."

"Did Warren do more than ye let on?" Aileen took her hand. "Ye can tell me, ye know."

"Yes, Rebekah," Gilbert's deep voice rumbled from across the carriage where he sat with Lindy. "If Warren did more than what you said at the police station, please tell us."

Aileen jumped, her grip tightening on Rebekah's hand. The Irishwoman probably hadn't intended for her words to carry across the carriage, but in the wee hours of the morning, the slightest of whispers could be heard.

"Did he force you?" Lindy coughed slightly, but the sound was far different from the deep, murky coughs that had been so incessant when Rebekah arrived a month ago.

"Only to kiss him." But though she'd been spared from worse, the headache he'd given her still came and went and the carriage jostled her bruised ribs. Her throat felt constantly parched regardless of how much water she drank, while simultaneously throbbing from Warren's stranglehold.

But the worst was when she closed her eyes. Closed them and saw Warren's face above hers as he yanked her hair and dragged her down the stairs, as he threw her against the wall and leaned his body into her before she could grab her fishing knife.

Her arms were already wrapped around herself, but she hugged herself harder, then tucked her feet up beneath her on the seat. If only she could curl up in a ball and drift into a painless sleep devoid of memories.

"You don't seem fine." Gilbert's tone was soft, beseeching even. He'd been the perfect gentleman to them all, holding the carriage door open, helping them climb inside, asking Lindy if she needed a pillow for her comfort or a lap robe to ward off any chill she might have. "You seem as though my brother harmed you in some way you refuse to speak of."

If only he was seated beside her rather than Aileen. If only he would wrap his arms around her, then maybe she could drift off into a peaceful slumber that seemed as distant as the horizon.

He had put his arms around her once. No, twice. That day when they'd stood together on the deck of the *Lassiter* during the storm, and the morning he'd kissed her. She'd threatened to gut him with her fishing knife if ever he touched her again. What a fool she was, because at the moment, she wanted nothing more than to burrow into his side and cry.

Why? Because of what Warren had done to her last night? Because of what he'd done to Aileen?

Because the next time she saw Gilbert, he'd be married to Marianne?

Because she was returning home a failure who hadn't earned her hundred dollars?

"Stay here." Gilbert announced as the carriage slowed in front of the train station. "I'll procure tickets and then have us driven around to our platform."

With the precision and efficiency of a military general, he disembarked from the carriage and strode through the fog toward the train station awash with lights. It was a precision and efficiency he exercised in all things, and she was going to miss it.

Miss him.

"I'm happy you thought to bring me along." Lindy said with nary a cough. "I've missed Eagle Harbor. It's so beautiful."

"Beautiful, mayhap, but it can't compare to Ireland." Aileen's accent thickened as she spoke of her home country.

"You best not go around saying that once you're there. It's a town full of Cornishmen, or didn't Rebekah tell you?"

Aileen stiffened and turned to Rebekah. "Cornish? Ye didna' tell me."

"You'll be welcome there." At least in her family's household, Aileen would. And after a month or two of seeing Aileen was harmless, those with strong Cornish roots would likely warm toward the Irishwoman.

The carriage door opened and Gilbert climbed inside. "I'm glad I had you wait here. Your platform is clear around the back."

The carriage lurched forward but soon turned and began crossing an endless number of tracks before reaching one of the last platforms. Gilbert and the driver needed only one trip from the carriage to the train to load their luggage, and Aileen and Lindy climbed aboard a train that seemed more empty than full.

"Don't you trust me to handle your luggage?" Gilbert's lips tilted in a half smile as he stopped beside where Rebekah stood on the platform.

Even in the gray, foggy mist, he had the features of an angel. Hair so rich a blond any woman would be jealous. Eyes so clear a blue they looked like the water when the afternoon sun beat upon it.

A heart so big and deep it made the waters of Lake Michigan seem small.

"I know you say you're all right, but you don't seem it." His voice rang deep against the puff and hiss of the train.

"I'm fine." Or she would be once she got away from Chicago and the memories of Warren yanking her hair and squeezing her wrist and wrapping his hands around her throat. When memories of Warren's hands creeping up her ribs and his lips forcing themselves on hers lay in the dust of Chicago.

"Are you certain Warren didn't—?"

She held up her hand. "Please don't ask me again. I waited here to say goodbye, not to keep putting you off."

He searched her face, his eyes flitting over her skin the way a butterfly did a flower, and if the intensity of his gaze warmed her skin? If she felt a slow blush spread across her cheeks?

He reached out and traced a finger over the aching part of her neck. "Your bruise is worsening."

She pressed her eyes shut. It was all too much. The way he'd fought Warren for her, the way he'd taken her to the police station and believed her story when no one else did. The way he'd worked tirelessly all night to get Aileen and her out of the city before

Warren could hurt them again.

Just like he worked tirelessly on his crane.

Tirelessly to help people like Lindy.

He claimed he wasn't supposed to have a family that loved him, claimed that God wanted him to build his crane instead. But here he was tending to people below him as though they were his family. As though he loved them.

"Rebekah?" He tucked a strand of hair behind her ear, his fingers lingering at the tender spot behind her jaw.

"I love you," she blurted before she could think better of it.

His hand stilled, his fingertips burning the patch of skin where they touched. "No, you don't."

Her eyes blurred. "But I do."

She didn't want to, could think of a million reasons why she shouldn't fall in love with Gilbert Sinclair. Like that he was an arrogant fool who assumed everyone had as much money at their disposal as he did. Or that he and Elijah had spent most of their lives fighting with each other. That he lived in Chicago and she lived in Eagle Harbor. That she didn't have sixteen thousand dollars to give him if they wed.

But they were useless, each and every one of them, because she'd gone and fallen in love anyway.

"You're tired and not thinking clearly." His voice grew tense, whether from anger or desperation, she couldn't tell. His hand left the soft spot behind her ear, and he gripped her shoulders so hard she nearly cringed. "You can't be."

"But I can, don't you see? You're the one who works endlessly to help people like Lindy and Aileen. Who buys train tickets for them regardless of whether you can afford it. How can I not love you after you do things like that? You listened to me last night when no one else would. And you're willing to see the truth about

Warren and Aileen, even though it would be much more convenient for you to look the other way."

He leaned his head down until his forehead touched hers, his skin warm against her own.

He was going to say it back. She could feel it in the way he pressed his eyes shut. Sense it in the way his Adam's apple bobbed.

The fog swirled around them, giving the platform lights an eerie glow and muting the footsteps of the handful of people headed toward the passenger cars as she waited for the words he was bound to say.

"Don't."

"Don't?" She pulled back from him. "Don't what?"

"Don't say things like that. Don't look at me that way, as though I'm someone to be commended and admired. I've told you before I'm no hero. I'm going to build a crane and sell hundreds of machines to ports all over the country and get terribly rich, richer than my father can ever hope to be."

"No, you're going to build a crane and sell hundreds of machines so that you can save lives and stop people from being injured. Thousands of lives and people." A man with such a tender heart deserved to have both the crane he longed to build and a wife and family that loved him. Didn't he see that? "It makes me love you even more."

She stopped talking then, because she could see it in his eyes, the cold, flat calculation. The look that told her he was thinking of numbers and business projections and goals he'd set for himself.

Goals he wouldn't waver from.

Like his crane.

He'd no intention to marry for love. He'd said it from the beginning, hadn't he? And he wasn't the type to change his mind because one of his friends got emotional.

And that's all they were, friends. Old friends, from a decade past.

The whistle blew, and he pulled away from her. One tiny step, but he might as well have been crossing to the opposite shore of Lake Michigan. "You 'pity the woman who ends up married to me.' Your words, not mine. Remember?"

The air whooshed from her lungs. Her words, yes. Spoken when they stood beneath the stars together after she'd learned he intended to marry for money. Had they hurt Gilbert that night as much as they now pierced her?

The train hissed and steamed behind her, and he gestured toward the passenger car where Aileen and Lindy had disappeared. "You best be going, or you'll miss your train."

She swallowed and licked her lips, sore and swollen from Warren's abuse. "Maybe I had it wrong. Maybe I don't pity the woman you marry, but rather I pity you. For thinking money will be enough to keep you happy."

A muscle clenched and unclenched in his jaw, and she sucked in a long, slow breath. Would he change his mind? Apologize? Yell at her for daring to challenge his carefully laid plans?

He said nothing, only turned and strode away, leaving her to walk across the large, empty platform to the train by herself.

~.~.~.~.~

She didn't love him. She couldn't.

Gilbert strode across the platform toward the carriage that awaited him. He didn't look back over his shoulder to make sure Rebekah made it onto the train like a proper gentleman would have done. This was the woman who wanted to join her brother's life-saving team. She could manage to get on a train that he'd left her ten feet away from.

So he kept his gaze forward, his back straight, his pace quick.

Because if he looked back even once, he might find himself turning around and walking toward her instead of away. Of declaring...

What was there to declare?

She probably wouldn't speak to him after he'd thrown her words so cruelly back in her face. And he had been cruel. Even he, as heartless as he was, understood the malice in what he'd said.

And why did it matter whether she'd speak to him again or not? Whether he'd hurt her?

He didn't love her. He couldn't. And even if he did, he'd no intention of building a marriage on a namby-pamby emotion that could fade at any time.

Which was why he was going to marry Marianne. She was sensible about this whole marriage business, smart enough to see the benefit to both of them if they forged an alliance, detached enough he didn't need to worry about letting his emotions rather than rational thought control him when he was around her.

And rich enough her dowry would finance his crane and the money he'd lost on the *Beaumont*.

Rebekah might quote that verse about a flood not drowning love and wealth not being able to buy it, but love wasn't powerful enough to replace the benefits that a logical marriage arrangement brought him.

Why was he even ruminating on this? There was no decision to make, not really. Only one choice made sense.

So why did his hands grow slick at the thought of not seeing Rebekah again until after he'd married Marianne? Why had he not been able to stay on the platform and watch her train disappear into the fog?

Chapter Nineteen

"You have to let me get up."

Victoria pressed a hand to his forehead and scowled at him. "If you t-tell me that one more time, I'll dump the next glass of water I bring on your head rather than let you drink it. At least then you'd have a good reason to be out of this b-bed."

Elijah leaned back against the pillows. There was no hope for it. His wife may as well be a captain in the army with how she'd been barking orders at him.

"I need to go to the sawmill." He'd been waiting for an opportunity to sneak off all day, but Victoria wouldn't leave him alone for more than ten minutes.

Was that intentional on her part? Did she suspect his plan?

His wife crossed her arms over her chest and tapped her foot on the floor—actions she must have learned from Rebekah, because he was fairly certain the sweet woman he'd married ten weeks ago had never looked at him like that before she'd moved into their house. "And what do you expect to d-do at the sawmill with a broken arm?"

He glanced down at the sling anchoring his right arm to his body. Yes, it hurt something fierce, and maybe Dr. Harrington had told him to keep it still and let it rest for the next six weeks, but

Doc Harrington didn't understand.

Victoria didn't understand.

He wasn't even sure Ma understood.

"I need to work."

"Elijah, dearest," Victoria sank down onto the bed beside him. "You're right handed. Even if it were p-possible for you to work at the mill one handed—which I doubt—you'd never be able to do the work with your left hand."

But not working meant not getting paid. He couldn't afford to keep his arm still for two days, let alone six weeks. "I'll manage."

She sprang from the bed and threw her hands up. "I've about had enough. Why didn't your family warn me how impossible you were before I married you?"

"Impossible? I'm not impossible. You're the one who—" He clamped his mouth shut before anything more escaped.

But evidently he didn't clamp it shut soon enough, because Victoria's eyes narrowed and her foot started tapping again.

"I'm the one who what?"

He swallowed and looked down. "Nothing."

"Oh, I don't think it's nothing. What aren't you telling me, Elijah Cummings?"

He clenched his teeth together. "Just give me some room. I'm the one who has to earn a living, and if I want to do so with a broken arm, then you've no business stopping me."

"I've plenty of b-business stopping you if you're going to only end up hurt worse. Why are you being so unreasonable?"

"You're the one wearing kidskin shoes, and you think I'm unreasonable?"

She looked down at her pristine slippers and then back up at him, confusion written across her face. "You're mad about my slippers?"

He looked away. "Sinclair was right."

"Sinclair? As in Gilbert? What d-does he have to d-d-do with any of this?"

"I can't take care of you, Victoria. Gilbert tried to warn me, though his warning came out a little different than how everything is ending up. Still, he was right. I'm ruining you. My lack of money will ruin you. And no matter how hard I try to make things better, they're just getting worse."

He sighed and let the rest of the words come tumbling out. "The roof is leaking, I'm running behind on the boathouse, I don't have anywhere close to the money I need to pay Mr. Foley back for damages at the general store, I haven't put any time into the benevolence project for the Thimbleberry Festival, and there you are working like a servant in your pretty dresses and hats and shoes, all of which I'll never be able to replace once they wear out, and—"

"Elijah, stop." She pressed a hand to his mouth, one that she should probably be using to wipe away the tears streaking her cheeks rather than stop him from talking. "Just be quiet. When have I ever asked you to replace my dress or b-buy me new—"

"But—"

"No, listen." Though more tears slipped down her cheeks, determination glinted in her eyes. "I d-didn't marry you so that you could pauper yourself trying to buy me things. I don't need half of what you mentioned. But do you know what I d-d-do need? You."

She took his face in her hands, framing his cheeks with her fingers, and forcing his gaze on her—not that he would have looked away on his own. The roof caving in on them wouldn't entice him to take his gaze off his wife at the moment.

"And I don't mean that I need to be married to a m-man that I never see or a man that forgets our picnics. I mean I need to be married to a man who loves me. Who has time for me. Who listens when I talk no matter how b-b-badly I stutter." She pressed her lips to his cheek in a simple kiss. "If I wanted the things you just described, fancy clothes and a roof that never leaks, then I could have had them. I c-could have married Gilbert."

He growled low in his throat. "Can you do me a favor and never mention his name again—and especially not that part about how you almost married him."

She laughed slightly and wiped at the tears on her cheek. "It's all right, Elijah. Don't you see? I could have had that, but I didn't want it. I wanted you more. And a family—one who would have t-time for me and listen to me and…" She swallowed thickly. "… And love me. No matter what I did or how embarrassing I was. You were the p-person who promised to do that. You were the man who gave me Bible verses about how I mattered to God and was fearfully and wonderfully made.

"I didn't want nice things, Elijah. I wanted you." She rested her head on his chest.

He couldn't help but slip the fingers of his good arm into her hair and toy with the silky tresses.

Dear Father, what was I thinking?

She was right. He'd been so concerned about money and providing all the things he wanted to give her that he'd lost sight of what was most important. His wife. Not the clothes she wore, but the person she was.

"I'm sorry, Victoria. Will you forgive me?"

She sighed contentedly against his chest. "Of course I forgive you. You were only trying to keep me happy. Though maybe next time you should ask me what I want first. It would have saved you a lot of trouble."

And quite possibly a broken arm.

Ignoring the pain, he sifted his fingers through her hair again and let his own chest fill with contentment as he held his wife close.

Chapter Twenty

Gilbert had been right—again.

She'd missed Eagle Harbor, every last bit of it.

The small natural harbor rimmed with sand, the treacherous rocks that lined the shore surrounding the inlet, the tree-covered hills rolling over the land beyond, and the tiny town of log and clapboard structures where she'd grown up. Rebekah swallowed the lump that kept rising in her throat as she put one foot in front of the other and headed down North Street with Lindy and Aileen.

"I was expecting something bigger." Aileen stepped around a rut in the road and continued past the general store. "This is smaller than the town I came from in County Clare."

"Anything is likely to seem small after Chicago." She blinked back the tears that had burned behind her eyes far too often since she'd left Chicago and quickened her pace. The sooner she got home...

Well, hopefully seeing her family again would distract her from thinking about Gilbert, at least for a few hours.

She'd told him she loved him. Loved him! And what had he done? Stiffened, told her she couldn't possibly love him, then stormed away.

What was she supposed to do on the trip north if not cry? It wasn't as though she went around confessing her love to every second man she met. He was the first man she'd spoken those words to.

The first man she'd kissed.

The only man she'd ever fallen in love with, regardless of how foolish the notion.

"I've missed this place." Lindy's quiet voice floated from a few steps behind her. "I'm glad to come home."

"Yes, you're home now. And don't you forget it." Rebekah slowed, waiting for Lindy and Aileen to both catch up. "Sorry. I didn't realize I'd gotten so far ahead of you."

"You're eager to see your family. I can't blame you for that." Lindy's chest rose and fell a bit harder than it should as she came to a stop beside Rebekah.

"Here, let me carry your bag for a bit. No sense in you getting sick again."

Lindy held the fraying carpetbag away from her. "I'm fine."

Rebekah planted her feet in the road in front of Lindy and held out her hand for the bag.

"Ye best give it to her, or we'll be here till the sun goes down." Aileen nudged Lindy in the shoulder.

Lindy's face rose in a half smile. "If I truly needed help with it, I'd let you know."

"How much farther is yer home? Maybe I need help with me bag." Aileen attempted to smile, but it fell flat, just like everything else she'd done on the journey north. Indeed, in some ways, Aileen seemed more sickly than Lindy.

Rebekah sighed. What a motley trio the three of them must make. Her with her sick heart, Aileen with her sick spirit, and Lindy with her sick body.

But she wouldn't think about her heart now. She only hoped

Gilbert stayed away from Eagle Harbor for a good, long time—perhaps even the rest of his life—because she fully planned to put him from her mind now that she was home.

Except she'd only been in Eagle Harbor a quarter hour and had thought of him twice.

She huffed and spun on her heel. The sooner she got to her family's cabin, the better.

"I wasn't needling ye about yer home. How much farther is it?"

Rebekah swung back around and faced Aileen. The woman had two bags to her and Lindy's one, which made sense seeing how Lindy owned next to nothing and Rebekah had left most of her possessions in Eagle Harbor. But it was a bit of a walk from the dock to her house.

"I'll take your second bag." Rebekah reached for it.

"Where are your brothers?" Lindy looked around the street. "I assumed one of them would help us."

"Don't know. Figured my entire family would have found us by now." In a town the size of Eagle Harbor, arriving home wasn't going to be a secret.

She'd imagined her return several times over the two and a half days it took to get here. One version included Mac spotting her from the lighthouse grounds and rushing to greet her before she'd made it off the pier. Another version had Elijah seeing her from the beach when he returned home from a day on the water and wrapping her in a hug so fierce it sucked the breath from her. And one version even included running into Mrs. Ranulfson near the general store and being forced to explain to the town gossip where she'd been.

Instead, she'd gotten nothing.

It was as though the entire town had disappeared for the afternoon. A few dockworkers unloaded the mail and other small cargo that had come with them from Houghton. Other than that, only a handful of strangers bustled around town.

"It's strange." She surveyed the general store, its porch usually filled with people at this hour of the afternoon. "Everything seems empty."

"I was wondering if a lot of people had moved away since I left." Lindy looked around the street again.

"No. If anything, the town has more people now." Rebekah hefted Aileen's bag, which was none too light, and started walking. "Let's go. My ma and Victoria should be home this time of day, even if Elijah isn't."

"Ye're sure it's not a bother if we stay with ye?" Aileen hastened to catch up with her. "Lindy and I can rent a room if we've a need."

"There's plenty of room at the cabin." How many times must she tell Aileen she was welcome?

"We don't intend to stay for long." This from Lindy, who'd gone back to trailing behind them, her chest still working harder than it should.

"You can stay as long as you want."

"I'll look for work then. I don't need to be taking yer family's charity."

Work or not, it didn't matter as long as Aileen was away from Warren. And if the woman needed a month or two before she felt up to working, Rebekah wasn't going to push her.

She turned off North Street and led the girls up the twisting drive lined with pines and maples. Hammering echoed in the distance, carrying on the breeze off the lake. Was Elijah fixing the roof on the cabin?

"Do you know of anywhere that's hiring?" Lindy panted, then loosed a small cough. "I need a job too."

Rebekah paused again, giving the woman a chance to catch her breath. "Are you sure you won't let me take your—?"

"Rebekah? Is that you?"

At the sound of Mac's voice, Rebekah spun around, only to find her body being drawn up and crushed in her adopted brother's big, bear-like arms.

She closed her eyes and wrapped her arms around him—or would have, if she'd been able to move—then drew in his scent. He smelled of sweat and sunshine and… Mac. So he hadn't found her on the pier, he'd found her in the drive. Either way, it was good to be in her brother's arms again.

"What gave you the hankering to head on down to Chicago? We were worried something fierce."

"Mac?" But his name came out muffled considering the way he held her crushed against his chest. At least one of her family members was still talking to her after how she'd left, though.

"Isaac wanted Elijah to run off to Chicago and get you the second he got that telegram from Sinclair. But your ma and Elijah talked him out of it."

Good. She would have been irate had someone come to Chicago for her, but she had a more pressing matter to deal with at the moment. "Mac?"

"We decided to wait. But waiting's none too easy when your baby sister's off in a big city by herself. We even—"

"Mac!" She shoved against his chest with every last bit of strength and managed to move him just enough to draw air into her lungs.

He stared down at her, a question written in his light brown eyes. "Were you saying something?"

She sucked in another breath. "I couldn't breathe."

"Oh." He dropped his arms from around her shoulders and

gave them a pat. "Sorry about that. I forget how tiny you are sometimes."

"It's all right." And it was. Feeling his arms around her for the first time in a month had been worth the temporary suffocating sensation. "I missed you too."

"Never thought I'd see you in a skirt again either." Mac slung his arm back around her shoulder and brought her in for another hug, though not quite as brutal as the last one, then looked at Lindy and Aileen "You hear that? My little sister missed m—Lindy Marsden? Is that you?" Mac released Rebekah and stepped around her only to take Lindy's hand and engulf it in his overly large one. "It's good to have you back."

Lindy's arm jiggled with Mac's hearty handshake. "Thank you. It's good to be back."

"And who is this beside you?" Mac's gaze moved to Aileen, whose freckles stuck out on her pale face like coffee grounds sprinkled on snow.

Rebekah stepped between him and Aileen. "Aileen, this is Mac Oakton, my adopted brother. And Mac, this is Aileen Brogan from Ireland."

"You brought an Irish lass to a Cornish town?"

Rebekah jabbed him with her elbow. "Don't be that way. She was in need of a home, so I offered one. Would you have done any different?"

Mac scratched the back of his head. "'Spose not. But next time you go gallivanting across the country, you'd do better to bring back a Cornishwoman. Now come on." Mac swiped up the carpet bags she'd dropped when he'd hugged her. "Everyone will be thrilled to have you home."

Rebekah glanced up the drive to where it curved out of view, but the sound of pounding hammers still carried on the breeze.

Lots of pounding hammers. "What's going on?"

"The town's here for a workday. Foley even closed the general store for a few hours."

"A workday? To fix the roof?"

"Yep. Victoria organized it when Elijah broke his arm."

"Elijah broke his arm?" she squeaked. "Is he all right?"

"Doc Harrington says he'll be fine in a few more weeks. Now give me your bags." Mac reached out and plucked the bag from Lindy's hand, but Aileen had edged her way to the side of the drive, where the path met the woods. "I'll carry that for you— Aileen, is it?"

Aileen shook her head and stepped into the weeds that lined the forest.

"There's no sense in you carrying your bag when I can do it." He took a step closer, and panic flitted over Aileen's face.

"Why don't you and Lindy go on ahead?" Rebekah moved between her giant of a brother and Aileen again, shielding the Irishwoman from Mac's gaze. "I need to talk to Aileen."

Mac scratched his head again and looked between the two of them. "At least let me take her bag."

"I... I can manage," Aileen answered quietly. "Th-thank you."

Rebekah sent Mac a pleading look, but whether her lovable dunderhead of a brother would understand the message was another matter.

"I'd love to go see everyone." Lindy stepped beside him and tugged on his arm. "It's been far too long. Rebekah says you're married now?"

Mac might not know what was going on with Aileen, but he turned and headed down the drive with Lindy in tow.

"I'd love to meet your wife." Lindy's voice carried on the breeze, along with a small cough.

"That man is yer brother?" Aileen peeked around Rebekah's shoulder and watched Mac and Lindy disappear around the bend. "Ye didna' say he was so big."

"I didn't know it mattered. He won't hurt you, Aileen."

Aileen kept her gaze pinned to the spot where Mac had vanished. "How can ye be sure?"

"Mac? He's nothing but melted sugar on the inside." If her friend was going to worry about one of her brothers, Isaac was a better pick. He was always brooding these days. "Now let's get going. I want to see everyone." She took her friend's hand and gave a tug.

But Aileen stood rooted to the ground, her eyes welling with tears. "I... I can't. I'm sorry. I thought it would be just yer family, which was bad enough since ye have three brothers. But it sounds like half the town is there."

Was Aileen truly so terrified of men? She hadn't cowered from them on their trip north, but she hadn't been expected to talk to any men either. Come to think of it, Rebekah had done almost all of the talking, and Aileen had always taken the window seat on the train. And Mac was something of a giant, which would probably frighten someone like Aileen.

But that didn't mean her brothers were ogres, either. "No one here will hurt you. Someone who hurts women the way Warren did, well, he's not the type to help put a new roof on a building."

"How do ye know?" Aileen sniffled and wiped the tears from her cheeks. "What if someone like that is at yer house, and ye do'na know? Warren visited me for a long time, and none of the Sinclairs would have known if not for yer telling them."

Rebekah reached out and squeezed her friend's hand. "I don't have all the answers, but I do know that every man isn't like Warren Sinclair. You're only going to make things hard on yourself if you treat all men like they mean you harm."

"I still can't meet everyone." Aileen tugged her hand away from Rebekah's hold and wrapped her arms around her middle. "I've got a dime novel in my bag. I'll sit by that tree over yonder and read."

Rebekah shook her head, but Aileen was already moving off the path. And really, what could she do? First Aileen's brother had been taken from her, then her virtue. If she wanted to sit in the woods by herself for a few hours, then Rebekah wasn't going to take that choice away from her.

Far too many choices had already been taken away as it was.

~.~.~.~.~

"You canceled dinner."

Gilbert set his pencil down and stood, coming around the desk in his office at Great Northern Shipping, where Marianne had just barged through the door. "Marianne, what brings you here today?"

He cast a quick glance about the room, with its stacks of papers and haphazard piles of books, and tried not to wince. Had he known she would stop by, he would have tidied things.

Marianne set her reticule on an armchair that held a book on engines and some drawings that Stansby had dropped by yesterday for that ridiculous pulley system—just in case Gilbert felt the urge to look at them and offer any insight.

"I received word that you canceled dinner. Again. That's the third day in a row."

"I'm sorry. I've…"

She raised her eyebrows at him, her chin coming up a notch.

"Been busy." It was a lie, really. Because as much as he'd tried to stay busy in the three days since Rebekah had left, he'd gotten hardly anything done.

"You're always busy. That's never stopped you from coming to dinner before."

"Yes, well, I fell behind while I was gone, and I've been working on my crane and possibly even a new pulley system." There was truth to that, at least. He'd looked at the drawings from Stansby last night. Using a pulley system to move cargo down the docks was still decidedly impractical, but Stansby had hit on something with the system itself. If the man was willing to modify it for factory use, then perhaps—

"Don't feed me lies." Marianne stomped her dainty little foot on the floor. Strange how when Rebekah did it, he found the action either infuriating or amusing. Marianne, however, seemed like a child throwing a tantrum. "You've been avoiding me ever since you got into that fight with your brother over the servant."

"I'm sorry?" He swept his gaze down Marianne, with her pale pink dress, dark upswept hair, and clear blue eyes. He was supposed to visit a jeweler this weekend to pick out a ring, and he couldn't even interest himself in sharing a dinner with her.

What was wrong with him? Friends had come and gone over the years, and he'd never been so bothered when he'd had to say goodbye.

But a *friend* had never told him she loved him before, either.

How long had it been since he'd heard those words? They were probably spoken freely in a home like the Cummingses', but never in the Sinclair household, not even by his mother.

"Gilbert. Dinner. Tonight." Marianne stomped her foot like a petulant child after she spoke each word. "Why did you cancel? I want the truth."

"I, ah… I'm tired, Marianne, and I'd make for rather poor company." At least that had more truth to it than the line about him being busy. "I'm sorting through some things, if you must know."

Except there was nothing to sort through. Rebekah had told him she loved him, and he'd walked away from her. She didn't have the money he needed to replace the *Beaumont* and build his crane, and those things were more important than love.

At least they should be. So why did that verse from Song of Solomon keep running through his head? *Many waters cannot quench love, neither can the floods drown it: if a man would give all the substance of his house for love, it would utterly be contemned.*

Was Rebekah right? Was he trading the things that were truly important for something of lesser value?

But how could he say helping people like Lindy was something of lesser value? Surely his crane was of greater value than his own future happiness, because it meant he'd be able to help others.

And why was he thinking about any of this at all? He didn't even love Rebekah. She was merely a friend.

A friend with thick auburn hair and a smile that made the hard places inside him warm, put feeling back into the cold parts of him he'd learned to numb long ago because of his father and brother. A friend who enjoyed the feel of the breeze on her face and the sight of stars on a dark night. A friend who left the town she loved to make sacrifices for her family. A friend who then made more sacrifices for penniless women she didn't have to help.

"Can I speak plainly with you, Gilbert?" Marianne crossed her arms over her slight chest and tapped her foot on the floor.

At least she wasn't stomping it any longer.

"Let me clear off a chair." He stepped to the chair opposite his desk.

"I don't want to sit." Stomp.

So maybe she wasn't done. He gathered an armful of ledgers off the chair nonetheless and headed toward the sofa along the far wall.

"I'm not one to embrace unrealistic expectations. I thought you knew that of me. It's one of the reasons I've entertained your suit. But I want to be clear on some things. If you marry me, I'm well aware we'll have the kind of marriage where you indulge in your… your… masculine pleasures. But I refuse to let you keep any of your women under the same roof as me. If a servant takes your fancy, set her up in her own apartment. I don't want her with us."

He dropped the books onto the sofa with a crash and turned. "You misunderstand. I fully intend to be faithful to you."

She quirked an eyebrow, much like Rebekah always accused him of doing. Did the gesture look so arrogant when he managed it?

"Then what was that little…" She waved her hand as though shooing away a mosquito. "…Incident the other night with the pretty servant?"

How could she think so little of them? Of their relationship? Of the hours he'd spent pursuing her over the past month? "Rebekah's a friend."

"Since when does a man such as you consider servants to be his friends?"

The room grew suddenly hot, and he shoved his hands into his pockets to hide the fists he couldn't keep himself from forming. "You forget my father started his business in Eagle Harbor. The town there isn't nearly as diverse as Chicago. I've known Rebekah all my life, attended school with both her and her brothers." This probably wasn't the time to explain that Rebekah's brother had wed his former fiancée. Or saved Gilbert's life.

"Lying is another thing I won't tolerate in our relationship." Marianne opened a fan with the snap of her wrist and fanned her face furiously.

"I'm not lying." He stalked toward her.

"You are. Your brother stopped by today and told me everything." Swish, swish, swish went the fan. "How you've been dallying with that girl for years and visiting her whenever you're in Eagle Harbor."

Warren had been to visit Marianne? Of course he had, because lying to the police wasn't enough, evidently.

"I've never dallied with Rebekah. She, of all people, wouldn't stand to be treated that way. Warren's the one lying." Gilbert hadn't given Marianne any details regarding his fight with Warren. There were some things a gentleman simply didn't discuss with a lady, but maybe he should have been more direct. "Warren tried to force himself on Rebekah while the rest of us were gathered in the drawing room. I barely stopped it."

Marianne's forehead drew down into a frown while she continued to bat her fan. "No. She propositioned Warren, and you found out about it. That's why you got into a fight."

One visit from Warren, and Marianne believed the worst? Gilbert opened his mouth to deny it, but what was the point? She didn't seem inclined to believe anything else he'd said. "Let me guess, Warren explained that part as well when he called on you earlier."

How was it his brother and father could both lie so convincingly, and he couldn't even get the woman he'd spent the past month pursuing to believe the truth? "I swear to you, Marianne, there's nothing besides friendship between Rebekah Cummings and me."

Friendship. And kisses. Afternoons spent sailing at the lake, evenings aboard ship staring up at the stars, and confessions of love.

Marianne's swishing fan slowed, but he didn't offer more in his defense, just stood there. He wasn't going to explain about Aileen when the woman had begged him to keep quiet, and if Marianne wouldn't take his word over Warren's, then was there any point in marrying her?

Marianne swallowed and met his gaze. "Well, what I said still stands. If we marry, it will be more of a business partnership than a relationship. I understand you'll want some masculine entertainment from time to time. To be honest, I'd prefer that you took it, as I consider it my duty to bear you children and nothing more. But I won't have you bring your women into my house or introduce them to our children."

"Let me understand something." He would have shouted, but an emptiness opened inside him, cold and dark. He was suddenly too tired to yell. Too tired to demand she believe him. Too tired to care one way or the other. "Once we wed, you don't even want me to be faithful to you?"

She raised a shoulder. "My brothers have arrangements such as the one I described. It works well for them."

He rubbed at his temples. This was what he wanted, wasn't it? A marriage that was a business arrangement rather than a relationship. A marriage that would meet society's expectations and further his business endeavors. Marianne had no romantic notions or false hope regarding what their marriage would be. She only wanted things to appear ideal to everybody else, much the same as he did.

She would make him the perfect wife. If that hadn't been clear before, it was abundantly so now.

So why did his dreams suddenly feel so empty?

~.~.~.~.~

The door creaked as Elijah let himself out into the warm evening air. Crickets and toads chirped evening's song, and the sun slanted low over the water, a big ball of orange that tinged everything it touched with gold.

He breathed in the scent of lake mixed with forest and headed toward the boulders that lined the shore. He may have made peace with Victoria about trying to do too much and needing to stay still and rest while his arm healed, but that didn't mean he cottoned to being an invalid for five and a half more weeks.

If Doc Harrington knew what he was up to, he'd probably have a lecture or ten coming about not climbing rocks with a broken arm, but Rebekah had climbed over the rocks and disappeared before dinner, and he'd barely had a chance to talk to her since she'd arrived home yesterday. He balanced himself on the first rock and then stepped onto the second. Of course Rebekah couldn't have plopped herself down on one of the rocks near the house, that would be too easy for his sister.

He followed the shore for a quarter hour or better, though the climb would have taken half the time if he didn't have to worry over his arm. The water spread before him, as clear and flat as the panes of glass in the cabin's windows, while the setting sun burned a solitary strip of orange across an expanse of grayish-blue. But when he reached the big pile of rocks that lay west of their house, he had to stop. Rebekah would be just on the other side of it, in the little nook carved out by time and wind and waves. It was where she'd always disappeared as a child. Had even gone through a spell where she'd dragged Gilbert Sinclair there to fish, though that was a decade or so back.

But how was he going to climb atop it with one hand, let alone get down the other side?

He scratched his head. Maybe he should just call for Rebekah. Except that might give her a mind to set off farther down the beach rather than—

"Are you trying to get yourself killed?" Rebekah appeared at the top of the pile, standing on the uppermost rock as she scowled down at him.

"I was looking for you."

She started toward him, flitting from rock to rock as though she was a bird with wings to aid her. "If I tried climbing these rocks with a broken arm, you'd haul me over your shoulder, drag me to the cabin, and tie me to the couch for a fortnight."

So he would. "Only because I love you. Only because I wouldn't want harm to come to you."

She came to a stop on the rock beside him, her throat working back and forth as she searched his face.

Was that a tear brimming in her eye? His sister who never cried? Maybe he should have hauled her down to the beach last night so they could have gotten their talking done.

"I love you too," she spoke into the air between them. "And I don't want you hurt just the same as you don't want me hurt."

He settled a hand on her shoulder and drew her into a one-armed hug. "So we're even then."

"Only if you get back off these rocks safely. You must have been climbing for a half hour."

"I'm not that much of a cripple. Besides, I figured the climbing would be worth it once I found you."

"I don't need you to come rescue me."

"I came because I wanted to talk, not because I was worried."

"Oh." She grew still again, which was strange, because *Rebekah* and *still* were two words he'd never put together before she left. "What did you want to talk about?"

Everything. Why she left. Why she came home. What she'd seen and done and learned in the time between. But he settled for, "I'm glad you're back."

Her chin trembled, and the strange moisture in her eyes that might have been tears earlier was back, about to crest. "Oh, Elijah. I never should have left."

She threw her arms around him, causing him to take a step back and wince as she pressed against his arm.

She didn't seem to notice, just hugged him tighter as she spoke into his chest. "I'm too stubborn by half. I don't know why you put up with me."

Rebekah was, in fact, too stubborn by half. And though he might have dreamed about his sister finally giving up her stubborn ways countless times over the years, he'd never envisioned her sobbing in his arms as she did so.

"I try to control too many things, and all I end up doing is making a mess of them. I never prayed about leaving Eagle Harbor, and I didn't tell you what I was planning because I knew you wouldn't like it. I was like Jonah, supposed to be going to Nineveh but then running in the opposite direction. Oh, I wanted to leave, all right. Even thought I needed to. You needed money for the roof and general store, and I was one more mouth to feed. Our fish were hardly bringing anything in, and after I tried to go on that rescue with you, you made it sound like you didn't want my help anymore."

She pulled back from him and raised her head so that their eyes met. "But I only made a bigger mess of things in Chicago. Instead of earning money for the family, I brought back two other women, both of which have no money and need help. And now I find that you've taken on extra work while I was gone and Victoria organized a work day for our house and…"

"Rebekah, you're part of the family. We'll always need your help, and I'm sorry if I made you think otherwise." He patted her shoulder in the soothing way he used to back when she'd been young and scared of thunderstorms. "I don't want you to go on my shipwreck rescues, but only because I want to keep you safe. In every other area, I want your help, need it, even."

"That's what Gilbert said."

It was? Since when did he agree with Sinclair?

She looked out at the lake, still bright and fiery beneath the setting sun. "I tell myself that I don't need to listen to others. Like when Pa drowned. I tell myself over and over that if I just would have ignored Mac and Isaac telling me to stay ashore and gone out to rescue him, he'd still be alive today."

She blamed herself? "Rebekah, no. I…"

She held up a hand, and he paused. "I tell myself that my way is always best, that I don't need to listen to others, and sometimes I get so set on my own plans that I don't even listen to God. That's what happened in Chicago. I was so determined that my way was right that I ended up making a mess of everything."

He shook his head. "I might not know everything that happened in Chicago, but you brought two hurting women to a place they can be cared for. That's not making a mess." And if he'd proposed to one of them five years ago and the other one fled the room whenever he entered, well, those were other matters entirely. Both Aileen and Lindy needed help, and he wasn't going to complain about giving it.

Though he could muster up a complaint or two about being the only man in a house full of five women.

Rebekah blinked furiously, trying to hold back tears.

He'd expected she would return home full of fight and determination, with stories of all the things she'd seen and heard and done. He'd never expected her to come back broken because she'd left without consulting God. "I'd wager bringing Lindy and Aileen here was part of God's plan. It might be the reason He had you go to Chicago in the first place, even if you didn't pray before you left—or leave in the best manner."

"Yes, I suppose I helped them." She sniffled and wiped away a tear with the back of her hand. "But that still doesn't make up for what I did to Gilbert."

Elijah's stomach clenched at the sound of that name on his sister's lips. "What did you do to Sinclair?" Did he even want to hear her answer?

"I just wanted him to realize that he was worth being loved. His family, they're terrible to him. He might have money, but he's never known what a family should be. And he's convinced he has to marry an heiress to replace the money he lost when the *Beaumont* went down and put his crane into production. I tried telling him he's going to be miserable married to her, but…"

She swiped at her face with the back of her hand again, his strong sister that was more likely to pull out her fishing knife and threaten to gut a person than cry. "He wouldn't listen, and why should he? Who am I to tell him not to marry someone? That love is more important than helping people? Gilbert will probably do just fine married to Marianne, and then he'll have the money he needs to finish his crane so people like Lindy's dad and Aileen's brother don't get killed, and everything will work out perfect for him, like it always does."

Cranes and Aileen's brother and Lindy's dad? Elijah didn't understand half of what Rebekah had just said, but one thing was clear. "If everything will work out perfectly, then why are you crying?"

"Because… because…" Tears coursed freely down her cheeks. "I don't want to talk about it."

A sick sensation filled his gut, his heart, his head. His sister had gone and fallen in love with Gilbert Sinclair. Though he might have found his own happy married life with Victoria, something told him there wouldn't be a happy ending to Gilbert and Rebekah's story, especially not if Sinclair was engaged to this Marianne person.

But happy ending or not, there was one thing he could tell his sister to do. "So pray. Ask God to forgive you, and He will. It's as simple as that. He forgave Jonah for heading away from Nineveh, didn't He? He gave Jonah a second chance to go back and obey. What's to say He won't do the same for you?"

Rebekah wiped away another bout of tears and offered a trembling smile. "It's as simple as that, isn't it? I've been trying to pray more lately, but I still seem to be rushing headlong into everything and making a bunch of mistakes."

"Don't be too hard on yourself. Nobody's perfect. I know I've sure made my share of mistakes this summer."

She sighed. "You're right, and maybe I'll stay here and pray a little longer, if you don't mind walking back by yourself."

And so he left his little sister there, sitting on the rock, her head bowed as she beseeched the Master of the Universe to forgive her and direct her steps.

Chapter Twenty-One

A hundred dollars. Rebekah stared at the series of twenty dollar bills that had been tucked inside her carpetbag's pocket along with a small note.

In the event you, Lindy, or Aileen need anything. Gilbert.

It was enough for the three of them to eat on for half a year, and it would also purchase boots, scarves, and other winter clothes for Lindy and Aileen. Rebekah slid the money into the pocket of her skirt and stowed her carpetbag under the bed in the loft where the three of them slept.

She should have known Gilbert would do this. Should have searched the bag before he'd loaded it onto the train. Though that was probably when he'd slipped the money inside, giving her no way of refusing.

And why was she so adamant about refusing anyway? Last week on the beach with Elijah, she'd been worried about the strain she, Lindy, and Aileen would put on the family's finances. Now she didn't have to worry, at least not for the next few months. And since both Lindy and Aileen had gone looking for jobs today, she might not need to worry at all.

Rebekah leaned forward and rested her forehead on the side of the bed. Why did Gilbert have to be so kind? It was much easier to envision him married to Marianne when he acted arrogant and selfish. But when he went out of his way to give her a hundred dollars, how could she not love him?

No. She wasn't going down that path anymore. She'd been home for a full week now, and she was done crying about Gilbert. Done thinking about him. She'd turned the situation over to God, and she was waiting on Him to guide her steps. The only thing she knew for certain was that those steps wouldn't take her back to Chicago and Gilbert Sinclair.

And that was fine with her.

Or rather, she wanted it to be fine with her.

Oh, if she was working so hard at turning things over to God, then why was she having such trouble moving past Gilbert? He'd probably not spared her a thought since she'd left and had likely put a ring on Marianne's finger by now.

What had Gilbert told her that night they'd looked at the stars? *Love isn't something you helplessly fall into. It's something that grows out of mutual respect, often aided by shared living arrangements, and it's hardly necessary for a marriage.*

Song of Solomon might claim that many waters couldn't quench love, and floods couldn't drown it, but King Solomon had evidently never met Gilbert Sinclair. The man was cold enough to freeze love and snap it like an icicle in winter.

Except for when he wasn't cold. Except for when he gave her a hundred dollars, and went to the police station with her, and believed the words of a servant over the claims of his own brother.

Rebekah gulped back a silent sob, swallowing thickly instead of letting out the wail that welled in her chest. She had to be done mooning over Gilbert. Now. Today. This very instant. He was doubtlessly moving on with his life in Chicago, and how could she let God direct her future when she was still stuck in the past?

She needed to move forward. Find something to occupy her.

No, she was still getting things wrong. She didn't need to move at all. She needed to wait. And pray. And pray some more.

Dear God, forgive me for getting so caught up in my feelings for Gilbert. Direct my steps and show me what you would have me do here in—

A knock sounded downstairs, then the creak of the door opening and the thumping of boots on the kitchen floor.

"Have you come to let me out of this sling?" Elijah called.

"Has it been six weeks?" Sarcasm tinged Dr. Harrington's southern accent.

Now there was a man who always seemed happy to see her. Seth Harrington always had a fond smile for her on his face and a soft look in his eyes. Rebekah placed a hand over her pocket just to make sure the money from Gilbert was really there, then climbed down the ladder from the loft.

Dr. Harrington already had the bandage off Elijah's arm. His eyes came up to meet hers as she approached, warm and green like dandelion stems in a field. "Rebekah. It's good to have you back."

A faint heat stole over her cheeks. "Thank you."

"And wearing a skirt, no less."

She glanced down at her blue and white calico dress. Donning skirts like every other woman in town had seemed the thing to do when she returned home, especially since she didn't have the excuse of fishing with Elijah to justify wearing trousers.

"My arm, Doc." Elijah raised his forearm, then winced. "You're here to tend my arm, not make eyes at my sister."

"But your sister is much lovelier to look at." The doctor's green eyes never left her as he spoke.

The faint heat in her cheeks began to burn in full. "How's my brother's arm?"

But her question didn't seem to distract the doctor. His eyes took on a knowing little gleam, and he winked at her before going back to Elijah. "The bone appears to be healing straight. Not much else to do but wrap it, keep it still, and wait until that six weeks is up."

"Three weeks, Doc. Three weeks," Elijah grumbled. "It'll be healed by then."

"You'll only make your arm worse if you use it before the bone is healed and strong." Dr. Harrington deftly wrapped the bandage back around Elijah's arm and placed it in the sling.

Eagle Harbor was fortunate to have a doctor like him, even if some of the older folk preferred the drunken Dr. Greely instead. Which brought her to another matter. "One of my friends from Chicago has a cough. I was hoping you could see to her, but she's out looking for work this afternoon."

Dr. Harrington—or maybe she should be calling him Seth?— closed his medical bag and straightened. "She can stop by the office any time. As can you. You know, Tillie is leaving in another week or so. Her husband wants to try his hand at mining rather than dock work. I'm in need of a nurse."

"You think I'd make a good nurse?" She could well imagine herself getting mad at one of his patients and pouring a bowl of steaming soup on his head rather than spoon feeding him.

But would God want her to try nursing? It was as stubborn to refuse an opportunity that presented itself as it was to force her way into the middle of situations. And she'd just been praying for God to direct her steps. Maybe after a week of such prayers, He was finally answering.

Seth stepped away from Elijah and bent his head until his lips were beside her ear. "A good nurse, perhaps. But I think you'd make a better wife."

"Oh." She dropped her gaze to the ground. She wanted this, didn't she? To move past Gilbert and start a family of her own? But Seth was so kind and gentle. She still had the inkling she'd trample him in any relationship they had.

"I... I don't think I'd make you a good wife at all," she whispered back.

"Rebekah, why don't you walk Dr. Harrington outside?" Elijah's voice echoed overly loud in the room. "Then I don't have to sit here and watch you two whisper and smile at each other."

"Shall we?" Seth winked at her again and offered his arm, leading her through the kitchen and entryway before stepping onto the porch.

The breeze off the water was a bit cool, the waves forming tiny whitecaps before washing into the rocks. She inhaled the clean scent of lake and forest that she'd missed so much while she was gone.

Seth set down his medical bag and laid his hand over hers on his arm. "I think you'd do fine if you gave yourself a chance."

She'd do fine? "Are you talking about working for you or being your wife?"

"Both. Will you at least let me call on you?" The corner of his mouth tipped up into a lopsided, relaxed smile.

Gilbert's smiles were never lopsided or relaxed.

And why was she thinking about Gilbert, who was either engaged or soon to be so? One thing God had shown her over the summer was that He wanted her in Eagle Harbor for now—which was where Seth Harrington happened to live. She couldn't deny he'd make a good husband. The only question was, would he make *her* a good husband?

What if he would? What if, in her stubbornness, she'd dismissed his request to write letters too quickly when she'd left at the end of June? What if she wasn't giving either of them a fair chance to see how their relationship developed?

That verse from Song of Solomon said a whole lot about love not being quenched or bought. But it didn't say anything about how love started. What if it started slowly? With small smiles and simple questions? What if sparking with Seth was part of God's plan for her?

She squeezed Seth's hand back and blew out a long, slow breath. "I'd like it if you called on me. A lot, actually."

~.~.~.~.~

Gilbert stared at the papers spread over the desk in his bedroom, not drawings of his crane or an analysis of friction drums or pistons, but business projections of a different sort.

A soft knock sounded on the door, and he pulled his gaze away from the papers. "Come in."

His mother stepped inside, her posture perfect as she crossed the room to him. "I thought you'd be headed to—"

"I canceled. One of the footmen delivered a message to the Mellars about an hour ago."

Her forehead puckered. "You haven't seen Marianne in a week and a half."

It was an honest statement, infused with curiosity rather than the accusation that had rung through Father's voice yesterday when he'd asked why Gilbert had suddenly stopped calling on Marianne.

"It's been a week."

Mother blinked at him.

"She came by the office a week ago today and said that Warren had paid a call." His jaw clenched at the memory, but he wasn't about to repeat what Marianne had said regarding him and Rebekah.

Mother sat in the armchair opposite his desk, her back as straight as the posters on his bed. "I don't think that's the only call your brother's paid on her."

It wasn't? A sickness churned in his gut, though he shouldn't be surprised. If Warren had paid one call on Marianne, what stopped him from paying a second or a third? It wasn't as though Marianne was betrothed.

But she could be.

If he wanted to marry her. If he hadn't ignored her for the past week. If he could muster up the will to care about a woman who thought him unfaithful and wasn't bothered by it. Gilbert stared at the papers in front of him and shook his head. "I can't face her, Mother. I just... can't."

Mother folded her bony hands tightly in her lap. "She would be a good match for you, would bring the money you need into your marriage."

"I know." He forced the words out of his suddenly dry throat.

"Then why did you cancel dinner?"

Why, indeed. He blew out a breath, long and hopeless. If only emptying his lungs of air would give him the answers he needed. "I don't love her."

Mother grew stiffer yet, straightening her neck until her collarbone stuck out from the neckline of her dress. "What does love have to do with it?"

Everything, evidently, and he may as well tell her, because after spending a restless week tossing and turning and unable to think about anything or anyone other than Rebekah, he'd reached the end of his wits. Did Rebekah know the havoc she'd wreaked on his life? She'd ruined not just his feelings for Marianne, but all that incessant rambling about love not being quenched or bought had somehow changed his feelings about marriage itself.

Gilbert set his papers down on his desk and looked straight at his mother. "I don't want a marriage like you and Father have."

Then what kind of marriage do you want? She didn't need to speak for him to read the question written in her eyes.

One like Hiram and Mabel Cummings's.

She'd laugh at him if he voiced it. He was part owner in a shipping company. How foolish was he to yearn for something a poor fisherman had?

But if he was letting God's Word guide his decisions, maybe he wasn't entirely foolish. "I love Rebekah Cummings. That's why I can't marry Marianne."

"Oh." The stiffness collapsed from Mother's spine, and she sank back in the chair.

Had he stunned her so badly she'd forgotten propriety? That was probably the first time in her life. "You think I'm a fool, don't you?"

But rather than agree like Father or Warren would have, something soft flitted over Mother's face. "I… I like Rebekah. She's smart, firm, a hard worker, a good thinker."

"She's also poor." No need to pretend that didn't matter.

"Are you going to marry her and ask your father for the money you need then?"

"You aren't going to try to talk me out of it?"

Mother paused for a moment, as though unsure of what she should say. "I don't know. You're a smart man, Gilbert, with a good head on your shoulders. And you're old enough to make your own decisions. If you weren't, then this crane of yours wouldn't exist."

"It doesn't exist now," he muttered.

But he understood what she meant. If he was going to let father control his every choice the way Warren did, then his idea for the crane would have stayed just that—an idea. It never would have been drawn on paper, let alone built the first time.

"Father won't give me the money I need. As soon as he saw I'd set my sights on Marianne, he started salivating. 'What a good team we'd make, the Sinclairs and Mellars.'" He deepened his voice to sound like Father when he talked business. "'Maybe Mellar would give us a couple of his shipping routes, and we could expand our holdings as far as Lake Ontario.'" Gilbert shook his head. "No, if I pursue Rebekah over Marianne, Father will push Warren toward her. He's probably the one telling Warren to call on her now. Then his goals can be accomplished with the golden son, the shipping heir."

And he'd be left behind. Again.

"Not quite so golden." Mother's sharp words echoed through the bedchamber.

Gilbert glanced up. It was unlike Mother to speak ill of Warren, even when he deserved it. Had Mother's opinion of her perfect oldest son fallen? She kept her chin raised, her eyes flat and bored, her face void of any expression. But she had gone out of her way to care for Aileen even though the Irishwoman had never admitted to being forced.

Perhaps she'd finally gotten tired of pretending Warren was perfect.

"So what are you going to do?" Mother asked, her hands still clenched tightly in her lap.

He looked down at the papers spread across his desk, then handed the first two pages to her. "I'd like to somehow get my hands on sixteen thousand dollars and put my crane into production. I have business projections, and after a year, I should be able to—"

"Start a charity to benefit injured dockworkers and their

families." Mother gazed intently at the papers. "It's a fabulous idea. I wish your father had done something like this long ago."

He gave a short, hard laugh. "Father only cares about pouring more profits into Great Northern Shipping."

"But not you."

No. Not him. "How do I choose? Which is more important? Rebekah, or setting up this charity?"

The Bible had verses about love, sure, but it also had verses about giving. *He that hath pity on the poor lendeth unto the Lord.* Along with, *Give, and it shall be given unto you; good measure, pressed down, and shaken together, and running over, shall men give into your bosom. For with the same measure that ye mete withal it shall be measured to you again.* He'd spent the past week scouring them.

Mother rose slowly from her chair and handed him the papers. "I don't think you need to choose between one or the other, son. You need to figure out a way you can have both, even if you take a different path than you were planning to get them."

A different path? What if there was only one path? He'd been agonizing over the situation all week. He had to choose one or the other.

Mother's slippers were whisper soft on the carpet as she headed toward the door.

"That's it? No other advice? I don't know of a path that lets me have both my charity and Rebekah."

"This from the man who thwarted his father about getting an engineering degree rather than a business one? From the man who spends more time in Eagle Harbor than Chicago where his father would like him to be? From the man who designed and built a crane without any support from his family? If you can't figure out a way to have the woman you love and your machine, then maybe you don't deserve either of them." She closed the door behind her with a thunk, leaving Gilbert to stare down at his business projection.

He'd been over it a thousand times in his mind. It was one or the other. If another possibility was there, surely he would have seen it by now.

But what if the solution wasn't as clear or logical as he thought? He liked understanding things, how they worked and why. How engines pumped and steam hoists got their power. How the wind over the water caused waves to form and how gravity equaled mass times weight.

What if God had a better plan, and he was so busy trying to force his own plan on everybody else that he'd overlooked the best plan?

God, what am I missing? If there's another way, show me, and I'll listen. We don't have to do things my way. He stared down at his business projection as an idea took shape.

Maybe he couldn't have both Rebekah and his crane, but what if he could have both Rebekah and his charity? He sucked in a breath as a plan burst across his thoughts.

The pieces had been there all along, in the recesses of his mind, just waiting to be put together. Or maybe his stubbornness had been blinding him to the possibility this whole time.

But it wouldn't be easy, not for him, and not for the others involved.

Could he make the sacrifice this idea would require?

Could he give up his crane?

Chapter Twenty-Two

"I have a surprise for you."

Rebekah flipped the fish sizzling over the fire on the beach filled with people and turned to find Seth standing beside her. "A surprise?"

"Sure is delicious, Rebekah." Ian Fletcher muttered around a mouthful of fish.

"Yes, you'll have to tell me how you season these potatoes." Ellie Spritzer popped one of the wedges in her mouth.

"Family secret, I'm afraid. No telling allowed." Rebekah slid the pan of fish off the fire and wrapped the fillets in brown paper before placing the hot pieces in the basket that would soon be taken to the serving table. A small crowd had gathered around her now, which was nothing unusual for any of their beach gatherings, whether it be a formal event or just a shindig.

But since this was the annual Thimbleberry Festival, the beach was far more crowded than usual. People milled along the sand from the north end of the harbor to the south, buying goods, playing games, and participating in any number of competitions. Some of the backwoodsmen who made their homes inland journeyed to town to sell their wares at the festival, and groups from the Central and Delaware mines always flooded the town as well.

"I'm going to steal her for a bit, I'm afraid." Seth rested a hand on her shoulder. "Isaac plans to take your spot." Seth nodded toward the edge of the crowd where Isaac talked to Mr. Foley as they walked toward the fire pit.

"Steal me?" That was the surprise? "Why?"

Seth's eyes danced, and he tapped a finger on her nose. "I told you, it's a surprise."

Something large fisted in her stomach. He wasn't going to propose, was he?

She'd enjoyed his suit well enough over the past couple weeks. He wasn't much for fishing, but they'd gone for their share of walks, and he'd come to dinner one evening. Yet he seemed rather serious about their relationship, while she was still…

Mooning over Gilbert.

She smoothed a strand of hair away from her sweaty face and concentrated on placing more fish into the pan above the fire. How long would it take her to move past Gilbert? He was likely married by now, and if not that, then betrothed.

Was he happy with Marianne?

Did she want him to be?

No doubt it was petty to wish him a dismal future full of contention with his wife, but she wasn't exactly ready to smile at the thought of him marrying another woman, either.

Would he one day regret setting her aside for Marianne?

Probably not. Gilbert made his decisions with too much methodical calculation to regret anything. Ever.

"Rebekah?"

She glanced away from the fish and over at Seth, who looked at her expectantly. Had he asked a question?

"Move over, sister." Isaac grabbed the spatula from her hand. "I can manage as well as you."

She snorted. Isaac wasn't as good a cook as she was, though he wasn't half bad. "I like doing the cooking."

"You'll like what I have planned more." Seth extended his arm to her.

She looked up into his expectant gaze and stifled a sigh. Whatever he had planned, she wouldn't be able to duck out of it without hurting him.

Please don't propose.

She laid her hand in the crook of his arm and let him lead her away from the fire.

Maybe she was going about things wrong. Maybe she needed to tell him about Gilbert and explain that she still had feelings for someone else—even if the man she loved was marrying another woman.

Oh, why didn't that verse in Song of Solomon say something about how love started? Was she wrong for accepting Seth's suit? How would she know whether their relationship would grow into love if she told him not to call?

"Is something wrong?" Seth leaned closer to her, causing the increasingly familiar scent of bergamot to tease her nose.

If only she knew how to answer that.

"Have you purchased any thimbleberry jam yet?" She gestured toward the booths set up on the sand near Front Street. "Mrs. Kainner's is always the best."

"Of course. Though I'm partial to Mrs. Foley's jam myself."

Seth led her away from the water, where children were gathering for the sand castle competition, and through the milling people toward Front Street.

They passed the area marked off for the logging contest that would be starting in a half hour or so, and a group of men had met at the far end of the beach for a horseshoe match sure to run long into the evening.

"Are we going to get a pie? Is that your surprise?" Those were mostly thimbleberry as well, though blueberries, raspberries, and blackberries were in abundance this time of year.

"No pie." He led her past the booths and onto the road.

"Then where are we going?" She looked over her shoulder at the festival. "I'd like to see Mac and Elijah in the log splitting contest. And I think Isaac has a booth for his toys set up. I haven't had the chance to—"

"Do you trust me or not?" Seth's voice was smooth and gentle, as though she were an unhappy patient he was trying to calm.

"Ah..." Yet another question she didn't know how to answer. Did she trust him to be a gentleman? Yes. Did she trust he wouldn't propose? That he wasn't more invested in their relationship than she was? Not at all.

"Yes," she muttered. "I trust you." She didn't want to think about what would happen if she gave him the other answer.

But maybe that was the answer she needed to give. Maybe she needed to tell him to take things slower, that he was more interested in her than she was in him. She blew out a breath. How was she making such a big mess of things with Seth? She hadn't rushed into anything with him, had been praying about him the whole two weeks they'd been courting. And it seemed as though God had led her right to Seth, or rather, that God had led Seth right to her when he'd walked into their cabin to check on Elijah's arm.

So how had she gotten herself in this predicament?

They walked along in silence, Seth probably assuming it was the comfortable kind, even though the desire to squirm away from him kept crawling into her chest. They followed the road to the hill on which the cemetery sat on the outside of town, the

Thimbleberry Festival growing more distant with each step.

"Will you tell me where you're taking me now?" Surely not to visit her father's grave in the middle of the festival. "I don't always do well with surprises."

He patted the top of her hand—probably another thing he did with contrary patients. "On a picnic. Isaac told me about your family's favorite spot on the river, and I thought it would be perfect for a picnic."

"Oh." And in all of Isaac's yacking about their fishing spot, evidently her brother had forgotten to mention how much she liked the Thimbleberry Festival and how she wouldn't want to miss it for a picnic she could go on at any point during the summer.

But picnics were always nice, especially ones on the river where they could fish—as long as Seth didn't propose. She swallowed. Maybe the picnic would be a good opportunity to tell him about her feelings, or lack thereof.

Or maybe she should tell him on the way?

The breeze toyed with wisps of her hair as they walked. The sky above was a cloudless, brilliant blue, the afternoon just hot enough for the children at the festival to splash in the water, but not so hot that everyone dripped with sweat—unless they'd been standing over the cook fire like her.

Did she really want to ruin the afternoon?

They crested the hill, and there, beneath the oak that stood at the edge of the cemetery, was a picnic hamper with a blanket folded over the top. He'd obviously put a lot of effort into today, and what was the likelihood he'd propose after only two weeks of courtship? Besides, she didn't want to stop seeing him, just to make sure they were both expecting the same things from each other. She'd let him take her on the picnic, and sometime next week she'd—

"Doc Harrington." Elijah's voice rang out from behind them.

She turned to find her older brother jogging up the hill.

"I'm sorry, but you need to come. Mrs. Ranulfson fainted, and Doc Greely's away attending a birth."

Seth's hand tightened atop hers for the briefest of instants. "I'm sorry, Rebekah. This shouldn't take too long. Why don't you take the hamper and head to the river without me?"

"I…" *Want to go back to the Thimbleberry Festival.* But she kept her mouth shut. His shoulders were already slumped, his eyes missing a bit of the life that had been dancing in them a minute ago. Seth Harrington spent every day of his life serving other people. The least she could do was make sure the picnic he'd planned turned out well. "Sure. I'll go on ahead."

⁻.⁻.⁻.⁻.⁻

The Thimbleberry Festival. Of all the times for him to return to Eagle Harbor, it had to be during the annual festival.

Gilbert worked his way through the crowd. Rebekah had to be here somewhere, but how to find a woman as short as her amid two hundred people? He scanned the people standing near Front Street, where various booths featured everything from homemade blankets and quilts to jams and pies—most of the foodstuffs being thimbleberry. But Rebekah's auburn hair and pale skin didn't appear there. A quick glance at the group of men throwing horseshoes near the pier told him she wasn't there either. He headed toward the several dozen onlookers gathered around the log-splitting contest.

An ax blade rose high in the air, glinting silver in the afternoon sun before it descended at breathtaking speed. *Thwack!* Gilbert shuddered and looked away. If he took up an ax and swung like that, he'd be lucky if he only lost his big toe.

"Mama, look at me!"

"Ah! That's cold."

Gilbert glanced at the group of children wading and splashing in the shallow water.

"Tell Johnny to stop splashing!"

No sign of Rebekah there.

Regardless, he shouldered his way nearer to the children, where it was less crowded. Most of them were busy building sandcastles for the competition, each child attempting to earn one of the ribbons that would be given for the best three castles.

Would his own children participate one day? He'd won every year he'd entered. Turrets and towers and moats with drawbridges. Who needed a normal castle constructed from a pail and damp sand when there were so many different structures one could build?

Not that his father had ever cared.

Gilbert turned his back on the children and headed into the thick of the crowd again. Rebekah usually took her turn frying fish. Maybe she was there. But when he reached the small fire over which fish and potatoes cooked, a quick glance told him Isaac Cummings, Rebekah's twin, was the one cooking.

"Gilbert." Mr. Foley stopped beside him. "Tell me your cargo hold is full of boots."

"Boots?" Gilbert barely looked at the mercantile owner as he stood on his toes and searched the crowd. Where could she be?

"I sent word to your father about needing more boots for the winter. We'll be through what Fletcher has stored in the warehouse by the end of November."

"I'm sure my father's looking into it." Though he'd heard nothing of the sort. Still, if Foley was prepared to purchase a shipment of boots, then one would be arriving shortly. Father never turned down a business opportunity. "Has Elijah paid for his half of the damages to your store from our fight in May?"

Mr. Foley's mouth opened, then closed. "I'm not sure that's any of your business, son."

"I assume that means no. I'll be by in the morning to pay his part of the bill. If that means there's money left over, put it on his tab." He scanned the crowd for Rebekah once more, then turned back to see Mr. Foley staring at him as though his brain had left his body and jumped into the water somewhere between Chicago and Eagle Harbor.

But he'd given it thought. Paying his portion of the bill had been as simple as drawing breath for him, but Elijah would probably need to pick up extra work for half a year to pay the same debt. It only seemed right he pay Elijah's half.

And since that was settled... "Have you seen Rebekah Cummings?"

"I... ah... Rebekah?" Mr. Foley blinked at him. "I thought she was cooking." He glanced at the cook fire, then turned around in a circle. "Don't see her. Maybe she went on a walk with the doc."

A walk with the doc? Why would Rebekah be on a walk with Dr. Greely? Or did Mr. Foley mean Dr. Harrington?

Gilbert's throat tightened. Tall and blond with a cultured southern accent, the young doctor would be a fool not to pursue Rebekah. And she'd be a fool not to consider him. "Where did they walk to?"

"I didn't say they went for one. It was just an idea." Mr. Foley looked at him, his brow wrinkled for a moment, then his face broke into a smile. "So that's the way of it? You got feelings for the Cummings girl?" He slapped Gilbert on the back. "Better hurry and catch her then."

Feelings? The word didn't begin to describe the sleepless nights he'd endured since figuring out how he could marry her, or the way his palms grew damp at the mere thought of explaining himself to her after how he'd left her at the train station. But he wasn't about to admit anything in a small town filled with gossips.

He hardened his jaw and gave Mr. Foley a deliberately cold stare. "I simply need to talk to Rebekah. That's all."

"Sure ya' do." Mr. Foley kept a goofy grin plastered across his face. "You might try seeing if one of her friends from Chicago knows where she is." He pointed toward the group gathered around the log-splitting contest, where Lindy stood at the front of the crowd, her gaze riveted to the two men swinging axes.

"Thank you." He headed back through the throng. And if he pretended like he didn't hear Mrs. Kainner when she called to him, well, who could blame him for not wanting to spend a half hour talking to one of the gossips he was trying to avoid?

"Lindy." He came up beside her. "Have you seen Rebekah?"

"I think she…" Lindy pulled her gaze away from the contest and glanced at him. "Gilbert? Aren't you supposed to be in Chicago?"

"I am, but…"

A cheer from the crowd drowned out his words, and he turned to see Mac Oakton placing his last log on the chopping block while his opponent still had half a dozen remaining in his pile.

"I wince every time I see him swing." Lindy coughed, but the sound was soft and light, nothing like the murky, wet coughs that had plagued her lungs a month earlier. "What if he misses the log?"

Exactly. But he wasn't there to watch Mac Oakton cut off his leg—or win the contest, whichever happened first. "I asked where Rebekah was."

She blinked. "Rebekah? She went… Oh! You're looking for Rebekah!" A wide smile spread across her face. "You came here for her, didn't you?" She sprang up onto the balls of her feet and clapped her hands. "I knew you were more than friends. I just knew it!"

More than friends. Sure. Great. Fine.

He nearly reached out and gripped Lindy's shoulders, but settled for clenching his hands at his sides instead. "Just tell me where she is."

"Oh." The smile dropped from her face. "You want to know where she is?"

"Yes."

"As in, where she is right now?" Her voice squeaked on the last word.

"Correct."

"Um…" She slanted her gaze away. "Well, it's… complicated."

"No, it isn't." Did he look like he was in the mood to play games? "I'm looking for Rebekah. You know where she is. Now tell me."

Lindy bit the side of her lip. "I heard something about her going to some fishing spot on the river."

Fishing on the river. He knew exactly where she was, had spent far too many an afternoon there with her a decade past. He started toward Front Street and the woods that lay behind the town, barely hearing Lindy as she called after him.

"I don't think she'll be alone when you find her."

Chapter Twenty-Three

Seth hadn't packed a fishing rod. Who had a picnic on the river and didn't bring any fishing supplies?

Rebekah propped her head on her hands as she lay on her stomach across the red and white checkered picnic blanket and stared at the river.

Water raced along the narrow bed, clear and cold as it headed down the hill toward Lake Superior. Leafy shrubs surrounded the clearing, along with saplings that struggled for light beneath the dense canopy of leaves from older trees above. She drew in a breath of fresh, clean air, listening to the rushing of water over rocks in the otherwise silent woods.

How long had she been waiting, anyway? A half hour? An hour? Two? She rolled onto her back and stared through the foliage above her to the sky beyond, still bright blue with afternoon sunshine.

Maybe she didn't have the patience to make a good doctor's wife, even if she could move past her feelings for Gilbert. Seth needed someone who would wait for him with a smile on her face, not someone who stewed whenever he was called away.

Would it be wrong of her to leave? What had seemed like a simple call for Seth must have turned into something bigger, or he would have come by now. It wasn't her fault the picnic he'd put so much effort into hadn't worked out. Surely Seth would understand she didn't want to stay here by herself. She could stop by his office, see how Mrs. Ranulfson was faring, and let him know she'd grown tired of waiting. And she should also set up a time to talk to him— somewhere much less romantic than a picnic.

She sighed and stood to her feet, brushing off the bits of dirt that clung to her skirt even though she'd tried to stay on the blanket.

A twig snapped in the woods, followed by the faint thudding of footsteps. She paused in the midst of reaching for Seth's hamper.

But the man who appeared on the path wasn't Seth.

She froze. She'd known Gilbert would come back to Eagle Harbor, but did it have to be so soon? She wasn't ready to face him yet, especially not if he'd brought Marianne.

She looked around the clearing behind him, half expecting the raven-haired beauty to appear beside Gilbert. Had they already wed?

"Rebekah," Gilbert breathed, his chest rising and falling as though he'd run through the woods. "Thank goodness. Lindy said… I was worried that…"

He clamped his mouth shut and headed straight toward her, striding across the picnic blanket.

"W-what are you doing here?"

"I came for you." He reached out and rested a hand on her upper arm. "Because I love you."

He loved her? She took a step back, her heart thudding, all the emotion from the train station ramming into her as though she'd been hit by the engine that had carried her away from him.

The sun slanted over his golden hair and handsome face in little patches as it made its way through the leaves above, causing him to appear even more angelic than normal. She pressed her lips together as she surveyed him. A squirrel nattered from a nearby tree, frogs croaked, and the water rushed behind them.

"Say something. Anything." Confusion flitted in his beautiful blue eyes, and he tightened his grip on her arm. "Please?"

How? Why? When? Her head swirled with questions. "What does Marianne think about this?" If he thought he could have them both…

No. Gilbert despised his father having mistresses and would never have one himself. So why had he—?

"I broke things off with her."

The air rushed from her lungs, and iron bands constricted around her chest until she forgot how to draw breath. He couldn't have. His crane meant too much to him.

"I love you, not Marianne." He smoothed a strand of hair away from her face—hair that probably stunk of smoke and frying fish. But he didn't seem to notice. "'Many waters cannot quench love, neither can the floods drown it: if a man would give all the substance of his house for love, it would utterly be contemned.'"

Moisture pricked the backs of her eyes. He'd listened to her? All those times his gaze had gone hard and his jaw clenched as she'd quoted that verse, had he really been paying attention?

"But… but… you have to marry Marianne, remember? Or did you decide you don't want to help people like Lindy after all?" It was an impossible choice and unfair of her to throw it between them, yet that's where they stood. If he married Marianne for her money, she'd despise him. But if he turned his back on those in need, she'd despise him too.

"No, and no. I realized I don't have to marry Marianne, and I still want to help the injured and their families, but with you by my side." He laid a hand on her cheek, his palm warm against her skin.

Her tongue was suddenly so thick and cumbersome she could barely force words over it. "How is that possible?

"I sold my rights to the crane." He brought his other hand up to cup her cheek, cradling her face as gently as he would one of his mother's fancy teacups. "For you."

She blinked once, then twice. His words swirled inside her, but they didn't settle into a semblance of order, into anything she could make sense of. "But you love your crane."

He bent his head until his lips were only a hairsbreadth from hers. "I realized I love you more. In fact, I think I've always been in love with you, but I was too..."

His breath fanned over her lips as he continued speaking, an intoxicating mixture of sweetness and dreams and Gilbert. Some of what he was saying didn't fully make sense, like how he could sell his crane and still have money to help people. But he'd never been one to spout falsehoods. And when he looked at her with his gaze open and sincere and vulnerable, how could she not believe him?

He kept talking, something about an inventor and poor business choices and the need for a partner. She should probably care. She should probably be listening better. But there were only two things she wanted at that moment, the first was to hear him say he loved her again, and the second, well...

She reached up and slid her hand along the back of his neck, pulling him down until she cut off his words with her lips against his.

His eyes widened in surprise, and it took a moment for him to place his hands on her back—a moment she took full advantage of as she pressed closer to him and set to giving him a thorough kissing.

Gilbert's lips slid over hers, not quite as eager as they had been when they'd kissed on the *Lassiter*, but more confident, more certain. As though he, too, understood there was no need to explain everything when they could be kissing instead. This must be what the Bible meant about many waters not quenching love, because Lake Superior could flood this very moment, and it wouldn't begin to dampen the love swirling through her.

Gilbert pulled away too soon, and she stared up at him. Or rather, at his mouth, which hovered just above her lips.

"No fishing knife this time?" He gave her a soft smile.

Her cheeks warmed. "No, but another kiss would be nice. Or two."

His smile grew bigger. One of his warm, genuine ones rather than the polished one he used for his business acquaintances. Yet just when it seemed he was about to kiss her again, he pulled back another inch and spoke instead. "Don't you want to hear about how I managed to sell my crane plus come up with a way to help injured workers?"

Sure, yes, of course. Just as soon as her brain decided it was worth thinking about. Which would probably be sometime after their third or fourth kiss.

"Later." She went up on her tiptoes to press her lips to his, but Gilbert chuckled and held her away from him, his grip gentle on her shoulders.

"Slow down, darling." He cupped her cheek once more, his hand cool against her warm skin. "There are things I want you to know. Were you listening to anything I said before you kissed me?"

Her cheeks grew even warmer. "I remember the part about you loving me."

"And that I do." He placed a kiss on her forehead, but then withdrew. "But this first. I didn't sell all of the crane, more like two-thirds. There's an inventor, Frobisher, who's been interested in my ideas since I was in college. He's got some brilliant ideas himself, but not an ounce of business sense. Then there's Carl Mellar, Marianne's father, who has more money than he knows what to do with but doesn't know a thing about engineering. I put together a proposal and I approached them. Three partners, equal shares, and the first thing we put into production is my crane. Carl is the monetary backer, Frobisher is the chief engineer, and I'm the business manager who will also handle engineering when needed. It'll take longer to earn money on my crane this way than if I were to marry someone like Marianne, true. But money isn't everything. Having a wife that loves me, on the other hand… Having a family that cares about each other…"

Her heart thudded against her ribcage like a miner hammering his pickax into rock. He'd figured out a way to have both her and his crane.

Because he loved her.

He'd said it himself, and more than once, but a hundred times wouldn't be too much. This must be why she hadn't been able to move past Gilbert despite all the time she'd spent in prayer. This must be why she'd felt so adamantly that he shouldn't marry Marianne, even if she hadn't brought the situation to God until she'd been in Eagle Harbor.

She went back up on her tiptoes and threw her arms around his neck. "And who do you have in mind for that loving wife?" she whispered against his lips.

His mouth curved against hers. "You, Rebekah Cummings. I love you, and I want to marry you, and have babies with you, and—"

For the second time in mere minutes, she silenced his words with her lips. His hands came around her back, pulling her closer, and she closed her eyes against the sensation of being wrapped in his embrace.

"What is going on?"

Her eyes flew open, and she stilled.

Gilbert pulled away from her enough to glance over her shoulder, another grin on his face. "I'm kissing the woman I love."

"The woman you love?" Dr. Harrington's voice carried a hard edge. "That's strange, because I could swear you're kissing the woman I'm courting in the middle of the picnic I planned for her."

Rebekah jerked herself away from Gilbert and whirled to find Seth stalking toward them. "Seth. I'm sorry. I—"

"Have feelings for someone other than me, evidently." Despite his southern accent, his voice was severe, possibly even cold, and nothing familiar glinted in his usually compassionate eyes.

"Since when do you love my sister, Sinclair? Last I knew, you'd set her aside for another woman, one with a fat bank account."

Rebekah's gaze flitted past where Seth had stopped at the edge of the woods to Elijah, who was standing where the pathway emptied out into the clearing. Elijah, of all people! As if having a kiss interrupted by her suitor wasn't bad enough.

"Since I was fifteen, I think." Gilbert wrapped an arm around her waist and squeezed her in a sideways hug.

She would have wrapped her own arm around his back and squeezed in return, but Seth strode onto the blanket.

"He's loved you for a decade?" Hurt radiated from him, from the slumped set to his shoulders to the murkiness of his usually clear eyes. "Why didn't you tell me?"

She glanced up at Gilbert, who had tightened his hold around her, then moved her gaze back to Seth. "I'm hearing it for the first time too."

"But you obviously return his feelings."

Why hadn't she told him sooner, on the way to the picnic like she'd thought about? "Yes, I do, and I planned to tell you."

"Don't you think that's something you should have explained when I first asked to call on you? That you were in love with another man?" Seth rubbed the back of his neck.

"It wasn't that simple. Gilbert was going to marry Marianne in Chicago, and I'd come back here to..." *Wallow. Mope. Pray.* "Move on."

"I was a fool to ever let her go." Gilbert spoke in a calm, measured voice that probably did nothing to persuade Seth of his feelings.

But he'd never speak words like that if he didn't mean them. Beneath the stony wall he showed others, he was sincere and vulnerable and compassionate, even if she was the only person here who could see it.

But something about Gilbert must have convinced Seth as well, because the side of Seth's mouth tilted up in a faint, sad smile, and his grass green gaze sought hers. "I wish you would have said something sooner, but I do want you to be happy."

She pressed her lips together to stem the moisture pricking her eyes and swallowed tightly. "I will be. Thank you for understanding."

Seth gave a brief nod and turned to go, his lanky form still slumped.

She'd never meant to cause him pain, not someone so gentle and unassuming. "Seth." She shouldered out from under Gilbert's arm and took a step toward him. "For what it's worth, I think you'll make a good husband one day."

"But not a good husband for you." He spoke the words so softly she doubted Gilbert and Elijah could hear.

She swallowed again and shook her head. "No."

His gaze dropped to the checkered blanket beneath their feet, then he scanned the picnic spread around them. "Do you mind collecting my things and dropping them by the office when you return to town?"

"Not at all."

"Goodbye, then." He turned and strode briskly from the clearing, a gait at odds with his hunched back, deflated shoulders, and bent head.

If only she could offer more than to collect his things, do something to assuage the pain that emanated from him. To return the bright light to his eyes and the happiness in his step that he'd had just an hour ago when he'd stolen her away from the festival. But what was there to do other than go back in time and decline his offer to court her? She'd never given him any promises, never done more than hold his hand.

Yet she'd still hurt him.

A hand landed on her shoulder, familiar in its weight and size. "I didn't realize things were so serious between the two of you."

She turned to the man she loved. "They weren't. At least not for me. But he's pretty intent on finding a wife to help with his practice, and he's right. I should have told him what happened between us in Chicago."

"And what, exactly, happened in Chicago?" Elijah straightened from where he'd been leaning against a tree at the edge of the clearing.

⌐.⌐.⌐.⌐.⌐

Elijah. Gilbert stiffened. The trip to Eagle Harbor had seemed interminable. So why, in all his time waiting and pacing and praying, had he not thought about the answer he'd give Rebekah's family?

Because I was too busy thinking about what I'd say to her, how I'd beg her to take me back.

But he hadn't anticipated another man would have taken up suit with Rebekah in the few weeks she'd been back, nor had he anticipated facing her family.

And he prided himself on planning ahead, preparing for all possible variables.

Rebekah took a step toward her brother. "Gilbert said—"

"I made a mistake." Gilbert cut her off. This was his mess, and he'd be the one to fix it. "Quite possibly the biggest mistake of my life. I like to have everything perfectly planned out. It's better that way. I can be prepared for anything. No surprises. Everything calculated, controlled. Like a steam engine. You figure out how hot the water needs to be to make steam. How quickly the pistons pump once the water reaches a certain temperature, and how..."

Warmth burned his ears, and he lifted the side of his mouth in a smile. Leave it to him to get distracted by such an example. "Well, the specifics of a steam engine don't matter that much at the moment, do they?"

But Elijah didn't smile back. If anything, his face grew sterner, his jaw more tense. And the hand on his uninjured arm had clenched into a fist at some point.

"I forgot to consult God, a better design engineer than I'll ever be," he rushed on before Elijah could deny him outright. "I pressed ahead thinking my plan made the most sense, and in so doing, I missed the best plan. Granted, selling most of my crane wasn't as obvious as marrying an heiress, but an heiress wasn't what I needed." He slid his gaze away from Elijah's stern face to the woman he needed so badly he'd spent the past two weeks drawing up proposals and sitting in endless meetings to convince both Frobisher and Mellar to partner with him.

"You're not the only one. I made mistakes too, left Eagle

Harbor without talking to my family, forced you to listen to my opinion about your relationship with Marianne." Rebekah's eyes were large and luminous, shining with that vulnerable quality that always made him ache to wrap his arms around her and hold her against him for hours—something he planned to do often in the days and months ahead.

He reached out and fingered a strand of hair dangling beside her cheek, tugging gently so she stepped closer to him. "I'm glad you said those things. They helped me realize what was most important. And I'm glad I'm selling my crane, because it allows me to have that future you talked about, with a family and love and Bible verses at the dinner table. With afternoons spent on picnics and days spent boating. With everything you had growing up. I want that, and I want it with you."

"I want that too." Her words were fast and fierce, then she wrapped him in a hug so tight she squeezed the breath from him.

He settled his arms around her back, his gentle grip a contrast to her intense, determined one, but just as full of promise.

"When we made peace at the beginning of the summer, you failed to warn me you intended to marry my sister." Elijah's voice was low and gravelly, but not with anger. It sounded like it had that day Elijah saved his life, when they'd reached across the room at Dr. Harrington's office and clasped hands as a promise of peace.

But making peace then didn't necessarily mean Elijah would bless a marriage to his sister now. Though they were standing in the clearing together without throwing punches, a definite improvement on both sides—even if Elijah looked tempted to fell him.

But if the situation were reversed, if someone had treated a person he loved the way he'd treated Rebekah, and then he found out the scoundrel intended to marry her, he'd have knocked the man cold long before now.

And while he didn't care one way or the other what his family thought of his marriage to Rebekah, Rebekah needed her family's blessing. Her family was too important a part of her life for her to thwart them in this. Marrying against their wishes would tear her in two.

Gilbert loosed his grip on Rebekah—though he'd every intention of sweeping her into his arms again the second Elijah left the clearing—and locked eyes with Elijah's stormy gray gaze. "I was still in denial over my feelings about your sister when we made peace."

"I knew there was something going on between you." Elijah sighed and rubbed his hand over his hair.

"He sold his crane for me." Rebekah inched closer to his side. "You have to understand what that means, Elijah. Please, say you favor our marriage."

Gilbert sneaked a hand behind Rebekah's back and rested it in the little hollow above her hips as Elijah looked at his sister.

This would be the perfect moment to remind Elijah that he'd given up his claim to Victoria because he'd known Elijah loved her, but he'd not play that game. *You owe me your sister because I gave you my fiancée.* How ridiculous. He wanted Elijah's blessing outright. No games, no bartering.

But perhaps a bit of begging.

"Give us your blessing. Please." He refused to consider what thoughts might be running through Elijah's head. Only weeks ago, he would have laughed at the irony of a Sinclair pleading with a fisherman. But he'd sign the *Lassiter* over to Elijah here and now if that's what it took for the man to assent. "I intend to cherish your sister, but I want your blessing. No, I need your blessing. Your opinion means too much to Rebekah. We want to start our life together with your support, not your anger."

A flicker of amusement passed through Elijah's eyes, then his mouth tipped up into a small smile. "She can be as prickly as a porcupine when she gets in one of her snits. You sure you want to take that on?"

Rebekah stiffened and stepped away from his side. "Oh, and you're a furry little kitten yourself, are you?"

Gilbert inclined his head to Elijah. "I don't mind a few prickles."

Rebekah planted a hand on her hip and stomped her foot. "I am not that—"

Her words trailed off as he yanked her back to his side—where he planned to keep her for a half century or better—and spun her to face him.

Her eyes flashed, and her mouth opened to...

Well, he didn't know what she planned to say, and he didn't much care, since he cut off any future protest with his lips and wrapped his arms around her, prickles and all.

She sighed into the kiss, her lips tasting of love and promises. Of dreams realized and achieved.

An overly loud groan sounded from Elijah's vicinity. "I'll give you my blessing, Sinclair. But I'm not about to stand around and watch you two canoodle."

"Then leave." He waved Elijah off and buried his face in his future wife's neck, smelling her scent and burrowing into the softness of her hair as it brushed his face. "I love you, Rebekah, and I'm not content to merely tell you. I'm going to prove it, over and over, day after day."

She smiled up at him, her eyes brimming with love and hope, with the future they'd have together. It wasn't a future married to a rich heiress with the fanciest carriages, newest yachts, and largest house on Prairie Street.

But a future full of love and happiness and children, and it would make him richer in the ways that mattered most.

Thank You

Thank you for reading *Love's Sure Dawn*. I sincerely hope you enjoyed Gilbert and Rebekah's story. The next full length novel in the Eagle Harbor Series is Dr. Seth Harrington and Lindy Marsden's story, *Love's Eternal Breath*. It will be available in winter of 2017.

To be notified when my next novel is releasing, consider signing up for the Naomi Rawlings Author Newsletter. Be sure to add naomi@naomirawlings.com to your safe email list so that the emails go through. I keep all subscriber information confidential, and I only send out newsletters when I have a new release or large sale.

Also, if you enjoyed reading *Love's Sure Dawn*, please take a moment to tell others about the novel. You can do this by posting an honest review where you bought it, or on GoodReads. I read every one of my reviews, and reviews help readers like yourself decide whether to purchase a novel. You could also consider mentioning *Love's Sure Dawn* to your friends on Facebook, Twitter, or Pinterest.

If you'd like to read more about Gilbert, Rebekah, Elijah, and Victoria, you might enjoy *Love's Every Whisper*, the book that comes right before *Love's Sure Dawn*. I've included an excerpt next.

Love's Every Whisper
Chapter One

Eagle Harbor, Michigan: May, 1883

The wind whipped off the lake, thrashing the skeletal tree limbs
back and forth like a bear tearing through the woods.

Victoria Donnelly stepped onto an ice-encrusted rock and
steadied herself. Hard white snowflakes spewed from the sky,
pelting her face despite the wide brim of the masculine hat she'd
donned. "E-e-e-elijah. Elijah Cummings!"

She held her lantern out and surveyed the beach; but with the
driving snow, gray sky, and foaming waves of Lake Superior, she
couldn't see more than ten feet in front of her. A sickening wave
rose in her stomach, similar to the one that crashed into the rocks
and sent icy spray to splatter the bottom of her cloak. Was the
Beaumont out there?

*Please, God, let them have sought shelter somewhere. Let Father
and Gilbert be safe.*

She turned away from the lake, though she couldn't block out
the ever-present roar of it, and scanned the rocky beach once more.

"E-elijah!"

Oh, if Mother heard how loud and unladylike she yelled, she'd
get lectured for an hour, and probably another lecture for
stuttering along with a comeuppance for being out here in the first
place.

She headed toward a large boulder jutting above the others. Maybe if she climbed atop it, she could see the light from Elijah's lantern—if she could glimpse anything besides the blinding snow and angry, froth-tipped waves, that was.

She stepped onto a wet rock and teetered for a moment before hurrying onto a dry one. How did Elijah search these beaches during storms without falling and breaking his neck?

"Elijah!" she called once more, then set her lantern atop the high boulder and searched for a nook to grab.

"Are you trying to get yourself killed?"

She jolted at the familiar voice behind her, and the heel of her boot slid out from under her. She tried to catch the boulder, but her hand gripped only air.

A strong arm wrapped around her ribs and she fell back into a solid wall of man. What a way to reintroduce herself to a friend she hadn't seen in three years.

"You shouldn't be out here," he muttered against her ear.

"B-but Father." She struggled to her feet and turned. No wonder she hadn't been able to find Elijah, snow clung to every inch of him, from his large hat to his woolen coat to the sturdy boots encasing his feet. "And Gilbert. The *Beaumont*. I th-think they're caught in the storm, and I knew you c-could help."

He released her and held his lantern up to survey the roaring lake. The mere thought of the ferocious waves crashing into the beach made her stomach roil. How did Elijah go out on rescues during storms like this?

"Have any other ships made it into harbor?"

"One about an hour ago. Said they almost m-missed the light."

"Glad they're safe." He glanced over his shoulder toward the lighthouse, or rather, where the lighthouse should be. Swirling white and gray smothered the orange glow.

Would Gilbert's ship be able to see the beam from the light in time to turn toward harbor?

A sudden burst of wind ripped across the beach, and she shivered against its chilling force. Elijah reached for her hand, encased in its soft-kidskin glove, and held it up. "These aren't going to keep you warm." He jutted his chin toward the dainty little boots Mother had purchased for her in Milwaukee. "Neither are those."

She pulled her hand away from him. "I w-wasn't planning to be out long. I just wanted to t-t-tell you about Father."

Elijah's gaze moved back to the wide, open waters of Lake Superior. "I know the storm came up quick, but it's unlikely he's still out in it. If anything, he would have sheltered up in Copper Harbor."

She looked helplessly out to the lake and raised her hands to her sides before letting them fall again. Moisture gathered in her eyes, but she blinked it away. "Th-their steamer was due in three hours ago, b-b-before the storm even started. Please, Elijah. You h-have to help."

⌐.⌐.⌐.⌐.⌐

Victoria's words ran like icy Lake Superior water through Elijah's veins. *Not someone else I know. Please, God. Not even Gilbert Sinclair.* This town wouldn't be able to handle another death at the hands of the lake.

Or maybe he was the one who couldn't handle another.

He pushed away the choking guilt that swelled whenever he thought of his father's empty grave sitting in the town cemetery. "You're certain the steamer left on time?"

She swallowed, the strained muscles of her creamy throat barely visible in the blowing snow. "Y-yes. F-father and Gilbert telegraphed Mother from Marquette last night. They meant to leave on the *Beaumont* this morning."

He nearly cursed. If Gilbert Sinclair's fancy new steamer had left Marquette by noon, it should have arrived before the storm. Had something else gone wrong? And what exactly did she think he could do about it? It was one thing to rescue men from a ship he knew was floundering. Taking his crew into dangerous waters to search for a vessel that could be miles away was quite another.

Victoria stared up at him, wisps of dark brown hair escaping from beneath her wide-brimmed hat. At least she'd had the sense to wear a good one of those, and a warm fur cloak, but her fingers and toes had to be nigh frozen. "Your father and fiancé probably harbored somewhere along the coast and are waiting out the storm."

Victoria's chin came up and her lips firmed into a straight line. "Gilbert's n-n-not my f-fiancé."

Yet. Though this was no time to start arguing about his choice of words.

Just then, the bell clanged, not the constant ringing that warned ships of fog, but three short chimes, a pause, and then another chime: the signal call to the life-savers.

"Maybe that's for the *Beaumont*. Come on." He grabbed her lantern off the ridiculous boulder she'd been trying to climb, snuffed it, took her other hand in his, and started crossing the slippery rocks.

How long had it been since he'd held her hand? A decade maybe?

The bell clanged again. Confound it. In the three years he'd been making these rescues, he'd never once gotten distracted. Now he couldn't keep his concentration for ten seconds.

"D-do you think F-f-father will be all right?" Worried shadows haunted the soft skin beneath her hazel eyes, the same hazel eyes that stared back at him from his dreams every night.

Double confound it. If only he had a moment to stop and take her in his arms, whisper that everything would be fine, hold her until she stopped trembling.

But she wasn't his to hold, never had been and never would be. And he could hardly promise everything would be fine in a storm like this. "I don't know, but your father and Gilbert, they're good sailors who know these waters. They've got a better chance than most."

He should drop her hand. Continuing to hold it was doing ridiculous things to his heart, despite the barrier of her thin, inadequate gloves. But he couldn't quite manage to let it go. "Quickly now."

They scrambled over the last of the rocks and climbed onto the lighthouse lawn. Above, the usually strong beam of the tower's light quickly diffused into the swirling snow. He raced with Victoria over the lawn toward Front Street and the sandy beach that rimmed the harbor.

"There." He pointed toward the shadow of a lifeboat pulled up alongside the surfboat his crew prepared to launch. "Maybe your father's already ashore."

She heaved in a breath and her grip tightened on his hand. "It's not the *Beaumont's*. Gil's dinghies are shorter than that."

She was familiar enough with Gilbert's ships to recognize his dinghies in a snowstorm?

Something tightened inside his chest. He'd known it was coming, that someday the woman he'd loved for as long as he could remember would marry another. He'd prayed every night it wouldn't be Gilbert Sinclair, but evidently God wasn't interested in answering that particular request.

"Do you still have that knack for nursing? Can you help those sailors to the doc's?" He pointed toward the snow-shrouded shadows staggering around the unfamiliar lifeboat on the beach. "Take them to the new doc, Harrington. Not Dr. Greely." Greely was probably slumped over on his bar stool at the moment.

"Of course."

The fog bell chimed again, though he was probably the only rescuer not at the surfboat. He dropped her hand and bent his head against the wind, starting forward.

She caught his arm and pulled him back. "Promise you'll do whatever you can for Father and Gilbert."

He put his hand to her wind-burnished cheek, never mind that he had no business doing such a thing.

A tear spilled onto her skin, freezing into a perfect drop before it reached his glove. "Please."

"I'll look for them as we head out, but if I don't spot the *Beaumont*..."

She dropped her head, staring at some unseen speck on the storm-ravaged grass. "I understand."

"Victoria..." But he didn't have any words of comfort for her, not with the wind whipping at them, the bell calling to him, the roaring waves carrying off half their words. So he crushed her against his side for one brief, sweet moment.

Then he let her go, just like he'd been letting her go for the past fifteen years.

He raced down the other side of the rocky incline to the sand below, where the surfboat rested on the ground. It was an appallingly small craft to take into a storm like this. But the twenty-six foot long boat was the exact size and shape as those used by the United States Life-Saving Service. He'd seen to that when he built it.

Shadows of men in oilskin coats and hats milled about the boat, likely checking the lifelines and oars and making sure woolen blankets were secured beneath the seats as he'd taught them.

Mac Oakton straightened from where he'd been hunched over the stern. Even with high waves pummeling the harbor beach, the man towered over the scene.

"Thanks for getting the men ready," he called to the man his family had unofficially adopted as one of their own.

Mac dipped his head and tightened the rope knotted to one of the life rings. "Spot anything from shore?"

"Not in this mess. Your wife all right back at the lighthouse?" The wind blew a burst of snow into his face.

"I left her at the light, snug as could be."

"You're sure?" Elijah wiped the snow from his eyes. Perhaps Mac had been going out on rescues with him since he started his volunteer team, but still, if something happened to the light while Mac was gone…

He glanced toward the orange glow muted by the blizzard.

"Don't worry, Elijah." Mac landed a bear-like hand on his shoulder. "It's not the first time I've left Tressa alone."

No, it certainly wasn't. Tressa had been tending the light ever since she and Mac married three years ago. So why the sense of foreboding that churned in the pit of his stomach?

"Where's the wreck?" Elijah headed to his own position and checked his ropes.

"About a mile to the east."

"East. Doesn't that just rankle? It's like the storm knew I was patrolling to the west." He glanced at the shrouded forms farther down the beach, the unmistakable silhouette of Victoria's fancy fur cloak among them. She'd see to the sailors that had rowed to shore right good, had always had a hand for things like that.

"The schooner was trying to make harbor when the wind caught her and threw her onto a sandbar." Mac hooked the life ring onto the side of the boat. "Twelve man crew on her, eight made it to a dingy and came for help, but she's got four left aboard, and we know one of them."

"We do?"

"Clifford Spritzer. The captain said he offered to stay behind and wait for us."

Clifford was aboard that ship? Something heavy fisted in his gut. He glanced down the beach toward where the Spritzer house sat just off to the right, but couldn't see anything in the snow. He'd been the one to teach Cliff to sail, the one to write Cliff a letter of recommendation to a shipmaster he knew two years ago.

What if something happened to Clifford in the storm?

"Elijah, you with us?" Mac's sharp voice carried through the storm.

Elijah tore his eyes away from the beach and checked his oar. Clifford wasn't the only one left aboard a ship that would be battered and sunk within hours at the rate the waves were rolling in. He didn't have time to get distracted. He drew the collar of his jacket up around his neck and ran his hands quickly along the blankets stowed beneath the seat. *Please, God, keep us safe. Let us reach those men in time.*

A sense of peace flooded him. The storm spat snow, the waves ravaged the coast, and the lake looked ready to shred anything that dared sail atop it. Yet somehow this was right. The rest of Eagle Harbor might sit huddled in their homes, but he belonged in the midst of this, heading out to rescue sailors so nobody else would have to stand over an empty grave.

One man. One person willing to help three years ago, and Pa might still be alive.

If only he would have been in Eagle Harbor to make that rescue.

"Stations men," he growled through the wind. The other figures hurried into their positions, and Elijah grabbed the portside gunwale near the stern. "Hope you're ready to get wet."

Across from him, Mac let out a howl, the crazy man. His best friend actually liked sailing in messes such as this.

"One." Elijah's voice boomed against the storm. The men heaved the boat inward then swung it out. "Two." Again the boat swung in and out, six men working together in unity to—

Wait. There weren't six men lined up, three on each side of the boat. There were... there were...

"Rebekah!" His nails dug through his gloves into the gunwale.

The slender form near the bow jumped, then turned to look at him. "Please, Elijah. Let me go. It's wild out there today. You know I can help."

He pointed toward town. "Go home."

"I didn't know she was here." Mac squashed his hat lower on his head. "She must have been hiding behind a rock."

And likely waited until he'd called the men to their stations to approach the surfboat.

"I'm a good sailor, and you can use the help." Rebekah didn't leave her position near the bow.

The five others looked between them. Each held the gunwale, ready to launch into the surf with a moment's notice. "You think this is helping? Men are on that lake in a sinking ship, and you're wasting our time arguing."

"Only because you're stubborn. If you let me go, then you'll see—"

"You're *not* going!" Ma would throttle him if he let Rebekah in the boat, not that he was too keen on the idea himself.

Rebekah dropped her hold on the gunwale. "Just this once?"

"No. And don't let me see you out here during a storm again." He pinned his gaze on the lake. "One!"

The boat heaved in then out, a fluid movement cultivated from hours of the team practicing on the beach.

"Two... three." They ran into the surf, six men, one purpose. The water churned at their boots and thrashed against their legs. Spray hit their faces and snow shrouded their vision. At the bow, Jesse and Emmett heaved themselves aboard, followed by Simon and Floyd in the middle.

Elijah launched himself out of the water at the same instant as Mac. "Fall in."

All six of them plunged their eighteen foot oars into the water and rowed.

In the three years since he'd started his volunteer life-saving team, he'd saved thirty-three people.

Tonight, he had every intention of making that number thirty-seven.

⌐.⌐.⌐.⌐.⌐

Love's Every Whisper is available now.

Other Novels by Naomi Rawlings

Eagle Harbor Series
Book 1—*Love's Unfading Light*
Book 2—*Love's Every Whisper*
Book 3—*Love's Sure Dawn*
Book 4—*Love's Eternal Breath*
(Seth and Lindy, available winter 2017)
Book 5—*Love's Constant Hope*
(Thomas and Jessalyn, available spring 2017)
Book 6—*Love's Bright Tomorrow*
(Isaac and Aileen, release unknown)
Short Story—*Love's Beginning*

Belanger Family Saga
Book 1—*Sanctuary for a Lady*
Book 2—*The Soldier's Secrets*
Book 3—*Falling for the Enemy*

Stand Alone Novels
The Wyoming Heir

Acknowledgments

Thank you first and foremost to my Lord and Savior, Jesus Christ, for giving me both the ability and opportunity to write novels for His glory.

As with any novel, the author might come up with a story idea and sit at her computer to type the initial words, but it takes an army of people to bring you the book you have today. I'd especially like to thank Melissa Jagears, both my critique partner and editor for *Love's Sure Dawn*. I'd also like to thank my family for working with my writing schedule and giving me a chance to do two things I love: be a mommy and a writer. I wrote *Love's Sure Dawn* while I was going through a difficult, high-risk pregnancy, and I'd like to thank all the people who encouraged and supported me during those uncertain months. And finally, a special thanks to my agent Natasha Kern for encouraging me to keep working on the Eagle Harbor Series.

Author's Note

Three years ago, when I was writing one of the first scenes for what would become the Eagle Harbor Series, Rebekah Cummings accidently popped onto the page, interrupting Elijah's attempt to launch a rescue boat. Ever since then, I haven't quite known what to do with her. I never intended for her to have a crush on Elijah's nemesis, Gilbert Sinclair. Oh, I knew Elijah and Gilbert were going to fight over a piece of land and Victoria, but I didn't expect for Gilbert to end up honorable and redeemed. In that regard the entire story of *Love's Sure Dawn* was a bit of a surprise. I never really intended to write a romance for Elijah's little sister and enemy; it just happened. However, I'm very glad I got the chance to delve into Rebekah and Gilbert's story. Being confident and strong, Rebekah needed a man who was going to challenge her, and I found that person in Gilbert Sinclair.

One thing I've tried to stress with the Cummings family is the importance of a godly heritage. Parents, obviously, can't control their children's lives forever. What happens to their teachings after those children grow up and start making their own choices? Do those children cling to the biblical truths they learned when they were young, or do they reject them? I've tried to explore these issues a bit with each novel that features a character from the Cummings family.

Gilbert is an industrialist, but right on the heels of the Industrial Revolution came the Labor Movement. As industry exploded across the United States, so did unsafe working conditions for the average laborer. Today there are laws and regulations that protect workers, but not during the late 1800s. It took a few decades for thriving industry and safe working conditions to find a balance, and unfortunately, that era of history is filled with thousands of Lindy Marsdens and Aileen Brogans, who lost loved ones and found themselves in dire situations due to poor treatment of workers.

I hope you're enjoying the Eagle Harbor Series. It's been my favorite set of novels to write, though I admit to being a little biased since I live in a little town on Lake Superior myself, only a couple hours from the real life Eagle Harbor. I look forward to writing many more books in this series, and Lindy Marsden and Seth Harrington will be next, with *Love's Eternal Breath* releasing in the winter of 2016/2017.

About the Author

A mother of three, Naomi Rawlings spends her days picking up, cleaning, playing and, of course, writing. Her husband pastors a small church in Michigan's rugged Upper Peninsula, where her family shares its ten wooded acres with black bears, wolves, coyotes, deer and bald eagles. Naomi and her family live only three miles from Lake Superior, where the scenery is beautiful and they average 200 inches of snow per winter. She's currently enjoying writing a historical novel series set in this unique area of the United States.

For more information about Naomi, please visit her website at naomirawlings.com or find her on Facebook at:

www.facebook.com/author.naomirawlings.

Made in the USA
Columbia, SC
07 April 2020